INTO THE DARKNESS

By
Amberly Evans

CREATESPACE EDITION
PUBLISHED BY
Amberly Evans

Into The Darkness © 2012 Amberly Evans
All rights reserved

CreateSpace Edition License Notes

Cover Design © Kelli Ann Morgan
Inspire Creative Services
www.inspirecreativeservices.com

Interior book design by
Bob Houston eBook Formatting
http://about.me/BobHouston

ISBN: 978-1478328278

CHAPTER ONE

Mia stared out the window of her apartment at the lights on the Manhattan Bridge. She loved the view from the fourth floor, but tonight she felt anxious and tense. The air all around her was vibrating with energy that always preceded one of her dreams. It was late and she was exhausted. She had stayed up most of last night painting and she couldn't fight off sleep any longer. Lifting the covers, she slid in and closed her eyes.

Mia felt the panic sweep through her from head to toe, racing like ice in her veins. There was nowhere to run, nowhere to hide. He was on her in an instant. She fell hard with him right on top of her. She hit him with all her might, but it made no difference. The knife in his hand still pierced her skin, going deep into her flesh. She tried to scream but all she heard was a low moan. Had it come from her? Again, the knife was forced into her body, only this time it didn't hurt as much. His face contorted into a grotesque mask of rage and hatred as he pushed the knife in one last time. She tried to cover her heart with her hand. She could hear her own breath billowing in and out of her lungs, and then a gurgling sound as blood flowed into her throat. The ringing in her ears faded and darkness surrounded her.

The darkness was all around her, closing in. She could feel it pressing against her, making it hard to breathe. Sirens, growing louder and louder, they were coming for her. She had to wake up. She had to wake up now. The voice inside her head screamed, 'Wake up now!'

Mia jackknifed into an upright position, panting as she tried to catch her breath. There were voices all around her, all talking at once, a cacophony of whispers. Her body was soaked in sweat, even her sheets were damp. She flipped back her covers and went to the window. The street below looked just as it should for a cold, dark, and snowy night in January. The street lights illuminated the snow even as the snow plow went by, clearing one dark strip of asphalt, unmindful of the flakes that were still falling from the sky.

Mia glanced at the clock on her nightstand. It read four-thirty-six.

The air in her loft was frigid and she started to shiver. She snatched her bathrobe off the back of the chair and wrapped herself in it. She continued to shiver, though not from the cold. The intensity of her vision had been terrifying. Mia took a deep breath. It was going to be bad this time. She could feel it in her bones. She pressed her forehead against the icy glass and begged out loud, "Please, please let this pass by me. I don't want to do this again."

She had to get the vision out of her head and there was only one way to do that. Flipping on the lights, all of them, she grabbed a fresh canvas, propped it on her easel, and began to sketch. The lines started to appear one after another. The shape of the girl's face was oval with a small cleft in the chin. A few strands of dark hair crossed her forehead, the rest framed her face. The nose was thin at the bridge and then widened with distinct nostrils. It was an interesting face.

Mia's hand grew tired from the frantic movements, but she couldn't stop, not until she had the image out of her head and onto the canvas. The girl's left hand rested lifelessly on her chest. Mia could still see it in her mind. There was a ring on her middle finger. She had to get this right. It was a sapphire, set in silver metal, with a rope band crossing over the stone. With eraser in hand, Mia removed what wasn't right and started over.

She kept working as the city came to life outside. She heard the streets below humming as the morning rush came and went. Still, she sketched. The clock in her apartment ticked off the minutes. Shadows shifted and lengthened as the hours passed. A dog barked then quieted. The chorus of horns and rhythm of engines told her that the afternoon rush was picking up. The last thing she sketched was her eyes. Dead eyes. Over and over she drew them until they mirrored what she saw in her mind.

When she was done, Mia stood back and looked at the canvas as a whole. It was all there-- the face, the blood, the snow in her hair. Mia didn't draw the trash she had seen in her vision. It would have demeaned the girl's death and she couldn't do that.

"I hope you're at peace," Mia whispered.

She sat on the foot of her bed exhausted, her hand cramping from hours of uninterrupted use. She wasn't sure how long she'd stared at the sketch, but when she heard the siren outside her window, she realized she had to hurry. She needed to get to Charlie's gallery and it was a long walk.

She showered and scrubbed the graphite off of her hands, though they never came completely clean. She put on her artist clothes-- black skirt, black tights, and black boots. And tonight, she'd wear her emerald green sweater and matching paisley scarf, along with her black trench coat.

The cold air surrounded her as the doorman opened the lobby door.

"Have a nice evening, Ms. Carrigan." Carl tipped his hat to her.

"Thank you."

It felt good to be outside. The openness soothed some of her anxiety, but only some. Mia knew she was standing on a precipice and with one wrong step she was going to fall. She had fallen before. That was one road she couldn't go down again because she knew she wouldn't make it back.

CHAPTER TWO

Nick walked into the gallery because the painting in the front window had caught his eye. His new apartment needed something on the walls and he was past re-hanging his old posters. He wanted something cool and sophisticated. A cop's salary wouldn't allow him to buy art from an upscale place like this, but what the hell, it couldn't hurt to look.

The place was warm, dry, and well lit, all pluses in his book. Several different artists had their work on display, but there was only one he was interested in, M. Carrigan. His paintings were sparse, with very little color. Most of them were of young women. Some were nude, but the paintings weren't sexual. If Nick had to pick an adjective, he would say peaceful. They looked at peace.

He knew it was almost closing time, so he quickly moved from painting to painting. Out of the corner of his eye he saw a young woman staring at one of the displays. She had been in the same spot since he'd arrived. All he could see was her back. She wore all black, from her boots to her hat. Her hands were shoved deeply into the pockets of her trench coat, even her hair was black.

Nick stepped closer and studied the same painting. The piece appealed to him. It was the face of a woman, partially submerged in water. Her lips were parted and her eyes closed. The water rippled around her face, covering everything but her lips and nose. The woman was drawn in black and white, but the water around her was a faded red. It was dramatic, yet simple in its presentation.

The painting made him feel as if she were floating somewhere quiet and alone. He could see himself looking at it after a long, stressful day at work, while trying to unwind.

He glanced at the woman next to him. She never looked at him or in any way acknowledged that he was there. She continued to stare, apparently deep in thought.

"Do you like it?" she asked, without taking her eyes off of the painting.

"Yes, very much."

"Why?" Her voice was very soft, not what he would have

expected.

She finally looked at him, her eyes watching him, waiting for his answer.

He thought for a moment. "Because she looks so relaxed floating there. It makes me feel calmer just seeing her."

Nick saw a Mona Lisa smile appear on her face as her gaze returned to the painting.

"Do you like it?" he asked, intrigued by her.

"I can't decide."

"You've been contemplating it for a while."

"A long while, but I still can't decide."

Nick's cell phone rang. He hoped his boss wasn't dropping a new case in his lap. He hadn't even made it home yet. He walked away, hoping for some privacy.

Discussing the details of a murder investigation wasn't a good conversation starter. It tended to creep people out, especially women. After the call was over, he was disappointed to see that the dark-haired woman was gone.

"I must have made a great first impression," he whispered to himself.

The gallery's owner nodded to him and said, "If you're interested, I might be able to get the artist to sell it."

"I'll think about it." Nick could see by the man's sour expression, that wasn't the answer he'd been looking for. As he walked out, the wind nipped at all his exposed skin.

Spotting an all night diner across the street, he went to grab something to eat before calling it a night. When he walked in, he was surprised to see the woman from the gallery sitting by herself at a small booth. She smiled when she saw him, so Nick made his way to her table. "Mind if I join you? We didn't get to finish our conversation."

She gestured to the empty side of the table. "Please."

For the first time, Nick got to really see her face. Her eyes and hair were dark brown, not black, and where his skin was light brown, hers was like cream. He wouldn't say she was beautiful, not like a model, but she was cute. There was something about her that intrigued him.

He picked up a menu and glanced at the usual choices. When the waitress came over he ordered a double cheeseburger and fries.

It occurred to him he hadn't waited for her to order. "I'm sorry, did you-?"

"I ordered already. Thanks." She smiled at him.

The waitress took his menu and walked away.

"So, how long have you been into art?" Nick asked.

"Since I was a little girl. My mom would take me to all kinds of museums and galleries. How about you? Is there a frustrated artist inside of you?"

"To be honest, I'm looking to cover the bare walls of my new apartment, but I can't afford that kind of real art with my paycheck."

As she lifted a cup of steaming hot chocolate to her lips, she asked, "What do you do?"

"I'm a cop." Nick didn't have to wait long for her reaction. Her cup stopped an inch from her mouth and her gaze flew to his face. She didn't say anything for a moment.

"Homicide."

From her tone of voice, Nick couldn't tell if she was asking or telling. Either way, it felt weird. "How did you know?"

The cup finally made its way to her lips and she took a quiet sip.

He had been a cop long enough to know when someone was trying to come up with a believable answer.

"You have an inquisitive look about you."

"Really? Can I have your name, ma'am?" Nick asked, as if he were on a case.

"Are you going to investigate me?" she laughed.

"Of course."

"Mia Carrigan, but that's not my real name," she said as she held out her hand.

"Nick White, but that's not my real name either," he replied, taking it.

The smile on her face faded for just a second and her eyes narrowed. Nick saw it. It was as if she knew that what he said was actually true. His real name wasn't White. But how could she possibly know that? This woman was odd, to say the least. Not that that was unusual. New York City was full of nutcases. At that moment he wasn't sure if *he* was one of them or she was.

"Here ya go." The waitress sat his burger in front of him and then slid a huge banana split, the size of his forearm, in front of Mia.

Nick chuckled quietly because he had figured her for the salad type. "You haven't told me what you do," he said, taking a bite of his burger.

"I teach art at several of the Boys and Girls Clubs in the city, and at the Freeman Academy. And, in my free time, I paint."

"The Freeman Academy? The prep school for rich girls?" Nick took another bite.

"That's the one."

He forced himself to swallow before he said, "Wow." He had heard you had to be somebody to even work at that place. "So what do you paint?"

She looked at him inquisitively and shrugged. "Whatever I'm in the mood to at the time. I also sketch and I pretend I'm a photographer."

"You pretend?"

"I'm not very good." Mia cut off a piece of banana with her spoon and ate it.

"I don't believe that."

"Why?"

"Because of the way you were looking at that painting tonight, examining it, evaluating it."

"More like critiquing it, finding the flaws."

"I think I'm in trouble then, because I have way too many of them." Nick smiled and said, "I think it's better to focus on the pluses."

"I'll drink to that." Mia lifted her cup of hot chocolate and he lifted his water. They made a hollow clinking sound when they touched.

Both of them took sips and set their drinks back on the table.

"It's after eleven. I better go." Mia dropped a fifty on the table.

"That was the most expensive banana split in history."

"I'm paying for yours too."

"No way," Nick protested.

"It's the least I can do for an honest public servant. And because you saved me from eating dinner alone again."

"How do you know I'm honest?"

Mia leaned forward and whispered, "Because if you were on the take, you'd be able to afford decent art." She winked at him.

Nick had to laugh. He couldn't help it. There was some kind of chemistry between them and he wanted to see her again. "I'll let you pay, if you let me take you to dinner, a real dinner."

Her smile started out small and then got bigger. "I'd like that."

He pulled a business card out of his pocket. "This has both my work and cell phone numbers on it. If you call me tomorrow, we can work out the details."

They walked out of the diner and Nick asked, "Where is your car?"

"I don't have one. I'll walk home or I'll get a cab."

"You can't walk home at this time of night! This is New York for crying out loud!"

"I'm perfectly safe. I do it all the time."

Nick could see she was serious. "Well, not on my watch. Come on, I'll take you home." He took her by the elbow, so she wouldn't slip on the icy sidewalks, and crossed the street to his car. As he opened the door for her, he said, "You shouldn't take rides from men you've just met either."

She glanced at him over her shoulder and laughed out loud. She had a great laugh.

"I can't believe you walked all the way to that gallery. I've gone like twenty blocks already. How much farther?"

"Pull over here." Mia pointed to an open spot at the curb. "There's a night club around the corner, so you better take this one."

"You live here?" All Nick saw was abandoned store fronts, dark industrial buildings, and warehouses.

"My building is around the corner, but the parking in front is impossible, being New York and all." Mia's eyes sparkled as she teased him.

"Sarcasm? Already? We're moving right along, aren't we?"

As he walked around the car, he could hear her laughing. He liked that she had waited for him to open the door. He liked independent women, but he wanted to show that he was a gentleman when he was with one.

Around the corner was an old warehouse that looked like it had been converted into lofts. Even in the dark, he could see that the building had been fixed up. Someone had poured a lot of money into it. And when he opened the door to the lobby for Mia, he could have sworn he'd walked into a fancy lobby on Park Avenue, complete with a doorman at the desk.

"They must pay really well at the Freeman Academy."

She smiled. "Thanks for the ride home." Mia started to head to the elevator.

"Any time, and don't forget to call me. I owe you a dinner." Geeze that sounded pathetic and desperate.

She smiled again and waved as the elevator doors closed.

The cold January air was a bold contrast to the warmth of the lobby. *At least the wind wasn't blowing here,* he thought as he headed back to his car. As Nick rounded the corner movement caught his eye. He stopped and looked, but the sidewalk behind him was empty.

Still, he had a strange feeling he was being followed. The hair on the back of his neck stood up, warning him. He started walking again, his hand on the gun that rested in its holster on his belt. It was probably some junkie looking for a few dollars to get a fix. He kept going, trying to listen for the sound of footsteps, but the street was eerily quiet. His own breathing was all he could hear. He glanced over his shoulder, truly expecting to see a person standing there, but again there was no one.

Nick looked down the street in both directions, nothing. He didn't normally spook easily, but hell, it was after midnight and only one of the street lights was working on the whole block. All the others were dark.

"Freaking New York," he muttered, feeling stupid. He knew he had seen something, probably trash blowing down the road. Still he didn't take his hand off of his gun.

He was almost to his car when, in the glass windows of the abandoned shop, he saw someone, in all black, not ten feet behind him. Nick turned around and shouted, "If you think---" he stood there, gun in hand, seeing a cold, empty sidewalk. His heart was pounding.

Someone was there, but there was no one he could see. He looked at the grimy windows. There was still a dark shadow in front of him. It was close enough that he could almost reach out and touch it.

As he stood there, staring at the reflection, the darkness faded and the glow from the street light glared off of the glass. He blinked his eyes a couple of times, but it didn't make any difference. His heart continued pounding. He could feel the rush of adrenaline all the way to his fingertips and toes. Sweaty goose bumps covered his whole body.

He could've handled a junkie, but this? He didn't even know what he had seen, but he *had* seen something. And Nick had a feeling it wasn't friendly.

He got in his car and locked all the doors, and as he drove away, he fish-tailed down the icy street. When he stopped at a red light a few blocks away, he went over everything that had happened again in his mind. Something had been there, he couldn't see it, but he'd felt it. It felt evil.

CHAPTER THREE

Mia had been looking forward to this night. She was disappointed that Nick wasn't feeling well. She sensed his indecision about whether he should reschedule once more or keep their date.

"I'm sorry it's taken so long for us to get together," Nick said, waiting for her to slide into the booth. "I caught two new cases and I've been working like a dog."

"We don't have to do this tonight. We can wait until your feeling better." Mia could feel the tension in him. He was in pain.

"It's just this stupid headache." Nick took his place opposite her. "Wait, how did you know?"

"Uh…you look really tense and tired." Mia covered her tracks.

"I worked like thirty-six hours straight and I'd only had about four hours sleep when it was time to come and pick you up." Nick pinched the bridge of his nose.

Mia knew she shouldn't do it, but she wanted to help him. "Give me your hands."

Nick opened his eyes and glanced at her hands on the table in front of him. He didn't hesitate. He placed both of his hands in hers. They were warm and he held onto her firmly. The contrast of his brown skin against her white skin was beautiful. She was going to sketch the image later on.

"Now lean back and relax. Try to clear your mind."

Mia closed her eyes and began to pull the negative energy from him, letting it flow into her body. When all of the bad energy was inside of her, she took a deep breath, as deep as she could, and exhaled slowly until there was no air left in her lungs. Again, she inhaled and exhaled. And again. Mia opened her eyes.

Nick was still leaning back against the booth looking totally relaxed. She could feel his heartbeat under the skin at his wrist. It had been a long time since she had touched another person like this. Suddenly, she realized how lonely her life had been, but the strange thing was, she felt lonely for him. A man she hardly knew. Her logical mind told her to stop thinking like that, it was going to lead to heartbreak, but her heart was beating in the same rhythm as his.

"What did you do to me?"

"Nothing." She shrugged.

"Yes, you did. I felt something go through me. What was it?"

Mia saw that he wasn't going to stop until he had a real answer. "I took away the negative energy that was giving you your headache."

His eyes narrowed in disbelief. "Okay."

His tone of voice with that one word told Mia all she needed to know. Nick White was not going to easily accept who she was. She started to take her hands back, but he wouldn't let go. Not until the waiter came to their table.

"Would you like a glass of wine?" The man held out a bottle of red wine for their examination.

"I don't drink, thank you," Mia said. "So, water with lemon please."

"I'll have the same," Nick told the waiter, who turned and walked away.

"You don't have to go without because of me."

"I don't drink, either. Both of my parents were alcoholics, so I decided not to go down that path."

"They've passed on?"

"My dad died when I was ten and my mom when I was thirteen. My grandparents took me in and I lived with them until I joined the Marines. How about you?"

Mia's nerve endings tingled. She had felt drawn to him the moment he had walked into the gallery. His revelation made her wonder if it was more than basic attraction.

"My parents died in a plane crash when I was thirteen."

"Really?" he asked. "Any brothers or sisters?"

"I'm an only child," Mia replied.

"Me too." Nick was silent for a moment. "That's quite a coincidence."

"Is it?"

"What do you mean?" His eyes narrowed.

"Maybe it was fate."

"I don't believe in fate. I believe things just happen."

The waiter sat their glasses on the table and took their order. When he left, Mia changed the subject. "Tell me about your grandparents. Do you see them much?"

"They live in Oklahoma… on a reservation. Frank and Josie Whitecloud." Nick was watching for her reaction. Mia could feel his apprehension.

"You don't like telling people that, do you?" she asked.

"There is still a lot of prejudice out there, so, when I left the military, I shortened my name to just White. I wanted to be judged by my own merits instead of some preconceived notion of what an Indian is. Here in New York and with my last name White, I can do that. Back home, with the last name of Whitecloud, I couldn't be who I wanted to be."

"Your grandparents didn't like that, did they?"

"They've accepted it now, but things were strained for a while."

The waiter came with their food and set it on the table. Nick took a fork to his lasagna and cut into it. The steam floated upward and dissipated.

Mia studied him closely. In Oklahoma his dark hair, eyes, and skin might have identified him as Native American, but in New York he could be one of a hundred different nationalities that gave a person those characteristics. Here he could be Nick White, with no questions asked.

"Don't tell me you don't like Italian?" Nick asked, nodding at her untouched plate.

"I love Italian."

"Good, because this place has the best in the city."

Mia stirred her Fettuccine Alfredo and then took a bite. The rich, creamy sauce coated her tongue and seemed to come alive in her mouth. She could only moan in ecstasy.

Nick laughed quietly. "I told you."

Mia liked his laugh. It made her warm inside.

They talked all through dinner. Mia had never been so at ease with a man. It was like they had been friends forever.

Nick paid the bill and as they were walking to his car, Mia noticed his hand on the small of her back. She had never had a man do that before. It made her feel special and protected.

He drove her home and circled the block twice.

"You can keep circling, but you're not going to find an empty spot until the bar closes at two."

Nick grumbled under his breath and took the next open spot, a hundred yards from her front door. He helped her out of the car and kept looking behind him. His good humor was gone.

"What's wrong?" Mia asked, feeling his stress.

"Nothing." Nick looked down the street once more and then into the windows of the abandoned stores that lined the streets.

He put his hand to her back once again and tried to get her moving, but she stayed where she was. "Tell me what you saw?"

"When I left your place the other night, I thought I was being followed, but every time I turned around there was no one there and…"

"And what?"

"Nothing, let's go."

He pressed against her back with more force and he kept up a quick pace until they were in the lobby.

"Evening, Ms. Carrigan," the doorman Carl called out to her.

"Hi, Carl," Mia replied.

Mia pushed the button to the elevator door and it opened with a ding. "Do you want to come up and see my loft?" she asked hesitantly. "I'm really proud of it."

"I'd like that." Nick stepped into the elevator with her. "I don't want to alarm you, but I think I busted the doorman for narcotics when I was new on the job."

"You're probably right. We have ten different people working the lobby, seven men and three women, and they are all on parole for one thing or another."

"That doesn't bother you?"

"It was my idea to hire them and give them a chance to fix their past mistakes."

"It was your idea to hire them?" Nick looked confused.

"It's my building. I own it. Remember the first time you brought me home and I said that's my building?"

"Yeah, but everyone says that, meaning that's where they live, not that they own the whole stinking building."

Mia shrugged and wondered if she should have told him. People always treated her differently when they found out she had money. Nick didn't seem like that kind of person and she needed him to know her, the real her. The feelings she had for him were growing stronger and she needed to be able to talk to someone who wanted to be with her, and not just for her money.

The elevator doors opened and Mia stepped into the long

hallway that divided her side of the building from the apartment on the other side. She pulled out her key and said, "This one is mine." She opened the door and flipped on the lights. Everything was just as she'd left it, but it felt different. *He* had been here, in her space. The air all around her was cold.

"I guess these old buildings still get pretty chilly in the winter," Nick commented.

"I'll turn up the heat." Mia pushed the button on the thermostat and flipped the switch for the fireplace. "That should do it."

"Are you okay? Your face is real pale. If you're uncomfortable having me here, just say so and I'll go?"

"No, please. I really want you to stay. I'll give you the grand tour."

Nick followed her into the living area. "Over here is the kitchen." Mia led him to her right and through her kitchen, pointing out all the commercial grade appliances.

"Nice," he said as he ran his hand over the granite countertop.

"And, the dining area. It has a great view of the Manhattan Bridge." Mia pointed toward the huge windows that ran almost floor to ceiling. She then took him back through the living area, where the fireplace was already warming the room, past the frosted glass panels that hung from the heavy wooden beams, and into her bedroom. "I guess I should have made my bed." Mia felt herself blush.

Nick laughed. "If you never made your bed again, no one would notice. This place is amazing."

"Thanks. I designed it myself."

"Is that the bathroom?" Nick nodded to the only enclosed space in the room.

Mia smiled and held her hand out towards the door.

"I'm almost afraid to look." Nick teased.

"Go ahead. It's part of the tour."

He opened one of the few doors in the apartment. Mia watched as he walked past the shower stall. "It's big enough for two." He grinned.

"I wouldn't know."

Nick stepped up onto the platform that held her tub. "It has its own dais."

"We had to raise it to hide the plumbing."

"I can't even imagine what a tub like this would cost."

"Between eight and ten thousand dollars," she confessed.

Nick looked at her with his eyebrows raised. "They must pay really well at The Freeman Academy." He watched her for a second and then pointed to the red roses on the vanity. "It looks like I have competition."

Mia glanced at her roses. "I bought them for myself. My mother loved red roses, so when I'm missing her, I buy roses." She couldn't bring herself to look him in the eye as she admitted it.

He didn't say anything else about the roses.

"What about privacy?" He tilted his head toward the windows.

Mia opened a drawer in the vanity and pulled out a small remote and pushed a button. Automatic window blinds came from the bottom and top of each window to fully cover them. She smiled. "All the windows have them. I often work at night and sleep during the day. With the touch of a button, I can make it as dark as night anytime I want."

"I think my entire apartment would fit in this room and my *old* apartment was as big as your bathroom." He closed the door behind him and made his way to some of her canvases hanging on the wall. Nick studied each piece. "This has the same style as that painting at the gallery, the one we were looking at the night we met."

"That's because it's my piece."

Nick turned around and looked at her. "M. Carrigan?"

"As in Mia."

"I'm such a moron," he said shaking his head. "Are there any other big secrets you want to let me in on before I make an even bigger fool of myself?"

"I have lots of them, but I think that's enough for one night."

"Okay. What do you want to do now?" he asked with a grin on his face.

"I umm, I really want to sketch you. Will you let me?"

"Why do you want to sketch *me*?"

"Because you have a great face." As soon as the words were out of her mouth, Mia regretted them. The heat burned her cheeks as they turned pink. "I mean, from an artist's viewpoint."

Nick's eyebrows arched and without saying a word, it was like he was asking her just what she meant by that comment.

Mia stammered. "I didn't mean it isn't a great face anyway. I meant…"

Nick laughed and put his hands on her shoulders. "Mia, relax. I'm flattered that you want to sketch me."

"Really?"

"Sure. Where do you want me?" He flung his arms out wide.

Mia quickly looked around the room. She had never sketched a live person in her loft before. A chair would be too uncomfortable, and she needed it anyway. "Is the bed okay?"

"I didn't think I'd get here on our first date, but I'm good with it." He winked at her, sat down on the bed, and leaned against one of her pillows.

Mia grabbed a blank canvas and a piece of lead. She propped the canvas on an easel and started working. Nick had his hands behind his head. She barely had the shape of his face outlined when she heard him snoring. Luckily, he seemed too tired to move so she kept sketching. Three hours passed before he shifted onto his side.

She kept sketching until her eyes were burning. If she kept going when she was this tired, she was going to ruin the whole thing. Stepping back, she studied what she had so far. It was him, but it didn't have the life in it that she wanted to see. Tomorrow, she would work on it some more.

As quietly as she could, Mia dimmed the lights and covered him with a blanket. She watched him sleep for several minutes. She knew she should wake him and send him home, but he was exhausted and she wanted to take care of him. It had been so long since she had had someone to care about and there was something between them. It was new and old at the same time. Mia wanted to nurture it to see how it would grow.

Mia crept into the kitchen, got a drink of water, and settled in on the couch with her last blanket. As she was dozing off, the voices came to her. One in particular kept calling to her. "Tell him to follow the ring. Follow the ring." Mia knew instantly who it was, the girl from her dream. "I can't. He won't understand and he'll think I'm crazy," she whispered into the darkness.

Again she heard the same words repeated, only more urgently. "Tell him to follow the ring. The ring has the answers. Tell him now."

Mia tip-toed into the bedroom and prayed Nick wouldn't wake up and think she had lost her mind. She leaned down and barely whispered, "She says to follow the ring. It has the answers. Follow the ring." Nick never moved and Mia figured she had wasted her time.

The wooden floorboards creaked and groaned as she got back to the couch. "Are you happy now? Now go away, all of you." Within seconds, the whispers were gone.

Mia punched the throw pillow on the couch and covered herself with the fleece blanket. Her hands and body ached from working too many uninterrupted hours and her eyes burned even after she closed them. She was almost asleep when the air around her turned ice cold and began to vibrate. The feeling nauseated her, like motion sickness.

In the kitchen was a black shadow. It was so large it blocked the blue numbers on the oven clock. Mia blinked to make sure her eyes weren't playing tricks on her, even though she knew they weren't. Still, the glowing blue numbers were obscured.

The shadow moved towards her and she froze with fear. The malevolence that surrounded her was terrifying. Her heart pounded in her chest so hard that it hurt and adrenaline raced through her blood. Her body began to shake from the effects.

The shadow hovered, as if it was waiting for her to make the first move, but she just sat there on the couch watching it. Then, slowly it started to move toward the bedroom.

Mia jumped up and ran to the open space that made up her bedroom door. She put her hands out as if she could stop the shadow physically. "You are not welcome here! I order you to leave!" Her voice was quivering. She was trying not to wake Nick. She didn't want to explain to him who, or what, she was kicking out of her apartment at three-thirty in the morning, while he was sleeping in her bed.

The black shadow grew thinner, but just as light began to filter through it, all at once it grew larger and solid black. Mia saw a book, that had been sitting on her end table, fly across the room and land underneath the dining room table with a loud thud. When Mia looked back, the shadow was gone. The frigid air around her dissipated and grew still.

Slowly, Mia took a breath and let it out. Her hand went to her heart, willing it to slow down. It didn't make any difference. She stood there, shaking uncontrollably, for at least ten minutes. The thought of sleeping on the couch by herself, well, she just couldn't do it. She put one foot in front of the other until she was right next to her bed. Pulling back the thick down comforter, she slipped in, trying not to wake Nick. It didn't work, he woke up anyway.

"Oh crap! I fell asleep. I'm so sorry. I better go."

He started to get up, but Mia grabbed his arm and begged, "Please don't leave! Please?"

Nick covered her hand where it rested on his arm. "Mia, you're freezing cold. What happened to you?"

"I was sleeping on the couch." It was partially the truth.

He shifted until they were both under the covers and he pulled her into his arms.

"Your skin feels like you've been sleeping in a freezer. You're shaking."

Mia didn't respond, she just let his warmth soak into her body until she could stop the trembling. His arms held her tightly with her back against his chest. Deep inside she knew she should have let him leave. She was afraid she wouldn't be able to protect him. She wasn't sure she would be able to protect herself. Mia pressed her body closer to Nick than she already was. She couldn't admit out loud that she was afraid for both of them.

CHAPTER FOUR

"So, you want to tell me about her?" Wayne Coleman grinned as he started the car.

"I don't know what you're talking about," Nick said, but he couldn't keep a straight face.

"Come on. I'm your partner. You're supposed to tell me everything. You show up today wearing the extra shirt you keep in your locker and with a five o'clock shadow at nine-thirty in the morning. That tells me you didn't go home last night."

"You're on top of it today."

"That's why I get paid the big bucks. Now, tell me all the details, and don't leave anything out." Wayne turned and looked behind him as he backed out of the parking space.

"There's nothing to tell."

"Come on," Wayne prodded.

"She's an artist and I think she's rich."

"What do you mean, you think she's rich?" Wayne wanted to know.

"She owns the building she lives in and has a ten-thousand dollar tub in her apartment." Nick smiled as he remembered how Mia seemed almost embarrassed as she'd told him that.

"What? Are you serious? Where is this building?"

"I'm totally serious. It's in Brooklyn. Over in DUMBO."

"That figures. If she's an artist, I mean. They seem to congregate there." Wayne laughed. "You should marry her as fast as you can."

Nick didn't respond. He just watched the abandoned buildings pass as they headed to the scene of a new murder. The reflection of flashing lights caught his eye. "Over there," Nick pointed.

"I see it now." Wayne made a hard left and pulled over next to a patrol car.

A beat cop, who didn't look old enough to shave, came over to them. "You guys from Homicide?"

"I'm Coleman. This is White. What do we got?"

"Dead woman over there in the empty lot." He gestured to where the crime scene tape was being strung up. "There's trauma to the body, a lot of blood..."The young cop took a deep breath. Nick thought the kid might puke. Wayne rolled his eyes and walked toward the dead girl.

Nick tugged his coat collar up against the freezing cold wind that was blowing. "This your first?"

The young cop nodded.

"Believe it or not, it gets easier." Nick told him as he followed his partner.

There, in the middle of a field, was the body of a young woman. She was fully clothed, but she had on a short skirt, a white blouse, and a rain coat. On her left foot was a black pump. Her right foot was bare. She wasn't dressed for the outdoors.

"She was brought here and then killed," Nick said, pointing to the mud on her foot.

"It's hard to say how long she's been here. Three or four days, maybe a week," Wayne observed. It's been so cold, she's frozen solid. There are three separate holes in her blouse, maybe more under her arm and hand."

"Looks like a thin bladed knife, or dagger, possibly a screwdriver. We'll know more after they thaw her out and do the autopsy." Nick began to walk around the body. "I don't see any sign of a purse."

"We may have to wait for prints."

"She's a pretty girl. Someone has to be missing her by now." Nick crouched down on the balls of his feet to get a better look. The girl's dark brown hair was partially covering her face and her left hand was over her heart. She almost looked posed. On her hand was a ring. It was blue, like a sapphire, set in either sterling silver or white gold maybe. He had never seen anything like it. The stone was set in what looked like a nest of rope with a piece of the rope crossing over it, securing it in place. He leaned closer and that was when he heard a voice whisper in his ear, "Follow the ring. It has the answers. Follow the ring."

Nick stood up and turned around, half expecting to see someone behind him. The whisper was that clear. "What the hell?"

"What's wrong?" Wayne asked.

"Did you hear that?"

"Hear what?"

Nick shook his head. "Never mind."

"I wonder where her other shoe is?"

"I'll look around." Nick walked away, grateful to be by himself and think through what he had just experienced. He hated when creepy stuff like that happened. He didn't believe in that mumbo-jumbo crap, déjà vu, weird dreams, the feeling of being followed when no one's there, and yet, he couldn't deny that strange things *had* been happening to him lately. It had all started when he met Mia, and what was even stranger was that he could have sworn it was Mia's voice he had heard.

Nick walked up and down the empty street, but there was nothing to be found. Back at the station he spent the afternoon going through missing person's reports. There were no matches.

"We're not going to find out who she is tonight." Nick was frustrated.

"We did get the tox screen on the kid in the abandoned warehouse." Wayne opened the file. "It looks like whoever killed him wasted his bullet because the kid had a huge dose of Oxy in his bloodstream."

"Maybe he took someone else's stash. Let's re-canvas the neighborhood tomorrow and see if we can get someone to talk. And I think we should take his picture down to the mission, the parks, and the homeless shelter. Someone has to know who the kid ran with."

"Sounds good, but I'm calling it a day." Wayne leaned closer and lowered his voice. "You gonna see her again tonight?"

"I'm going home to a hot shower and my bed."

"Don't be such an old man. Call her." Wayne went on, "Take her dancing."

"Mia doesn't strike me as the dancing, partying type. She's kind of…" What was the word he was looking for? "Reserved."

"Whatever." Wayne pointed his finger at him. "Bright and early tomorrow. Don't make me wait for you."

***

Nick shaved, showered, and sat on his couch, remote in hand, flipping through channels without ever pausing to see what was on. After his fourth rotation of all available channels, he tossed the remote, picked up the phone, and dialed her number. Her machine came on and just as he was about to hang up, he heard her voice.

"Nick?"

"How did you know it was me?"

"No one else would call me at this time of night, except maybe Charlie."

"Charlie?"

"Charlie is the owner of the gallery where we met. And his wife wouldn't let him call me for anything but business. She's really scary."

Nick laughed and shook his head. "What are you doing?"

"I'm on my way to DiMilo's to get a pizza. Why?"

"I was on my way to DiMilo's to get a pizza too," Nick told her even though he had no idea where the place was.

"Really? Meet me there and we can share one."

"Are you taking a cab?"

"It's only five blocks, I'm walking it."

"Don't you dare!" Nick warned. "It's dark outside. I'll pick you up. Give me twenty minutes."

"I'll wait for you in the lobby."

The thought of old Carl in the lobby made Nick think twice. "What's your cell phone number and I'll call you when I'm close?"

"I don't have a cell phone," Mia admitted quietly.

"Okay, I'll come to your apartment."

"I'll be waiting."

Nick was going to double-park, but when he got to her building she was outside waiting. She waved and climbed into the car.

"Why are you waiting outside? It's only twenty degrees out there."

"I know, but I didn't want you to have to wait. Besides, I'm starving."

"Mia, put your seat belt on and promise me you won't walk the streets of New York after dark. It's not safe."

"I think you're jaded because of your job," she teased.

"Definitely." In his mind, Nick saw the young woman in the field.

The restaurant was a small family place with red and white checked plastic table cloths, a juke box playing oldies, and an arcade area filled with teenagers. It wasn't nearly as classy as the place he had taken her before, but she looked right at home.

"Mia!" the gray-haired man behind the counter called out when they took their seats.

"Hi, Sal." Mia waved.

Sal came to their table and in his heavy Italian accent said, "You never bring a friend in here before, this is good. You want the usual?"

"What's the usual," Nick asked her as her cheeks turned pink.

"A large pizza with pepperoni, mushrooms, and onions, and a large Coke to drink."

"Sounds good to me." After they were alone he asked, "Tell me why you don't have a cell phone."

Mia played with a napkin she'd pulled out of the metal dispenser, folding it into smaller and smaller squares. Nick could see he had touched on a sore subject.

"I used to have one, but anyone who needed to call me always called me at home, so I got rid of it."

"What about your family?"

"They're all gone."

Mia looked at him and for a moment he saw the incredible sadness she kept hidden inside of her.

"I'm sorry. I didn't mean to-"

"That's okay." She waved her hand dismissing what he was about to say. "It's old news. I'd rather talk about now. Tell me about the cases you're working on."

"No way, you don't want to know about them. It would give you bad dreams."

"I already have bad dreams."

Before he could ask her what she meant by that, their pizza came. Between the two of them they ate it all.

Nick smiled at Mia until she finally said, "What? Do I have cheese on my chin or something?"

"No. I think it's funny that you ate four pieces of pizza. Most of the girls I've dated were on perpetual diets. That can get on a guy's nerves after a while."

"When I eat at home, I try to eat healthy, but when I go out, it's a free-for-all, except for all the ice cream I have stuffed in my freezer. It's kind of my dirty little secret."

Nick leaned in and whispered suggestively, "I like dirty little secrets."

Mia giggled. "Maybe we should go back to my place and share some."

"I think we should."

As they drove back to Mia's apartment, Nick couldn't stop glancing in her direction. Her dark hair framed her face and her cheeks looked like satin. She must have sensed him watching her because she smiled that same Mona Lisa smile he had seen the night they'd met in the gallery.

Nick found a spot only a half block from her building and shut off the engine, but instead of getting out of the car, he sat there. Mia watched him, her dark eyes wide and curious as to what he was doing. He wanted to take her in his arms and kiss her, but instead he touched her cheek with his fingertips. Her skin was cold from the walk to the car.

"I had to know," he said quietly, "if you are as soft as you look." He took a lock of her hair and let it slip through his fingers.

"Am I?"

"Yes."

"I think you should," Mia whispered.

"Should what?"

"Kiss me."

Nick didn't need any more encouragement than that. He closed the distance between them until he felt her warm, moist lips against his. It was a kiss, the likes of which he had never experienced before. His heart started pounding and, all the way to his toes, a sensation of warmth filled him. It was just supposed to be a simple kiss, but it wasn't simple at all. As he pulled away, he kept his hand on her cheek, so there was still a connection. He didn't want to stop touching her.

"Do you always kiss like that?" he asked, trying to calm his racing pulse.

"Like what?"

He could see by her expression, she wasn't being coy. That was a relief because he was tired of playing head games with the women he dated. Mia seemed more sincere than all of them.

Her lips were still wet from his kiss, so he let his thumb slide over her bottom lip. "You're just as soft here." It was only his thumb, but it was as intimate as anything he had ever experienced. He didn't know why it felt that way, it just did.

"We better go." He opened the car door and it was like reality rushed in. Somewhere close by, a siren blared and the frosty air snaked down his neck.   He helped Mia out of the car, making sure she didn't slip on the icy sidewalk.

When they reached the lobby, Nick held the door. They had only taken two steps when Mia stopped dead in her tracks. Sitting inside the lobby was an older woman, dressed all in black, but for the bright red scarf that covered her graying hair.

As soon as the woman saw Mia she rushed toward her and started talking in English that was heavily accented. "Mia, I call you and I call you, but I don't hear from you."

"I'm sorry, Silviana. I've been very busy."

"You are Nadja's only child and I have to hunt you down like a stranger."

It was obvious from Mia's body language that she did not want to talk to the woman. Her accent, he guessed, was eastern European.

"Silviana, I will call you tomorrow and we can talk."

"No! No! I have to talk, now!" The woman took Mia's face in her hands. "You are in danger, Mia. The spirits have shown it to me. There is darkness all around you. It will be like a storm and you will lose your way in the darkness."

"Please, Silviana, I can't talk of this now. Tomorrow." Mia started to walk past the woman, only to have her grab Mia's arm and pull her back hard.

"Hey, let her go," Nick said before he could think better of it.

The woman turned on Nick. "Who are you? Her lover? Are you the man who betrays her? I have seen it," she hissed, before turning her attention back to Mia. The old woman's voice got louder as she spoke. "Tell me you have not denied the visions. Tell me you know what is coming for you?"

"Yes, I do!" Mia answered in a tight angry voice. "I will call you later and you can tell me all that you have seen. Now, please go."

The old woman took a deep breath, as if she was relieved of some heavy burden, and then she started to fumble in her coat pocket. She pressed something into Mia's palm and closed her hand over Mia's. "I made this for you, but I think it will do no good."

Mia said nothing else as the woman walked out the lobby door, letting in a gust of ice cold wind. Mia didn't even look at him as she headed straight to the elevator and jabbed the button.

Nick trailed after her, confused by what had just happened. He wanted to know what it was all about, but he felt like Mia had closed herself off to him. They rode to the fourth floor in silence. In the hallway, her hands were shaking so badly she couldn't get her apartment key into the lock.

He covered her hand with his and guided it in. As soon as she stepped inside, Mia flipped on the lights and turned up the heat. When she looked at him, he saw she had no color in her face at all. Nick thought she might faint.

"Are you all right?"

"I don't know," she spoke very quietly.

"Mia, you don't believe what that old woman said, do you? I mean, I don't know her, but all that crazy talk about spirits and darkness, you don't buy into that stuff do you?"

Mia wouldn't look at him. "I'll get the ice cream," she said, ignoring what he'd asked her.

As she moved to the kitchen, Nick took her arm and stopped her. "Who was that woman?"

"She is my mother's oldest sister, my aunt Silviana."

"She believes she can talk to spirits?" He hadn't meant to sound so sarcastic, but he did.

"Is that really so hard to believe? I mean, you come from people that have great faith in spiritual things."

"*I* believe in things you can see and touch and nothing else. One of the reasons I left home was to get away from all of the old ones, like my grandfather, and their superstitions and myths."

Mia hesitated. "What about love? You can't see or touch love. Is that a myth?"

There was such a look of disappointment on her face that he didn't respond to her question. After an awkward silence, he asked, "Why does your aunt think you are in danger?"

"You don't believe in anything you can't see, or touch, so it doesn't matter, does it?"

Nick didn't say a word. Somehow their worlds had collided and he wasn't even sure how it had happened. His childhood had been filled with legends and lore, but he had walked away from it all, and he wasn't going back. That would mean becoming Nicholas Whitecloud again and he wasn't about to do that. He had worked too hard distancing himself from that Indian kid on the reservation.

"I have something I want to give you before you go." Mia walked into the studio part of her bedroom and came back with a gift bag the size of a small suitcase. White tissue paper was poking out of every square inch of the top of the bag.

"What is it?" Nick asked.

"It's something I want you to have, but don't open it until you get home. If you don't like it, you don't have to keep it."

Nick had no doubt that the evening was over. He took the gift from Mia's hand and she walked him to the door. As he stepped out into the hallway he said, "I'm sorry, Mia."

"I guess we can't help who we are. Goodbye, Nick."

She closed the door and he stood there staring at it. This was so far from how he thought the night would go he couldn't believe it. Nick put his hand up, intending to knock and try to fix it. His knuckles were against the cold steel. For some reason he opened his hand and pressed it flat against the door. There was no sound at all coming from Mia's apartment. It dawned on him that she was on the other side, touching the same door. She hadn't walked away. In his gut he knew it. It was like he could feel her through it. How could that be? Nick jerked his hand away. She was making him as crazy as she was, apparently.

Nick hurried to his car, bag in hand. He tossed it into the passenger seat and started the engine. From where he was parked, he could see Mia's apartment. The lights were still on and he could see her standing in the dining room looking out the window. Right before his eyes he saw a dark shadow surround her. It was so dark it obstructed the light glowing behind her. She didn't move. She gave no indication she saw it at all. Nick blinked, thinking he was seeing things, but when he opened his eyes it was still there. His whole body grew cold and goose bumps broke out on his flesh as he remembered the old woman's words. "There is darkness all around you."

Nick slammed the car into gear and raced down the street. He couldn't get away fast enough.

CHAPTER FIVE

"You're sure quiet today. You want to talk about it?" Wayne sat at his desk going over an autopsy report.

"No." Nick's mood was foul and talking about it wasn't going to make it any better.

"Okay." Wayne moved on. "We got an ID on the girl in the field. Her name was Kelly Langford, twenty-eight and single, as far as we know. We have her last known address. The cause of death was six stab wounds, one that pierced her lung and another, her heart. The weapon was a long, thin, double-edged blade. Maybe a dagger, or even a letter opener, the doc said."

"Any next of kin we need to notify?" Nick tapped his pen on the desk top.

"None that we could find. She had been in the system since she was four. Mother was a junky, father unknown."

"Really?" Nick questioned. "I wouldn't have thought that when I saw her. She was too clean."

"She went to college and had a job at one of the big finance companies."

"Let's go find out who wanted her dead." Nick grabbed his coat, grateful to have something to take his mind off of Mia for the rest of the day.

As Wayne drove, Nick flipped through the autopsy photos. When he came to a close up of the ring, he remembered the voice that whispered in his ear. He could still hear it, and that was enough to make the hairs on the back of his neck stand up all over again.

"Do you believe in anything paranormal?" Nick asked hoping he wouldn't regret it.

"What?" Wayne took his eyes off the road and stared at Nick. "What are you talking about?"

"Do you think it's possible that some people can talk with spirits and stuff like that?"

"Why? Are you having visitations from little green men or something?" Wayne laughed.

"That would be aliens, not spirits. Forget I said anything." He *was* sorry he'd brought it up.

Wayne once again looked at him and the smile left his face. "What are we talking about here, seriously?"

"Last night Mia and I met for pizza. When we got back to her place, her aunt was waiting in the lobby. She started going on and on about how Mia was in grave danger and there was darkness all around her, and she was going to lose her way, and all this kind of stuff."

"I take it you didn't believe it?"

Nick shook his head. "No, but I could see that Mia did. She looked really scared. I kind of made fun of the whole thing and that was the end of it. She showed me the door."

"She was pissed?"

Nick thought about it for a moment before he replied. "She seemed more… hurt, like the fact that I thought it was all bull made her sad or something."

Wayne didn't say anything, which wasn't like him at all. He had opinions about everything and anything.

Nick couldn't take the deafening silence any longer. "What?"

"I didn't say a word." Wayne shrugged.

"I know. Why not? I know you've got something to say, you always do."

"You won't like it."

"That never stopped you before."

"You're very closed minded about certain things and that's one of them."

"I am not closed minded," Nick denied angrily.

"Yes, you are. It's one of the hazards of being a cop. We start to think in nothing but cold, hard facts, physical evidence, and what will stand up in court. We won't acknowledge anything we can't use."

"So?"

"So, we forget that part of our job is gut instinct," Wayne continued, "and I think sometimes, maybe we get help with that gut instinct."

"What are you talking about?"

"One of the very first cases I worked when I came to homicide was the murder of a boy. He was thirteen. He was found beaten to death in an ally. I just couldn't get a handle on the case, until one night…" Wayne hesitated and glanced at Nick. "I had a dream."

"Go on," Nick prompted.

"In my dream, the kid was whole, not all messed up like when we found him. He was smiling and laughing. I asked him who killed him and he said two words to me. He said, 'Papa knows.' That broke the case wide open. The family had been smuggled into the country by human traffickers. The coyotes had demanded even more money from the father when they'd gotten here, and when the father couldn't pay, they killed the boy in retribution.

"I have never heard you talk about that before."

"Because most cops are closed minded about things they can't use in court and I didn't want to have to hear it all. Can you imagine if Shilling and Wentz heard that story?"

Nick thought about Shilling and Wentz. They were good cops, but they were miserable to work with. They would have given Wayne so much grief if they'd heard that story. Suddenly, Nick felt a little sick to his stomach. He had treated Mia just like Shilling and Wentz would have treated Wayne. Nick leaned his head back against the head rest and pressed his thumb and forefinger to his eyes.

"Maybe you should give her a chance to explain. Or, are you too afraid of what the truth might be?" Wayne asked cautiously.

"What's that supposed to mean?"

"It means, I know how you feel about your heritage and your grandfather's beliefs. Don't let that ruin your relationship with Mia because you're hardheaded."

"After last night, I'm not sure I would even call it a friendship."

Wayne laughed loudly. "You've done nothing, but think about and talk about her since the night you met. It's a relationship, whether you want to admit it or not. I was the same way when I met Kathy, so I know the signs." Wayne thought for a second. "We should go on a double date. Kathy would love to meet Mia and she's been complaining I never take her anywhere anymore. What do you say?"

"If Mia ever talks to me again, maybe."

They spent the next few hours going through Kelly Langford's apartment and talking to her neighbors.

"You'd think she would be friends with someone in her building after living there for four years," Nick complained as they left her building.

"That's why some people like New York. You can be

anonymous."

"Maybe we'll have better luck at her work, Stanton and Bingham Financial."

***

The offices of Stanton and Bingham Financial screamed big money. After flashing their badges, they were ushered into the office of one of its presidents, Martin Bingham.

"We're here investigating the murder of one of your employees, Kelly Langford." Wayne took the lead while Nick paced around the room and gauged the man's reaction.

"Kelly's been murdered? When? How? Are you sure it's her?"

"Yes. We're sure. She was stabbed to death over a week ago."

Nick would put Martin Bingham at about fifty-five, with silver hair and a slight build. Nothing about his demeanor was off. He seemed genuinely shocked.

"I can't believe it, she is, was, one of our brightest associates."

"Didn't anyone notice she hadn't shown up for work lately?"

"She had taken a few weeks off," Bingham explained. "She just finished an extremely intensive project that lasted six months. She was tired and needed a break. She mentioned going to Tahiti and basking in the sun, but I don't know that she ever made the reservations. I offered our travel service. They would know."

"We'll need a name and number. What else can you tell us about Kelly?"

"I assume you know her background. She was a foster child until she turned eighteen. A friend of mine is a social worker and told me how bright Kelly is." Bingham took out a handkerchief and wiped at his eyes. "I arranged to pay for Kelly's schooling. She has a master's in Business Administration specializing in International Finance, and graduated summa cum laude. It was Kelly's accomplishments that convinced me to start a scholarship program for foster kids."

"That's nice." Wayne nodded at Nick. "What about Kelly? Did she have a boyfriend? Was she close to anyone here at work that you know of?" Was she on good terms with her co-workers?"

"Kelly never would have spoken to me about a boyfriend. She was very private and I think she had a hard time getting close to people. I'm sure her childhood had a lot to do with that. This is such a tragedy. She had so much to live for."

"How much did Kelly make? Did she carry around a lot of cash that you know of?"

"Does anyone carry cash these days?" Bingham looked surprised at that. "Her base pay was around three-hundred and fifty-thousand and she just received a large bonus of a quarter of a million dollars."

"She got a bonus of two-hundred and fifty thousand dollars?" Wayne's asked incredulously.

"Her work on the Saudi Project more than warranted such a bonus. She would have gotten bonuses every year, over the next ten years. If the project goes as expected, it should net our company over three billion dollars. So, you can see, she was a valuable asset to us."

"How many people do you employ here, Mr. Bingham?" Nick asked.

"We have forty-two on the payroll. We're a small firm, but profitable."

"We would like to speak with all of the employees and Mr. Stanton also."

Bingham picked up his phone. "Marie, print out a list of all current employees, with addresses and phone numbers and give it to the officers. And get the address and phone number of the travel service." He hung up the phone. "I am afraid that James is out of the country right now. He and his wife are in Hong Kong, and they won't be back for another week."

"Is that Mr. Stanton?"

"Yes, James Stanton is my partner. James is going to be devastated. He worked very closely with Kelly. I'm going to have to call him."

"Thanks for your help, Mr. Bingham. If you think of anything else." Wayne tapped the card he placed on Bingham's desk.

"Of course. Good luck, gentlemen. I hope you find whoever did this."

The rest of the employees told the same story. Kelly was well liked, a hard worker and quiet. She kept to herself.

"There has to be someone who knows what she was about," Wayne observed. "How many women do you know who don't have girlfriends they complain to about their boyfriends?"

Nick thought of Mia. She didn't seem to have very many

friends, or did he just not know of them? Was she telling all her friends what a jerk he was? Probably. He needed to call her when he had a chance, to straighten things out. Even if she didn't want to see him again, he needed to at least say he was sorry.

"How about her foster family?" Wayne asked, pointing to the file. "Does it have anything about them in there? Like an address."

Nick shuffled through the papers until he found it. "Yeah, Crescent Street, that's not too far from here."

"Let's go." Wayne hung a u-turn and headed north.

He pulled to a stop and Nick double checked the address. "This is it?"

"I've seen a lot worse foster homes than this place," Nick commented.

"Middle-class neighborhood, house looks neat from the outside. Let's see what's going on inside."

Nick knocked and a middle-aged woman opened the door, holding a sleeping baby in her arms. She had tears on her face and her eyes were red and swollen like she had been crying for a while.

"Mrs. Shaffer?"

"You're police officers, aren't you? And you're here about Kelly?" she asked.

"Yes, ma'am."

"They just said her name on the news. I was praying it wasn't really her, but it was, wasn't it?"

"Yes, ma'am. Can we ask you a few questions about her?"

"Come on in. Let me put Alicia down in her crib." The woman left and then came back without the baby.

Nick noticed framed pictures on the wall with, what appeared to be, school photos inside. The kids all looked healthy and happy, black, white, and Hispanic, two had obvious disabilities, but they were all smiling.

"The one on the end is Kelly." Natalie Shaffer pointed to the brown-haired girl with a space between her teeth. "She was thirteen when she came to us."

"Our paperwork has her in the system when she was four." Wayne stated.

"She bounced from home to home for years until she came here," Mrs. Shaffer explained. "She was very scared and had extreme trust issues. Kelly was very bright though. All those years in foster care and she still managed to get straight A's. It's almost unheard of."

"When was the last time you talked with Kelly?" Nick flipped open his note pad.

"I called her once a month if I hadn't heard from her. I wanted her to know we still loved her, but it wasn't easy with her. She kept everyone at arms length. Vannessa is the only one I know of that Kelly let get close to her."

"Vannessa?" Nick asked.

"Vannessa Gomez. She lived with us for six years. She's going to school at NYU during the day and waiting tables at night. Vanessa and Kelly were very close. I think Kelly helped her with money sometimes. I just got off the phone with her. I could barely understand her because she was crying so hard." Tears ran down Mrs. Shaffer's cheeks. "I can't believe she's gone. Kelly accomplished so much and was such a good example to the other kids. What am I going to tell them when they get home?"

Nick and Wayne glanced at each other. There was never an answer to that question.

"Could we get Vannessa's number, address, and place of employment?"

"I'll write it down." Mrs. Shaffer went into the kitchen and came back with a slip of yellow paper.

"Thanks, and we're very sorry for your loss." Wayne told her as they walked out the door.

"Let's go by Vannessa Gomez' place. She doesn't live too far from here," Nick said, looking at the address.

They pounded on Vannessa's door and tried her phone number before they gave up .

"Should we try the restaurant where she works?" Wayne asked.
Nick nodded.

The manager at The Living Oak restaurant looked at their badges and said, "Vannessa called off. Said there was a death in the family?" The man was looking for confirmation.

"That's why we're here. Her sister was murdered."

"Murdered? No wonder she was crying."

"If she calls in or shows up, tell her it is imperative we speak to her right away." Nick handed the man his card.

As they got back into the car, Wayne said, "This day was a

bust."

"We'll find her tomorrow." Nick pulled out the picture of the ring again and wondered if he was crazy.

"You going to call Mia?"

Nick thought about it for a minute. "I don't know. I'm gonna head home, shower, and eat. Then, if I'm not too tired, maybe."

Wayne chuckled under his breath. "You're gonna call."

Nick tossed the file onto the dashboard. "You're a pain in the butt."

***

Nick used his hook shot to get his empty carton of Chinese into the trash can.

"Two points," he said out loud.

Grabbing a wash cloth from the sink he wiped up the rice he had spilled on the counter top, carefully avoiding the gift bag that Mia had sent home with him. He hadn't felt right opening it last night and he still wasn't sure he should. Finally, he tossed the cloth in the sink and grabbed the gift bag.

He sat on his couch, with the bag between his feet, and began pulling out the white tissue paper. Inside was a rectangular box wrapped in more tissue paper. When he picked it up, he realized it wasn't a box, it was a canvas. He pulled off the extra wrapping and just stared at the image before him.

Nick recognized it instantly. Mia's small white hands resting in his large dark ones, all sketched in charcoal. The shading was amazing. The details perfect.

Nick set it at the end of the couch where he could see it from farther away. The more he looked at it, the more he knew he had made a horrible mistake leaving Mia's last night. She was odd, there was no getting around it, but he was drawn to her. He grabbed his coat and his keys and started for the door.

As his hand gripped the knob, he paused. If he went to her, there would be no going back. He would have to accept that whatever it was that was around her was real. Could he do that? Could he set aside logic and rational thinking to believe in something…paranormal? Was he just being hardheaded? After everything he had seen and felt since he met her, he couldn't think of a logical explanation on his own. He had to know what was going on. He had to hear it from Mia.

The drive to her building seemed to take forever. When he got there, he found a parking spot down the block and started walking.

"Freaking New York," he muttered as the snow blew in his face.

Nick walked into the lobby headed straight for the elevator, but before he could get there, the doorman said, "She's not here."

"Do you know where she went?"

His name tag said Jimmy. Nick had never seen him before, but he knew an ex-con when he saw one. Jimmy kind of shrugged and remained silent.

"It's really important that I talk to her."

"She doesn't like to be disturbed when she's working."

"Then she *is* home?"

"Naw, she went out with her camera about an hour ago." Jimmy pointed in the opposite direction Nick had just come from. "There's a small park down the street, toward the bridge. She goes there sometimes and takes pictures."

Nick nodded. "Thanks."

Back out into the cold he went. It had been snowing all afternoon and the snow crunched under his feet as he walked. In the distance, he could see the dark form of the Manhattan Bridge overpass. When he got to the corner park, there was no one there.

"Damn it," he said under his breath.

A lone street light barely lit up the darkness. He took a step toward it when a voice called out, "Don't move." Nick knew it was Mia.

"Why not?"

"You'll ruin my shot, and I've been waiting forever to get it." Her voice sounded high up.

Nick heard the whirr of her camera, but he couldn't see her. "Where are you?"

"On the fire escape."

The sounds of her feet moving on the cold metal rang out. Then, in the darkness, he saw something move. Mia emerged from the shadows with a somber expression on her face. She was dressed all in black, including a black knit beanie on her head. She belonged to the night. Nick couldn't tell if she was happy to see him, or not.

She stopped three feet from him and waited to see what he was going to say. Her dark eyes seemed larger than ever and they were watching him expectantly.

"I had to see you and I'm not sure why, except there are things that are happening that I don't understand. I can't find an explanation that makes sense to me. There's a part of me that wants to walk away as fast as I can and not look back, but for some reason I can't. It's like a moth to flame."

Mia thought for a minute before she spoke. "Maybe you should trust your instincts. Sometimes the moth gets too close to the flame and I wouldn't want you to get hurt." Tears filled Mia's eyes. She turned away from him as if she was ashamed of them.

Nick put his hand on her arm. "Tell me what's going on Mia. I want to understand."

"Do you? Because my world is very different from yours."

"I kind of got that. I *want* to understand."

As they stood there in the cold darkness, snow started to come down heavier. The flakes landed on Mia's beanie and then on her cheeks. She didn't brush them away. She let them stay where they landed.

"I don't let very many people get close to me."

Nick could see the conflict raging within her. She was trying to decide if she could trust him.

"Mia, I don't know what will happen between us. All I know is that since the first time I saw you in the gallery you have been in my head. I have never believed in love at first sight, not real love anyway, but there is something going on between us that I have never experienced before. And all I know right now, at this minute, is I can't get closer to you until you help me understand who you are." Nick reached for her and she stepped into his arms. Their bodies seemed to move with a will of their own, drawn together like some kind of magnetic force. "I don't know what's happening here." Nick whispered just before his lips met Mia's for a long, passionate kiss.

When the kiss ended, she said, "Let's go back to my apartment." Mia took his hand. "I'll try to help you see what my world is like."

CHAPTER SIX

Mia pushed her door open and Nick followed her in. She knew this moment would come, but she didn't know how it would end. Her heart was pounding in her chest and her hands were trembling.

The people she had loved most in her life accepted her for who she was, her parents, her Grandma Behan, Holly, and Joe. With everyone else she didn't care if they thought she was a freak, including her father's family. It mattered with Nick though. It mattered a lot.

Nick sat on the couch and Mia perched on the old chest that was her coffee table. She was so nervous, she didn't know where to start or how much to tell him. If she told him everything, he might run out the door and never look back.

"You look so scared, Mia."

She forced a smile. "I am."

Nick rested his hand on her knee. "Start at the beginning."

"Okay." Mia held her own hand to give her courage. "My mother was adopted when she was five by my grandparents, Walter and Maggie Behan. They had tried for years to have children, but my grandma never could get pregnant. My grandfather worked in Europe for the U.S. government. It was there they met another couple who had just adopted a child from an orphanage in Romania. The adoption wasn't working out for them, they couldn't seem to bond with their little girl. So, my grandparents adopted her from the other couple."

"They just gave your mother away?"

"It sounds bad, but the other couple had been trying to give my mother a home she could thrive in and they recognized that they weren't the right parents for her. They had my mother's best interests at heart." Mia dreaded the next part.

"Okay. It sounds like it worked out for the best."

"My grandparents had my mother for over a year when they found out that she and her two older sisters had been taken away from her parents. My mother was only four at the time. They were taken away because they were...Roma." Mia waited for Nick's reaction.

His eyebrows shot up. "Gypsy?"

"Yes, my aunt Silviana, my aunt Mirella, and my mother, Nadja, were taken because their parents were nomads moving from place to place. The gypsies were thought of as thieves, prostitutes, and fortune tellers."

"Were they?"

"I don't know, maybe." Mia shrugged. "I never met any of my mom's family, except my aunts. My parents brought them over years later and tried to help them, but there were a lot of problems mostly because of my parent's money. Money changes things."

"So, your Aunt Silviana, she is a fortune teller?"

"She has second sight. More than my mother did, although she had it too. Silviana uses her gifts for money and not always in honorable ways. She is very much a performer and she likes the attention it brings."

"And where do you fit into all of this?"

Mia took a deep breath for courage before she spoke. "I can communicate with spirits."

Nick's dark brown eyes narrowed and he chuckled. "I see dead people," he quoted the line from an old movie.

When she didn't smile, Nick stopped laughing. "Are you serious?"

"My mother told me that when I was a baby I would babble to empty spaces as if there was someone standing next to my crib. That's when she knew I had the gift. As a child, more spirits would come to me. And the older I got, the thinner the barrier became between this world and theirs. Now, I see things and hear things that others can't. I have impressions come to me, feelings when I touch things. Everything is made up of energy and that energy gives off vibrations I can feel and interpret most of the time."

Nick sat back on the couch, his brow furrowed in thought. "Wow. I don't know what I was expecting you to say, but that wasn't it."

Mia felt her heart sink all the way to her toes. She looked at her hands so Nick couldn't see her disappointment. Jumping up she headed for the kitchen. "I need a glass of water." She tried to keep her voice steady, but she couldn't.

"Mia, wait." Nick followed her into the kitchen and watched as she got ice and water from the dispenser on the fridge. "I'm not trying to hurt your feelings, it's just such an incredible story. You've got to give me some time."

Mia kept her back to him and walked to the dining room window and stared out into the night. Nick was right behind her.

"Is there some way you can show me?"

"I don't do parlor tricks, if that's what you mean."

"I don't want parlor tricks, I...I don't know what I want."

When Mia turned around to look at Nick, she smiled. "You want proof. How about that?" She pointed into the kitchen where every door and drawer now stood wide open.

Nick looked over his shoulder and jumped back until his back hit the wall. "What the hell?"

"They want you to know they're here."

Nick's mouth hung open and he lost several shades of color in his face. Mia took his hand. "Don't be scared. They're teasing you."

"How? How did that happen?"

"I find my stuff moved around all the time. It's what I live with everyday. When I get tired of it, I can order them away for a while, but they always come back."

"This happens to you all the time?"

Mia nodded.

"What else?"

"I can hear them, sometimes I see them."

Nick looked at her closely. "You can hear them right now?"

Mia nodded again.

Nick let go of her hand and walked into the living room, grabbed his jacket off the rack, and shoved his arms into the sleeves.

Mia's heart started to hurt, physically hurt, when she realized he was leaving. She thought about begging him to stay, but she didn't say a word. He knew who she was now, at least he'd had a glimpse, and if he couldn't deal with it, it was better that it end now. It wouldn't be the first time someone she thought was a friend walked out the door without looking back. It *would* be the first time she cried herself to sleep over it. She could already feel the tears burning her eyes.

Nick stopped with one foot in the hallway and glanced back at her over his shoulder. To Mia, it seemed like time stood still as they stared at each other. She knew he was the key to the life she wanted.

He was the other half of her, just like her father was for her mother, but he had to come to that conclusion on his own. So, she waited in silence.

"I've spent most of my life trying to get away from my grandfather's beliefs in visions and spirits walking the earth and in the old ways, and now you're asking me to believe, just like that."

"You don't have to accept it all in one night. If you can just open your mind to the possibility that there may be more to life than what you see."

Nick continued to stand in the doorway, battling within himself. She could feel his conflict. Finally, he came back inside, took off his coat and hung it back on the hook. The door closed behind him. The metal on metal sounded louder in the quiet tension that permeated her apartment.

"There is a part of me that wants to leave and not come back, but I can't do it. I know that walking out that door would be a terrible mistake. I don't know why and I don't know how, but I can feel it in my gut."

Mia couldn't speak, so she held her arms out to him and he walked into them.

Once again they were drawn together. Nick's long arms slid around her waist and hers wrapped around his neck. Their bodies pressed against each other so closely that Mia could feel his heart beating in his chest. She closed her eyes and reveled in his warmth and his scent.

"Mia, what do you want from me?"

His body was hard and muscular under his skin. She felt his strength and knew she was safe in his arms. "Can you hold me like this forever?"

He kissed her neck just below her ear and whispered, "Yes." His fingertips worked their way under her top and glided across the bare skin on her back.

Mia shivered at his touch.

"You're so soft," he said, as he did it again.

Mia pulled away just enough to look into his eyes. His pupils were wide and black. She entwined her fingers in his hair on the back of his head and brought his lips to hers. The kiss was gentle at first and then it became more, much more. It became a kiss filled with need. Nick held her even tighter. His tongue teased and tasted her as their hearts started racing within them. His body was taut with desire.

Nick leaned down and with an arm behind her knees, he picked her up and took her to her bed, laying her there like she was a fragile piece of glass. He kissed her again and then opened the drawer on the nightstand next to her bed. When he didn't find what he was looking for, he climbed across her and the bed to open the drawer to the matching nightstand on the other side.

"What are you looking for?"

"Condoms," he said. "I didn't bring any."

"I don't have condoms," Mia admitted shyly.

Nick stretched out next to her on the bed, put his hand around her waist, and pulled her closer to him. "Are you on the pill?"

"No."

"Well, what do you use for birth control?"

Mia could feel the heat rising on her cheeks. "I've never needed it."

For the second time that night, Nick's eyebrows shot up. "Mia? Are you telling me that you've never…?"

"Never."

Nick stared at her, looking confused and unsure. "Why?"

Mia felt her eyes filling with tears and the lump in her throat made it hard to speak. "I was waiting for you."

Nick's swift intake of breath was almost imperceptible, almost.

He rested his forehead against hers, but said nothing. She could feel a different kind of tension fill his body. When he looked at her again, he had tears in his eyes. Mia's heart skipped a beat.

"Did I say something wrong?"

"When I was eighteen, I stayed out late with a girl and my grandfather gave me a bad time. We got into a huge fight and during that fight I said, 'I'll never get married!' and he got real quiet and said, 'You will find your woman. I know this and she will be waiting for you.' He said the spirits told him. I laughed at him."

Mia could feel the different emotions running through him, sadness, regret, disbelief, and confusion one after the other. He was being bombarded. Mia took his face in her hands and called to the negative emotions that were flowing through him. "It's not too late, Nick. You can fix it." She held onto him until she felt him start to relax.

He leaned in and kissed her once again. Then, he rolled onto his back and Mia snuggled up next to him and laid her head on his shoulder. She was so glad he hadn't left.

Mia ran her hand over his chest. She liked the feel of him and she couldn't help but wonder what it would have been like if they had made love. It would be intense, she was sure of it. Intensity was a part of his nature. It was what made him a good cop.

Fate had had the last laugh in this situation, a homicide detective, for heavens sake. Mia pictured all the sketches and paintings she had done the last few years. The girl with the sapphire ring was sitting ten feet away, in her cabinets with all of her art supplies, along with a few of the others. The rest were in her storage space in the basement. If Nick saw them he would think she was crazy. Sooner or later she would have to tell him, but not now. Not now.

CHAPTER SEVEN

Nick began to stir long before dawn. Mia was lying next to him. The soft curves of her body pressed against his back. It seemed odd to him how familiar it felt, as if he had been sleeping in her bed forever. He hadn't slept all night in a woman's bed in a long time and never without having had sex beforehand. Everything about their relationship was different. Mia was different.

Outside the windows of her apartment he could see snow falling. *Please don't let the traffic be bad,* he thought to himself. He couldn't show up to work again wearing the same clothes he'd worn the day before. Wayne would give him grief all day. Nick needed to go home and shave, shower, and change before he went in, and that was going to take some time. In his head he mentally added the time he would need to do it all, then added in an extra thirty minutes for good measure. He figured he would have to leave by six to make it to work on time.

He closed his eyes to rest for just a minute, but when he opened them again an hour and a half had passed. Nick cursed under his breath and slipped out of bed trying not to wake Mia. He waited until he was in the bathroom before turning on the light. On the bathroom counter he was surprised to find a toothbrush, still in the packaging, toothpaste, a brand new razor, shaving cream, deodorant, and shampoo. The creepy thing was, every single item was his exact brand. It gave him goose bumps and proved to him that Mia was the real deal.

Nick shrugged and figured he'd shave and shower at Mia's and save the time. He opened the linen closet to grab a towel and there was a note.

Clothes in closet, was all it said. Nick pulled open the door to Mia's walk in closet and saw plastic clothing bags hanging on a hook. Price's for Men was printed on the bags. He lifted the plastic and found three brand new dress shirts, freshly pressed. The last three bags had new suits. A smaller bag in the back had three matching ties, socks, and even underwear. Everything he could possibly need and all of it in the right sizes.

Nick wondered if he should accept them. On one hand he felt like it would be taking advantage of Mia and her obviously healthy bank account, while on the other he knew it would hurt her feelings if he refused them.

After seeing the look on her face when he was standing in her doorway the night before, he knew he had to accept them. He didn't want to be responsible for that kind of emotional pain again.

He took his time in the shower. After all, now he didn't have to go all the way home and he had plenty of time. Mia's shower had more jets than JFK International Airport and he tried out every one of them. She even had a sound system inside the bathroom, but he didn't turn that on because he didn't want to wake her. As he dried off he realized that her bathroom had double sinks. In his head he heard Mia's voice softly say, "I was waiting for you." Nick stopped drying off and wondered if she really had been waiting just for him.

After dressing and running a comb over his closely cropped, black hair he stepped out of Mia's bathroom oasis as quietly as he could. He glanced at the bed, but Mia wasn't there. That's when he heard her moving around in the kitchen. At least, he hoped it was her. After last night he couldn't be sure. He walked through the apartment and saw Mia moving something around on the counter. When he went into the kitchen he saw a brand new coffee maker. Spread out in front of her were filters, the instructions, and his favorite coffee.

"I haven't quite figured out how to do this yet." She smiled and looked him over from head to toe.

Nick obligingly turned a full circle and he heard her laugh. The sound of it made him feel warm inside.

"You look really nice."

"I should. I have a hunch that these probably cost a month's worth of my pay."

Mia looked unsure for a moment. "I didn't know if you would accept them or not."

"I wasn't going to, but," he hesitated for a moment, "I wanted to make you happy."

Mia's smile was radiant and her eyes came alive.

"Please don't over do it, okay?"

"Is the coffee maker too much?" she asked with a touch of sarcasm.

"No. I need coffee in the morning to get me going." Nick chuckled.

"I know." Mia picked up the instructions again. "Do you know how to work this thing?"

"Filter here, coffee here, water here, and turn it on."

"Well, that was easy." Mia stuffed all the packing material back in the box.

"So, what are you going to do today?"

"I have to teach classes at Freeman in the morning, at the Boys and Girls club this afternoon, and sometime today I need to go to the gallery and talk to Charlie. He called and left a message yesterday sounding frantic about something."

"He's sort of a high stress kind of guy, isn't he?" Nick asked, remembering the gallery owner from the night he and Mia had met.

"You have no idea." Mia's laugh filled the air. "I was going to make myself a quick omelet, do you want some?"

"That sounds great. Thanks to you, I have time."

Mia began pulling things out of her fridge and cupboards. She moved like a chef, completely comfortable with what she was doing. Nick watched every nuance of her body. Her hands were small, but her fingers moved with grace and dexterity as she chopped up an onion, tomato, and what looked like spinach. It was easy to picture her sketching on a canvas, her brow furrowed in concentration. He regretted falling asleep the night she sketched him. It would have been interesting to watch her work.

"I never got to see the sketch you did of me."

"Would you like to see it?"

Nick couldn't help but notice how her eyes had lit up when he'd asked. She was like a kid on Christmas morning. There was something about seeing her so excited that made him smile. It was strange how, if she was happy, he felt happy. But last night, when she thought he was leaving, he couldn't go, knowing it was going to make her so sad. He wondered about her psychic powers or abilities. Did her emotions influence the people around her?

The smell of coffee drifted through the air. Mia opened a cupboard, grabbed a mug, and set it on the counter.

"Help yourself."

Nick poured his coffee slowly, careful not to spill. "Do you need any help?"

"No, I do this all the time." She set two plates on the counter, cut the omelet into two pieces with a spatula, slid a section onto each plate and added slices of an orange.

By the time she set the plate down in front of him, Nick's mouth was watering. He cut a piece off with his fork and took a bite.

"This sure beats stale donuts and bad coffee."

"I'm glad you like it."

"I want to ask you something. How did you know to buy me all the right stuff in the bathroom and how did you know my sizes for the clothes?"

Mia's eyes dropped to her plate. "Does it matter?"

"It does to me."

"Sometimes I just know things. I can feel them. When things are the way they are supposed to be, there is a peaceful feeling inside of me, and when things are wrong…"

"What?" Nick asked, fascinated.

"I feel uneasy, nervous." Mia shrugged.

He sensed she didn't want to talk about it, but he had to know.

"Sometimes I can touch something and I can feel the emotions attached to it. I can usually tell when someone is lying by the energy or vibrations they give off. I can feel them."

Nick undid his watch and offered it to her. "Show me."

Mia reluctantly took the watch from his hand. He watched as she held it and let her fingers run over the face and down the silver metal band.

"There is a lot of love surrounding this. Whoever gave you this watch loves you very much. It's a man and he's far away from you, not only in space, but emotionally." Mia closed her fingers around it. "There is a great sense of loss, of sadness-."

"Stop! That's enough," he told her, his tone harsher than he meant it to be. Nick took the watch back and strapped it onto his wrist.

Mia sat silent for a minute, not touching her food. "I have to get ready."

"Mia," Nick watched her practically run to her bathroom. He felt like a first class jerk. He just hadn't expected her to be so dead on. It took him by surprise. The water in the shower went on and he watched the clock, waiting for it to go off. As the time ticked by, he knew if he didn't leave, he would be late for work. Still he stayed.

After forty-five minutes, the shower went off and he heard Mia moving around in the bathroom.

He softly knocked on the door. "Mia, I need to talk to you."

Silence was the only response.

"Please."

The door opened about eight inches and Mia stood there wearing nothing but a towel. Her hair was tousled and a few strands still had water dripping from them. He thought about unwrapping her like a gift, until she looked up at him and he could see she had been crying. Her eyes were red and puffy.

"Aren't you going to be late?" She wiped her hair with a second towel.

"Yes, but I couldn't leave until I'd said I was sorry. I shouldn't have asked if I didn't want to hear the truth." He touched her cheek with the back of his fingers. "You keep surprising me at every turn. I didn't mean to make you cry."

"I wasn't crying. I got shampoo in my eyes." She blinked and looked away.

"I may not have your insight, but I've been a cop for a while and I can usually tell when someone isn't being truthful."

Mia smiled just slightly.

"I'll do better next time."

"Okay."

"Thank you for the clothes and all the rest. And for breakfast, and the coffee, and for letting me see you in your towel. Now, I won't be able to concentrate all day."

They both laughed.

"Will you have dinner with me? I'm buying." It was the least he could do.

"I would rather eat in, if it's okay? How about you pick up something on the way home? I mean on the way here."

"I will." He liked that she had said home.

"I might not be here until seven-thirty."

"Seven-thirty it is." Nick leaned down and kissed her, and he couldn't stop his gaze from drifting to the cleavage showing above the towel.

"You keep thinking like that, you'll never get to work and you'll get fired."

"It would be worth it though."

"Goodbye, Nick." Mia shut the bathroom door and Nick left with a smile on his face.

Nick sat down at his desk thirty minutes late. Wayne was just coming back from his morning trip to the can.

"What? My bran flakes kicked in." Wayne looked him over. "You look real pretty this morning. Did you fall off the cover of GQ magazine?"

"Mia bought these for me."

Before Wayne could say anything else, his phone rang. "Detective Coleman. Yes, I did. It's real important that we speak to you right away. Can my partner and I come over now? Thank you, we'll be there as soon as we can."

"Vannessa Gomez?" Nick asked, grabbing the coat he had just taken off.

"Yep."

As soon as Nick turned the key, Wayne started in.

"So, what's going on with you and the new girl?"

Nick cocked his head. "I'm not sure yet."

"Did you ask about her aunt and all the things she said?"

"Sort of." He never had gotten around to asking about the details of what Mia's Aunt Silviana had said. He'd have to ask her tonight.

"So?" Wayne prompted.

Nick hesitated. He usually told Wayne everything. They had been partners for four years. He'd been the best man when Wayne married Kathy, but this felt different. On the other hand, sooner or later Nick would have to tell him. It was too big not to.

"Mia has...she is...um," Nick tried to find the right words to explain.

"A man?"

"What? No!"

"Dying?" Wayne offered.

"No!" Nick shook is head.

"A lesbian?"

"Will you shut up?"

"I'm trying to help." Wayne shrugged.

"Well, you're not helping."

"So, what is the big secret?"

"Mia can communicate with spirits."

Wayne didn't say a word for a minute. "For real? How do you know she isn't full of it?"

"Ever since I met her, all of this really weird stuff has been happening to me. I thought I was going nuts or something, but now I think it all has to do with Mia."

"Like what?"

"Like the first night I drove her home, when I was walking back to my car, I felt like I was being followed, but when I turned around there was no one there. I was almost to my car when I saw the shadow of a man right behind me in a store window. I thought I was about to be mugged. I even pulled my weapon, but there was still no one there. "

"Could it have been your imagination?"

"Maybe, but the night Mia's aunt showed up and talked about Mia being surrounded by darkness, I was getting in my car and I glanced up to her window. I could see her standing there and all of a sudden there was this black cloud all around her. That wasn't my imagination. I saw it. And last night, when she was telling me how she can talk to spirits, we were in her kitchen, I walked right through it, everything was normal and two seconds later, I turned around and every cupboard and drawer was wide open. There was no sound and a person couldn't have done it in that amount of time."

"Okay, you're freaking me out."

"Tell me about it. And this morning, I go into her bathroom and laying on the counter was toothpaste, a razor, shampoo, deodorant, everything I use to get ready for work and it was all the exact same brands I use. If I didn't know better I would think she'd raided my bathroom."

"Maybe she saw it all at your place?"

"She's never been to my place."

"So she's like…psychic."

"I guess. Mia didn't say that, but I guess it fits."

"And you think she's the real deal?"

Nick thought about it. "I know she is."

They pulled up to Vannessa Gomez's apartment building. A small dark-haired young woman opened the door when they knocked.

"Come in." She stepped aside to let them in.

The apartment was small, but nice.

"We're very sorry for your loss, Miss Gomez." Nick watched as tears filled her eyes and she dabbed at them with a tissue.

"So, you two are going to find out who killed Kelly?"

"We're going to do our best," Wayne said, taking out his notebook and a pen. "What can you tell us about Kelly?" he asked. "Who were her friends, boyfriends, the people at work? Who would want to hurt her?"

"Kelly and I are…were like sisters, but even with me, there were things she really didn't talk about. I know she dated a guy at work, but she would never tell me who. It was like this big secret, only it was more a secret from Ben than me."

"Ben?"

"Ben Carlyle. He owns a motorcycle shop and sells Harley Davidson's to dentists who want to play road warrior on the weekends. He and Kelly were pretty serious. And I only know about him because he showed up at Kelly's when I was there."

"She ever say anything about this Ben being violent or jealous?"

"He could be jealous. That's why she didn't want him to know about the guy at work."

"Did you ever see signs of Kelly being abused, things like bruises or black eyes?"

"Once, Kelly had a bruise on the back of her neck. I only saw it because she had just gotten out of the shower and had her hair up in a towel. When I asked her what had happened she took off the towel really quick and made up some lie about getting hurt at the gym, but I knew she wasn't telling me the truth."

"How did you know that?" Nick pressed her.

"I could see the finger marks on her neck."

"She never said who did it?" Wayne scribbled in his notebook.

"There were things Kelly wouldn't even tell me."

"What about her money? Did she carry large amounts of cash on her? Did her boyfriends have access to it?"

"Kelly was very careful with her money. She didn't really carry cash and no one had access to it, but her. She splurged on her apartment and she helped me pay for my classes, other than that, she just had basic living expenses. I think she was afraid she would wake up one morning and it would be gone. A lot of foster kids are like that."

Nick and Wayne spent almost two hours asking questions until they had an idea who Kelly Langford was. They were about to leave when Nick remembered the picture of the ring in the file he held in his hand. He took it out and showed it to Vannessa.

"Do you know anything about this ring?"

"It was Kelly's. Did she have that on when she…"

"Yes."

"That's odd. She stopped wearing it a while ago. She broke up with the guy who gave it to her."

"Thanks for your help." Nick handed her his card. "If you think of anything else, call us."

When they got back in the car, Wayne asked, "What's up with the ring? Is there something I should know?"

"I think it's the key to this case."

"Really, how do you know that?"

"A little bird told me." A little bird named Mia. He didn't say it, but he knew she had something to do with it.

CHAPTER EIGHT

"Okay, everyone put your paints away, quickly," Mia told her students. Her class was supposed to be done by four and it was a quarter after already.

She couldn't wait to get home and spend the evening with Nick. A smile found its way to her lips. Being with him was right. She could feel it deep inside of her. He hadn't walked out when she'd told him her secret. The secret she only shared with a handful of people.

Holly and Joe knew, but they were clear across the country in Los Angeles. She missed them. Now that she was pretty sure Nick was going to be around for a while, Mia needed to call Holly and tell her all about him. She could hear Holly's voice in her head saying, "It's about time."

Mia took a cab to the gallery because of the heavy snow that blanketed the city.

Charlie was waiting for her in his usual state of excitement. "Mia, the Times wants to do a piece on you."

When Mia didn't say anything, Charlie looked exacerbated. "Did you hear what I said? The New York Times! Think of what that would do for your career, not to mention my gallery. It could put us both on the map, so to speak."

Mia still didn't say anything.

"What's wrong?"

"I don't think I want the New York Times poking around in my life."

"Have you lost your mind? Do you want to be an artist or not?" Charlie was getting agitated.

"I'm already an artist. I don't need them to tell me so."

"Mia don't you want to be famous for your work."

"Most artists aren't famous in their own lifetimes, so I guess I can wait."

"You don't understand what this could do for *me*. It would increase the foot traffic in here and maybe I could sell a few things. The economy has been an albatross around my neck for two years now."

"I won't let you go under, Charlie."

"I appreciate that you want to help, but I want to make a success of this place on my own."

"I'll think about it."

"Here," Charlie handed her a business card. "This is the woman you should call if you decide to go for it. And I do hope you decide to go for it because it would be awesome."

Mia walked around the gallery for almost an hour. She always spent time here whenever she came. It was a peaceful place and Mia felt calm and relaxed. There were three other artists whose work hung in different sections. It was pleasing to her to see their work. Jose Cortez was one of her favorites. His work was mostly abstract and it was very dark. Abigail La Shayne was a sculptor and her work was really taking off. Mia had heard that several big celebrities had recently bought a few of her more erotic pieces.

Mia studied a sculpture of a man and a woman that appeared to be making love. His hand was on her breast and her arms were wrapped around his neck as they kissed. It gave Mia a strange feeling in the pit of her stomach. She couldn't help but wonder what it would be like to make love to Nick. She knew he wanted her, but when he found out she was a virgin, he hadn't pressed her. She wondered why. Her old boyfriend, Mark, had hounded her constantly, but she hadn't been ready back then. And Mark was totally the wrong guy.

Mia saw a man staring at one of her paintings. Feelings of overwhelming sadness washed over her like a wave at the beach. The man was mourning someone very close to him, a wife or a daughter maybe.

The painting he was viewing Mia called, 'Girl Under Glass,' but Mia knew her real name was Celia Burke. She had been murdered two years ago and her killer had never been found. Worker's discovered Celia's body in a trash bin at a construction site. Mia had seen Celia's physical death, just as she had seen the girl's who had now been identified as Kelly Langford on the news.

Mia's first instinct was to go and talk with the man, try to ease his pain, but voices came to her, warning her to stay away from him. The word danger was whispered over and over again. Silviana's words came back to her, danger, darkness all around, betrayal. Mia never did call Silviana back, now she wished she had.

As she left the gallery, the cold wind tore the door from her hand. It slammed so hard Mia thought the glass would shatter. She walked down the street quickly, trying to put as much distance as she could between herself and what ever danger there was lurking around her.

Mia didn't pay attention to where she was going, she just kept walking, block after block. The feeling of impending doom was all around her. It was as if a hand was reaching out to grab her from behind. Her heart pounded and she was beginning to perspire, despite the cold winter air all around her. Six blocks, ten, still she didn't slow her pace. She looked up and down the street for a cab, but there were none to be found.

A car pulled up next to her and someone called her name.

"Mia? Mia!"

It was Nick. He pulled over and she ran to the passenger door and jumped in. Once she was in his car, she felt relieved, and safe for the moment.

"What the heck are you walking in this weather for?" He sounded irritated.

Still, Mia sat there shivering, not from the cold, but from fear.

"Mia? What's wrong? Are you okay?"

"I'm fine," she lied.

"Why are you shaking like that?"

"It's cold outside."

The expression on his face told Mia he didn't believe her, but he didn't say anything else. When they got to her building, they parked and went inside. She turned the heat up as soon as the door closed behind them. Mia didn't want to talk, so she went and pressed the button on her answering machine.

"Mia? It's Holly. Are you home? Why haven't you called me? I better hear from you soon or else." Holly giggled at the end of her message and then the usual beep.

"Hey, it's Charlie. I need to talk to you. I have been calling all over town trying to catch up with you. Why can't you get a cell phone? Call me." Beep.

"Mia! It's Evan. I have been trying to call you, so we can talk. It's urgent! Do you hear me? You better call me back."

"Who is Evan?" Nick asked, as he set down a couple of bags of what smelled like Chinese food on the kitchen counter.

Mia never should have played back her messages. Now there was going to be questions she didn't want to answer.

"Mia?"

Nick's dark eyes were boring into her and he wasn't going to be satisfied until he had an answer.

"Evan is my cousin."

"Why is he leaving you threatening messages?"

"Because he is my uncle's son and they all hate me."

Nick thought that over for a minute. "How could they hate you?"

"Because of the money. I control several accounts and trusts that they think they should be entitled to and I won't let them have." Mia plopped down in a chair scared, discouraged, and irritated.

"Man, you look like you had a bad day." Nick crouched down before her and put his hands on her knees.

"I had a great day, until I got to the gallery"

"What happened there? Does it have something to do with Charlie's message?"

"Yes." Mia took a deep breath. "There is a New York Times art reporter that wants to do a story about me."

"That's great! That would be awesome exposure."

When she didn't respond, Nick carefully studied her face. "Wouldn't it?"

"Yes, normally it would, but it has taken me years to find the peace I have now and I don't want to change that. When my parents died, the following five or six years were awful. I had paparazzi following me everywhere I went. The few friends I had were hounded constantly and I don't want to go back to that. No one really knows I'm here and I want to keep it that way."

"That must have been terrible."

"It was." Mia glanced to her phone. The slight vibration she felt in the air told her it was about to ring. "Excuse me." Mia was about two feet away when it rang. She hesitated, her hand only inches away. Someone was here. It was someone she didn't want to see. Nervousness and agitation flowed over her like hot water. Finally, she picked up the phone, "Hello?"

"Miss Carrigan, there is an Evan Carrigan here to see you. He says it is urgent that he speak to you, right now."

Mia closed her eyes. She didn't want to do this in front of Nick, but she had no choice. There was no telling what Evan would do if she turned him away. His erratic behavior had always kept her on edge.

"Send him up." She turned to Nick, "Would you mind waiting in my bedroom. I don't want him to know you're here. It's nothing personal. I'll explain after he leaves."

"Of course." Nick walked into the darkness and was swallowed up. With the lights off in there, Mia was pretty sure that Evan wouldn't realize it wasn't just the two of them, at least that's what she hoped.

The hard pounding on her steel door sounded all through her apartment. Even his knock was arrogant. She opened it intending not to let him step foot inside, but he pushed past her. Mia left the door slightly ajar.

"What do you want, Evan?"

"You can't even say hello? We haven't seen each other in over a year." Evan's dishwater blond hair was slicked back and his blue eyes were as hostile and conniving as ever.

"Hello. Now, what is it that you want or should I say how much?"

Evan took in her apartment from where he stood. "Nice place. Do you like living here?"

"Yes."

"That doesn't surprise me. This neighborhood suits you, run down, trashy, and full of freaks. You fit right in here."

"If that's all you came to say, you can leave now." Mia had a really bad feeling that this wasn't going to end well and she didn't want Nick to see and hear it all. She knew he was watching. Not that she blamed him. Evan's hostility was palpable.

"I want to talk to you about the business accounts. We need that money, Mia. We are trying to expand and we can't do that without the extra capital."

"Richard has already talked to me and I'm sure he has talked to Uncle David, so you already know what my answer is."

Evan reached out and grabbed her arm, intentionally digging his fingers into her hard enough to cause pain. "Look you little freak, we've been working on this deal for almost a year and I'm not going to let you ruin it for me. Now, call Richard and tell him to order the release of the funds.

Mia tried to jerk her arm away. "You know where you can go."

Evan raised his hand as if he was going to slap her.

"You remember what happened the last time you tried to hurt me, Evan?"

Mia saw her cousin's eyes get wider.

"You may have been drunk, but you remember."

"Let go of her, right now." Nick was in full cop mode. Mia wouldn't have been surprised if he had his gun in hand.

"Who the hell are you?"

"I'm the guy whose gonna kick your ass if you ever touch her again."

The tone of Nick's voice told her and Evan that he meant it. Mia had never heard him sound angry before, not like this.

"You have no idea who I am."

"You're a man who would hurt a woman, that's all I need to know. You're lucky I don't haul you in and throw your butt in a cell with some gangbangers."

He let go of Mia's arm with a shove. "I'll be in touch, little witch."

Evan's nick name for her opened the gates to all the memories she had tried to put out of her mind for years. She remembered the insults and the way she was treated for three long years. Mia could feel the anger raging within her. Evan was barely out the door when Mia waved her hand and the heavy steel door slammed closed so hard the floor shook. When she realized what she had done, she froze. She never let anyone see her use her powers physically. She instantly regretted losing her control. Tears formed in her eyes as the last few hours took their toll.

"Mia?" Nick was almost breathless with shock. "How did you do that?"

"I'm sorry. I lost my temper." Mia stammered, trying to figure out what to say to lessen the strangeness of it all. "You can leave if you want to."

Tears were running down her face, but she didn't say anything. Nick didn't either. Mia figured he was trying to find a way to leave without looking like he was abandoning her. Not that she would blame him. She was just too different for most people to handle. It made for a lonely life.

"I'm not leaving." Nick put his arms around her and pulled her to his chest. "I'm never leaving."

Mia leaned against him drawing his strength and warmth into her body, she needed it desperately. "I'm sorry," she whispered.

"It's okay."

"Something bad is going to happen, Nick. I can feel it. This is the same way I felt right before my parents died. I haven't had this feeling since, but I remember it."

"Does it have something to do with Evan?"

"I don't know, but I'm…I'm afraid."

Nick put his hand on the back of her head and held her tighter. "I'll keep you safe, Mia."

"How are you going to do that?"

"Like this, for starters." Nick took her hand and led her into the kitchen. He opened one of the bags and handed her a cell phone. "It's already activated and my cell is number two on your speed dial."

Mia took the phone into her hand.

"If you don't like it, we can exchange it."

"No, it's great. But why?" she managed to squeak out past the lump in her throat.

"Do you know how many times I've wanted to call you today to see how your day was going? Now, I can call you or you can call me, you know, if you need me."

"Thank you," Mia said, holding the phone tightly.

"Don't be afraid. Everything is going to be okay." Nick framed her face with his hands and kissed her slowly. "Tomorrow morning I think we should go talk with your Aunt Silviana. Let's get to the bottom of this, once and for all."

"Don't you have to work?"

"I'll take a few hours of personal time."

"Won't you lose some of your pay?"

"It's okay. My girlfriend's rich," Nick chuckled.

It was the first time Nick had called her his girlfriend and it made her smile, but the best part was, there was no desire for her money behind his words. She knew that even if she offered it to him, he wouldn't take it. That made him all the more special to her.

CHAPTER NINE

Nick saw Mia standing by the window looking out over the snow laden streets.

"Mia? Is every thing alright?"

She didn't move.

"Mia?"

She turned to him. "Go back to sleep. You still have an hour until dawn."

"Then come back to bed and keep me warm."

She made her way to the bed, tossed her thick cotton bathrobe on the foot of the bed, and climbed in. He put his arm around her and she snuggled up against him. The feel of her so close to his body made his mind go in its usual direction.

"Is your still being a virgin a religious thing, or what?"

Mia shifted and looked at his face with a huge smile. "I was thinking of entering a convent."

"What?"

Mia laughed into his chest. "I'm just kidding, relax. I went to an all girl's school for high school, remember?"

"What about college? You did go to college, right?"

"I had two boyfriends in college, but I didn't sleep with them because it didn't feel right. Needless to say, they weren't boyfriends for long. Besides, I was studying really hard and I didn't want the distractions."

"What did you major in? Fine arts? "

"I minored in art, but I have my master's in business. It's what my dad wanted."

"Did he want you to take over the business?"

"Yes, and I think he wanted me to be able to protect myself from the rest of his family. My uncle has always run a couple of the divisions for my dad, but he doesn't always make smart decisions. More than once, my dad had to bail him out of near financial collapse. For the last few years I have been cutting ties between my father's and their part of the business. When Evan takes over, I think they will go under. He has less self-control than my uncle, and he is arrogant and impulsive."

"Wow, I knew you were smart, but..."

"But what?"

"What is a girl like you doing with a schmuck like me? You could have your choice of the blue bloods in this city."

"Blue bloods don't want gypsy blood contaminating the blood lines. My father's family showed me that. When my dad and mom got married, his family basically turned their backs on him. They couldn't believe he would marry a gypsy over some debutante. Not that their family was that prominent at the time. It was my dad who made Carrigan Industries what it is today. But they didn't approve and they let him know it. Besides, I like schmucks."

Nick ran his hand down her back. "I have to tell you that sleeping in your bed and not making love to you is getting harder and harder."

Mia rolled onto her back and laughed out loud.

"What is so funny?"

"You are. When the time is right, you'll know it."

Nick leaned up on his elbow and stared down at her. "I think the time is right pretty much whenever I'm with you."

"I bet you say that to all the girls."

"I know that's probably what you're thinking, but it's different with you. I want you to understand that. It seems crazy, since we've only known each other for a couple of weeks, but it is different."

"I know how you feel. It's hard for me to get close to people because...," Mia hesitated, "either they can't handle who I am or I can feel their hunger for money."

"I don't care about your money. I'm not rich and my job doesn't pay a lot, but I'm good at it. I feel like I'm right where I need to be right now. And that includes being here with you."

"Do you? There's nothing in your past that maybe you want to rethink?"

Nick had the distinct feeling she wasn't talking in generalizations, there was meaning in her words. "What are you talking about?"

"What do you think I'm talking about?"

"It sounds like you're talking about my past." He wanted her to understand. "I had legitimate reasons for making the choices I did. I wanted a different life, a better life than my parents. They were good people, but they had no hope for their future. They didn't realize they had to reach out and take it, not wait for it to come to them. You grew up with money. You don't know what it is like to have no Christmas presents under the tree on Christmas morning. You don't know what it's like to see your father drink himself to death and then watch your mother self-destruct because of it."

Mia didn't speak, didn't move. He looked at her, but only saw shadows, even though it was almost dawn.

Mia leaned up and kissed his cheek. "I'm sorry you see so many negative things in your childhood. I'm sorry you don't see the good."

Nick heard her words and it felt like the breath was being pulled out of his chest. He pushed Mia away, got out of bed, and went into the bathroom. His mind told him to shave, shower, and get ready for the day, but he couldn't bring himself to look in the mirror. He didn't want to see his own reflection. He sat on the edge of her tub in nothing but his underwear.

Mia's words had brought it all back so vividly, he couldn't stand it. He could still smell the dust and the poverty of the reservation. He could hear his grandfather praying for miracles that never came, whispering to spirits that weren't there, talking about the old ways, and how Nick was a part of it all. He always thought it was foolishness on his grandfather's part, but if Mia could see spirits, maybe his grandfather could too. Nick had thought of his grandfather as almost delusional. He could hear the words the old man had told him so many times, "Your heart is closed and you will not see until you open it."

The bathroom door opened slightly and Mia poked her head inside, her expression fearful.

"You can come in."

Mia came to him.

"You're changing everything I thought I knew about my life, my childhood, my parents, and my grandparents. Am I going to recognize myself when I get to the other side?"

"You're not changing." Mia put her hand on his cheek. "You are still the same man, you are just seeing through different eyes. We all are here on a journey, with things we need to learn and experience. It helps us grow. You are who you are, but you are still traveling."

"When I was eighteen, I left home thinking I could leave who I was behind me. I became a soldier. I changed my name. Became a cop. I thought I would feel different, but I don't."

"Because you're still Nicholas Whitecloud."

"I *am* seeing through different eyes. And I am seeing who my grandfather really is. I'm not worthy to even call him grandfather."

"It was him that gave you the watch, wasn't it?"

"For my graduation from high school." Nick took a deep breath. "And to thank him, I left home, got rid of my name, and in a way, my heritage. I wouldn't blame him if he never spoke to me again. I turned my back on him, my grandmother, and all the rest of my family. I cut myself off from all of them. I deserve to be alone."

"You are never alone, Nick. Many of your ancestors are with you. They watch over you and protect you."

Nick didn't want to believe that it could be true. "Do they talk to you?" Nick could hardly get the words out of his mouth.

"There is one, he is very old. He told me you never knew him in life, but you know him in your heart. He said you have great honor and I can trust you."

"What else?"

"He said there is no joy in your life and that I should make sure to tell you to find the joy. And he said you should listen more. His exact words were, 'listen to Three Fingers when he speaks to you."

Nick sat on the edge of her tub, chills running all over his body.

"Do you know of him?"

"When I was little, my grandfather would tell me stories about his great- grandfather. He was a respected warrior among my people. They called him three fingers because he was missing his little finger and his ring finger on his left hand."

"Did he lose them in a fight?" Mia asked, her eyes wide with curiosity.

"No, he got bit by a rattler while he and his brother were hunting, and to keep from dying, he cut them off with a knife, cauterized the wound and kept hunting."

"Are you teasing me?"

"That's the story that has been handed down for generations." There was no way for Mia to know anything about his grandfather's great-grandfather. If ever he'd had any doubt about Mia's gift or power or what ever she called it, he couldn't deny it now.

He kissed Mia on the forehead. "I better get ready so we can see

Silviana first thing this morning."

"I'll go make you some coffee. Do you want some bagels and cream cheese to go with it?"

"Whatever you're having is fine. Should you call your aunt and make sure she's home?"

"She's always home."

Nick showered and put on the second pair of pants and shirt Mia had bought him. Just like the first ones, these fit perfectly. And all he got her was a cell phone. There was no way he could keep up with her. She had too much cash at her disposal. Nick had a feeling that the old saying, 'it's the gesture that counts,' would hold true for Mia. She didn't seem too taken with her money. As he tied his tie, he made a mental note to stop and get her some roses on the way home tonight.

He could smell the coffee as soon as he opened the bathroom door.

"Perfect timing, your bagel is ready."

Nick laid the new suit jacket over the chest in front of the couch and went into the kitchen. Mia handed him his mug of coffee and he took a sip. "That always tastes so good first thing in the morning."

"You look amazing."

"Thank you, madam. Did you get a hold of your aunt?"

"I didn't call her." Mia didn't look at him as she spoke.

"Why?" Nick's cell phone rang before she could answer. It was Wayne calling. That could only mean one thing.

"White."

"We caught a new case. I'm gonna text you the address. Meet me there. It'll be faster and watch out, the snow's bad. There are accidents everywhere."

Nick snapped his phone closed and looked at Mia. "You knew I wasn't going to be able to go, didn't you?"

Mia nodded her head.

"How did you know that?" Once again Nick's cell phone began to ring. "I've got to go, but I want to talk about this more tonight." Nick put his phone to his ear. "No, I didn't get it, text it again."

Nick grabbed his jacket and his coat and headed to the door.

"Nick wait, I have something for you." Mia handed him a key. "Just in case you need to get in and I'm not here."

"Where are you going today?"

"I'm not planning on going anywhere. I have some work to do. Besides, it's going to snow for several hours before it stops."

"How do you know that?"

"I saw it on the news when you were in the shower." She smiled at him.

"Oh." Nick kissed her quickly and out the door he went.

Wayne's text finally came through as Nick scraped his windshield clear of snow, which was still falling. "Please let the body be *inside*. Someplace nice and warm," he mumbled to himself. Nick was grateful when he pulled up to an apartment building and saw the crime scene guys headed in. He followed.

"About time," Wayne said quietly.

"Traffic. What do we have?"

"Her license says her name is Michelle Wong, twenty-six. According to her neighbors, she lived here alone. She was strangled to death last night or early this morning."

Nick saw the girl, crumpled on the floor right next to her kitchen table, her arm extended over her head like she was asking a question in class. "With what?"

"His hands. And she was strangled from behind."

"Someone she knows who couldn't look her in the eye as he killed her. Anyone know of a boyfriend, or an ex-boyfriend?" Nick was sure it was someone close to her.

"The neighbors said the only visitors she had were female friends and her family. They never saw her bring any guys home with her, but I've only canvassed this floor so far. We need to go upstairs and downstairs and talk to who ever will open their doors."

"What about next of kin?" Nick asked.

"A patrol unit was dispatched to tell her family."

He was grateful. Telling the family was always the worst part.

It was almost one o'clock before they left.

"What's next on the list?" Wayne asked.

"I say we pay a visit to Kelly Langford's jealous boyfriend and find out where he was the night she was killed."

"I think we need a few more cases to work at the same time, just to make life interesting," Wayne complained. "We need to distribute the fliers with the warehouse kid's picture on it."

"I had a couple of patrol units do that." Nick opened the car door and climbed inside. "We'll still have to re-canvas the area, but at least the fliers are out there."

"Delegation. I like that." Wayne turned to look at him with a grin on his face. "So, what's going on with Mia? Any more weird happenings?"

"I don't want to talk about it."

"Okay, let's talk about the sex."

"I don't want to talk about that either." Nick knew he would never hear the end of it if Wayne knew he was sleeping at Mia's, but they hadn't had sex.

"Come on man, you gotta give me something here."

"Let's talk about *your* sex life," Nick offered.

"I've been married for three and a half years. What sex life?"

The tone of Wayne's voice told Nick something was wrong. "You and Kathy have a fight?"

"No more than usual."

"What's going on?"

"I don't know, she's only my wife. Every time I say something to her she starts freaking out and then two seconds later she's crying. It's like she has permanent PMS. I think she hates me."

"Kathy doesn't hate you. I've seen you two together." Nick laughed.

"Not lately."

"Well, let's have our double date?"

"I told Kathy about Mia and she would love to meet her." Wayne pointed to the motorcycle shop. "That's it right there."

A bell rang when they walked in the door. A short, fat guy came out from what had to be the garage, with a burrito, the size of a small dog, in his black and greasy hands. The grime didn't stop him from taking a huge bite and when the cheese oozed onto his fingers, he licked it off.

"You Ben Carlyle?" Nick asked.

"Who wants to know?"

Nick flashed his badge and Wayne did the same. "I'm Detective White and this is Detective Coleman."

"You here about Kelly?"

"Yeah, we're here about Miss Langford."

"Come this way."

He led them through the garage and into another part of the building that looked like it was being lived in.

"Ben's real broke up over Kelly. He's been drinking since he heard about it on the news yesterday. Go easy on him."

Wayne glanced at Nick and he knew they were both thinking the same thing. It wouldn't be the first time some low-life had tried to pretend they'd just heard that someone they knew had been murdered, to cover their tracks.

Greasy fingers pounded on a door three times before it opened.

"What the hell do you want?" Ben Carlyle yelled as he opened the door.

"Cops are here to see you, man." A greasy thumb was jerked in their direction.

Nick and Wayne flashed their badges. "We need to talk to you, Mr. Carlyle."

He opened the door and stepped aside so they could go in. Nick was surprised to find a studio apartment that wasn't half bad, considering it was in the back of a mechanics garage. It had a small kitchenette with new wood cabinets, granite countertops and a pub table. To the right was an alcove with a king-sized bed that took up most of the floor space, but the bed was made with a lot of pillows. A woman's touch, Nick thought. A nice leather couch had a pillow and an old ratty quilt on it, obviously where Carlyle had been sleeping. Across from the couch a huge TV hung on the wall with two chairs bracketing it. The chairs looked like they had never been sat on.

"Have a seat." Carlyle pointed to them. "And let's make this quick. I have a hangover you wouldn't believe."

Nick couldn't picture Kelly Langford with this guy. He looked a step up from being homeless, holey jeans, a Metallica t-shirt with the sleeves cut off, and his long brown hair in a pony tail that was hanging a skewed.

"Okay. Where were you the night of January sixteenth?"

"I was at the hospital with my mom. She had gallbladder surgery and was in the hospital for three days. Her doctor is Andrew Merriman. Here's his card. You can call and confirm it. Rosie was my mom's nurse that night. She can tell you that I was there all night. I didn't leave until nine in the morning."

"We don't usually see someone quite so prepared."

"When I heard about Kelly on the news, I knew you'd talk to Vannessa and she would tell you about me." Carlyle scrubbed at his face with his hands. "I can't believe she's gone."

"How is it that you didn't know she was missing? Don't you talk to her every day? Hook up at night? Or, did you find out about the guy she was seeing at work and get pissed off about it? Things get a little out of hand?" Wayne was pressing the guy to see if he had a temper and if he would lose it.

"She asked me to give her some time to work things out, so I did. Kelly liked her space. And I knew about the other guy all along, but when I asked her to marry me, she said she was going to break it off for good. The guy treated her like crap. Always threatening her job if she didn't do what he wanted. Once she showed up with bruised ribs. That's who you should be looking at."

"Can you give us a name?" Wayne asked.

"She would never tell me his name. Vannessa might know. She and Kelly were tight."

"Can you think of anyone else who might want to hurt Kelly?" Nick asked.

"To hate someone enough to kill them like that, you have to get close, and aside from Vannessa and me, Kelly kept everyone at arms length, except the guy from her work."

Wayne scribbled in his note pad. "You have access to Kelly's money? Maybe in her will?"

"I don't need Kelly's money. I brought in over a million dollars last year selling custom and antique bikes and restoring cars."

"Why do you live here then? With that kind of money you could have a nice place?" Wayne questioned him.

"This is New York man, if I don't stay here at night, there won't be a hub cap left in the morning. Besides, Kelly helped me remodel it. She picked out everything."

"Don't leave town until this is cleared up." Wayne held out his card. "If you think of anything later, call us anytime, day or night."

"How 'bout you call me when you figure out who did it and give me a fifteen minute window, that's all I'd need. Think of the tax dollars you'd save the public."

Nick was almost out the door when he remembered the ring. He pulled out the picture and put it in front of Ben Carlyle. "What can you tell me about this ring?"

"It's Kelly's. That's a real sapphire. He had it custom made. It cost like ten grand or something, she said."

"Thanks, we'll be in touch." Nick was reaching for the photo when Carlyle took it back.

"Wait, did Kelly have this on her when---?"

"Yes," Nick confirmed.

"That's impossible. She hocked it and gave the money to Vannessa for her tuition."

"Are you sure?"

"That's what Kelly told me. I guess you would have to check with Vannessa to be sure."

Nick took the picture back and left.

As they got in the car Wayne said, "How did you know there was something up with the ring? Did Mia tell you? Does she know something about this case?"

"I don't know, not for sure." Nick had a sick feeling in his gut. Something about this whole case didn't feel right.

CHAPTER TEN

Nick read the text that had just come through. "Meet me at the ice skating rink in Central Park. Mia."

What the hell does that mean? Nick hoped she didn't want to skate. No, she couldn't mean that.

"Hey, I think I'm done for the day." Nick slipped his cell phone back into his pocket. "Let me know what Vannessa says about the money."

"Okay. Where are you going?"

"Mia wants me to meet her in Central Park by the ice skating rink."

"Really? That should be interesting." Wayne laughed.

Snow was starting to fall again when Nick got there. He walked all around the rink, but couldn't find Mia.

"Hey," he heard someone calling. Mia was on the ice, moving like a pro.

"I didn't know you could skate."

"I had lessons when I was a kid."

"Of course, you did." Nick couldn't stop the grin that spread across his face as he watched her. She looked free on the ice.

"Have you ever ice skated before?"

"No. And I'm not going to start now."

"Go rent some skates. I'm waiting for you. I have something to show you."

"Mia."

"Hurry!"

Against his better judgment, and before he could talk himself out of it, he was walking like a robot on the ice. "Is this supposed to be fun?"

"It *is* fun."

Mia glided over to him and took his hand. "Hang on, I'll lead you."

"I'm going to fall and break my butt, I know it."

"I won't let you fall. Trust me."

Nick gave up control and let Mia pull him all over the ice. It hurt his pride when a little girl, not more than five, passed him by. He was about to tell Mia he'd had enough, when she turned around and smiled at him.

"You're doing great. Keep going."

When they were in the middle of the rink, Mia let go of his hand and skated into his arms.

"Thank you for coming and for being a good sport."

"Why are we doing this?"

"I'm trying to bring you joy."

Nick wanted to say, 'you bring me joy,' but held his tongue. He had never seen her look more beautiful. He leaned down and kissed the tip of her nose. "Your nose is so cold."

Mia pushed herself backward until she was about five feet away from him. "That's because it's snowing." She started spinning until she was just a dark blur on the ice. She stopped herself in an instant. Nick clapped and laughed at the same time.

"You're really good. How often do you come here?"

"I try to come every two weeks."

"You do?"

She skated back to him and took both of his hands in hers. "It's a lot more fun with you here."

"Have you had enough for tonight?"

"I guess, since I've been here for an hour already."

Nick wobbled over to the bench and Mia glided gracefully. "We're not much of a match on the ice are we?"

"You'll get better. I'm going to help you."

"I don't think ice skating is for me."

"Sure it is. You can come with me next time."

"I think I'll be sick that day."

Mia laughed. "I'm going to take one more spin around the rink."

"I'll wait here."

She was at home on the ice, so sure of herself. It was amazing to watch her move. Nick realized he'd fallen in love with her. He had been fond of some of the women he'd dated before Mia, but he had never felt like this before. Someone sat down next to him on the bench, but Nick never took his eyes off her.

"She can skate."

"Yeah, she can."

Nick realized he knew that voice and looked at Wayne. "What

are you doing here?"

"I had nothing to do, so I thought I would stop by and see if she could really get you onto the ice."

Nick grunted.

"At least you held your own and didn't fall," Wayne chuckled.

Mia skated over, her cheeks were pink and she was out of breath. When she saw Wayne, she became quiet and looked to Nick for an explanation.

"Mia, this is my partner, Wayne Coleman. He was just leaving."

Wayne offered Mia his hand. "Hi, it's nice to meet you, finally. Nick talks about you all the time."

Mia took his hand and enclosed it with her other hand. "It's nice to meet you too. How long have you two been working together?"

"Oh, about four years, give or take. I taught him everything he knows."

"Yeah, right," Nick huffed.

"How would you like to get together with my wife, Kathy, and me for dinner sometime?"

"Is Nick invited too?"

Wayne laughed out loud. "If you insist."

"I'd like that." Mia smiled with excitement. "What night should we do it."

"How about Friday night?" Wayne offered.

"That would be great." Mia's smiled.

"I'll tell my wife."

"I think you should go now," Nick suggested. "And stop holding her hand."

Mia let go and giggled under her breath.

Wayne pushed Nick's shoulder and winked at Mia as he got up and left.

"The man doesn't understand boundaries," Nick complained.

Mia sat on the bench and started to undo her skates. Nick picked her foot up off the ice and put it in his lap. With half frozen fingers he picked at her laces.

"You're not really jealous."

"How do you know that?"

"Because you have no reason to be." Mia brushed some of the snow off of his head. "I love you, Nick."

Nick jerked his gaze from her skates to her face. She had the glow of a woman in love, there was no denying it. He found it funny she seemed to come to that conclusion at the same time he did.

"You don't have to say you love me," Mia told him. "I just wanted you to know."

Nick leaned closer to her and kissed her softly on the lips. Her lips were warm, but the rest of her face was cold.

"Let's go before we freeze to death."

"Okay, what do you want to get for dinner on the way home?"

"I don't know what I'm hungry for," he said trying to think of something good.

"Decide fast because I'm starving. Skating always makes me hungry for something really fattening."

"Let's get ice cream," Nick suggested knowing how much she loved the stuff.

"That's a great idea."

They returned Nick's skates and were on their way to the car when Nick said, "I can't believe I didn't fall on the ice. I would have put money on me landing the hard way."

"Like this." Mia leaned against him hard, causing him to lose his balance and land in a huge pile of snow with Mia right on top of him. She was laughing so hard she couldn't talk.

"Yeah, just like that." Without warning, Nick rolled and Mia was buried in the snow beneath him. She grabbed a hand full and tried to toss it in his face, but it fell right back into her own.

"That didn't work out so well," she said blowing it off of her face.

Nick leaned down and licked a clump of snow off of her cheek. Mia stopped smiling and her eyes took on a glassy sheen. Just then, a man walked by and said, "Somebody ought to call the cops."

Nick glanced at Mia and then back to the man who kept on walking. "I am a cop. You want your car towed?"

Mia started laughing all over again, even as the snow had turned into droplets of water and were running down her cheeks.

Before he knew what he was doing, he asked, "Will you marry me?"

Mia's eyes widened in surprise.

"Don't think about it, just answer what's in your heart."

"I would love to marry you, but it has to be for forever."

"I can do forever," Nick said quietly and he meant it.

"And I think you should know I want children. Lots of them, so I won't ever have to be alone again." Nick knew she had been alone for a while, but until that moment he hadn't realized how deeply it had affected her.

"I think I can handle that." Nick pressed his body against hers and kissed her until she was gasping for air.

"I can't breathe. Get off me," Mia laughed.

Nick grinned. "Okay, but you're never going to get any babies with that attitude." He got up, helped Mia to her feet, pulled her into his arms, and gazed at her until she looked up at him. "I love you, too."

"I know." She smiled her Mona Lisa smile. "But, it's nice to hear you say it out loud."

Later that night, he was lying in bed thinking about what had happened. He had asked Mia to marry him. He kept waiting for the voice in his head to say, *what the hell were you thinking?* but it wasn't there. He was completely at peace. He waited for Mia to come to bed, so he could ask her if she was okay with it all. It was probably the worst proposal ever. Ten minutes passed and still she didn't come out of the bathroom. Nick knocked on the door, but there was no reply. He turned the knob and it swung open. Inside the bathroom, Mia was sitting on the floor sobbing.

"Mia, what's wrong?" Nick sat down on the floor in front of her.

"This isn't how it's supposed to be. It's all wrong."

"I know. I didn't do it right, because I didn't plan it and I didn't have a ring or anything, but I'll do it again and I'll make it right. Really, I'll get down on one knee and everything. Please don't cry, Mia." He held her, but she just cried harder. It took a while for her to calm herself enough to choke out the words.

"That's not it. I love how you proposed, but you want to know what my first thought was?"

"What?"

"I want to call my mom and dad and tell them I'm getting married, but they aren't here and I miss them so much. Other than Holly and Joe, I don't even have anyone to invite to a wedding who isn't on the payroll. I feel so alone."

"Mia, honey, you aren't alone." Nick held her face in his hands. As he spoke, more tears ran down her cheeks and he wiped them away with his thumbs. "Wherever they are, they love you, and they're watching over you. *You* taught me that. And I love you and we'll make our own family. Please don't cry. I hate seeing girls cry. It'll be okay."

She nodded and repeated his words. "It will be okay." Mia tipped her face to his and kissed him softly on the lips.

Nick kissed her back and within minutes what had started out as comforting, had become something else. Mia was lying on her back with her arms around his neck holding him close to her. Between them was just enough space for Nick's hand to caress her breast. When he glanced down into Mia's soft brown eyes he saw the passion he had ignited within her. He could make love to her right then, she would accept him. Heaven knows his body was crying out for it, no, screaming for it, but he stopped.

"What's wrong?" she asked, her breath unsteady.

"I can't do this. Not like this. I don't want to make love to you for the first time on the bathroom floor."

"We could move to the bed."

Nick closed his eyes and groaned in frustration. "I can't believe I'm going to say this, but this isn't the right time." He gently took his hand off of her breast, rolled onto his back and stared at the ceiling. "I think we should wait until our wedding night."

"Are you sure?" Mia asked, laying her head on his shoulder.

"The only thing I'm sure of is, I'm losing my mind and it's a good thing your bathroom floor is heated."

Mia smiled and kissed his cheek.

"Now, go to bed. I'm going to take a shower, a cold one."

Twenty minutes later, Nick came out of the bathroom to find Mia sitting up in her bed waiting for him. In her hand was a ring box.

"What's that?" he asked as he climbed into bed.

"It's my mother's wedding ring. I was wondering if you wouldn't mind if we use it. It's her original."

Nick took the little blue box from Mia and opened it. Inside were two rings, The engagement ring was what he assumed to be white gold with a huge center stone, a smaller stone on each side and four small stones going around the band on either side. "Whoa, this ring is amazing."

"I've always loved it, and the only reason I have it is because my dad bought my mom a new one the year before they died."

Nick slipped the engagement ring on his little finger. It wouldn't even go over his first knuckle. Under the light from the lamp on the nightstand, he watched it sparkle.

"Do you think it's weird that I want to wear my mother's ring?"

He heard the tentativeness in her voice and turned to Mia. "Not at all. I think it's

a nice way of making your parents a part of it all, even though they aren't here. Besides, this is better than any ring I could afford on my salary."

"It's platinum, and the center stone is a two carat asscher cut diamond. With the side stones and the wedding band the ring is a little over four carats."

"Everyone's gonna think I'm a dirty cop."

"A dirty cop with really good taste."

Nick took Mia's left hand and slid the engagement ring on her finger. She wiggled her fingers and watched it sparkle.

"Now, it's official, unless you want me to get down on one knee."

Mia touched her lips to his, put her arms around his neck, and held him tight. Her body was so warm and soft, and she clung to him as if she was afraid to let go.

"I've been alone for a long time and I don't have the words to tell you how having you come into my life has made everything come alive again."

There was such a haunting tone to her words that Nick couldn't help but ask, "Mia you have other friends besides me, don't you? I mean you never mention anyone, except that one friend, what's her name?"

"Holly?"

"Yeah, Holly."

"I had other friends in high school, but right after graduation, well, we drifted apart. Holly and I were real close, but she met Joe and they got married. Joe's an architect and he got this great job offer in LA. They left a little over a year ago. I talk to Holly, but it's not the same as having her across the hallway."

"Holly used to live in the apartment across the hall?"

Mia nodded. "And then she and Joe lived there, until they left for LA. It's been really quiet without them around."

"Why didn't you rent the apartment to someone else?"

"I don't know. I guess because I keep hoping they'll come back. They probably won't though. Joe loves his job and he thinks I'm a little…odd."

"I can't imagine why." Nick tried to sound serious, but even Mia couldn't help but laugh.

They snuggled down under the covers and Mia turned out the light. Nick didn't go to sleep right away though. The events of the night kept replaying in his mind. The more time he spent with Mia, the more he learned about her.

Nick drifted off to sleep with Mia right beside him. When he woke up it was still dark outside. He reached for Mia, but she wasn't there. He sat up and looked around. Out of the corner of his eye he saw her walk out the door of the apartment, leaving it wide open. "Mia, where are you going?"

He got out of bed, followed her downstairs, out the lobby door, and onto the street. It was snowing heavily and he could hardly see anything. Even the sounds of the city were muffled by the large flakes. Nick held out his hand and they landed on his skin. He thought it odd that he wasn't cold. Mia was standing near him, smiling and laughing, and then she started walking down the street.

"Mia, where are you going?" he called to her, but she didn't turn around. He tried to follow, but the snow was getting so deep. *I don't have any shoes on.* He looked down to see where to step and that's when he saw it, blood on the snow. It was just a few drops, but he knew it was blood. He fought to go a few more feet, more blood. "Mia, stop!" he yelled to her. "There's blood on the snow!"

She kept walking, keeping the same steady pace. No matter how hard he ran she was always just ahead of him and with each step he took there was more and more blood on the snow.

"Mia!" he screamed and she finally heard him. She turned back toward him and held out her hands to him, which were covered in blood. It was dripping onto the ground. He reached out to her, but she faded away right in front of his eyes.

"Mia!" he screamed. "Mia!" No matter which way he ran, she was gone. "Mia!"

He knew she had gone some place where he couldn't follow. Still he screamed her name with everything inside of him.

"Nick! Wake up!"

Nick opened his eyes and found himself still in bed with Mia right beside him. He was soaked with sweat and shaking. Taking a deep breath to calm his nerves he pulled Mia to him.

"It's okay," Mia whispered. "It was only a bad dream."

"I've never had a nightmare like that before. It was so real. We were outside on the street and you were bleeding badly. I tried to catch up with you, but I couldn't, no matter how hard I tried."

"I'm here. I'm here. Try to go back to sleep."

Sleep was a long time in coming. Nick knew the dream was telling him what Silviana already had. Mia was in danger somehow. Every ounce of protectiveness inside of him roared to life and he held her tighter. How could he protect her? What if the threat to her wasn't anything from this world, but something from Mia's world? How could he protect her from that?

CHAPTER ELEVEN

Mia saw the apartment building out of the taxi window. Silviana was waiting for her and Mia made sure she brought her checkbook. She always needed it when she visited her aunt.

Silviana opened her door before Mia could knock.

"Come in," Silviana said, her tone impatient.

Mia looked around, expecting to see her aunt Mirella. "Where is Mirella?" she asked.

"She has gone to Atlantic City with Esteban."

"I see. And where is Jacobo?" Mia wondered where her aunt's husband was lurking. She didn't feel his presence in the apartment.

"He is visiting his mother. She is very ill."

Mia was relieved they were alone. The silence grew uncomfortable as the two women looked at each other.

"Please sit down." Silviana nodded to a chair. "I know why you are here, Mia. You want to know what I have seen for you."

"Yes."

"You have never asked me before."

"Things are different now."

"The man I saw you with. He is your lover?"

"No."

Silviana's eyebrows went up in disbelief. "But you love him?"

"Yes."

"He is the one who makes you unsure?"

"No. Yes. There are many things to consider. I need to have time to think everything through, but-"

"You have no more time, Mia. You already know this." Silviana's words were stern. "You already know what you must do. I can sense that. You are afraid to act upon it. If you wait too long, the choice will be made for you."

"Silviana, you said someone will betray me. Do you see who it is? I need to know."

The older woman reached out her hand and touched Mia's cheek. "Mia, I should be asking you. For generations our family has had the gift passed from mother to daughter. Sometimes it was strong and sometimes it was weak. Your mother had it, but you, Mia, I have never sensed such power before. Tell me what *you* see."

Mia hesitated. She wasn't sure how much she should reveal to her aunt. Her gift had been used to hurt her in the past and she knew she had to be careful, but she needed to talk to someone who wouldn't think she was crazy, so she took a chance.

"I have dreams of people I do not know. I can see what they see and feel what they feel...at the moment they die. Their deaths are violent. I am haunted by them. It is as if they want me to help them and I have tried, in my own way."

"It is not enough, is it?"

"I don't want to disrupt my life. I am happy now and, for the first time in a long time, I am not alone. Nick has asked me to marry him and I accepted. I want to be a normal woman and a normal wife."

"It will never be. You are special, Mia. But you know this also, so why do you come to me when you already know what to do?"

Mia sat and thought about what her aunt had asked. Why *did* she come here? She came because she needed to know about him.

"There are times when I have visions where I feel as if I am in danger. My life is being threatened."

"Is he back?" Silviana looked frightened. "Is it him, the one you called Man when you were a little girl?"

Mia was stunned. She didn't think anyone knew about the spirit that had haunted her on and off since she was a child. Mia found it hard to admit. "Yes, it is him. Sometimes I feel his presence. How do you know about him?"

"Nadja came to me when you where about six. She felt something around you and then she heard you talking to him." Her aunt said nothing more. She just stirred her tea and thought.

"I have felt the presence of many spirits in my life. Some have been very lost and some have been very angry, but the spirit that I called Man, is not like the others. When he is near me, I can feel him. His emotions are powerful and they are all negative, rage, hatred, and a hunger to destroy." Just speaking the words out loud to her aunt gave Mia the chills. She wrapped her arms around herself to keep from trembling. "He is the most terrifying spirit I have ever encountered."

"I do not think Man is a spirit, Mia. I believe he is a demon and he has attached himself to you."

"How can that be? I have done nothing to invite him into my life!"

"I believe he wants you because of your gift. He must see your strength and he either wants to possess it or he wants to destroy it."

Mia sat in her aunt's apartment, her mind racing with the possibilities of what was to come. None of them were good. "What about Nick? How much danger could he be in?"

"Demons can be very powerful, Mia. They can harm you. You must not underestimate him."

"Thank you for your help, Silviana. You've given me a lot to think about."

Mia felt the bond growing between her and her aunt and then Silviana said, "Jacobo's mother is very ill and very poor."

Her hope for a different kind of relationship with her aunt crumbled as she took out her checkbook. Mia played the game she always did with both of her aunts. "I would like to help Jacobo's mother." She handed Silviana a check, just as her mother would have done.

"Jacobo will be very happy," her aunt said tucking it into her bra.

Mia doubted that Silviana's husband would ever know of the check.

"I have to go. Tell Mirella I said, hello." Mia made her way to the door. When she was about to close it behind her, she heard Silviana say, "God be with you."

Mia walked part way home and then hailed a cab when the wind picked up. As she walked into the lobby of her building, Joe, the doorman, stood up. "There were two men here to see you, Miss Carrigan."

"Did they say what they wanted?"

"No, but they did say they would be back."

"Thank you." Mia started for the elevator.

"I'm pretty sure they were cops." Joe's words held a note of warning.

"Was it Detective White?"

"No, ma'am."

"Thank you, Joe."

Mia rode the elevator with an ominous feeling surrounding her.

"You have no more time," those were Silviana's words and she knew they were true. Whatever was coming, it was already knocking at the door.

She slipped off her coat and hat and went into her studio. She opened one of the four cabinets that she'd designed and had had built into the studio part of her bedroom and pulled out a new canvas and a few fresh pieces of charcoal. Mia loved the way the cabinets had turned out. Even from the bed, which faced them, you couldn't tell they were there. It looked like wood paneling on the wall, but with a slight push in just the right spot, the cabinet door would open. Inside there was tons of storage space for all her things.

Mia hid her life in those cupboards. The first one held everything precious to her, that she didn't want the world to see at first glance, all of her family's photo albums, her awards for ice skating when she was a kid, her scrapbooks, her baby clothes, and special gifts from her parents. The second one held blank canvases, art supplies, and her photography stuff. The third one was filled with paintings and sketches, things she was still working on, or pieces she hadn't yet given to Charlie to display.

The fourth one held the paintings of the women and girls she had seen in her dreams. There were twenty-one of them in all. The original paintings were hard to look at because each canvas was of the unnatural death of something sacred, a human life. Mia almost never opened that cabinet. She preferred to see the women the way she painted them the second time, with their wounds covered and their expressions beautiful and at peace. Eight of those were hanging in the gallery.

Mia still felt uneasy about that decision. If Charlie hadn't seen two of them and insisted that those were the ones he wanted to display, she never would have let them out of the apartment. It was like having herself on display, naked for the entire world to see. And yet, she felt compelled to show them.

Mia placed the new canvas on the easel and started sketching. After an hour, the image of a pretty Asian woman began to emerge. Her black hair was long and it fanned out around her head. Her arm was raised and lay on top of her hair.

Mia sketched faster, trying to get the vision she had seen the night before out of her mind. She had always been able to work out the images she saw right away, but now Nick was in her life and she hadn't told him about her visions. Flashes of the girl's murder had been replaying in Mia's head all day long. She had felt the girl's disbelief when his fingers had tightened around her throat and cut off her air. Even as things grew dark around her, she was sure his fingers would loosen and she would be okay. It wasn't until she'd looked down on her own body that she'd known he had killed her.

In her dreams, Mia heard the girl scream out in agony. That's what had awakened her, that and the ice cold air surrounding her own body. She'd known he was there, hovering near by, watching her, but there had been no shadow in the dark this time.

She'd managed to get out of bed without waking Nick and had wrapped herself in her thick chenille bathrobe. How long she'd stood staring out the window she wasn't sure, but eventually, she had climbed back in bed and had snuggled closer to Nick. She had just been drifting back to sleep when she'd heard Nick screaming her name and talking about blood on the snow.

Mia wondered if her dreams were infectious because Nick had been trembling and sweating with fear when she'd woken him. He'd held her so tight. Just remembering the feel of it made her eyes misty. She loved him and being with him made her feel a sense of completion she had never had before, but she was afraid for him. They were meant to be together, but there were so many questions that had no answers. What kind of danger was she in? Was it something in the physical world or the spiritual world? Was Nick in danger also? Who would betray her?

She stopped sketching and sat on her bed to give her eyes and muscles a break. Her fingers were black. Mia lay back and stared at the ceiling. She always found it fascinating to see the wood beams above her, some were new and had been put in place to give the building the structural integrity it needed to be safe, and others had been there since the building had been built in 1917.

Mia closed her eyes and listened to the sounds outside, cars honking, trucks rumbling by, and somewhere far away, a siren. The heartbeat of the city began to fade and around her the room grew dark. When she opened her eyes she was still lying on her bed, but above her, the heavy wooden beams were gone and there was darkness. Then, one by one, snowflakes began fluttering down, only a few at first then more and more.

That was when she noticed the pressure on her chest. It felt like someone was pushing on her. It grew harder and harder to breathe. Mia tried to get up, but she couldn't move. She knew she was passing out when the darkness floated down and enveloped her.

The wind was blowing, she could hear it and feel it against her skin. Mia looked all around in the darkness as she became aware she was no longer in her physical body. The lightness and freedom she felt was incredible. It was as if her soul recognized this new state of being and rejoiced in it. Now she knew how birds felt when they were soaring on the wind. She wanted to fly forever.

Mia sensed that there were others around her. She could hear the whisper of their voices. Still the darkness surrounded her and the wind caressed and supported her. Never had she been more aware of the limitations of her physical body. She was totally free.

The wind grew stronger and louder. It started pushing against her and yet going through her at the same time. She wasn't in control of herself any longer. She was being forced downward. Instinct made her want to grab onto whatever she could for her own safety, but she was no longer in possession of a body. She didn't want to go back, but she heard different voices saying, "This isn't the right time. You must return. Your journey isn't finished." It was her mother's voice.

Mia felt as if she had been slammed back to Earth from where ever she had been. The breath was knocked from her lungs. When she opened her eyes, she could see the thick beams above her, but they were obscured by a misty black form hovering over her.

A different kind of darkness was closing in around her. There was no freedom or joy or lightness in it. It was evil. It was Man. Mia gasped for air and tried to fight against his overwhelming power, but her body was so weak she couldn't raise her arms off the bed. Why was this happening? She wanted to scream, but she couldn't even do that. Mia had the sensation of something touching her, all over her body, all at once. It was touching her face, her legs, her breasts, her arms and her stomach, everywhere. It was like having large bugs crawling all over her. Mia was breathing hard. The wind that had been so warm and embracing was now roaring in her ears like a tornado.

In her mind Mia cried out for help, praying she would be heard. Instantly, the room was quiet, no wind and no black mist. Everything was as it should be. Her ears rang and she gulped down air like she was starving for it. In her chest, her heart beat so hard and fast she was afraid she would faint.

Mia wanted to sit up, but her body wouldn't respond. Every muscle and nerve was numb. She was paralyzed. Thoughts raced through her mind so fast she almost couldn't finish one before another one came. What if she never had feeling in her body again? Would Nick come home and find her like this? How could she explain what had happened? Would he still love her or would he leave her? Tears started to pool in her eyes. If he was smart, he would leave anyway. If *she* was smart, she would force him to go because she knew that Silviana was right. Man was dangerous and she didn't know if she could protect herself, let alone Nick.

It took a few minutes for the feeling to start coming back into Mia's limbs. The pins and needles sensation started in her belly and moved outward all the way to her fingers and toes. Gradually, she was able to move. She forced herself to sit up and, with her hands on her lap, she tested her fingers, wiggling them in different ways. When her heart rate returned to normal, she stood up. Her legs were shaky, but she could stand.

She went into the bathroom and turned on the light. When Mia saw her reflection in the mirror, she could see she had no color, even her lips were white. She splashed water on her face and dried it vigorously with a towel. Mia didn't want to look like she had seen a ghost when Nick got home, so she turned on the shower, hoping the hot water would bring color back to her skin. As Mia undressed, she caught a glimpse of her body in the mirror. All over her were red marks, scratches on her arms, stomach, and legs. Some were deeper than others, almost to the point of drawing blood, but not quite.

Suddenly, a memory from when she was a little girl came back to her. Mia had had a nightmare and her mother had come rushing into her bedroom. She'd turned on the light, only to discover what looked like three distinct bite marks on Mia's arms. The look of fright on her mother's face scared Mia, even more than the marks did. Mia's mother told her that she had to forbid anyone or anything from hurting her. She made her say the words out loud. I forbid you to hurt me, over and over, until she'd sounded angry.

Mia grabbed a towel, wrapped it around her, and stormed into her bedroom. "I forbid you to hurt me!" she yelled. "I forbid it. Do you hear me?! You are not allowed to touch me." The only response was silence, but Mia knew that he was there, listening.

Mia took her shower and felt better. Most of the marks had faded away. She put on clean clothes and brushed her hair, but when she opened the bathroom door she gasped. All the sheets had been torn off her bed and were on the floor. All of her cabinets were wide open and her things had been pulled out and knocked to the floor. Mia was used to things being moved around, but this was different. The air around her still vibrated with rage, a deep murderous rage. Goose bumps ran over her skin and she shivered. Mia wondered for the first time if he could kill her.

CHAPTER TWELVE

Mia waited in the lobby for Nick to pick her up. They were supposed to have dinner with Wayne and his wife Kathy, but he was late. She checked the time on her new cell phone again and thought about calling, but she had already called twice and Nick had assured her that he was on his way. She saw him pull up and walked out into the cold to meet him.

He hurried to get the car door for her. "I would have come up for you," he said. As he got back in the other side, Mia told him, "That's okay. I don't want to be

any later than we already are."

"You're forgetting that if I'm late, so is he. We both had to stay late. In fact, we will probably beat them to the restaurant."

"Do you think they'll like me?" Mia had butterflies in her stomach as she asked. Meeting new people always made her anxious.

"Of course, they'll like you. Who couldn't like you?" Nick took her hand, raised it to his lips, and kissed the back of it.

Mia felt a little less nervous since Nick seemed so sure.

When they got to the restaurant, Mia was determined to be as normal as everyone else. She wanted it to be a night out with friends, like she used to have with Holly and Joe. She missed the camaraderie of their friendship.

Mia was taking her seat when she saw a red-haired woman walk through the door, followed by the man she had met in Central Park. Wayne pointed his wife in their direction and after weaving through the crowded room, they made their way to the table.

"Nothing like Friday night in New York City, is there?" the woman said with a smile and a kiss on the cheek for Nick. "It's been too long since I've seen you, Nick. And this must be Mia." Kathy took Mia's hand in hers.

"And you must be Kathy."

"It's a good thing we made reservations because I'm starving," Wayne said as he held the chair for his wife.

"I have wanted to meet you ever since Wayne told me that Nick had finally found a woman he couldn't escape from. Let me see the ring."

Mia held out her hand.

"So, what bank did you rob?" Wayne asked with raised eyebrows.

"Wow!" Kathy exclaimed. "That is *some* ring."

"It was her mother's. It's Mia's way of remembering her mom," Nick explained.

"It's amazing how much you and Nick have in common. Neither of you have siblings and both lost your parents at such a young age. What are the chances that you would meet in New York City? The odds must be astronomical." Kathy kept talking. "All of his other girlfriends were polar opposites."

"You'll have to tell me about all of his other girlfriends." Mia smiled conspiratorially.

"And there is so much to tell." Kathy was having a great time teasing Nick. "We'll have to have lunch sometime, just the two of us."

"I knew this was a bad idea. Kathy knows too much about me." Nick shook his head and they all laughed at his misery.

"I do, don't I? If I had thought about it in advance, I could have hatched a little blackmail scheme."

"On our pay, you wouldn't make much," Wayne chimed in and Nick nodded in agreement.

The waiter came and took their order, and the small talk continued until their food came.

Kathy and Mia chatted about their favorite places to eat and then Kathy told her all about the vacation they took to Mexico last winter and how Wayne got so sick he couldn't leave the hotel. "At least there wasn't a foot of snow outside."

Just when Mia was beginning to relax and really enjoy herself, Kathy said, "So, my husband tells me you're a psychic. Is this true?"

Mia could barely swallow the food that was in her mouth. She looked at Nick, who grew uncomfortable under her gaze.

"Was I not supposed to tell him?" Nick looked like a deer caught in headlights.

Mia didn't respond, but her hopes for a normal friendship went right out the window. She knew exactly how the rest of the evening would go. Taking her fork, she stirred the pasta on her plate. The men got really quiet. Kathy, however, kept talking as if she didn't sense the tension in the air.

"I would love to know how that works. Do you read tarot cards or tea leaves or something? Wayne told me you're a gypsy."

"Yes. I'm also Irish, English, and Scottish on my father's side." Mia hoped that Kathy would let it drop, but she could tell it wasn't going to happen. Kathy had a very inquisitive nature. At least there were no feelings of contempt or hostility coming from either Kathy or Wayne.

So many times in the past, when people would confront her about her abilities, she could sense they only wanted to make fun of her and point out how different she was. Some of the girls in high school would do that, and so would Evan. He delighted in trying to humiliate her in front of his friends.

"I just get feelings or impressions about certain people or things, like emotions. It's nothing, really." Mia tried to downplay their expectations.

"Okay, so tell me what I'm feeling?" Kathy was smiling, enjoying what to her seemed a game.

"I don't like to do that," Mia tried to discourage her. "People think they want to know things, but it doesn't always turn out the way they plan."

"Yeah, tell us what Kathy's feeling," Wayne nudged her, ignoring what she'd said.

Mia turned to Nick, who looked at her like he expected her to comply with their request. She wasn't going to get any help from him. Kathy's blue eyes were boring into hers, and Wayne was staring with intense interest.

"I really don't think this is a good idea."

A wave of disappointment rolled across the table.

"Please, Mia. I really want to understand how it works." Kathy was so hopeful. Mia didn't want to do this, but she couldn't just say no to Nick's friends.

"Let me start with your husband, since I met him first."

Kathy clapped her hands together excitedly. "Oh good! Tell me all of his deep, dark secrets."

"When I shook your hand in Central Park, I felt confusion, fear, and I was overwhelmed with sadness. I could feel your reluctance to go home. Home isn't where you want to be right now. There is a void between you two that is getting deeper."

Kathy turned to Wayne. "That isn't true is it?"

Wayne didn't respond, he simply stared at Mia with his mouth hanging open. His body language said it all. It was hard to tell whose expression was more shocked, Wayne's, Kathy's, or Nick's.

Before Wayne was forced to answer, Mia tried to save him.

"Kathy, there is something you're keeping from your husband, that you shouldn't be. You're causing more pain than you realize. You should just tell him the truth and the tension you have been sensing will take care of itself."

Everyone sat in silence for a full minute before Wayne whispered, "What is she talking about?"

Kathy stared at Mia. "How could you know?" Her already pale skin turned as white as the table cloth. Mia thought for a second that Kathy might faint.

"What secret is she talking about?" Wayne asked his wife, louder this time.

"Excuse me." With tears in her eyes, Kathy jumped up from the table and ran to the ladies room. Wayne followed her.

"Well that was fun." Nick tossed his fork on his plate. "What're you doing, Mia?"

"I told you, I don't do parlor tricks. This is why. And thanks for your help."

"If you didn't want to do it, why didn't you just say so?"

The accusatory tone in Nick's voice not only made her mad, it hurt her feelings.

"Because they are your friends and I felt like I had no choice. And I thought you would back me up the *first* time I said no." The more Mia thought about it the madder she got. "This isn't a game and it isn't entertainment. I thought you understood that." Mia got up from the table and headed for the door. She passed Kathy and Wayne on their way back to the table.

"Mia, wait!" Wayne called out after her.

The only consolation was that Mia could tell they had made up and both of them were very happy.

As soon as she was out the door, she hailed a cab. On the way home she couldn't help but regret the whole evening. She never should have gone. Maybe she was meant to be alone. The cell phone in her pocket began to hum. Mia took it out and looked at the screen. It said, *Nick's cell.* She couldn't bring herself to answer it. As soon as it stopped humming, she turned it off.

The cab stopped right in front of her building. Mia paid the fare and hurried inside. She wasn't sure why she felt like she needed to hurry, but she did.

Once she was inside, she slipped out of her coat and glanced around her apartment. It felt so empty, dark, and cold without Nick there with her. Mia bit back a sob and proceeded to turn on every light in the apartment and turn up the heat. There was nothing she could do about the emptiness, but she could fix the dark and the cold. She put a tea kettle on the stove and went to change into her work clothes, old ratty things that didn't matter if she couldn't get the stains out.

Mia was going to work all night, since she wouldn't be able to sleep anyway. Just as she was pouring the steaming hot water into her mug she knew Nick was coming to her. She could feel his presence in the air around her.

What if he was coming to break off their engagement? Mia tried to feel for his mood, but she was too upset to get past her own emotions. She wished she hadn't turned on all the lights. If she had left them off, he might have thought she wasn't home.

She heard the elevator door slide open and voices coming to her door. If she wasn't mortified enough, he had brought Wayne and Kathy with him. Could this night get any worse?

Nick knocked on the door. The sound of it echoed through the apartment.

"Mia? Mia, I need to talk to you. Let me in." His tone was soft and contrite.

She stood there in her kitchen, her mug of tea sending wisps of steam into the cool night air, wondering what she should do, what she should say. If she didn't open it or respond, would they go away?

"Mia, you gave me a key. Don't make me use it. Please open the door."

Mia forced herself to move. She turned the lock and cracked the door, only to find Nick looking really uncomfortable. Kathy and Wayne were right behind him. Kathy's eyes were red and swollen.

"Can we come in for a minute?"

Mia tried to remember how graceful her mother was when her

father's family would come to their house. Always the perfect hostess, even when her uncle and aunt made veiled comments about Mia and her mom. She was going to use that example to get through this night.

"Of course." Mia swung the door open so they could enter. "I was making some tea, would you like some? Kathy?"

Kathy was barely inside the door when she started talking.

"Mia, I am so sorry about tonight. I shouldn't have bullied you like I did. I didn't expect you to be so right and it surprised me. I hadn't told Wayne I was pregnant again because I've already had three miscarriages and I wanted to be sure I could carry the baby this time. I didn't even realize he sensed that something was going on with me. I've been so preoccupied for the last few months. I haven't been myself and that includes tonight."

"It's okay. It wasn't your fault. It's mine. I wanted to make a good impression for Nick's sake and..." Mia felt the tears pooling in her eyes once again, even though she was trying to smile, and wished she was anywhere but where she was. "I'm going to get us all some tea before it gets cold."

Mia escaped into the kitchen and got three more mugs out of the cupboard. She was sure she wouldn't be able to choke down any tea. Nick followed and was watching her as she tried to pour the water into the cups with shaking hands.

Carefully, he took the hot kettle from her and finished pouring it. He didn't say a word, but Mia could feel him staring at her.

"After they leave, we'll talk," he whispered.

Once again, Mia tried to feel what emotions he was experiencing, but her own sadness and fears were too overwhelming for her to sense anything else.

Mia went back to Kathy and Wayne and handed Kathy a mug of tea.

"Your apartment is amazing," Kathy said. "I don't know where to look first, the fireplace, the glass panels, or the view outside. It's like eye candy."

"I hope so or I'm out of a job."

"I forgot that you're an artist. Nick says you have your work on display somewhere. I would love to go see it."

"I'll give you Charlie's business card. It has the address and the hours printed on it."

"Thank you."

Both Kathy and Wayne were taking everything in, so Mia asked, "Would you like a tour of the apartment?"

"I would love that." Kathy smiled.

As Mia showed them the apartment, she sensed the tension begin to ease.

When they got to the bathroom, Wayne said to Kathy, "Honey, that is a ten-thousand dollar tub."

"I can see why. You could swim laps in that thing."

"It has its own heating unit, so the water stays at whatever temperature you set it."

Wayne played with the remote for the automatic blinds. "This is really cool."

"Boys and their toys," Kathy whispered into Mia's ear. "He loves remotes of any kind."

"I think it's something in that Y chromosome," Mia whispered back. When they both began to laugh, Mia finally began to feel better. She genuinely liked Kathy and Wayne.

"I still would love to get together for lunch sometime." Kathy waited for her reaction.

"I would like that."

"Really? How about Wednesday? That's my day off."

"That's my day off too, so that should work. Let me give you my phone number and my cell phone number and we can talk about it next week." Mia grabbed a pen and a piece of paper and jotted down the two numbers and handed it to Kathy, along with Charlie's card.

"Thanks. I'll call you." Kathy then looked at Wayne. "Let's go, honey. I'm getting tired."

The door shut behind them, leaving Nick and Mia in silence.

Mia gathered the mugs of tea and put them in the sink.

Nick followed her. "I want to talk to you."

"About what?" She grabbed a clean wash cloth and wiped off the counter top.

"About tonight."

Mia moved into the dining area and wiped up the table, even though nobody had sat there, then back into the kitchen. After a quick rinse of the cloth, she went into the living room to wipe down the coffee table and end tables, all the while Nick was right behind her.

When she started for the kitchen again, Nick took her by the arm. "Mia, stop. Talk to me."

"I don't want to talk because I don't want to fight with you."

"All couples fight. There are going to be times when we disagree about things and get on each others nerves."

"That's not what happened tonight. Why did you tell them about me?"

"Wayne is my partner. It's like having a brother. I tell him everything and he tells me everything."

Mia felt her cheeks get hot. "You tell him everything? Then he knows that we…that you and I haven't…"

"No. I haven't told him that we haven't made love." He chuckled softly. "No man would understand that, especially since we've practically been living together. So, there is no need to blush." Nick touched her cheek with his fingertips.

His cool caress was a relief against her flushed skin. Mia turned her cheek to his palm.

"Why do we have to fight? My parents never did."

Nick started to laugh until he saw that she was serious. "Your parents never fought?"

"Never. I saw them discuss things and I saw them making out." Mia pulled on the front of Nick's shirt until his lips met hers. He wrapped his arms around her and held her tight as they kissed and kissed some more. Mia couldn't stop the little moan from escaping her as his tongue slid past her lips. She loved the way he tasted and she loved the way he smelled. She loved him.

"I love you, Nick, and tonight when you got mad at me, I felt like you were blaming me for Kathy and Wayne being upset. I only told them what I did because they wanted me to and I wanted them to like me, for your sake. I don't do parlor tricks and when I say that, I mean it. I need you to understand whatever abilities I have are, for lack of a better word, sacred. Misusing them is like cursing in church or defacing a great work of art."

"Or, peeing in a sweat lodge," Nick added. "Is that why it bothers you so much that Silviana likes to show off with her powers or gifts?"

"Yes. My mother used to say, misusing what we know is like spitting in the face of God."

"Okay, I get it. I'm sorry I was such a jerk and I wish I could say it won't happen again, but it will. I try really hard not to get angry and lose my temper like I used to, but it's a long and bumpy road for me. And just when I think I have it under control, it flares."

"I thought you didn't love me anymore and it hurt me." Mia laid her head against his chest, unable to look in his eyes as she said the words.

He cradled her head with one hand, while his other ran up and down her back, soothing her fears. Mia was calm enough now that she could once again sense his emotions, just as she could hear his heart beating in his chest.

There was regret and happiness, but mostly love. It fed her soul.

"I've had three serious girlfriends in my life. One I dated for over two years, but I never felt about her the way I do about you."

Mia wanted to cry, but she held it in. "Good. I want forever, remember?"

"I remember."

They stood for the longest time, just holding each other.

"Mia, I hope you won't be upset, but I have to go home tonight."

Nick loosened his hold on her and glanced at her face for her reaction.

"I have a couple of things I need to get from my apartment and I need to see if the super fixed the leaky faucet in the kitchen. Is that okay?"

"That's fine. I have some work I need to finish too."

"You do?"

"Yes. I usually work at night, but with you here I haven't been getting as much done because you need to sleep."

"I didn't realize that was a problem. You should have said something."

"If I need to work at night when you are here I can just go across the hall to Holly and Joe's apartment. I already have some of my stuff over there anyway. At certain times of the day, I like the light that comes in through those windows."

Nick nodded. "Oh, good. That reminds me, you never showed me the portrait of me that you did the night of our first date."

"That's right, I didn't." Mia panicked a little bit. The portrait was in her cabinet with her other unfinished work. Right next to the cupboard with the sketches and paintings of all of the women she had seen in her visions. If he saw her open the cabinet he would know what all four of the panels were. She wasn't ready to show them to him. It was too soon. And they had just made up. And he might not understand them.

"Mia?"

"Um, I'll grab it. Would you mind putting those mugs in the dishwasher for me while I do?"

Nick looked at her like it was the strangest request he had ever heard.

"Sure, okay." As he headed to the kitchen, Mia sprinted to the bedroom and before she opened the cabinet, she turned out the lights. The door clicked quietly when she pushed on it and it popped open just a couple of inches. Mia reached inside and grabbed the canvas, hoping Nick was too busy to notice.

Mia heard the dishwasher close and hurried into the living room where Nick met her. She held it out for him to see. On the canvas was his image. His face totally relaxed in sleep. His hair and eyebrows were black against his tan skin. His lips were perfect. If there was anything that was off slightly, it was his nose. *Maybe a little narrow at the bridge,* Mia thought.

Suddenly, she realized that Nick hadn't said a word. "It's okay if you don't like it. I know the nose is a little off. I was going to fix it."

"Is this how you see me?"

Mia studied the canvas once more. "Yes."

Nick leaned in and kissed her on her head. "Don't change anything. I like it just the way it is. Call me in the morning when you wake up."

"Aren't you going to kiss me goodnight?"

"If I kiss you again, I won't be leaving. I'm only human."

Nick smiled a smile that Mia suspected very few people ever got to see from Nick White or Detective White or Nick Whitecloud or whoever he was when he wasn't with her. When he was with her, he was just her Nick, and nothing else mattered.

CHAPTER THIRTEEN

Walking into his apartment was like coming home after a vacation. The apartment felt stale and empty. Nick grabbed the remote, turned on the television just for the noise, and sorted through his mail. It had been a week since he had picked it up and his box was full. Most of it was junk, with a few bills thrown in and a baby's birth announcement. The little post card had blue booties embossed around the edge. His cousin Tawna had had a baby boy and they were naming him Franklin.

Nick could picture his grandfather's look of pride to have a child named after him. His family had been on his mind a lot more now that he had met Mia. She reminded him of his grandfather in how she accepted things beyond herself as fact. Nick could remember as a boy talking to his grandfather about the elder man's beliefs in spirits and the power in things you couldn't see or touch. Now, he wished he had paid more attention.

Nick turned down the sound on the TV, picked up the phone, and dialed his grandfather's number.

"Nicholas, how are you?" his grandfather asked, as he answered.

"How did you know it was me?" Nick asked, thinking it was some kind of premonition.

"We've got caller ID now."

Nick rolled his eyes. "How are you, Grandfather?"

"I am well."

"And how is Grandmother?"

"Her diabetes has been acting up. The doctor's are trying a new medicine. She misses you."

Guilt washed over him, making him wish he had called more often. "I know. I miss her too. I have something to tell you."

"You have met a woman."

"Yes, how did you know?"

"I can hear it in your voice. You are less angry than you used to be."

"Grandfather, I wish I could tell you this in person, but I'm sorry for being so prideful and angry when I was younger, and for not listening to you when you were trying to teach me about the spiritual things you believe, and about the ways of our ancestors."

There was only silence on the other end.

"Grandfather? Are you still there?"

"Yes. Tell me about your woman. Is she responsible for these feelings?"

"She is different from any other woman I have ever known. She is an only child and both of her parents died in a plane crash when she was thirteen. She is an artist and can sense people's emotions and," Nick wondered if he should tell his grandfather the rest, "she can communicate with spirits. She is gifted. I've seen it."

"Does she have a name?" His grandfather sounded happy at his news.

"Her name is Mia and I am going to marry her."

"Are you sure she is the one?"

Nick remembered the love in Mia's eyes the night she told him she was a virgin. "She told me she has been waiting for me."

"Ah," Grandfather replied in understanding. "You should bring her home to meet your family, especially your grandmother."

"If I can arrange time off work in the next couple of months, I will try."

"That would make us very happy."

"I see you have a new great-grandson named after you."

"It is a good name," he replied.

Nick could tell his grandfather was smiling. "It *is* a good name. Goodnight, Grandfather. Tell everyone I said, hello."

Nick hung up and leaned back on his couch with a smile on his face. He was just reaching for the remote when the phone rang.

"Hello."

"Is this Nick White?"

"Yes."

"My name is Richard Sharpe. I need to speak with you. It's urgent."

Nick hesitated and tried to remember if he knew a Richard Sharpe. No one came to mind. "How did you get this number? It's unlisted."

"Yes, I know. I'll explain everything when we meet. I could come to your apartment."

"I don't know who you are. You come to my apartment and you

may be leaving feet first."

"Would you be willing to meet me at the restaurant across the street from your building?"

A part of him wanted to tell the guy to take a hike, but curiosity got the better of him. He'd go, but he wouldn't be alone.

"Across the street. Give me thirty minutes."

"I'll see you then."

Nick took out his cell phone and hit number two. After three rings, Wayne answered.

"What's up?"

"I need your help." Nick explained the situation.

When he walked into Buck's a half hour later, he knew Wayne was already there, watching his back.

The hostess came to him and asked, "Are you Detective White?"

"Yes."

"I'll show you to your table."

He followed the young woman to a table that was more private than the others. A man, who looked about fifty, was already seated there with a drink in front of him. Several thick manila file folders rested on the table next to him.

Nick sat down and the two men sized each other up.

"Richard Sharpe?"

"Yes."

"I'm Nick White."

"I know who you are, Detective."

"So, who the hell are you and what do you want?" Nick didn't like the man's expensive three piece suit and the way Sharpe was looking at him, as if he was being appraised.

"Can I get you a drink, sir?" the waiter interrupted.

"No, I don't think I'll be staying long."

The waiter walked away and Nick waited for the man to continue.

"Paul Carrigan was my best friend. I was his personal attorney and now I handle all of Mia's personal matters. I also supervise a team of lawyers, accountants, and financial advisers who take care of all of her business affairs."

"So, this is about Mia?" He should have known.

"Yes."

"When Mia called me and told me that she was engaged after

only knowing you for three weeks, I was very concerned. It's not like her to rush into things. She has always been a good judge of character, but when she started talking about changing her will and giving you power of attorney, I knew I had to do something."

"So, you hired a private investigator to check me out."

"I hired a team of private investigators and called in favors from some very connected people." Sharpe tapped his fingers on the manila folder. "Your whole life is in this file, starting with your grandfather's service in the Korean War. Your parent's deaths. Your military records. The court documents from when you changed your name from Whitecloud to White. Your rise to detective at the age of thirty. Where you have stayed for the last four years. Your bank accounts and credit cards, all the way down to when you paid your cable bill last week. It's all here."

"You think that paperwork tells you who I am?"

"In a way. It tells me you are a hard worker who lives within his means. You don't drink, you're well respected by your co-workers, and you have dated many different women, but have never been married. So, my only question is, why Mia?"

"You're afraid I want to marry her for her money, aren't you?"

"The thought crossed my mind." Sharpe sat back in his chair as if he was contemplating what to say next. "If I offered you a million dollars, tax free of course, to walk away from Mia and never see her again, what would you say?"

"I'd say, 'how would you like to step out into the back alley for a couple of minutes?'"

"Are you willing to sign a prenuptial agreement, stating that if the marriage ends, you leave with what you came with?"

"Let me ask you something, Sharpe. Are you afraid of getting a smaller piece of the pie if I marry Mia? Is that what is really going on here? Are you afraid of losing your Christmas bonus?"

"You do think like a cop, don't you?" Richard Sharpe laughed quietly. It was the first emotion the man had shown.

"Occupational hazard."

"Paul was a generous employer. If I were to die tomorrow, my great-grandchildren will be taken care of. So, the answer to your question is, no. I promised Paul that I would look after Mia if anything happened to him and Nadja. To this day my concern is for her happiness and her safety. Do you have any idea how much she is worth?   There are a lot of unscrupulous men that would love to sweep her off her feet and gain access to her money."

Nick had to admit the man seemed sincere and if he was in Richard Sharpe's shoes he might be thinking the same thing.

"First of all, Mia's money is Mia's money. I don't want any of it. I may not make a fortune, but I can support myself. Second, if it will make you feel better write up a pre-nup and I'll sign it. And third, I care about Mia's happiness and safety too."

"I already suggested a pre-nup to her and she wouldn't hear of it." Sharpe shook his head. "I had to see for myself what kind of man you were."

"So, did I pass your test?"

"For now." Sharpe tapped his finger on the stack of folders, "Keep in mind I have a long reach. And I will do everything within my power to protect her, just like I always have." Richard Sharpe's words held a, not so veiled, threat.

Nick knew the man meant what he said. Sharpe tossed a fifty on the table and was slipping his arms into his expensive overcoat when Nick thought of one thing he had to know. "Do you also represent Mia's uncle and her cousin Evan?"

"No. I only deal with them on Mia's behalf. Why do you ask?"

"Evan came to Mia's apartment and wanted to talk to her about some money for the business. If I hadn't been there, I think he might have gotten violent with her."

Sharpe mulled over what Nick had said for a few minutes. "David Carrigan, Mia's uncle, is not the businessman Paul was, but he is harmless, except for driving his portion of the business into the ground about every ten years or so. Evan, on the other hand, he..." Sharpe was choosing his words carefully. "He is arrogant, spoiled, and at times erratic, and I would advise against letting him near Mia."

Nick wasn't surprised at Sharpe's assessment of Mia's cousin because that was his impression also.

Richard Sharpe offered Nick his hand and Nick took it. "I hope you are who you appear to be, for Mia's sake," he said as he placed his files in a briefcase and clicked the latches closed. "I'll be seeing you."

Nick watched Richard Sharpe head to the door and no sooner had the door closed behind him than Kathy and Wayne joined him at the table.

"What are you doing here, Kathy?" Nick asked, surprised that Wayne would bring her along.

"You don't think you could keep me away from all this cloak and dagger stuff, do you?" Kathy smiled.

"I thought it would seem less suspicious if I brought her with me," Wayne explained. "So, what did he want?"

"He's Mia's personal attorney. He's been checking me out."

"What do you mean?" Wayne asked.

"Apparently, he's had a team of investigators doing a complete background check."

"I'm not surprised," Kathy told them as both men looked at her. "With that kind of money on the line, I mean."

"What are you talking about, Kathy? What do you know?" She had Nick's attention now.

"You don't even know who Mia is, do you? Have either of you heard of Carrigan Industries?

"Mia mentioned it a while ago."

"Mia's grandfather started Carrigan Steel and Mia's father expanded big time, manufacturing, chemical, pharmaceuticals, shipping, and a dozen other businesses. It was huge news when her parents died. It was in all the papers and on TV. When her grandmother died, there was a custody battle between Mia's mother's family and her father's family."

Nick remembered Silviana, Mia's aunt, and wondered if she was the one who fought for custody.

"You couldn't open the paper without seeing Mia," Kathy continued. "She was like royalty. The paparazzi hounded her constantly and then, after a while, she just seemed to fall off the face of the earth. I hadn't heard about her until Wayne told me you were dating someone named Mia Carrigan. I didn't think it was the same girl, but it's her."

***

Nick left Kathy and Wayne at the restaurant and as soon as he got home, he grabbed his laptop and sat on the couch with it. He typed Mia's name into the search engine and watched the information load onto the screen.

Everything was there, from her birth announcement to pictures of Mia with her parents at charity events throughout her childhood, articles about Mia competing in the Junior Nationals for ice skating, to eventually, her parent's plane crashing in bad weather. Her whole life was right there for everyone to read, but what haunted Nick were the pictures of a happy, smiling, little girl who turned into an older, sadder image of herself.

From his computer screen, Nick stared at the pictures of Mia, her dark eyes and solemn expression staring back at the camera. She looked so young and so scared at her parent's funeral and that same lost look stayed on her face throughout her teenage years. There were pictures of her at school, getting out of cabs, and at restaurants with friends. They must have made her life miserable.

No wonder Mia was hesitant about letting the New York Times do a story about her art. No one in their right mind would want to live under that kind of scrutiny.

Nick glanced at the clock. It was two-thirty in the morning and he had to go to work in a few hours. He brushed his teeth, made sure his alarm clock was set, and climbed into bed.

His body craved sleep, but his mind wouldn't let him rest. All the things he had learned about Mia kept going through his head. He loved her, but he realized there was so much he didn't know about her. It was as if she had hidden away the real Mia.

And tonight at her apartment, when he'd asked to see the sketch she had done of him, she'd been hesitant. She had turned out all the lights in her bedroom and then opened up a door in her bedroom wall. It was obvious she hadn't wanted him to see that what he thought were just wood panels was some kind of storage space. Why? What was she hiding from him and why did she need to hide it at all? He needed answers.

There was so much more to Mia than met the eye. He finally fell asleep, but it was a restless sleep, where strange dreams haunted him and all of them were about Mia.

CHAPTER FOURTEEN

Nick was feeling his lack of sleep as he sat down at his desk.

Wayne didn't say anything. He didn't have to. The look on his face said it all.

"Shut up," Nick warned.

Wayne chuckled and sipped his coffee.

"Did we hear back from Vannessa about the money for her tuition?" Nick wanted to change the subject.

"I had a message this morning. Kelly did give Vannessa the cash for school, but she wasn't sure where the money came from."

"If Kelly did pawn the ring, we have to find out where and who bought it back."

"And how the ring got back on her finger."

Nick knew they were onto something big. "Follow the ring," Nick mumbled under his breath.

"What did you say?"

"Nothing." It still bothered him that those words were in his head. What bothered him even more was that it was Mia's voice he heard saying them. How could she know anything about this case? He had never discussed it with her and they had been very careful about what had been released to the media. As far as he knew, he and Wayne were the only ones who knew anything about the ring being important in the case. The whole situation made Nick uneasy.

"I'm going to fax a picture to every pawn shop in the city and see if we can't shake something loose."

"James Stanton, from Stanton and Bingham, should be back from his vacation by now. We need to go and talk to him. Also, we got a tip about the kid in the warehouse that we need to follow up on, and then there are all the interviews to go over in the Michelle Wong case."

"It's going to be another long day." Wayne smiled.

"I need some coffee before we go." Nick filled his travel cup to the brim, sure he was going to need it.

***

The office of Stanton and Bingham was a hub of activity as they waited in the reception area for James Stanton. When the secretary finally did show them into James Stanton's office, he was no where to be found.

"Just have a seat, gentlemen. Mr. Stanton will be right with you."

Nick checked the time on his watch. "You'd think having two homicide cops in your office would make someone a little more prompt."

Wayne walked around the plush office, checking everything out. "How much do you think this guy makes?"

"More than we'll ever see in our lifetimes put together."

"Not you. When you marry Mia you'll be in the money."

Nick was about to respond when James Stanton walked in, his tie askew, and his shirt sleeves rolled up.

"Sorry, gentlemen. I had an overseas conference call."

Nick didn't like the man already. He was so assured of his own self-importance it was irritating, but Wayne's comments about Mia's money had already rubbed Nick the wrong way and had soured his mood. "We need to speak with you about Kelly Langford. What can you tell us about her?"

James Stanton sat down in his big chair and leaned back. "I don't know what I can tell you that you don't already know. She was a bright, hardworking, young woman who had a great career in front of her. It is a tragedy that she's gone."

"When was the last time you saw Kelly?" Wayne asked, notepad in hand.

"The night we wrapped up the Saudi deal. By the time everything was finalized, it was about one in the morning."

"One? Did you and Kelly often work late nights together?" Nick's alarm bells were going off.

"Yes, quite often."

"So, you would know who it was that Kelly was sleeping with here at work?" Nick asked bluntly trying to shake the man up.

"She wasn't sleeping with anyone here that I know of. I believe she had a boyfriend outside of work, though. You might want to check him out. I got the feeling from Kelly he was a little rough around the edges. I'm sure you know about Kelly's background."

"Are you referring to her being a foster kid?" Nick tried to lead him to say more.

"Yes. Kelly accomplished a great deal, considering her background, but it's hard to overcome that kind of upbringing and go the distance. You know what I mean?"

Stanton's cocky smile was the worst. The man's money and charm had taken him a long way, but Nick saw right through him.

"No. What do you mean?" Nick forced himself to smile back like they were two guys talking about women.

"You know the saying, 'you can take the girl out of the ghetto, but you can't take the ghetto out of the girl'? Kelly knew the score. That's all I'm saying."

"When exactly did you leave for Hong Kong?" Wayne cut in.

"My wife and I left on the fifteenth."

"Thank you for your time, Mr. Stanton," Wayne told him. "If we need anything else, we'll be in touch."

Nick and Wayne left the office and as they passed the desk in the reception area, Nick spotted a brochure that had both Martin Bingham's and James Stanton's pictures on the cover. Nick flashed it at Wayne and slipped it into his suit pocket.

Once they were outside the office, Wayne didn't waste any time voicing his opinion about James Stanton. "What a sleazebag. It was like he was blaming Kelly for her own murder."

"I got a bad feeling about him," Nick told Wayne. "He was Kelly's boss, so he could hold her job over her head. They worked late at night together."

"But he was on his way to Hong Kong. He couldn't have been in two places at once."

"Maybe. Maybe not. The time of death isn't for sure because of the weather. What if he killed her and hopped a plane to Hong Kong a few hours later?" Nick speculated.

"We'll have a hard time proving that with so little DNA evidence."

"Let's go find some *circumstantial* evidence and wipe that smile right off his face."

***

Nick was glad Mia's building had an elevator because he was dead tired. As soon as the doors opened on the fourth floor, the aroma of food cooking hit him. His stomach growled in response.

Inside, Mia was in the kitchen making a salad. When she saw him, she smiled and came and put her arms around his neck.

"Hi. You're late. How was your day?"

Before he could answer, her lips were on his. None of his other girlfriends ever welcomed him home like that. He had to admit, he liked it.

"My day was long. What smells so good?"

"I have a pot roast in the oven. Take off your coat and rest. The food isn't quite ready, so I'm going to take a quick shower."

He could tell she had been working. She had black stuff on her face.

"Okay, but hurry. I'm starving."

As Mia headed to the bathroom, Nick sat on the bed and slipped off his shoes. On the easel near the bed was a canvas with Mia's latest piece. It was a girl standing on the edge of a cliff with heavy ocean waves at the bottom. The sky was dark, with gray storm clouds. It was foreboding. Nick wondered what was behind its bleakness. The water went on in the bathroom.

As he sat there, he noticed the easel was sitting right in front of the wall that Mia had somehow opened the night before. He hadn't paid it much attention before, but now he was curious. Nick got up and got closer, trying to find something. The brick wall that surrounded the front door stopped about twelve feet from the windows that faced north. Now, he could see that the wall had been covered with bead board paneling and some wood trim. There were no knobs or pulls anywhere.

"I must be crazy," he muttered to himself as he inspected the wall. He could have sworn that he had seen Mia open the wall. As he ran his hand over the painted wood surface, he thought he must have been mistaken, until he pushed on it just a bit and the door popped open a few inches. "I'll be damned."

A little voice in his head mentioned something about invading Mia's privacy, but he told it to shut up as he swung the door open. Inside were shelves, top to bottom, each filled with small boxes, photo albums, and plastic bins. Nick slid one of the boxes closer. Inside was a collection of small ice skating trophies, ribbons, and medals. He picked one up and inspected it. Mia's name was engraved on the tarnished gold plate on the bottom. He put the box back and took out another one. He lifted the lid and inside was some baby clothes, dresses for a little girl. They must have been hers when she was a baby.

The whole cabinet seemed to be filled with keepsakes from her childhood. On an upper shelf he saw a couple of old stuffed animals. There was an old gray rabbit that looked well loved by a child. Nick could picture Mia as a small girl holding onto the rabbit as she went to sleep at night, afraid of the dark.

He closed the cabinet and moved to the next one. Pressing in the same spot it popped open just as the first one had. Inside this cabinet the shelves ran only half way up. The open space at the top held several different sizes of canvases, all brand new and ready for Mia to use. On the shelves were art supplies and her camera equipment. Nick noticed a stack of pictures sitting right next to her camera. When he picked them up he recognized them instantly. They were the pictures she had taken at the small park down the street. From where Mia had been on the fire escape she had taken a picture of the empty park as the snow fell. The street light was the only illumination and the black and white photo seemed eerily lonely. The picture felt sad, but he couldn't stop staring at it.

The low hum that had filled the apartment stopped and Nick realized that the water in the bathroom had gone off. He put the pictures back, shut the cabinet and walked into the kitchen just as Mia came out of the bathroom in her pajamas.

She walked into the kitchen, grabbed a couple of pot holders, headed straight for the oven, and pulled out a small roasting pan and set it on the stove top.

"I hope you like it."

"It smells great and right now, I could eat just about anything."

"Good. Sit down and start on your salad while I serve this up."

Nick ate a few bites of the salad, but what he really wanted was the meat and potatoes he had seen in the pan. His mouth watered as the air became saturated with the aroma. He watched Mia open the bottom oven and take out a pan of rolls that looked like they had melted butter already on them.

"That looks and smells so good." As soon as she set his plate on the table he started eating. The chunks of beef swam with carrots, onions, and potatoes in thick and creamy gravy. "This is so good. I didn't know you could cook like this. What's in the gravy? It has a different taste to it."

"It's a white wine cream sauce. It's my mom's recipe and she was a really good cook."

Nick cleaned his plate, had two rolls, and polished off his salad.

"Do you want more?" Mia laughed as she asked.

"If I eat more, I won't be able to get out of bed in the morning without a crane."

They did the dishes together and Nick changed into his old flannel pajama bottoms and a t-shirt. He normally slept in his underwear, but it was too cold in the apartment for that. Mia was sitting on the couch, watching the early news, when Nick came out of the bathroom. When he joined her, he saw that she had tears in her eyes.

"What's wrong?" he asked, thinking he had done something to upset her.

"This story on the news is so sad."

Nick glanced at the TV and saw a man and a woman holding onto each other with tears in their eyes. "What happened?"

"Their son died two weeks ago from cancer and now their house burned down. The husband lost his job as a janitor and they still have three little kids to feed. It's just so sad and unfair."

"Life isn't fair sometimes." After he said it, he realized how jaded it sounded.

"I think we both know that from experience."

Mia snuggled up next to him. He liked the smell and feel of her hair, it was so soft. He ran his fingers through it. It was still a little bit damp.

"Was it hard for you, after your parents died, to go and live with your grandparents?" Mia wanted to know.

"Not really. My dad died three years before my mom so when my mom went to work I stayed with them anyway. The last year of her life she lost her job and didn't come home very often, so it wasn't a big change. Plus, my cousins were always there, so I had someone to hang out with. How about you? Who did you live with after your parents died?"

"I lived with my grandma Behan. She was my mother's mom and she was great. She would drive me into the city for school every morning. On the way we would stop at a coffee shop and she would get her morning pick-me-up, as she called it, and I would get hot chocolate. And she would be there when I got out of school."

"She sounds like a great lady."

"She was. I was sixteen when she died."

Nick could still hear the regret in Mia's voice. "What happened?"

"She had a massive stroke in the middle of the night and died in her bed."

"I'm so sorry you had to find her like that, Mia."

"I didn't find her. I just called 911 and let the firemen take care of it. I never saw her body until her funeral."

"How did you know to call 911?"

Mia didn't say anything for a moment. "She came to me right after she died. We talked for a while and she told me to call 911."

Nick pulled Mia tighter against his body, trying to offer what comfort he could. At times, he forgot that Mia wasn't what she appeared to be. She could seem so normal, but she was unique. And, as if to prove the point, she started to get up.

"Where are you going?" he asked, taking her hand before she was out of his reach.

"I have to get the phone." It began to ring as soon as the words were out of her mouth.

The hair on the back of his neck stood up. He stayed on the couch and listened to the one-sided conversation.

"Hello. Hi, Charlie. Yes, I know. I didn't forget. I won't back out. Just remember our agreement. I know. Don't worry. I will. Bye." She hung up the phone with a worried look on her face.

"Mia, what's wrong. What was that all about?"

"It was Charlie. He wanted to make sure that I wasn't having second thoughts about Friday."

"What's going on Friday?"

"I'm doing the Times interview."

"I thought you didn't want to do it?"

"I owe it to Charlie. He's been good to me."

"What's this agreement you were talking about?"

"That we talk only about art, not about my past." She sounded skeptical as she sat back down on the couch.

Nick noticed her furrowed brow and the tension around her mouth. She looked nervous. He held her close as they watched the rest of the news. The next thing he remembered was being shaken awake.

"Nick, wake up."

He opened his eyes and saw her standing in front of him.

"You must be exhausted. I have been trying to wake you up for ten minutes."

"Sorry." Nick made his way to the bed and climbed in. Mia got in next to him and snuggled close. His mind was half asleep when he remembered the question he had been meaning to ask her. "Did you tell me to follow the ring?" His mind was giving into sleep.

He heard Mia say, "It's what she wanted you to know." Questions entered his mind, but he was too tired to respond.

CHAPTER FIFTEEN

"Luckily, he was so high he never even knew he had dislocated his shoulder and the doctor had popped it back in before he sobered up." Kathy's blue eyes scrunched up when she laughed. "I should write a book. *Tales of the Emergency Room.*"

"That is quite a story." Mia laughed. "I could never be a nurse. I don't know how you do it."

"I could never be an artist. I can't even draw a straight line."

Mia stabbed another piece of chicken with her fork and ate it. "This place is really good. I'm going to have to bring Nick here."

"He's been here before. It was Pam's favorite restaurant."

"Oh." Mia nodded, knowing that Pam must have been one of Nick's former girlfriends.

Kathy held still for a second. "I'm sorry, Mia. I shouldn't have brought up Pam. Sometimes, I talk too much."

"That's okay. What was she like?"

"She was great, but I don't think they were ever really serious about a relationship. At least it didn't seem like it to me or Wayne."

"Why not?" Mia asked.

"Pam was a flight attendant. She was always here one day, gone the next. When she was offered a job transfer to Paris, she took it and was gone for good. It seemed as if she was, um…" Kathy put her finger to her chin, "convenient. Not that they didn't get along, it was just never going to be for the long haul. Not like *you* and Nick."

Mia smiled. It made her feel good inside to know that Kathy could see what she felt. "I knew the night we met that it was fate."

"It's a good time for Nick. He was so driven to get ahead in his career, I've never seen anyone work so hard, and now he's established and not working such insane hours."

"I work insane hours."

"I have worked my share of graveyard shifts, mostly to earn extra money for the down payment on a place of our own. I think we've looked at fifty houses and we've narrowed it down to two. One is affordable and I can stay home with the baby. The other is out of our price range, but I love it.

"Tell me about them."

"I could show them to you if you'd like. They aren't too far from here and my cousin Jimmy, our real estate agent, lent me the keys, but don't tell anyone. He could get in trouble." Kathy's excitement was contagious.

"I'd love to see them, but don't we need to make an appointment?"

"They're both empty."

"Let's go." Mia dropped a fifty on the table. "It's my treat today."

"I can't let you pay for my meal," Kathy protested.

"I'll let you pay next time."

"I'm gonna hold you to it, and thank you."

Mia could sense that Kathy was genuine in her emotions. She was a 'what you see is what you get' kind of girl and Mia appreciated that. Her own family always had ulterior motives for everything they did, her uncle, his wife, and Evan. And her aunts were no better. Everything had an angle that would benefit them.

As they drove, Kathy talked about all the different qualities she liked or disliked about each of the houses. Mia realized how lonely she had become. She had shut herself off from people after Holly and Joe left. Her work had kept her busy, but it was a solitary occupation. Being with Kathy was like picking up where she left off with Holly. Mia smiled. She couldn't help it.

"I'm talking too much again, aren't I?" Kathy asked when she noticed the smile on Mia's face.

"I was just thinking how much fun I'm having. I love looking at real estate. I went with Holly when she and Joe were thinking of buying a house. We must have looked at a hundred different places, never finding one they both liked, so they moved into the apartment across from mine. The next thing I knew, Joe got a great job in California and they were gone."

"I'm sorry, Mia. That must have been hard for you."

"It was at first, but I got used to it. And then I met Nick and he introduced me to you and Wayne, so it all worked out."

"I'm glad you gave me a second chance after I behaved so badly at dinner." Kathy's cheeks turned pink. "I'm still so embarrassed that I acted that way."

"At least you didn't call me a witch and suggest burning me at the stake."

Kathy laughed, until she saw that Mia wasn't joking. "Are you serious?"

"Yes," Mia said, looking out the window at the houses as they passed by.

"That's awful. Why would someone do such a thing?"

"Some people are just mean."

"Here is the first one. It's a fixer-upper." Kathy's excited smile returned and she almost skipped up the walkway with Mia trying to keep up. "I think this is the right key." She turned the lock and opened the door.

Mia immediately felt the presence of others in the house. As Kathy moved from room to room, pointing out the woodwork and the built in cabinets in the dining room, Mia was hearing voices and seeing shadows.

"I think we will take out this wall and make the kitchen open up into the back bedroom and make that a family room. What do you think?"

"How long has this house been on the market?" Mia wanted to know more of the house's history.

"It's been for sale for over two years. That's why the price is so low. They just want to unload it."

Mia stopped at the bottom of the staircase and looked toward the second floor. On the landing were three distinct shadows. When Kathy saw her staring, she stopped talking and followed Mia's gaze to the top of the stairs.

"What's wrong?"

"I don't think you should buy this house."

"Why not?" Kathy whispered. Her shaky tone of voice told Mia that Kathy was pretty sure that something strange was going on.

"They don't seem to be finished with it yet." Mia told her.

"Who are they?"

"The family who's still living here. There's a father, a mother, and a little girl."

Kathy inhaled with fear. "Wayne told me this place gave him the creeps."

Mia read the vibrations all around her and listened to the voices. "They won't harm you, but they aren't going to leave. If you buy this house, you will be sharing it."

Kathy's face went a little bit white. "I don't think I want to do that."

"Maybe we should go look at the other house." Mia took Kathy's arm and steered her toward the front door.

Kathy sat in the car for a minute before turning the key. The car started and the heater came on, cold at first and then it warmed up.

"My cousin told me that some of the neighbors said the house was haunted."

"They're right," Mia confirmed.

The second house was beautiful on the outside even with the front yard piled with two feet of snow. Mia could tell that the Craftsman style house had been painted and fixed up.

"It looks like the owners put in all new windows."

"They did. You have a good eye, Mia. I should have taken you with me when I toured all the other houses I've been through." Kathy turned the key and pushed open the door. "That would have made Wayne happy. This isn't his thing. He would much rather have me pick the house and he will live in it. Men." She rolled her eyes.

Mia stepped in first and glanced around. She could see the living room, the dining room, and part of the kitchen.

"Well?" Kathy asked.

Mia walked into the dining room and glanced up the staircase. "So far, so good."

"The kitchen has the original cabinets, but they were all stripped of the old paint and stained." Kathy ran her hand over one of the cabinets. "And the hardwood floors were refinished, so we wouldn't have to do any of that."

"What about the water damage in the corner over the sink?" Mia pointed to a spot where the paint was peeling.

"I never noticed that before. Do you think it's serious?"

"I don't know, but I would get an extensive home inspection before settling on a price."

"They're asking five-hundred and forty-nine thousand." Kathy looked disappointed. "Even if they dropped the price a hundred grand we couldn't afford it, but isn't it a great house? Let's go upstairs."

Mia followed Kathy into the master bedroom. The putty gray on the walls looked good with the white trim. "Do you like the paint?"

"I do. That would mean one less thing to do if we bought it."

Kathy pointed to the wall with the sloped ceiling, "This would be where we put the headboard for our bed. And there is room for a cradle and still room to walk to the bathroom."

"Maybe even a small rocking chair."

"That's such a good idea." Kathy's smile faded. "I shouldn't get my hopes up like this. I'm going to be so depressed when it doesn't happen." Kathy grabbed Mia's hand, "I have to show you the room we would make into the nursery."

The bedroom next to the master was cute with a small window seat and brand new carpet. As Kathy talked about how she would decorate it, Mia could see it all in her mind. It made her wonder where she and Nick would be living when their children were born. She could picture Nick holding their baby, patting his back or maybe her back.

Mia studied the house in a different light. Would Nick want to live in a house like this, to raise their family? Images began to flood her mind and her senses. She put her hands on her belly, imagining it was full of new life. Another vision of Nick smiling at her made her breath catch. He loved her. She knew it.

"Mia? Did you hear what I said?" Kathy asked.

"Sorry, my mind was wandering. What did you say?"

"I said, wouldn't it be a great house to raise a family in? I can see living our lives in this house."

"I think it fits you." Mia wanted Kathy to have her dream. "There is someone I know who is an expert in New York real estate. He's the one who worked out the deal on my apartment building. I could call him. If anyone can find a way to make this house affordable, he can."

"I don't know. I feel obligated to my cousin. I could never face my aunt again if I cut him out of the deal. He's taken me through so many houses."

"I will make sure he gets his full percentage."

Kathy clasped Mia by the shoulders. "That would be so great. I love this house. If we could get it without going broke, I would be so happy."

"I'll make the call as soon as I get home."

They walked through the rest of the house and Kathy talked about it the whole way back to Mia's apartment. "Do you want to come up?" Mia offered.

"I better get home. I promised Wayne I would make real food tonight. So, I have to pick something up, get it in the oven, and get rid of the evidence before he gets home."

Mia laughed.

"Don't forget to call me after you talk to your real estate guy. I want to know word for word what he says. Okay?"

"Okay."

"I had such a great time. We should shop for houses every Wednesday, only next time, I'm paying for *your* lunch."

"You're on."

"And if you still want me to go with you to do that interview thing I'd be happy to. It will give me a chance to see your work. Call me."

Mia was so relieved that Kathy had agreed to come with her. She knew Nick had to work and she didn't want to face it alone. She was dreading it.

***

When Nick walked through the door, it was after eight-thirty. He took off his coat and holster and draped them over the console table next to the front door. Mia was on the phone, but she smiled and kissed him anyway.

"How was your day?" she whispered.

"It was busy. How was yours?" he whispered back as his arms went around her waist. While she waited for Richard to come back on the line, Nick started kissing her neck. His breath was hot against her skin and his teeth nibbled her earlobe.

Her heart started beating in double-time and she forgot she was on the phone until she heard Richard's voice on the other end of the line.

"It's all been taken care of," he confirmed.

"Thank you, Richard. I knew I could depend on you. And I'll let you know about the other property as soon as I hear back from Levi."

"I'll be expecting your call. And Mia, how is everything working out with Detective White?"

Nick was so close that he'd heard Richard's question and he whispered in her other ear, "How am I working out?" as he cupped her bottom and then pinched her, just hard enough to make her squirm.

"He's working out great, most of the time." Mia pretended to push him away, but he wouldn't move. "Bye, Richard." When she heard the phone disconnect, she slipped her arms around Nick's neck, "That was devious. How am I supposed to concentrate when you're kissing my neck like that?"

Nick lifted her off the ground and she wrapped her legs around his waist.

"For right now, I only want you concentrating on me." He kissed her softly until their tongues met and the passion flared.

Mia held him tighter. She couldn't get close enough. His hands were hot as they burrowed under her shirt and caressed her skin. Nick moved to the bed and laid her down. He stood there, staring at her for a few seconds. Then, he yanked off his tie and started unbuttoning his shirt.

It was taking too long, so Mia reached out to help. She knew she shouldn't, but button after button slipped through its hole. She wanted to touch his skin and feel the heat. She wanted to hear his breath, heavy in her ear, and know she was the one causing it. She wanted him to love her in every way possible.

The white shirt against his tan skin was beautiful, but she was glad when it was off. Mia ran her hands up his chest. The muscles were hard and soft at the same time. Nick wore his hair short, but there was just enough for her to thread her fingers through and bring his lips to hers.

Mia had never let a man get this close to her. Now she understood why women had lovers. She was on fire.

Nick was gliding his hand across her belly when the entire apartment went black and the air around them got cold.

"What the…"

As he started to get up, Mia grabbed his arm. "Don't move, Nick."

"What?"

"Don't move. We're not alone."

"Tell your spirit friends to get out."

Mia started to tremble with fear. "This isn't a spirit and it isn't a friend."

"What are you talking about?"

A loud bang shook the apartment. "It sounds like someone's trying to come through the door." Nick began to move, but Mia held his arm.

"Where are you going?"

"I'm going to get my gun."

"Nick, that won't help."

He kept pulling away from her.

"Stay here, you're safer right where you are."

"Mia, it will be okay."

Nick hadn't taken three steps when the sound of glass breaking in the kitchen echoed in the darkness, followed by a loud thud from the opposite side of the room.

Mia watched Nick's silhouette turn one way and then the other. Another bang on the door and the lights flickered several times, staying on just long enough to blind them once again.

Nick cried out in pain. Instantly, Mia found him in the dark and stepped in front of him. The warmth of his touch in the frigid air gave her courage.

"Stop it!" Mia yelled. "I command you to stop! Get out!"

Something heavy hitting the floor in the kitchen made the floor shake and then there was silence. Total silence. There wasn't even the hum of the appliances. It was dead quiet.

"Mia, what the hell is going on?" Nick whispered right next to her ear.

The lights came back on as if nothing had happened. The refrigerator clicked on and began to hum, and all the clocks flashed twelve o'clock.

Mia stood in the middle of her apartment, not knowing what to do. She turned to Nick, who was still shirtless. "I heard you cry out. Are you okay?"

"I felt something scratch my back." He turned around as he spoke, so Mia could see.

Mia gasped in shock. Three deep gouges ran down Nicks back at an angle. Blood droplets were forming in a few places where the skin was broken.

"What? What is it?" Nick asked

Mia couldn't respond. Her mind was racing as fast as her heart.

"Mia? Are you going to faint?"

She still couldn't form any words, but she managed to shake her head, no.

"Are you sure?"

"You're…you're bleeding."

Nick walked to the bathroom with Mia following right behind him. He turned on the light and looked in the mirror. One small stream of blood was starting to run down his back.

Mia grabbed a clean washcloth, wet it in the sink, and without saying anything, she dabbed at the blood.

There is blood.

It was all she could process in her mind. Whoever or whatever had been tormenting her since she was little had now hurt Nick. The entity she called Man, had made him bleed. This had never happened before and Mia didn't know what to do. She doctored his wounds as best she could. With bandages covering the deepest gouge marks.

In the kitchen, the floor was littered with shattered glass and several of her cookbooks that had been knocked out of the cabinets. All over her apartment Mia could see things that were out of place. It looked like someone had come through while having a temper tantrum.

Nick started sweeping up the glass. Mia went to help him.

"Stay back. You don't have any shoes on."

Mia picked up a cookbook and put it back in the cabinet.

"Where is your dustpan?" Nick asked, getting the last pieces of glass into the pile.

She handed it to him and he finished his task.

"What the hell was that all about?" Nick asked, sounding irritated and confused at the same time.

She knew the questions were coming and she tried to think of a way to explain it all to him, without sounding like she was crazy.

"Mia, if that wasn't a spirit, what was it?"

"That was a demon," she blurted out.

Nick hesitated. Mia could see the doubt in his eyes and then the realization that there really was no other explanation for what had happened.

"A demon?"

"Yes."

"What does he want?"

Mia blinked over and over trying to get rid of the tears that were filling her eyes. "I think he wants me."

CHAPTER SIXTEEN

Nick saw the fear on Mia's face. He wanted to comfort her, but as he stepped closer to her, she moved away. She went into her bedroom and came back with the shirt and tie he had tossed onto the bed only minutes ago.

"I think you should go home, at least for tonight." Mia handed him his things.

"What are you talking about? Ten minutes ago, I thought we were going to make love, and now you're kicking me out?" After what had just taken place he couldn't believe she was trying to make him leave.

"Please, you have to go. I don't know what's happening here and I'm not sure I can protect you."

All at once he understood. She was worried about him. He hadn't had anyone worry about him like that since he'd left home when he was eighteen. "Who's going to protect *you* if I go?"

Mia didn't say anything.

"I'm not leaving. If he wants you, he has to come through me."

"It doesn't work that way. Your gun and your strength are useless here."

Nick knew that was true. He had nothing to offer. In this situation, Mia had more authority than he did. It was a strange realization for a cop.

"I'm not leaving." Nick took his shirt and tie from Mia and wrapped his arms around her. She was trembling. Nick visually searched the apartment, looking for any sign that whatever it was, was still there. His gun still sat on the table by the door, untouched, not that it would have done him any good. It had just been instinct that had made him go for it. "How do you know it was a demon?"

"I just know."

Nick leaned back and looked down at her. He needed to see her expression. "Mia, talk to me. Tell me what you know about this."

"It isn't the first time I have felt his presence. I have sensed it off and on during my life, but it wasn't until long after my parents died that I knew he was...evil." Mia's brown eyes were big, round, and frightened.

Nick pressed a kiss to her forehead, hoping it would reassure her.

As the minutes ticked by, nothing else happened until the phone rang. Mia jumped, startled by the loud sound in an otherwise quiet apartment.

"Let the machine get it," Nick said when she started to pull away.

"Okay." Mia once again laid her cheek against his chest.

An unfamiliar voice began speaking. "Mia, this is Levi. I checked on that property and I believe it's way over priced for the neighborhood. I have placed a call to the listing agent and as soon as I hear back from her, I'll give you a call."

"What was that all about?"

"Kathy and I went house hunting today. There is one she really likes, so I called Levi to check it out for me. He helped me get this place."

Before Nick could respond, his stomach growled long and loud.

"With everything that's happened tonight, I forgot about dinner. You go change and I'll get it out of the oven." Mia headed for the kitchen.

"You better put some shoes on. I swept up the glass, but I may have missed a few pieces."

Nick walked into the bathroom and glanced at his back in the mirror. He could still see three distinct scratches. They were a little too far apart to have been made by a human hand. The hairs on the back of his neck stood up once again. A small voice in his head asked him why he was still here. He should have left and not looked back. Another voice told him to take Mia and get out, but that would be pointless and Nick knew it. She was the key to all of this and he knew that wherever Mia went, this thing would follow.

He thought back to the night he was followed to his car. It had to have been this entity, but why? And how much danger were they in? Was it capable of killing? How ironic would that be, a homicide detective getting murdered by something you couldn't put in cuffs? He had worked his butt off to make detective and he'd be damned if he was going to become the laughing stock of the station house. Whatever this thing was, he would deal with it. How? He wasn't sure, but first chance he got, he was going to call his grandfather and seek his advice.

After they ate, they sat on the couch and watched a couple of shows on TV. Mia had been leaning on his shoulder, but now her head rested in his lap. Her soft rhythmic breathing told Nick that she was falling asleep. He felt around for the remote and was about to turn it off when Mia yawned. "Leave it on. The news is coming on."

"You're falling asleep?"

"I need to watch it tonight." She yawned once more.

"Okay."

Mia shifted as the anchors each read their parts. Nick played with a lock of her hair as they droned on. He loved the feel of it between his fingers.

On TV, they were doing a follow up story from the night before about the family who had lost their son to cancer. Nick watched as they showed clips from the previous night, where the husband held his crying wife.

"Tonight the family would like to thank the anonymous benefactor who not only supplied them with a place to stay and a new job for Mr. Gomez, but also paid off their sons medical bills." Nick glanced at Mia as the anchor went on. "Isn't it nice, with all the stories we do about the darker side of life here in the Big Apple, that we get to do a story like this?"

The female anchor nodded her head. "It sure is an amazing story, Bill."

A house, a job, and their medical bills paid off? Only a person with lots of money could do all that in a day. "Mia, did you have anything to do with that? Mia?" Nick leaned forward to see that she was sound asleep.

He waited until the sports segment was over and then turned off the TV. Carefully, he slipped out from under her and went about the apartment turning off all the lights and pulling the covers back on the bed.

When he went to wake her up, he noticed the moonlight was shining down on her through the window. She looked so young lying there with her hands under her cheek. Her skin was white and flawless against her dark hair and eyelashes. She reminded him of Snow White. His cousins Tawna, Sandra, and Ashley would watch that movie over and over again at his grandparent's house, until he could hear the dwarfs singing in his sleep. It had gotten to the point where Nick and his cousins had to escape outside, even if it had been the dead of winter. That was a long time ago, but the memory made him smile. Now, he had his own Snow White.

Nick leaned down and kissed her cheek. When she didn't move, he kissed her again. "Mia, it's time for bed."

Her lashes fluttered. She opened her eyes and smiled. "Carry me." She wrapped her arms around his neck and held on tight.

Nick slipped one arm under her knees and one behind her back and lifted. "It's a good thing you're light or I might slip a disc." He laid her gently on the bed and covered her up with the covers, tucking them around her in a fatherly way. Then, he walked to the other side of the bed and climbed in next to her, pulling her into his arms. The warmth of their bodies, so close together, soon made Nick feel tired and his eyelids drifted shut.

"No one's tucked me in like that since my mom died," Mia whispered, her voice tight with suppressed emotion. "I'm so glad you're here." Mia lifted his hand to her lips and kissed the back of it.

"I'm glad I'm here too. Now, go to sleep."

When Nick woke up the next morning, he could smell coffee brewing all through the apartment. Wayne was going to be ticked if he was late again, so he got out of bed and went straight into the bathroom. The hot water in the shower felt good until it hit the scratches on his back. Nick winced and muttered a few choice words. When he dried off, he did it carefully. He was pretty sure he set a new speed record in getting ready.

"I made pancakes," Mia told him as he walked into the living room and put on his holster and gun.

"I don't have time this morning, but thanks."

Mia came out of the kitchen and watched him with a strange look on her face.

"What?"

She forced a smile. "Nothing, just be careful while you work. I worry about you."

"I'll be fine. I'll call you later." Nick kissed her and ran out the door.

✳✳✳

Wayne took one look at him and glanced at the clock.

"I'm not late," Nick said before Wayne could say a word.

"We got a call about Kelly Langford's ring. Pawn shop downtown said they thought they recognized the ring from the pictures we sent out."

"Really? Let's go see if they know who bought it back."

"Let's give it thirty minutes, until the morning traffic lightens up and my bran muffin kicks in." Wayne took a sip of his coffee. "What are Kathy and Mia up to? Kathy was smiling like the Cheshire cat all night."

"I don't know, but I think it has something to do with a house they looked at yesterday."

"I told Kathy not to get her hopes up. The house she wants is way over our budget." Wayne frowned.

It was a look that Nick knew well. He had seen it often when Wayne and Kathy had first gotten married and her large Irish Catholic family couldn't keep out of their business. Nick made a mental note to tell Mia to stay out of whatever she was into, before Wayne got irritated.

As they drove to the pawn shop, Nick thought about how worried Mia seemed to be when he left that morning.

"Does Kathy ever worry about you being on the job?"

"When we first started dating she would worry, but not so much anymore. Why?"

"Mia, told me to be careful today. She's never done that before and there was something in her tone of voice. It was creepy"

"You think it was a premonition?"

Nick laughed. "No, I think she was being a woman."

"You better be careful how you say that. You'll get yourself in all kinds of trouble."

"I know. It's like asking a woman, who's acting crazier than normal, if she's PMSing."

It was Wayne's turn to laugh. "I asked Kathy that once and only once. She picked up a glass sugar bowl and threw it at my head. I've never been so glad for all those duck and cover drills you do in grade school in all my life."

"Was she PMSing?" Nick asked.

"Of course, but I'm not allowed to ask her if she is. I have to guess. They get to make up all the rules."

By the time they pulled up in front of Bayside Pawn, Nick and Wayne had commiserated on most of the ups and downs of having a woman in your life.

The pawn shop was like a thousand other pawn shops all over New York, with its flashing neon sign that said open in the window, and all kinds of stuff on display underneath it. Nick carried the file under one arm and followed Wayne through the door.

"I'm Detective Coleman and this is Detective White. Someone here called about a ring?" Wayne asked the man behind the counter.

"That was me," the dark haired man replied.

His accent told Nick the man was a native New Yorker. He handed him several photos of the ring, each taken from different angles. "Is this the ring?"

The man looked over each photo carefully, "That's it. I only remember it because I ain't never seen one like it before. I'm pretty sure it was custom made."

"Do you have the info on who sold it and who bought it?" Nick's adrenaline was pumping now. They were digging up another piece of the puzzle that was Kelly Langford's death.

"I got the papers right here. A Kelly Langford sold it. Here's her address, a copy of her ID and a thumbprint."

Nick glanced at the papers while Wayne flipped through them. "What about the person who bought it?"

"We don't ask questions when we're selling jewelry, especially if they are paying in cash." The man smiled.

"What can you tell us about the guy?"

"Older, expensive suit, paid with one hundred dollar bills."

"How much?" Nick wanted to know.

"He dropped seven grand. I was gonna sell it for five, but the guy had an attitude, like he was better than me. It pissed me off."

Nick reached into the file and took out the Bingham and Stanton brochure he had taken from their office and showed the shopkeeper the picture of James Stanton.

"That's him! That's the guy who bought the ring." He tapped the brochure with his finger.

"Are you sure?" Wayne asked.

"Positive."

"Sure enough to testify to that in court?" Nick studied the man for any signs of hesitation.

"I'm sure. Hell yes, I'll testify."

"Well, now we know who killed Kelly Langford," Wayne said

as they got back in the car.

"All we have to do now, is prove it." Nick buckled his seat belt.

"I gotta hand it to you. You thought it was him all along." Wayne started to go at the light. "How did you know?"

"He just felt wrong to me." Nick shrugged.

"I think you've been spending too much time with Mia." Wayne smiled, suddenly the smile vanished and he screamed, "Look out!"

Nick heard the screeching of tires and then everything went dark.

CHAPTER SEVENTEEN

When Nick opened his eyes, he wasn't sure where he was. His head hurt and his ears were ringing. Somewhere far away, he could hear Wayne's voice, but he couldn't make sense of his words. The ringing went on and on. The realization came to him, it wasn't ringing he heard, it was a siren. He was in an ambulance, but why? Was he shot? He tried to remember, but nothing came to him.

Once more he heard Wayne's voice. "Hold on, Nick. We'll be at the hospital in a few minutes."

"What happened?" he managed to say with the oxygen mask on his face.

"Some idiot ran the light and smashed into the passenger side." Wayne looked concerned. "You've got a gash in your head and the paramedics think you've got a concussion."

At the hospital it was X-rays, CT scans, stitches and all the rest. It felt like it took forever. Outside the hospital windows it was already dark. It was like he had lost a day of his life.

"They're going to keep you overnight for observation," The nurse told him as she wheeled him into his room. "You have some people who have been waiting to see you."

When the door swung open, Nick saw Wayne leaning against the window sill. As the nurse pushed him further into the room, he caught a glimpse of Mia sitting on the edge of a chair. She waited for the nurse to get him into bed then came and took his hand. She didn't say anything. She didn't have to. The look on her face said it all. She was pale and there were a few smudges of mascara at the corner of her eyes where a few tears had been shed.

He pulled her into his arms, "I'm fine, just a bump on my head." When he let her go, Nick reached up and felt the bandage on the side of his head.

"He's got the hardest head in the world. I should know." Wayne tried to add a little humor to the tense situation.

"Are you really okay?" she asked softly.

"My head hurts a little." He *had* to lie to her. In reality, his head felt like it had lost a fight with a sledgehammer.

"Thank goodness it was only his head, a mild concussion. A few days rest and he'll be back on the job," Wayne informed her.

"A few days? No way." Nick shook his head and instantly regretted it. "I'll be in tomorrow. We have work to do on the Langford case."

Wayne leaned over, pretending to whisper in Mia's ear. "Did you ever notice how stubborn he is? It's all part of the hard headedness."

"I did notice that. It's always about him." Mia smiled for the first time.

"Get out of here." Nick pointed to the door. "Go home and pester your wife. And, I'll see you in the morning."

Mia started to back away from the bed, but Nick grabbed her hand. "Not you. You stay here."

Wayne was part way out the door when he said, "If you need anything call me."

"I bet this isn't what you thought your day was going to be like," Nick said when he and Mia were finally alone.

"I'm just happy you're going to be okay, but you're not serious about trying to go to work tomorrow, are you?"

"I have to. We caught a big break in a case."

"Can't it wait until Monday?"

"I don't think so. Besides, by morning I'll be fine." As he said it, he hoped it would be true.

Mia looked skeptical, but she kept her thoughts to herself.

"Should we watch TV? See what we're missing in the evenings?" Nick pushed a button on the side of his bed and the TV that was hanging from the ceiling came on. Using the up and down buttons on his bed, he scanned through all the channels. "Should we watch the news or the news?"

"I think the news." Mia pulled up a chair to the side of his bed and that was how they spent the evening.

The glare off the screen hurt his eyes, so he closed them. At some point he must have drifted off to sleep. When he woke up, it took him a minute to remember where he was. The chaos of a daytime hospital had been replaced by the rhythmic beeping and whispering of the machines in the other rooms. Occasionally, an alarm would go off and then he could hear the scurrying of feet, until the offender was dealt with. He searched the room for Mia, but she was gone. *It's for the best,* he thought, *she should get some sleep.*

The door opened and Mia walked in looking disheveled and tired.

"I thought you'd left."

"I couldn't just leave without saying goodbye. I went down the hall to get something to drink from the vending machine." She held up the cup in one hand. "Do you need anything? You were sleeping when they brought your dinner."

Nick was confused. He couldn't believe he had slept through people coming and going in his room. He must have slept for a lot longer than he'd thought.

"What time is it?"

"It's almost four in the morning," Mia informed him as she put the back of her fingers against his forehead, like she was checking for a fever.

"I don't think you get a fever with a concussion." He smiled at her.

"Just humor me."

"What did you get to drink?" he asked as the steam came off her cup.

"It's green tea. Do you want some?"

"I don't drink grass clippings?"

"Ha, ha. You must be feeling better."

Nick took inventory, turning his head one way and then the other. I feel pretty good. My head doesn't hurt anymore."

Mia smiled a knowing smile.

"Did you do that?"

"Do what?" She pretended she didn't know what he was talking about.

"You did that on our first date. You took my headache away. How do you do that?"

She shrugged and sipped her tea. "I don't really know how to explain it."

"Try. I want to understand," Nick prompted her.

"It has to do with touch." Mia set her tea down and took his hand in hers. "After a few minutes and a little concentration, I can feel your pain. It's like two bodies becoming one. I can pull the pain away from you and into me, like water being absorbed by a sponge. And when I let go, I force the negative energy from my body and it's gone."

"I like the sound of that, two bodies becoming one." He couldn't help himself.

"You must be feeling better." Mia laughed quietly.

"I am. Let's go home. You look like you need some rest."

"What do you mean? We can't just leave. It's four in the morning."

"Sure we can." Nick hit the call button and the nurse at the desk down the hall answered.

"Can I help you?"

"I'm leaving now, so if you want me to sign anything you better have it ready."

"The doctor hasn't released you yet!" The nurse sounded upset at the breaking of the rules. "You can't just walk out!"

"Yes, I can, and in fifteen minutes, I am going to." Nick swung his legs over the side of the bed and glanced around. "Where are my clothes?"

"I don't think this is a good idea. Why don't we wait until the doctor clears you?"

"Thanks to you, I feel great."

Mia pressed her lips together disapprovingly.

"I'm fine." Nick took her by the hand and pulled her close until she stood between his legs. "And, I'll rest better at home, with you in my arms." Nick leaned forward until his lips touched hers. He kissed her once, twice, three times, and each kiss was a little longer, a little deeper. "Will you marry me?"

Mia shook her head. "Short term memory loss. The doctor told us that could be a problem with concussions." She held out her hand where her engagement ring sparkled.

"My head may be broken, but the rest of me is working just fine." Nick winked and kissed her again.

The nurse walked in and handed him a clipboard with a stack of papers to sign and gave him a lecture about leaving early and the danger signs of a concussion. All the same things he'd already heard. Nick signed and initialed until he wondered if checking out was worth it. "Is that it?"

The nurse snatched the clipboard out of his hands and left.

"So, where are my clothes?"

Mia walked over to a long cupboard and opened the door. All of his clothes were neatly hung.

"Did you do that?"

"That's a six hundred dollar suit. It shouldn't be thrown in a plastic bag."

"Mia," he chastised. "My first car didn't cost that much."

"It must not have been much of a car."

"It got me where I was going, mostly with me pushing from the rear, but I got there."

Mia handed him his socks and shoes and then laid out the rest on the foot of the bed.

In minutes Nick was dressed and ready to go. They hailed a cab and watched the snow fall out the windows as the cabbie negotiated the icy streets.

"I wish this awful weather would be done already," Nick complained.

"I like the snow. It's so quiet and peaceful." Mia sighed.

There was something in her tone of voice that made her seem sad. "Are you okay?"

"Tired, I guess. But I'm not the one with a concussion, so I shouldn't be complaining."

Nick took her hand, "Thanks for being there for me. If you hadn't stayed, Wayne would have felt obligated, and working with him when he's tired is like poking a pissed off rattler."

"You two sound like an old married couple." Mia smiled.

"More like brothers. I trust him with my life."

Mia was quiet for a moment. "You're lucky to have that. Not everybody does."

"Mia, you have family and friends. What about Holly, your friend in California?"

"I liked it better when she was Holly who lived across the hall, but she's doing great. Did I tell you she started her own business?"

"No, you didn't."

"She's excited. I guess it's really taking off."

"That's great." Nick said the words, but he had the feeling Mia didn't think it was so great. She stared out the window as the storefronts passed by, not saying another word until they entered the lobby of her building.

"Morning, Miss Carrigan," Carl, the doorman, said as he tipped his hat.

"Morning, Carl."

They rode the elevator in silence. Mia pushed open the heavy steel door to her apartment and headed straight to the thermostat to turn on the heat.

"I'm dying to take a shower. Do you want me to help you get in bed first?" she offered.

"I'm fine. You go ahead." Mia went into her bathroom and shut the door.

As he heard the water turn on, Nick glanced around the apartment. He could tell no one had been there, no one human at least. He listened carefully to see if he could hear or feel another presence. There was nothing, so he went to get a glass of water from the kitchen. He stood at the kitchen sink with a glass in hand, when out of the corner of his eye he saw something move. A piece of paper floated to the floor. The hairs on the back of his neck stood on end and he didn't move for what seemed like hours. Not two feet away, rested a picture of a girl in a long white wedding dress.

When he could force himself to move, he picked it up and looked at it closer. It was a picture of a wedding. The girl was on the arm of the groom inside a large cathedral with every pew filled with onlookers. On the dining room table were stacks of magazines and piles of paper. All of them were covered with brides. The papers were pictures that Mia had cut out of the magazines and like the first picture, every one of them were of lavish weddings, with formal china and fancy cakes.

Nick smiled to himself. Now it begins, she's been planning all this and hasn't told me yet. He would have to rent a tux. Strange, he hadn't noticed all this stuff before. Nick figured she was probably going through it when Wayne called yesterday and told her about the accident. She must have left in a rush and had forgotten to put it all away. Why hadn't she showed it to him before, he wondered? Was she afraid he wouldn't take an interest in their wedding? The water went off in the bathroom, so Nick put the picture back into the pile, sat on the couch, and turned on the TV.

Mia came out of the bathroom in her old sweats. Her hair was brushed, but still wet. "Don't you want to lie down and rest?" she asked as she sat down on the chest in front of him.

"I don't think I can sleep right now."

"I'm going to make a bagel, do you want one?"

"That sounds fine." Mia watched him for a few seconds too long. It made him start to worry. He took her hand as she started to get up. "Mia, what's wrong?"

"Nothing." She tried to smile.

"Why do women always say that when they're mad, and leave us poor dumb men to try and figure out what we did wrong?"

Mia laughed for real this time. "You didn't do anything wrong. I was just thinking how awful it would have been if you had been hurt any worse."

Nick pulled her until she fell into his lap and held her tight. She wrapped her arms around his neck. He could swear she was trembling a little bit.

"Don't be scared Mia. I'm fine. Remember what Wayne said? I have the hardest head ever."

"Thank goodness for that. I don't know what I would do without you."

The sadness was there again and it tore at his heart. "I'm here and I always will be. Forever, remember?"

"I remember."

She said the words, but there was no conviction in them. Something was wrong. Whatever it was, she wasn't ready to tell him. He hoped it would pass.

CHAPTER EIGHTEEN

"I don't see why you can't take one day off," Mia said worriedly.

"I already told you, we caught a break in a case and we have to follow it up. I'll take it easy. I promise."

Mia knew Nick well enough to know that when it came to work, he didn't know how to take it easy. He never would.

"Don't forget, I have that interview at the gallery this afternoon," Mia reminded him.

Nick kissed her and took her chin in his finger tips. "You'll do great. Be yourself. Is Kathy still going with you?"

"Yes. She's picking me up at three."

"Why don't we all meet for dinner afterward? Would you like that?"

"That would be fun." Mia tried to be positive, but it was hard with the way she was feeling.

"I'll talk to Wayne and let you know where. You should go back to bed and get some more sleep. You look tired." With that Nick walked out. The sound of the steel door slamming behind him gave Mia the chills.

She went back to bed and tried to sleep, but it was impossible. The few times she dozed off, she woke up terrified, her heart pounding in her chest like she'd had a bad dream that she couldn't remember.

Finally, she gave up and showered. After putting on her painting clothes, she started sketching a new piece. Her fingers flew across the canvas. As her heart beat faster and faster, her movements followed. The energy all around her was vibrating so fast she felt sick. Mia knew the canvas was ruined, but she couldn't stop. She felt out of control. She picked it up and threw it across the room. It slid, face down, coming to rest under the dining room table. The vibrations had stopped, like the final crescendo of an orchestra. It was silent.

Mia sat on the end of her bed, her face in her hands. "I don't want to do this," she whispered to no one. She thought Nick's accident was the reason she had been feeling so upset all week, but it wasn't. Instead of feeling like the worst had passed, she was more anxious than ever. There was only one other time she had felt this way, the night her parent's plane crashed.

She had stayed with her Grandma Behan for the weekend while her parents went on a business trip. She'd been sick. Anything she'd eaten or drank had come right back up and the dizziness had been unbearable. Her grandma had treated her like she'd had the flu, but Mia had known it was something else.

Sunday night, after being up for thirty-six hours straight, she'd fallen into a restless sleep. And then she'd dreamed.

Mia knew instantly where she was. She had been in her father's jet hundreds of times. The beige carpet and the burl wood consoles next to the plush chairs, even the smell was familiar. The plane ascended into the air, the whine of the engines growing louder and louder. Her parents were strapped in their respective chairs, one on each side of the aisle. Her mom was talking.

"It will be good to get home. I'm worried about Mia."

"Nadja, all kids get the flu once in a while. Don't worry, your mother can handle it."

"I know, but I want to be there when she's sick."

Her father reached out his hand and Nadja placed her hand in his. "I'll make sure Roger is there with the car when we land and we'll go straight to Mia."

Her mother smiled for the last time.

A loud explosion shook the plane violently. Her mother screamed as the aircraft turned on its side. Her father grabbed her mother's hand with both of his and held on tight.

As the lights went out inside the plane, Mia heard her father scream and her mother's last word. "Mia!"

She tried to call out to them, to let them know she was there, but she couldn't make herself known over the horrific noise. The plane was going down. She could feel it descending, picking up speed as it went. Everything disintegrated on impact. There were flames all around her. She was burning, her flesh was on fire. She needed death to come to stop the pain.

Mia'd sat up in bed screaming. Her grandmother had come running in, unsure of what had happened.

"Their plane crashed! I saw it!" Mia had cried inconsolably.

Her grandmother had rubbed her back and told her it had been a bad dream and that happens when people have the flu.

At four-thirty in the morning, the doorbell had rung. Her grandmother had gone downstairs and peeked out the peep-hole in the door before she'd opened it.

Mia had followed her down and had waited on the steps.

Grandma Behan had opened the door to a uniformed police officer.

"Ma'am, I'm officer Jimmel. Are you the mother of Nadja Carrigan?"

Her grandmother had nodded.

"I'm sorry to have to tell you this, but there has been an accident. Your daughter's plane went down shortly after take-off. There were no survivors."

Her grandmother had said nothing. She'd just turned around and stared at Mia. As long as she lived Mia would never forget that look on her grandmother's face.

The pain of losing her only child had been almost too much for her to bear.

Remembering it all now made Mia feel sick to her stomach. Her life had changed forever that day and now something was happening again and she couldn't stop it.

How she wished it wasn't Friday, with that stupid interview. She thought about calling Charlie and telling him she was sick and to cancel it, but he would see right through that charade and never forgive her.

She picked up the canvas she'd tossed and shoved it into the cupboard, along with all of her other art supplies, and then went around her apartment cleaning up. She made the bed, dust mopped the floor, put the few dishes from the sink into the dishwasher, and tried to take her mind off of everything.

That was when she noticed the bridal magazines she'd left on the dining room table. She wondered if Nick had seen them. She hoped not. Her cheeks burned. He would think she was turning into one of those bridezillas. In truth, she didn't really care about the wedding, she only cared about the marriage and the life they were going to share.

Mia picked up all the magazines and the pictures she had cut out and took them to the chest in front of the couch, opened it, and dumped them all inside.

She managed to waste the rest of the afternoon until two when she started getting ready. Kathy was picking her up at three. The interview was scheduled for four, so in rush hour traffic, they would need an hour to get to the gallery.

Kathy was right on time. Mia met her on the street, so she wouldn't waste time trying to park.

"Are you excited?" Kathy asked as soon as she was in the car.

"Not unless you consider severe nausea excitement."

"You're just tired from being at the hospital all night. What time did you guys get home?"

"Nick checked himself out at five this morning."

"What? He didn't wait for the doctor to release him?"

"No. He said he'd rested enough."

"I guess that shouldn't surprise me. That is one man with a mind of his own. I hope you can get used to that."

"Don't most men have minds of their own?"

"Wayne used to have a mind of his own, but then we got married." Kathy laughed. "I don't know if you will be able to break Nick though. He is very much a Leo, prideful, arrogant, thinks he's always right. He's also gentle and loyal, despite the roar. I know because Nick and I were born on the same day, four years apart. That's why we get along so well. I totally understand him. What sign are you?"

"Pisces."

"Are you serious? Wayne's a Pisces too. That can be a good match as long as you don't let him walk all over you."

"My mom knew a lot about astrology. She knew a lot about everything."

Mia was glad Kathy had come with her. It helped to take her mind off of her worries. Mia even smiled when Kathy laid on the horn and then gave some taxi driver the finger.

"Sorry, I have a little bit of road rage sometimes," Kathy explained unashamedly.

It took Kathy ten extra minutes to find a parking spot, but they were still a few minutes early. Mia's cell phone rang.

"That will be Charlie, freaking out because I'm not there yet." Mia answered her phone. "I'm right outside, Charlie. I won't be late."

"He sounds a little bit uptight," Kathy commented.

"You have no idea."

"Well, let's go. I can't wait to see your work."

Before Mia could respond, Kathy was out of the car and on the sidewalk, waiting. Mia got out, but didn't move to go inside.

"Are you okay? You look a little pale."

Mia nodded, took two steps, but couldn't go any further. Panic threatened to overwhelm her and she couldn't breathe.

"What is it? What's wrong?"

"I can't do this. Something is wrong, I can feel it."

"How can doing an interview for the New York Times be a bad thing? It's going to help your career." Kathy took her by the arm and pulled her along until they stepped into the gallery.

Mia couldn't believe how crowded it was. There must have been fifty people packed into the small storefront gallery. A buffet table had been set up and champagne was being passed around. This wasn't what she had agreed to. It was supposed to be a friendly chat, thirty minutes and she would be done.

Charlie rushed over to her, "Here she is. Mia, this is Amanda Baker from the New York Times. And this, is Mia Carrigan."

Mia was going to let him have it later.

Amanda Baker held out her hand. "I'm pleased to meet you, Miss Carrigan."

Mia took her hand. "Please, call me Mia." To Mia's left was a man with a camera.

"Shall we get started?" Amanda Baker asked as if she were in a hurry.

As Miss Baker flipped open a notepad and started asking questions, Kathy wandered away and checked out all the different pieces of art.

"You are the daughter of Paul Carrigan, the CEO of Carrigan Industries, who died in a plane crash eleven years ago?"

"It was twelve years ago. And, yes." The clicking of the camera bothered Mia. "I would rather not talk about my parents."

"Okay, let's talk about art. Your paintings are different from anything I've seen before." As she talked, she moved toward Mia's display.

Mia looked at her painting, Girl Under Glass, as Amanda pointed to it.

"Where do you get your inspiration?"

Mia wondered what the sophisticated, blonde reporter would think if she said, *from my nightmares.* Every time she looked at the paintings, she remembered them all so clearly. It was like reliving it all over again. The smells, the sounds, the fear, and the pain. She never forgot any of it. The hardest part was feeling their emotions all over again. Mia forced herself to stay calm, at least on the outside.

"Mia?" Amanda Baker pressed, looking at her with an odd expression.

"They just come to me."

Amanda continued asking questions about art for another half an hour. When they were about done, the reporter glanced at the ring on Mia's finger and asked with a smile, "I don't suppose you want to talk about him, either?"

"I value my privacy more than you can know."

Over Amanda's shoulder, Mia saw Jose Cortez and Abigail La Shayne waiting in the wings with Charlie hovering nearby. How convenient that he just happened to have the two other artists' whose work was on display in the gallery, at the party. All the other people at the gallery must be their friends and family.

Amanda, and her picture taking cohort, were just about to walk away when two men approached Mia. Her heart sank. She'd almost made it through the evening.

The first of the two men reached into his pocket and pulled out a badge. "I'm Detective Shilling, Miss Carrigan. This is Detective Wentz. We have some questions for you."

"About what?" Mia asked.

"I don't think this is the proper place to do this. You should come with us to the station and we can get it all sorted out."

Out of the corner of her eye, Mia saw Amanda Baker's notebook flip open once more. She glanced at Charlie.

"Unless you tell us what this is about," Charlie stepped in, "she's not going anywhere."

Detective Shilling pointed to the painting hanging on the wall. "We have a few questions about the murder of Celia Burke."

Mia went cold. The clicking of the camera continued, the only sound in the now silent gallery.

"Miss Carrigan, I think you should come with us now. We wouldn't want to make more of a scene than we already have." The detective pointed his arm towards the door.

Next to her, the reporter scribbled notes with a look of extreme satisfaction on her face. Mia was sure this wasn't what Amanda Baker had been expecting from their interview tonight.

"Miss Carrigan. I have to insist." The smile on Detective Shilling's face was anything but kind. He was very satisfied with himself and Mia sensed his arrogance. Detective Wentz watched her closely, examining her responses.

Mia went with them because she had no choice. The ride down to the police station was awkward.

The two detectives tried to make small talk as if they were old friends, but Mia said nothing.

"You don't need to be afraid, Miss Carrigan. As long as you tell the truth, there won't be a problem." Shilling, who was driving, turned around to look at her while Wentz spoke. Even though he said nothing, Mia could feel the hostility pouring off of him.

She was scared, not of them, but of what the consequences were going to be to all of this.

All the years she had spent trying to get lost in the city were over, just like that. Mia blinked back tears. For so long, she had been standing on the precipice of a tall cliff, looking into a black abyss, and now she was falling.

CHAPTER NINETEEN

Detective Shilling and Detective Wentz took Mia to the police station and led her upstairs to a large room filled with desks. About fifteen people, mostly men, were watching her carefully. Mia felt like a bug under a microscope.

She glanced around, hoping Nick was still here, so he could help her. She knew instantly which desk was his because she could feel his energy all around it. Mia took a step toward it, wanting to use it to shield off everything else, but Detective Shilling took her by the arm, to a room with the number two on the door. He unlocked the door with a key and pushed it open. When he did, Mia gasped and stepped back. The room was no bigger than her closet at home and it was so full of negative energy that it was like getting slapped in the face. Some truly evil people had been in this room.

"Is there someplace else we could talk?" Mia wouldn't move even though Detective Wentz was nudging her from behind.

"What? Are you claustrophobic?" Shilling asked her.

"No."

"Then, take a seat." He pointed to a chair on the other side of a small table.

Mia sat down. "Could you at least leave the door open?"

"No," Shilling told her.

Both men pulled up chairs, sitting directly across from her. Detective Shilling was about Nick's size, with blond receding hair, ruddy cheeks, and hard blue eyes. Detective Wentz looked like a high school science teacher, wire-rimmed glasses and small in stature.

"You know why you're here, don't you, Miss Carrigan?" Shilling asked.

"Not really."

Detective Shilling opened a file he had in his hand and set a photo of Celia Burke, young, beautiful and alive, on the table in front of her.

Mia looked at it and then back at the detectives.

"Do you know who this is?" Shilling tapped his finger on the picture.

"Celia Burke." She barely managed to get the words out.

Mia saw the man's eyes narrow and his facial muscles harden.

"How did you know her?"

"I didn't. Her picture was in the paper when she was murdered a couple of years ago."

He whipped out another picture and set it right next to the first one. It was a crime scene photo, showing Celia Burke in a dumpster with a large piece of glass on top of her. Detective Shilling pulled out one more. It was a picture of her painting 'Girl Under Glass' and placed them side by side.

"How is it that your painting and the crime scene photo of her are almost identical?"

Mia remained silent while she tried to figure out what she should do. If she told them the truth, they wouldn't believe her. If she lied, they would know it. Silviana's words echoed in her mind. "You have no more time, Mia. It is coming for you." Mia tried to control the trembling that was taking over her body, but she couldn't.

"So, tell us how you knew Celia Burke?"

"I didn't know her."

"This picture tells me you did and that, if you didn't kill her yourself, you were there when she was killed and you know who did it. What I want to know is, why? Why did you kill her? Was she a rival for a boyfriend? Were you jealous of her? Did you have a fight and it got out of hand?"

"No! I told you, I never met her."

"You expect us to believe that?" Shilling shoved the picture of Celia Burke's dead body under her nose.

"It's the truth."

"Miss Carrigan," Detective Wentz finally spoke up. "I see you attended the Freeman Academy."

"Yes." Mia was almost afraid to answer. It was like they were ready to spring a trap, so strong were their feelings of self-satisfaction.

"Did you ever go to the coffee shop down the street called Dina's?"

"Yes. My grandmother and I used to go there before school sometimes."

"Celia Burke worked at Dina's for two years. Coincidently, two of the same years you attended school just down the street."

"She did?" Mia looked from one man to the other and her heart started pounding even harder. "I didn't know."

"I think you're a liar," Shilling said with contempt.

Over and over they asked her the same questions in different ways, putting words in her mouth and trying to trick her.

Shilling stood up, put his hands on the table, and leaned so close that his face was only inches from hers. "You sit here and think about that, and when we come back I want the truth."

Mia watched the hands on the clock spin, sure that Nick was going to walk through the door any second and make it all stop. Kathy had to have called him. He had to know where she was. Why wasn't he here to get her?

***

Nick pulled up in front of the station at the same time as Wayne.

"Kathy called you?" Nick asked as they ran up the stairs.

"Why would Shilling and Wentz bring Mia in for questioning about a murder?"

"How the hell should I know?" And, at the moment, he didn't care. All he wanted to do was beat Shilling to a bloody pulp. The man had been an ass since the day they'd met.

Wayne grabbed Nick's arm and stopped him in his tracks. "I know you and Shilling have never seen eye to eye, so try to keep your temper."

"That's up to him," Nick replied, once again heading up the stairs.

"That's what I was afraid of," Wayne muttered as he followed Nick.

Nick walked in and saw Shilling across the room and headed straight for him. Shilling held out his hands like, bring it on.

Before Nick took three steps, there were five cops between them. Wayne had him around the neck and his arms were being held so tight he couldn't move.

"I'm gonna kick your ass, Shilling!"

"Is it my fault your girlfriend is some kind of gypsy freak, Chief?"

Nick struggled to break free again. He wanted nothing more than to get his hands around Shilling's neck.

"Shilling! Shut your mouth," Captain Webster yelled from across the room. "Coleman, bring your partner into my office."

Nick felt Wayne loosen his grip slowly. "You good?" he asked quietly.

Nick nodded, shrugged Wayne and the others off of him, and they headed to the Captain's office. Nick straightened his tie as he sat down in front of the beat up old desk.

"What the hell is this all about? If Shilling is doing this to get to me, I swear---"

"I asked Shilling and Wentz to look into this. If I had known you were involved with her, I would have put someone else on the case, but that's beside the point right now. How well do you know Mia Carrigan?"

Hearing the Captain ask the question made Nick's blood run cold. Whatever was going on was serious. The Captain wouldn't have had Mia investigated unless they had come up with something substantial. Nick glanced at Wayne. He too had a worried look on his face.

"We're engaged."

"I see. How long have you known her? The Captain picked up a file about an inch thick.

"Four weeks." Nick felt like a fool. It wasn't a feeling he enjoyed and he didn't like it at all.

The Captain opened the file and placed a picture on the desk in front of Nick.

"Do you recognize this?"

"It's one of Mia's paintings. 'Girl Under Glass,' I think she calls it. She's an artist."

The Captain opened up the file again and took out another picture. Nick recognized it as a crime scene photo. Captain Webster set it right next to the first one.

Nick swallowed hard and tried to keep any emotion from showing on his face.

"Frank Burke is a retired cop with a lot of old friends on the force, so he's been kept up to date on the case since his daughter was murdered, including seeing the crime scene photos." The Captain went on. "About a month ago, he walked into an art gallery and saw this hanging on the wall. It's more than a coincidence, I'd say. She even has the same earring twisted in the same direction."

Nick noticed the upside down daisy in her ear.

"Right now, there is a team of investigators on their way to her apartment to execute a search warrant."

"That's it? Two pictures that look similar and a judge gives you a search warrant?"

Captain Webster opened the file for the third time and placed another picture on the desk with a corresponding crime scene photo and then another and another, until he was staring at eight dead women.

Wayne cursed under his breath.

"Did you know that Mia Carrigan spent four months at Elmhurst in Connecticut when she was seventeen?"

"Elmhurst?" Wayne asked for him. "What's Elmhurst?"

"It's a private psychiatric hospital for rich folks. It's very hush, hush, and very expensive."

Nick felt like puking. He began to question everything he thought he knew about Mia. He picked up the picture of another woman and the picture of Mia's painting. It was almost an exact match, except Mia's painting had turned something horrific and violent into something beautiful. Gone were the blood and bruises, replaced with flowers and vines, strategically placed on her body to cover every knife wound. The victim's necklace was a precise match in both pictures, a metallic rose with a red stone in the center.

Wayne leaned over to Nick. "Are you going to tell him?"

"Tell me what?" Captain Webster asked.

Nick looked at Wayne, but said nothing.

"There may be another explanation as to these paintings."

"Wayne, shut up."

"Why? Would you rather they think she's a murderer?"

"What are you talking about, Coleman?" the Captain demanded this time.

"Mia is psychic. I don't know what that has to do with this, but I know it does."

The Captain sat back in his chair with a disbelieving expression on his face. "You've got to be kidding me."

"I know how it sounds," Wayne went on, "but it's true."

"Nick?" Webster was waiting for his response.

"I need to talk to her, privately."

The Captain nodded, got up from his chair, and left his office.

Nick could feel Wayne's gaze boring into his back. Finally, he couldn't take it anymore and he turned to his partner. "What?"

"I'm not sure you should talk to Mia with the mood you're in."

Nick got up and started for the door. "That's too damn bad!"

CHAPTER TWENTY

The detectives left the room and still the clock ticked away. Another half hour went by. Mia hadn't slept for more than a few hours since Wednesday night and she was exhausted. They were trying to break her down and it was working. She knew she couldn't take much more.

When the door cracked open and Nick walked in, she breathed a sigh of relief.

"I'm so glad you're here. Where have you been? Can I go home now?" Mia stood up, took her coat off of the back of the chair, and started for the door.

"No, you can't go home. This is a murder investigation." Nick's anger permeated every word.

"They can't honestly believe that I had anything to do with any of them."

"Yes, they do. As a matter of fact they are executing a search warrant at your apartment right now."

"What? They can't do that," Mia could hear the panic rising in her voice, but she couldn't control it. "You have to stop them. I can't have them touching my things!"

"Mia, I couldn't stop them even if I wanted to. This. Is. A. Murder. Investigation."

The way he said the words made Mia stop in her tracks. "You...*you* don't think I had anything to do with them... do you?"

"I don't know. Did you?" Nick's dark brown eyes were as cold as the Hudson River in February.

Mia felt dizzy. "This can't be happening."

"What the hell were you thinking? I'm a homicide detective for crying out loud! I have worked my ass off to get where I am now and I don't appreciate being made to look like a fool."

Mia's eyes started to burn. She desperately tried to blink away the tears.

"In about two minutes Shilling and Wentz are coming back in here and they are going to want answers. They're going to want to know how you painted pictures of murder victims and why they are hanging in a gallery in the city." Nick pressed his temples with his fingers. "What are you going to tell them? I don't want any more surprises."

Before Mia could answer, the door opened and she watched the detectives come back into the tiny room, followed by another man. Nick took her by her elbow and steered her back to her chair. With his touch, Nick's emotions flowed into her. His show of anger was nothing compared to what he was holding in. He was furious, filled with indignation, and shame. He was ashamed of her.

Wayne poked his head in the doorway. "Mia? Would you like some water or something?" He took one look at her face. "Are you okay?"

She couldn't respond. Her heart was being squeezed in her chest.

"Just bring a bottle," Nick replied for her.

"I'm Captain Webster, Miss Carrigan. I am going to listen in to what you have to say."

Detective Shilling slid Celia Burke's picture toward her once again. "Let's start here." His words were heavy with disgust.

There was so much hostility in the room that Mia thought she might be sick. She took a deep breath trying to calm herself, but that just made her light-headed.

"Tell us what you know." Shilling nodded toward the picture.

Mia picked it up and studied it. She didn't want to remember, but they were giving her no choice. She glanced up at Nick to find his manner and expression to be that of just another cop, not a man that was supposed to love her.

"She died in the summertime, during a heat wave. I went to bed at about eleven that night and I fell right to sleep. They come to me in my dreams. When I opened my eyes, I was in a room that was unfamiliar."

"Describe it," Shilling demanded.

"It was a small, studio apartment. On the walls, the paint was peeling and the furniture, what there was of it, was old and worn. There was a man there. He belonged there. I think it was his apartment. She was the guest."

Mia forced herself to remember. "She had been there before, but not in a long time. He had been drinking and she was scared. When she tried to get up to leave, he wouldn't let her go. Celia thought to herself, 'He knows my dad's a cop. He wouldn't dare hurt me.'"

"You heard her say that?" Wentz asked her.

"She thought it. I could hear her thoughts," Mia explained and then continued. She tried to leave again, but he threw her onto the bed, face down. She started to get up, but he got on top of her, grabbed her by her hair, and pushed her face into a pillow. He kept pushing harder and harder. She opened her mouth trying to get air, but she only inhaled the fabric from the pillowcase into her mouth."

Mia had to take a breath. She had to make sure she could still breathe.

"She started to panic. She reached out to him, found skin, and dug her nails in deep, trying to draw blood. She struggled as hard as she could, but he was too strong. Everything went red and then black. Her last thought was, 'He's killing me! He's killing me!'

"The next thing I knew, I was being tossed into a dumpster and stuff was being put on top of me." Mia realized what she had said and tried to fix it. "I mean her. He put a large, thick piece of glass on top of her, followed by strips of pink insulation."

Mia set the picture down and realized that none of the men in the room had said anything. When she looked up, they were all staring at her.

Wayne opened the door and walked in with a bottle of water, set it in front of her, and walked out without a word. Mia's hands were shaking so badly she couldn't open the lid. Nick took it out of her hand, twisted the top off, and set it back on the table in front of her. She could feel his anger radiating from him like the burning rays of the sun, and to a lesser extent, she could feel them on the bottle he'd handled. Mia didn't touch it again.

"Tell us what this man looked like," Detective Wentz said.

Mia brought back that image into her mind. For her, it was like watching a movie from Celia Burke's point of view. It was all so clear. "He's white, thick and muscular, not tall. He had his hair cut short. You could see his scalp underneath, and he had a tattoo."

Detective Shilling sat up straight and turned and looked at Detective Wentz who got up and left the room. "Tell me about the tattoo."

"It was a snake and it wrapped around his left arm three times between his elbow and his wrist. You can see the snake's rattles on the inside of his elbow and down on his wrist the snake's mouth is open and there is venom dripping off of one of its fangs."

Detective Wentz came back with papers in his hands. "If I show you some pictures, would you be able to identify the man you saw?"

Mia nodded and the officer put down a paper with the pictures of six different men on it. She studied each picture. "It's none of these men."

"Are you sure? Look again."

"It's none of them."

Once again there was silence in the room until Captain Webster said, "Would you excuse us for a moment?"

Mia could feel all of their emotions at once, doubt, anger, wonder. It was overwhelming to her. All of them filed out of the room. Mia put her arms on the table and rested her head on her arms. It was two in the morning and she was so tired she wanted to cry. The stress had given her a massive headache. Her eyes closed and she drifted into the darkness.

When she opened her eyes she was back in the apartment where Celia Burke was murdered. Her lifeless body lay face down on the bed.

Slowly Celia's face turned to Mia and she whispered, "You're in danger. You have to get out."

The air all around Mia went frigid and she could see her own breath floating in the dark. A few stray hairs tickled her cheek as someone whispered her name next to her ear. She spun around, but there was no one there. The sound of laughter filled the room. It was like nothing Mia had ever heard before. It was demonic. Man was in the apartment with her.

"Run!" Celia Burke told her, even though she was dead.

Mia grabbed the door knob and opened the door, as she was about to step out into the hallway, someone took a hold of her. She struggled to break free. Glancing behind her, she saw an arm holding onto the fabric of her coat. The fabric looked like skin being pulled away from flesh.

She grasped the doorframe with all the strength she had and broke free, running down a dark and dreary hallway. Heavy footfalls were right behind her, getting closer with every step she took. The weight of a hand on her shoulder made her heart pound. The fingers were digging into her tender flesh. The sound of a woman's screams echoed down the never ending hallway. The pressure on her shoulder grew more intense and she began to shake. A different voice came to her in the darkness.

"Mia, Mia. You need to wake up."

She opened her eyes to find Nick with his hand on her shoulder, trying to wake her up.

"We need to talk. They found the other paintings at your apartment." The expression on Nick's face was dire.

Mia knew which paintings he meant. She put her hands on her face for a moment to give herself time to think. The only way out was to tell Nick the truth and hope he understood.

"I paint them because it's the only way I can get the images out of my head. If I don't, they haunt me. I see them over and over, every time I close my eyes. After I paint the first one, I do the second one to try to give them back some dignity, some beauty. No one was ever supposed to see them, but Charlie came over one day unexpectedly and he bullied me into letting him use them at the gallery." Mia waited to see what he would say, but he said nothing. "Do you understand?"

"What about Elmhurst?" Nick asked her.

Mia sat back in the chair, too stunned to speak. The quiet ticking of the clock was the only sound.

"We know you spent four months there when you were seventeen. Why were you in a mental hospital for four months? They're going to want to know. And I *need* to know."

"How dare you throw that in my face? And it's none of *their* business. That had nothing to do with the deaths of these women. I had nothing to do with the deaths of these women."

"Except that, in a way, you witnessed their murders." Nick crossed his arms across his chest. "You saw Kelly Langford's murder didn't you?"

"Yes." Mia looked down and closed her eyes.

"They might think that you had something to do with these murders and that our relationship is nothing but a way for you to keep track of the investigations."

Mia's eyes were already burning and now her heart joined in. She had to get out of that tiny room and away from the pain his words were causing her. "I need to use the ladies room."

Nick's gaze and his pursed lips told her he didn't believe her, but he stepped aside anyway, "Down the hall, to the right."

Once Mia was inside the ladies room, she locked the door

behind her. She went to the sink and splashed her face with water and dried it with a rough paper towel. That didn't help. Mia slid to the floor. Her body hurt like she had been beaten and bruised. In one day her whole world had come undone. All the hopes and dreams she had for the future were gone. Her career was going to be ruined when the reporter told the world that Mia Carrigan, daughter of Paul Carrigan, was a suspect in several murder investigations.

Her apartment, her haven, was being ransacked by police. She couldn't stand the thought of strangers touching her things. The worst part of it all was Nick's lack of faith in her. She sensed his emotions as easily as if they were her own.

She felt so betrayed. Silviana was right. Mia recalled her aunt's words, "There is darkness all around you. It will be like a storm and you will lose your way in the darkness." And then Silviana accused Nick of being the one who betrays her. Mia never would have guessed it would be him. She should have known that Silviana would be right.

There would be no wedding. There would be no babies. She would be alone for the rest of her life. Mia clamped her mouth closed to keep from crying out at the thought. She had been so lonely when she'd met Nick, though she hadn't recognized it. He had given her hope and now he had taken it away. That was the worst part. If he hadn't made her see the possibilities, she could have been satisfied with her life, but not now. Her mother's ring sparkled on her finger. For the first time, it didn't make her happy. She slipped it off and held it tight in her fist.

Mia barely heard Nick tapping on the bathroom door. "Mia, we're waiting for you."

After a few minutes, she got to her feet and opened the door.

"They want to ask you some more questions."

"I'm exhausted. I can't."

"We're almost done." Nick hardly looked at her.

They walked back into room number two. Shilling, Wentz, and Captain Webster were waiting for her with a huge stack of files sitting on the table.

"We have some more questions for you." Shilling pointed to the chair.

Mia moved to the chair where her legs almost gave out. Her coat still hung on the back of it, so Mia slid her hand into the pocket and dropped the ring inside. She wondered if Nick would even notice and if he did, would he care?

Shilling pulled out one of the files and put it in front of her, just like he did before. "La Tanisha Jones. Tell us what you know about her."

Mia hesitated. They didn't understand that it wasn't like telling a story. For her it meant reliving it. She knew their fear, their pain, and the horror that filled them the moment they knew they were going to die. She knew reopening herself to all of it was not something she should be doing, but what choice did she have? All of their eyes were on her, waiting, expecting, and judging.

"La Tanisha was being stalked." Mia hesitated as the memories came flooding back to her. "When he grabbed her, she wasn't surprised and she knew she was going to die. He forced her into the trunk of his car and drove her out of the city where they could be alone. It was dark outside and there were tree limbs overhead. She begged him to kill her because she knew what awaited her, but he kept her alive for a while. He would strangle her until she passed out and then revive her. He raped her over and over. When she finally died, it was because she willed it. "

They spent another half hour asking her questions before putting a bunch of pictures in front of her. Mia pointed to the man she knew was guilty.

"You expect us to believe this crap?" Shilling yelled at her.

"Shilling!" Captain Webster intervened.

Mia could feel the rage that Detective Shilling was keeping barely controlled.

"If any of this is true, if you had come in and told us what you know two years ago, this man might be in prison now," Shilling said accusingly.

"If you check the phone records, you'll find that I called in twice to tell the detectives working this case, what I knew. I did it anonymously, of course," Mia replied. "None of what I tell you is admissible in court anyway. You still have to prove it."

Mia could sense Shilling's contempt for her from four feet away. Still, she chose to focus on *his* emotions instead of Nick's. It hurt less.

It was Detective Wentz's turn to slide another picture of a young woman in front of her. Mia's heart hurt when she saw it was Brittney

Parrish. Mia closed her eyes and turned away. "Please, I can't do anymore. I can't." Mia could feel her chin quivering and she knew she was about to fall apart.

A knock on the door drew their attention and Wayne poked his head in.

"Her attorney's here. He wants to see her, now." Wayne looked almost ashamed.

Richard pushed past Wayne, came in and knelt down by her side. When he saw her face, he gasped. "What have you done to her?" He accused every man in the room.

"Richard, help me!" It was all Mia could say before she broke down, sobbing.

"I will. I will. We are leaving right now."

Richard pulled her to her feet, though Mia wasn't sure she would be able to stay up as she swayed.

As he led her past Nick, she heard Richard say, "You bastard! Letting them do this to her."

If Nick replied, Mia didn't hear his words.

"We're going out the back way. There are reporters and cameras out the front."

Everything Mia was afraid of was happening. The life she had painstakingly built for herself, was over.

CHAPTER TWENTY-ONE

Richard talked all the way home, but Mia didn't hear a word he said. She dozed off twice, only to jolt awake when images of dead women entered her mind.

Outside her apartment, a crowd of people stood, waiting for her. There were news vans parked down the street and reporters and camera crews on the sidewalk outside the lobby. She didn't have the energy to face it all.

"Take me around the back and through the alley," Mia told him as she dug in her purse for keys. *Please let the basement door key be on there,* she prayed. It was.

"Do you want me to walk you up?"

"No. I need to do this myself." Mia's legs were wobbly as she got out of the car. "Thank you, Richard."

"Mia, don't talk to them again unless I'm with you. You should have called me right away, you know."

"I was so scared. I didn't think of it." In truth she thought she would be safe with Nick. Just the thought was like getting punched in the stomach. "I'm turning off my cell and unplugging my house phone. I will call you in a couple of days to see how this is going to affect the business."

"Okay," Richard nodded.

Mia ran down the cement steps and faced the solid steel door which led to the basement. She put the key in and tried to turn it, but it wouldn't budge. "Oh, no." She tried again and again. Finally, on the fourth try, it gave and just in time. She could hear people's voices coming up the alley.

"I saw that car turn in here," a man said.

Mia pulled the door open as quietly as she could and stepped inside. She closed it the same way. She relocked all the locks and hoped they hadn't seen her. Making her way up the stairs, she peeked out into the lobby and saw that Carl and Jose had locked it down, but the curtains were open.

"Carl, I want you to close the curtains and turn out the front lights."

"Miss Carrigan, is that you?"

"Yes, please hurry."

The two men did as she'd asked. When Mia was sure no one could see in, she came into the lobby. "Keep the doors locked. Do not answer the phone. And I want you to make sure we have two people here at all times. Carl, set up a schedule and tell everyone they will get double time for acting as security guards."

"Yes, ma'am. I'm sorry about letting them in. The cops, I mean. They had a search warrant and there was nothing I could do. Sorry." Carl looked like he was afraid he might be fired.

"You did the right thing, Carl. Don't worry about it. For the next few days I would like you to go out and pick up all the papers and tabloids that have my name on the front cover and leave them outside my door. You can use the money in the petty cash lock box. I will call you if I need anything else. I don't want to be disturbed otherwise."

"Yes, ma'am. Anything you say."

Carl looked like he had something else he wanted to say. "Is everything okay, Miss Carrigan?"

"I don't know yet."

Carl was very loyal to her. Too bad his loyalty had to be bought.

Mia stepped into the elevator and her cell phone started to vibrate in her purse. She was pretty sure she knew who it was. She fished it out and glanced at the screen—Nick's cell. Mia didn't answer it. The doors opened, but Mia didn't get out right away. In her mind she knew they had been here, but in her heart she was hoping it wouldn't be as bad as she'd thought. She was wrong.

She pushed open her door and felt the different energies hit her, one after the other, hostile, angry energies. There had to have been at least ten people in her apartment. Then, the condition of the apartment itself shocked her. Everything was in disarray. It was like she'd been robbed.

Mia took a few steps and stopped. It was overwhelming. Her home, her sanctuary, was ruined. She headed into the kitchen, sensing that every drawer and every cabinet had been gone through. They had walked into her dining room and looked out the windows. The chest that sat in front of her couch was out of place. Mia lifted the lid and cringed. Everything in it had been examined. The bride magazines had been thumbed through. Mia trembled with anger, indignation, and plain old exhaustion.

She went into the bedroom where the sheets had been pulled off of the bed and left in a heap on the floor. The mattress was still slightly askew. All of her cabinets were open and everything had been moved. Some of her things were gone, taken in an effort to blame her for murders she didn't commit. Her photo albums with all of her parent's pictures in them had been touched. Her bin full of baby clothes that she had hoped to put on her own daughters someday, were ruined by their touch.

They had gone through all of the photographs she had taken, some of which were still on the floor, trampled under uncaring feet. Mia picked up the picture she had taken at the little corner park the night it had been snowing and Nick had come. That was the night she'd told him about her abilities. She couldn't bring herself to call them gifts. A curse was more like it.

That picture had been one of her favorites. She'd waited for weeks for the right moment. The snow had to be falling and the street light had to be shining on undisturbed snow. Looking at the picture now made her lonely, a reminder of how her life was before Nick, with his strong personality and loud laugh. Mia held it close even though it made her very uncomfortable.

The cupboards with her paintings were empty, totally empty, and her art supplies were scattered all over the place. Mia walked into her bathroom and she knew the only things they hadn't touched were her toothbrush and toothpaste. She snatched them up and held on to them. What she found when she pushed opened her closet door with her toe, showed her the police had been thorough. The shoeboxes were emptied on the floor, along with most of her clothes. All of her pockets and purses had been searched. The drawers with her underwear and bras were ajar. Her cheeks burned with humiliation.

Mia left the bathroom and spotted a pillow behind the headboard of her bed. She tugged on it and knew instantly it was Nick's pillow. Tucking it under her arm, she noticed it smelled like him. She bit down on her lower lip to keep it from quivering, but it didn't help. Tears filled her eyes, spilling over. Mia wandered around the apartment once more, trying to figure out how to make it better. She couldn't stay here. Everything about her apartment was wrong.

If she wasn't such a freak, none of this would bother her. If she wasn't such a freak, none of this would have happened in the first place.

Out of the corner of her eye, Mia saw something move on the roof of the building across the street. Two men with telephoto lenses were trying to get pictures of her. She grabbed her remote from the end table next to the couch and closed the shades on all the windows. Now, the apartment was dark. It felt dead to her. She felt dead.

She couldn't leave the building, so there was only one place left for her to go. Mia took her keys and went across the hallway to Holly's old apartment. The only thing left inside was a large black couch and a matching chair Holly had left behind. They'd been covered with a couple of old sheets to keep the dust off.

Mia tossed a sheet to the end of the couch and sat. She didn't dare turn on a light, even though the apartment was dark, because then the reporters and the paparazzi would know where she was. It had been like this when her parents died, when her Grandma Behan died, and during the custody battle between her Uncle David and her Aunt Silviana.

Mia put the pillow on the arm of the couch and laid her head on it. Nick's face came in to her mind along with more tears. She reached into her pocket and pulled out her mother's ring. It wasn't meant to be. Mia set the ring on the floor where she could look at it. Next to it, she set the picture of the park in all its solitude and drifted off to sleep.

***

Nick sat at his desk staring at the Kelly Langford file. He'd read the same page three times and still had no idea what was on it. He kept hearing Mia beg Richard Sharpe for help. The memory of it sat like a brick in his belly.

Wayne sat down at his desk, "Are you okay?"

"I'm fine."

Wayne was quiet for a moment, "That was pretty intense. Do you think Mia's okay?"

Nick tossed the file on his desk and leaned back in his chair. "I don't know. She won't answer my calls. I hope she's sleeping."

"I have something for you." Wayne handed him a file that was at least an inch thick.

"What is this?" Nick asked as he opened it up and saw Mia's picture inside.

pointed at Mia's left hand. "Her engagement ring is gone."

CHAPTER TWENTY-TWO

Nick looked at his watch and then at the body of the homeless man who had been stabbed to death. It was already after five by the time he got through rush hour traffic. It would be six-thirty before he could get to Mia's place.

"Go ahead and take off. I'll finish up here," Wayne told him.

"You sure?"

"Yeah, I got it."

Nick didn't need to be told twice. He was dead tired and still had a headache. The thought of facing Mia didn't help his pain much. By the time he had finished going through the file on Mia, it had been almost eight in the morning. He'd stayed and worked his shift on no sleep.

From the outside, the building looked deserted, no lights could be seen and the expensive curtains in the lobby were pulled closed. The crowd of reporters loitering on the sidewalk told him it wasn't.

After watching the replay of the interview, he was sure she was…what? Furious? Hurt? Hate-filled? He wouldn't blame her if she hated him. Right now, he hated himself.

"Poor Mia," Nick whispered under his breath at the thought of her having to face such a cannibalistic crowd. "Freaking New York."

Nick had to park further away than he ever had before, due to all the news vans and cars parked around her building. He made his way through the crowd, pulled on the door, and found it locked. He knocked a few times, but got no response, so he pounded on the glass until the curtains moved. Carl, the doorman, peeked out at him, hesitated for a second, and then opened the door.

"What do you want?" Carl let him in, relocked the door, and pulled the curtains back over the door.

"I need to see Mia." Nick headed straight for the elevator and poked the button.

"She doesn't want to be disturbed."

"Then I won't disturb her." Nick stepped inside and was relieved when the doors closed. He watched the numbers go from one to four as the elevator arrived at the top floor of the building, a sense of dread in his gut.

When he got to Mia's door he hesitated. He wasn't sure if he should knock or go right in. He opened the door and knew in a heartbeat she wasn't there. All the lights were off and the blinds were closed. The apartment was cold, dark, and empty of the life Mia put into it.

As Nick stepped inside, a part of him was relieved he had avoided the confrontation and a part of him was disappointed.

He looked at the mess his fellow officers had made of the place and cussed under his breath. The bed was torn apart and one of her hidden cabinets was open. Nick got closer so he could see what kind of damage had been done. On the floor were some of Mia's pictures, mixed in with her art supplies. It had all been trampled like the confetti in Times Square after the New Year's partying was over. He picked them up, wiped them on his shirt, and put them in a nice neat stack.

When he set them on the shelf, he knew it was a waste of time. He couldn't fix this. Oh, he could clean up and put Mia's things in their rightful place, but he couldn't undo the effect this was going to have on her. For the first time, he understood what all the people must have felt when he and Wayne executed search warrants. His and Mia's privacy had been violated and it ticked him off.

Nick reached into the cabinet and straightened up what he could, then moved onto the next one and did the same. The last two cabinets were empty. All of her paintings had been confiscated. She would get them back, eventually, but he couldn't even imagine what she'd thought when she'd come home and seen this place.

He put the mattress into its proper place and put the sheets back on. Then he went into the bathroom to take a leak. As he passed the open closet door, he saw the chaos they'd left behind. It took him well over an hour just to match all of Mia's shoes and put them in the right boxes.

"What is it with women and shoes?" he muttered to himself as he started on her clothes and the few things he had there. When everything was back on the hangers and hung up the way Mia usually had it, he noticed her underwear drawers had been gone through. She always kept them perfectly neat and they were a mess.

He straightened the rest of the apartment and sat on the couch, intent on waiting until she came back from wherever she'd gone.

Another hour passed with no Mia, so he called Carl down in the lobby.

"Where is she?"

"What are you talking about? She went up there early this morning and I haven't seen her since."

"If I find out you're lying to me," Nick started.

"Hang on." Nick heard him ask, "Jose, you didn't see the boss leave, did you?"

"No, man. She's still upstairs as far as I know."

"We never saw her leave," Carl confirmed.

Nick hung up and wondered if he should go home. It didn't feel right sleeping in Mia's apartment without her, but the thought of the long drive back to his place when he was this tired just wasn't an option.

He took four Extra-Strength Tylenol, stripped down to his underwear, and climbed under the covers.

He must have slept for several hours before he realized how cold he was. He reached out for the down comforter that covered him earlier, but couldn't find it. He turned on the light and saw it on the floor in front of Mia's empty cabinet, ten feet away.

Nick froze. The comforter couldn't have gotten that far away from the bed without help. He walked over to it and picked it up. Looking around the bedroom nothing else seemed out of place. Still, it was creepy. He tossed it back on the bed and got back in. He turned out the light and was just dozing off again when he had the strangest feeling he wasn't alone.

Sitting up quickly, he turned the light back on and glanced around the room.

"Mia? Is that you?"

He saw someone move in the kitchen and got out of bed to investigate. The kitchen was dark and very cold. When Nick hit the light switch nothing happened. He flipped it a couple more times, still nothing. A loud bang shook the floor. The hair all over Nick's body stood on end. It sounded like someone on the floor below was smacking it with a sledge hammer. The problem was, he knew the entire third floor of the building was empty.

His heart pounded in his chest and he thought about grabbing his gun, but like Mia had said before, his gun was useless. Whatever was in the apartment was not going to be afraid of a gun, because it wasn't human. He wondered how Mia had lived her life like this.

"Look, Mia's not here so get out." A gust of frigid air passed by Nick's left side, making him jump back. His gut instinct was to double up his fist and swing, but there was nothing to hit. Another loud bang shook the floor beneath his feet. He was being toyed with and he didn't like it. Something didn't want him here and was trying to scare him off.

Nick wondered why? It wasn't as if he had never been there before. Why would the spirit, or demon, or whatever the hell it was care that he was here now?

"I'll leave when I'm damn well ready, so shove off."

Nick felt the floor shake again as heavy footsteps headed to the door and kept going. The freaky thing was that it felt as if someone was walking on the ceiling of the third floor. If it wasn't three-thirty in the morning, he would have left, but he vowed not to sleep there tomorrow night if Mia wasn't there.

He managed to doze off a couple of times, but he couldn't rid himself of the feeling he was being watched.

When the morning finally came, it wasn't soon enough. Nick showered and left for work. He arrived ten minutes early, much to Wayne's surprise.

"Since when do you show up early?"

"Since now," Nick grumbled.

"What happened with you and Mia?" Wayne asked, taking a sip of his coffee.

"Nothing."

"What do you mean nothing?"

"I mean, I went to her apartment and waited for her to show, but she never did."

"Maybe she checked into a hotel." Wayne bit into his bran muffin.

Nick thought it over. "Maybe, but the doorman was sure she was there. He said he never saw her leave and her place is surrounded by reporters."

"I know. I saw it on the news this morning."

"What?"

"That New York Times art reporter has been a busy woman. She has been giving interviews, showing pictures of Mia's paintings and then," Wayne hesitated, "the matching pictures from the crime scenes."

"How the hell did she get those?!"

"My guess would be that someone she knows at the paper has a friend on the force. Maybe even from Celia Burke's father. He's a retired cop."

Nick's head started to ache again and as he reached for the aspirin he kept at his desk, he wondered if Mia knew.

***

When Mia woke up it was full daylight. She leaned up on her elbow, dug her cell phone out of her purse and turned it on so she could check the time.

"Eleven-thirty?" she mumbled. At first, she thought she had only slept for a few hours, until she noticed the date. She had slept for more than twenty-four hours. That would explain why her phone showed so many missed calls. The majority were from Nick. Mia's heart sank when she thought about him. She closed her eyes against the pain and laid her head back on his pillow. The scent of his skin on the pillowcase only made it worse.

Mia knew she had to get up and force herself to do something, but what? It was Sunday, wasn't it? She didn't have classes at the Freeman Academy or the Boys and Girls Club today. Maybe she should go shopping for new clothes? If she did that, she would have to face the reporters or sneak out the back way. Could she make it to the street and get a cab before the media spotted her? Just the thought brought back so many bad memories of trying to hide from the paparazzi when she was a teenager. Why did they have to go through her clothes? They left her with nothing but the clothes on her back.

Mia walked to the window and pulled back the lace curtains, only an inch. Holly had chosen them over the more expensive remote controlled blinds because she only cared about letting the light in, she didn't want to look out and see the city the way Mia loved to do, because she was scared of heights.

"I wish you were here right now, Holly. I could use a friend," Mia whispered as she saw the news vans still parked down the street. She thought about calling Kathy, but decided against it. Nick was their friend, not her and when things like this happened, friends usually stuck together.

Mia's stomach growled and she started feeling nauseated. How long had it been since she'd eaten anything? She couldn't remember. She had needed to go the grocery store before all of this happened and now she didn't know what she had in her fridge, if anything.

Mia opened the apartment door and peeked out into the hallway. On the floor was the stack of newspapers she'd asked Carl to get for her. On the front page she saw her name in bold print and cringed. She knew she had to read through them, even though she didn't want to. She had to know what people were thinking and saying about her. Evan and her Uncle David would use any bad publicity against her, however they could. When she reached down to pick up the papers, she knew it wasn't going to be good. It would bring back all the memories of her parent's death. It was going to be painful.

The second Mia opened the door to her apartment, she knew Nick had been there. His energy was everywhere. The blinds were closed and it was dark inside, despite it being almost twelve in the afternoon. Mia turned on the light and saw that he had tidied up the place. The cabinets were closed with all of her things back inside and the bed was made. As Mia moved closer to the bed, she knew Nick had been on it recently. His energy was the strongest one coming to her from the bed. It dawned on her suddenly, he had slept there. She was as sure of it as she was her own name.

Mia stood, rooted to the floor wondering why. Why would he come here after everything that happened? As she stood there, the room grew darker and colder. The air around her began to move and her emotions came under attack. Wave upon wave of anger, despair, and hopelessness covered her. Mia gasped for breath against it all, but she was worn down and she couldn't fight back the negative feelings like she usually could.

She glanced at her cabinet where she kept her art supplies and wanted to reach for them. She needed to exorcise the feelings by putting them on paper and then destroying the sketches, but all of her things were untouchable to her now. Mia was vulnerable in a way she hadn't been in years and the panic welled up inside her.

"Please give me the strength to get through this," Mia whispered to the heavens, but she knew it was futile. The darkness gathered around her tighter than before, making it hard to catch her breath. The spirits that followed her so casually were gone. The room was empty except for the darkness. She was truly alone.

Her stomach growled, so she hurried into the kitchen,

determined to grab something and get out. When she opened the fridge, she was disappointed there was so little to choose from. She took a yogurt from the very back corner and a water bottle, and was going to go back to Holly's apartment when she saw the light blinking on her answering machine. Without thinking it through, she hit the play button and listened. Nick's voice was the first one she heard.

"Mia, call me." That was all he said, his voice cold and hard. It was like wrapping her heart in ice.

The next three were from reporters wanting a statement. Then the voice of the head mistress of the Freeman Academy came on.

"Mia, this is Mrs. Yeats. I think under the circumstances you should take a break from your art classes. I'm sure you understand that we don't want that kind of publicity to tarnish the school's reputation."

Mia heard the click as the phone hung up. The woman hadn't even said goodbye or ask if Mia was okay, she'd just hung up the phone.

The next six calls were from more reporters. Mia hit the delete button as soon as she heard them identify themselves. The seventh call was from her supervisor at The Boys and Girls Club.

"Mia, this is Gwen. I was told to call you and ask you not to come in until this situation is resolved. I'm sorry. I told them it had to be some kind of horrible mistake, but they wouldn't listen. I'm sorry."

Mia's eyes filled with tears. She had been fired from both of her teaching jobs. Could you *be* fired from a volunteer position? Was that the right word? They didn't want her back, that's really all that mattered.

The next call was from Richard. "Mia, I know you said you would call, but I wanted you to know that Evan and David are going to try to have you kicked off the board of directors. It is a shameless grab for control of the board, but with all the bad press, I don't know what will happen. I have a few ideas to stop it, but we have to wait until they make their move. I'll talk to you later. Are you okay? Call me if you need me."

Mia was sure she had turned to stone. She couldn't move. The next message began to play. It was someone whose voice she didn't recognize.

"You think because you have money you can go around killing people? Someone should kill you and show you how it feels." The caller then proceeded to call her every obscene name he could think of.

Still, Mia couldn't move. Another voice came on and threatened her life. The anger and hostility came through the phone line and settled on her skin, making her tremble.

"You don't even know me," Mia whispered back to them, even though she knew it was useless.

When the fourth crank message began to play she jerked the plug out of the wall and undid the phone line. She couldn't listen to any more.

She found herself in Holly's apartment, but she couldn't remember walking back over. She sat on the edge of the couch in a state of shock. It was all falling to pieces right before her eyes and there was nothing she could do about it. Everything she had worked for and accomplished in the years since her parents had died was being destroyed.

With shaking hands, she picked up her cell phone and dialed a number she hadn't used in years, but one she would never forget.

"Please answer. Please," Mia prayed.

"Dr. Whitaker," the voice said on the other end.

"Dr. Whitaker, it's Mia Carrigan."

"Mia, I was hoping you would call. I saw all the news reports and I was wondering if you're okay?"

Mia's tears couldn't be contained and it took her a minute to be able to speak. "I'm not okay. I need my medications. Can you call in the prescriptions for me?"

"Why don't you come to Connecticut and spend a few days here?"

Mia laughed through her tears. "I can't even leave my apartment. There's media everywhere."

"I'll call it in, right now. Do you have the number of your pharmacy for me?"

Luckily, Mia had an empty bottle of antibiotics in her purse with the number on it from when she'd had bronchitis two months earlier. She gave him the number. "Please, hurry."

"Is there anything else I can do to help?"

"Yes. There is. There is a police detective named Nick White, he's a homicide detective. He might show up there wanting to know about the time I spent there."

"Don't worry, I won't tell him anything."

"You don't understand. I want you to tell him *everything*. He can have copies of all of my files, even the pictures. And you can answer all of his questions."

Dr. Whitaker was silent for a moment. "Are you sure?"

Mia wasn't sure about anything, but she said, "Yes, I'm sure."

"Okay, if that's what you want me to do."

"It is."

"Mia, you can call me any time day or night. You know that, don't you? Or, you can come to Elmhurst. We can register you under a false name if you're worried about the press."

"Thank you." Mia wondered if she had done the right thing. "I'll keep it in mind."

CHAPTER TWENTY-THREE

Nick stopped by Mia's apartment to see if she had come back. Everything looked exactly as he'd left it that morning. He looked in her closet to see if any of her clothes had been taken, but it looked the same to him. The same pink panties were on the top of her stack of underwear. If she had come home and gotten clothes, those would be gone right?

He wandered into the kitchen for more Tylenol and saw that the phone was unplugged. She *had* been here. Nick plugged it back in and hit the play button. He listened to his own voice sounding so distant and cold. No wonder she hadn't called him back. Wayne was right, he was an ass. It would serve him right if she never spoke to him again and it was beginning to dawn on him that that was her plan. Whatever she thought her future held, it didn't include him.

A woman's voice came on next, just as cold and distant as his had been as she told Mia not to come back to the Freeman Academy. The next caller dismissed her from her job at the Boys and Girls Club, but at least that woman sounded sincerely sorry. The next caller threatened Mia's life and so did several others. That really pissed him off.

When the messages finished, he had to restrain himself from throwing the phone against the wall and smashing it to pieces. What a mess.

"Where are you, Mia?" He needed to see her and make sure she was okay. He was starting to get really worried. He glanced around the apartment once more trying to find some kind of clue.

As he went through the lobby, he saw two of the doormen sitting at the desk, looking beyond bored.

"Have either of you seen Miss Carrigan today?" Both looked him over with suspicious eyes. Her entire staff was made up of ex-cons, so it didn't surprise him much.

"No," the smaller of the two men said.

"So, you don't know where she is?"

They shrugged. "As far as we know, she's in her apartment."

"She's not in her apartment," Nick informed them through

clenched teeth.

"We were told to stay here and keep the doors locked. That's what we do."

"Unlock it, so I can leave."

"No problem." The shorter man opened the door and relocked it right behind him. The number of reporters hanging out at Mia's building, looking for a story, had diminished some, but there were still some diehards hanging around.

The long drive home didn't improve his mood. He pulled out his cell phone and left one more message for Mia, only this time he made sure he didn't sound like he was calling to sell her insurance. "Mia, it's me. Please call me when you get this. I'm really worried about you." Nick hesitated for a second. "I understand that you're mad. Please, let me know that you're okay. Please." He hung up, knowing she was never going to call him.

A sense of foreboding came over Nick that he hadn't had before. Something was wrong. Something was very wrong. A sick feeling sat in his gut. He had to find her, and soon.

He was in the elevator going up to his own apartment when his phone rang. He dug in his pocket as fast as he could, hoping it was Mia, but he recognized Wayne's number.

"Nick, where are you?"

"I'm at home."

"Well, I'm standing outside your apartment and you're not here."

"I'm in the elevator." The doors opened on his floor and Wayne and Kathy were standing in the hallway. Nick put his cell back in his pocket. "What's going on? Hi, Kathy."

Kathy smiled. "Nick."

"We need to talk," Wayne snapped at him.

Nick could tell Wayne was ticked off about something. He unlocked his door and let them in. Wayne dropped a large envelope on his coffee table and sat on the couch. Kathy sat down next to him, but she didn't look the least bit upset.

"So, what is it?" Nick asked.

"Do you know what this is?" Wayne pointed at the envelope.

Nick picked it up and took out the sheath of papers, flipped through the pages, and saw words like deed, property, and lot number. "I don't know. It looks like some kind of real estate contract."

"That's exactly what it is. Mia bought us a house."

"Not *a* house, *the* house," Kathy corrected him.

Wayne rolled his eyes at Nick. "The house Kathy liked. Mia bought it. It's been put in our names free and clear. No mortgage."

"Oh."

"Oh," Wayne parroted him. "That's all you have to say? Oh. What kind of a person goes around buying houses for people without their knowledge?"

"I guess Mia does. She's done it before. You know the family that was on the news last week? The ones who lost their son to cancer and whose father lost his job and their house burned down?"

"I saw that. It was so sad," Kathy said.

"I think Mia was the Good Samaritan who paid off their medical bills, got the father a job, and paid for a new house for their family." Nick couldn't help but smile at the memory of how Mia had insisted on watching the news and then fell asleep on his chest before the story aired. He couldn't believe how much he missed her. The sick, heavy feeling in his gut came back.

"I need to talk to her and straighten this out," Wayne said.

"I don't know where she is. And right now, Mia buying you a house is the least of my worries. I have to find her. I have to make sure she's okay because some really weird things were going on at her apartment last night."

Nick told them everything, from the comforter being across the room, the light in the kitchen not working, the cold air blowing by him, to the banging on the floor. He wasn't sure what their reaction would be, but both of them took it seriously.

"That's really creepy," Wayne said. "Like something you would see in a horror movie."

"Try living through it."

"I tried calling her," Kathy told him. "But I think her cell phone is shut off."

"I know. I've probably left fifty messages."

"I don't think she's going to call you back." Kathy put her hand on his shoulder as she spoke, in a gesture of support or sympathy, Nick wasn't sure which.

"I know this is my fault. I have to fix it," Nick hung his head.

"Nick, you can count on us to help in any way we can," Wayne added. "I really like Mia, even if she did buy us a house."

Wayne and Kathy left and Nick sat in silence. He wandered into the bedroom and stared at his bed. He hadn't been there in so long it felt like he was a visitor in his own apartment. The place felt stale and unlived in. From there he went into the kitchen and opened the fridge. The leftovers were green and the milk was curdled. It took him half an hour to clean it out and still it was only eight-thirty.

He flipped through all the channels on TV then shut it off and went to take a shower. In the mirror, he could still see the scratches on his back, though they had faded some. Nick couldn't shake the feeling that Mia was in danger and he couldn't protect her if he couldn't find her.

As he climbed in bed, he wanted to reach for Mia and pull her into his arms. He wanted to smell her hair and touch her soft skin as he fell asleep. The thought entered his head that he may never do those things again. He may never see her again.

He grabbed his cell and called her one last time. "Mia, it's me. I hope you get this. Even if you hate me, will you please call me? I need to hear your voice. I need to know you're okay."

Nick tossed and turned until two in the morning when he finally fell into a restless sleep. In the middle of the night, he heard someone calling his name. When he opened his eyes, he wasn't in his apartment. He was walking down the street by Mia's apartment. It was snowing, but he wasn't cold, even though he didn't have on a coat.

On the sidewalk there was blood. Little drops at first and then more and more. It led to her building. He pushed open the door, but the lobby was empty. He followed the blood into the elevator. It was all over the floor and on the buttons too. When the doors opened onto the fourth floor, there was blood everywhere, but the trail didn't lead to Mia's apartment, it led to the one across the hall. Nick turned the door knob and pushed the door open. The empty apartment was bathed in red, sticky blood. He never wondered if the blood was Mia's, he knew it was. Nick called out Mia's name and from somewhere far away he heard her answer. He followed the sound of her voice down a long dark hallway.

"Mia? Where are you? You're bleeding." There was no answer. He called out to her again. "Mia?" He started to run. The faster he ran the darker it became until he couldn't see anything. He kept running with his hands out in front of him trying to find her in the blackness.

"Mia!" he screamed as loud as he could.

Nick sat up in bed, the sound of him screaming Mia's name had woken him from his nightmare. He was soaked in sweat and he couldn't catch his breath. His heart was pounding so hard he could hear it in his ears. This was the second time he had dreamed of Mia bleeding. He had to find her. He had to find her now.

Nick dressed as fast as he could and drove to Mia's apartment. For the first time, he got a parking spot close to the door because it was almost four in the morning and the bar across the street had closed.

He had to pound on the door several times before he could get anyone's attention. The curtains moved and the door was unlocked.

"Do you know what time it is?" Carl asked, obviously having been woken up.

"Don't you ever go home?" Nick replied, heading straight for the elevator.

"Not when it's double time."

Being in the elevator after having such a vivid nightmare gave him the creeps. He kept seeing it covered with blood.

When the doors opened he went to the apartment door across from Mia's. To his surprise it was unlocked. He pushed it open and looked into a cave. It was dark inside, pitch black just like his nightmare. The hair all over his body stood on end. With his hand he felt the wall for a light switch and finally found it, but when he turned it on, the only illumination he got was the under-cabinet lights in the kitchen.

The apartment was empty except for a couch that faced the windows. As he got closer, he could see someone sleeping on the couch, using a white sheet as a blanket against the cold. It was Mia. He didn't want to scare her so he shook her gently. "Mia, Mia, wake up."

She didn't move at all. Nick put his hand on her mouth to make sure she was breathing. He could feel the warmth of her breath on his fingers. He exhaled the breath he had been holding in fear. The nightmare was still very much on his mind. Nick shook her again. Still she didn't wake up.

Nick moved his foot and knocked something over. He reached

down and felt a pill bottle. As his eyes adjusted to the darkness he saw that there were two of them. He picked them up and went to the kitchen where the light was better.

The first bottle was Prozac and the second, Ambien. "Anti-depressants and sleeping pills, no wonder she can't wake up." Nick felt sick inside that she had to resort to this. He looked to see when the prescriptions had been filled. They were both dated two days ago. The Prozac was a thirty-day prescription, one pill a day. The Ambien was a two week prescription, one pill at bed time. Nick counted the pills and found only two of each one missing. Relief swept over him as he realized she hadn't taken too many.

He tried to wake her once more, but it was no use. On the floor was a pile of newspaper clippings, most of them were about her and the supposed connection she had to the murders. A few others were about her art and they weren't very flattering. She had cut them out like souvenirs. As Nick put the clippings back, something on the floor caught his eye. It was Mia's engagement ring. She had set up her own little alter, it seemed to him, the newspaper articles, her engagement ring, and her pills. Sadness and guilt washed over him like a wave.

Nick sat down in the chair at the foot of the couch. It was angled so he could watch Mia sleep from where he was. That's when he noticed she had stuck her feet under the couch cushion and all she had covering her was a sheet. She had to be freezing, he was. He went to Mia's apartment to get a blanket, but the door was locked and he had left the key Mia had given him back at his place in the pocket of his other coat.

"Damn it," Nick whispered as he went back to the other apartment and tried to find the thermostat, but couldn't. He searched the rest of the rooms, but there was nothing else to use to keep them warm. Improvising, Nick took the chair cushion off and placed it over Mia's body hoping it would help.

As he sat there watching her sleep, he thought about his nightmare. If he hadn't had it, he never would have found her. If someone had told him a month ago, that he would find his missing girlfriend from a dream, he would have told them they were insane. Now, Nick wasn't sure if Mia's abilities were rubbing off on him or if he was just going nuts. Looking at the big picture, he supposed it didn't matter how he'd found her, just that he had. The relief was unbelievable.

Dawn came and she didn't stir, but that didn't matter. He would wait until she woke up. He didn't care if he had to wait for a week, he would be there when she opened her eyes.

CHAPTER TWENTY-FOUR

Mia woke up and saw the snow falling out the window. The sky was gray and dark just like her mood. She pulled the sheet up to her chin and tried to stop shivering. The air in the apartment was freezing. She was going to have to find out why the heat wasn't working before she froze to death. The sound of her pills being shaken in their little plastic bottle startled her.

Nick sat in the chair, not six feet away, with her pills in his hand.

She stared at him for a minute, trying to decide whether it was really him or a figment of her imagination. "What are you doing here?" Mia asked.

"I have been looking for you for three days. I've probably called your cell phone a hundred times."

"It's off, but why would you call it?"

"I wanted to talk to you and make sure you were okay."

"I don't want to talk to you. And now that you've seen that I'm fine, you can leave."

"Is this 'doing fine'?" He shook the pills once more.

"*That* is none of your business."

Nick didn't say anything for a few seconds. "Mia, I'm sorry about what happened. I want to—"

"Don't," Mia interrupted as her throat begin to burn and tighten. She had to blink faster to keep the tears from filling her eyes. "It's too late, Nick."

"You wanted forever, remember?"

Mia felt her mouth drop open and she shook her head. "Not anymore. Not with you or anyone else."

"What does that mean?"

"It means that I think it would be better… that *I* would be better off alone. Not everyone is meant to fall in love, get married, and live happily ever after."

"That may be true, but it's not true for you."

Mia pushed away the sadness and was starting to get angry. She sat up and tossed off the sheet and cushion that covered her. "It doesn't matter what you think. It's my decision and it's final."

"It doesn't matter that I have been searching for you for three days? And why are you still in the same clothes?"

"Because all my clothes are ruined. They ruined everything in my apartment. I can't even stay there anymore. And that's not any of your business either." Mia's words were getting louder the angrier she became.

"Is that why you are living in a meat locker? I don't know how you don't have hypothermia with the temperature in here."

Mia flopped back against the couch. "What difference does it make to you?"

"I care about you, despite what you may think. I have been worried sick."

"You didn't seem to care much when you fed me to those sharks. I was depending on you and you betrayed my trust." Mia's voice cracked.

"Mia, how often do you take these sleeping pills?"

"I only take them when I need them. I just got the prescription filled, as I'm sure you know, and I have been taking them as prescribed."

"What do you mean, as I'm sure you know?"

"Are you going to sit there and tell me you haven't counted every pill and done the math?"

Nick shook his head and looked confused. "How is it that you know me so well, and yet the other day at the station house, I felt like I didn't know you at all? Why didn't you tell me you painted pictures of murder victims and why didn't you tell me you were only twenty-four? And that you are worth like a billion dollars? And that your birthday is on March first? And that you spent four months in a mental hospital? And that you filed a police report that accused your cousin Evan of trying to rape you?"

That was the last straw. Mia's barely controlled reserve shattered and she stood up, screaming. "He did try to rape me and I called the police to protect me, but by the time they got to my uncle's house, Evan and his mom had cooked up this elaborate lie that I was suicidal and that all the scratches and bruises on the both of us were from him heroically trying to save my life."

Mia's fists were clenched by her sides. "Do you have any idea what happens to someone they think is suicidal? They take them to a hospital of horrors, strip them naked and toss them in a padded cell for forty-eight hours." Mia's voice began to fail her. "Do you have any idea how traumatic that is for a seventeen-year-old girl? If it wasn't for Richard forcing them to move me to Elmhurst, they would have left me there. And I stayed at Elmhurst for four months because it was only four months until my eighteenth birthday. And it was the only place I felt safe." Tears were running down her cheeks, but she didn't brush them away.

Though he said nothing, the look on Nick's face told Mia that he was as horrified by what she'd said as she was.

"How pathetic is that? All that money and I had nowhere else to go. I was all alone." Mia choked back a sob. "And nothing has changed."

"I'm so sorry, Mia."

Nick's cell phone rang, but he turned off the ringer.

"I never told you all of that stuff because you never asked and now it is none of your business. Please leave." Mia wasn't sure how much longer she could keep from totally breaking down. She wanted to cry, but she wouldn't do it in front of Nick.

Nick's phone vibrated again.

"You should answer it. The city obviously needs you."

He did. "Hello? Yeah, I found her. She's in the empty apartment across from hers. No, I don't think so. I'm not coming in today. I don't care. Tell them I need a personal day. I'll call you later."

"Don't take the day off on my account, because you're leaving. I don't want you here and I don't need you here." It took every thing she had to say the words calmly.

"You may not want me here, but right now you do need me."

"No. I needed you last Friday night when they were accusing me of murder. I needed you when I was so tired from being at the hospital with you that I couldn't think. I needed you when they made me relive the murders of those girls. But I don't need you now. You chose your career over me. Fine. Now you have to live with it and so do I." She couldn't believe how painful the last four words were.

"Mia, I didn't choose my career over you."

Mia plopped down on the couch in frustration. "Don't lie to me, Nick. It insults my intelligence. I felt your every emotion. From when you wondered if I did have something to do with their murders, to the shame you had in even knowing me. I felt it all." Mia covered her face with her hands so he wouldn't see her tears.

Nick didn't say anything for a long while. "When I walked into the Captain's office and I saw the pictures of your paintings and the crime scene photos right next to them, I didn't know what to think. It crossed my mind that maybe you were using me to try to find out more about the investigations."

"I never once asked you about your investigations."

"I realize that now, but it took me a while to think that through." Nick hesitated. "I'm not your father. I'm not perfect. I make mistakes and I think maybe because of your parents, you have unrealistic expectations of what a real relationship is."

"Maybe I am naïve about some things, but I would never have abandoned you when you needed me. When things get tough for you, you just walk away. You walked away from your grandparents, your heritage, and now me."

Mia saw the hurt in his eyes, but he didn't deny it.

"That's where you're wrong. I make mistakes, but I try to learn from them. I'm not walking away this time. When I know you're going to be okay, if you still don't want me around, I'll leave, but not now. Not like this."

"I can't do this." She couldn't hold back the sob. "Please. I'm hanging on by my fingernails here. I don't have the strength to do this with you. If you care about me at all, please go and forget about me."

"When was the last time you ate anything?"

The sudden change of subject took Mia off-guard. "What?"

"What is the last thing you remember eating?"

She had to stop and think. "I had some yogurt."

"That one?" Nick pointed to the counter in the kitchen where a half-eaten cup of yogurt sat out.

"I'm not hungry, anyway."

Nick got up and came to her, taking her hand in his. "I'm going to go and get you some of the stuff you need. I'll be back."

Mia grimaced. She didn't want him to come back. It was like rubbing salt in an open wound and the wound was in her heart.

By the time she found the strength to tell him not to come back, he was gone. She went to the bathroom and looked at her reflection in the mirror. No wonder Nick was worried. The dark circles under her eyes were awful looking. She had been here before, fighting the darkness that threatened to overtake her. Mia splashed her face with water and dried it with toilet paper because there were no towels.

"You have to pull yourself together," Mia told her reflection. "You can do it." Even as she said the words, she had her doubts. She'd always had hope that she would find someone to love and to love her in the future. She didn't have that anymore. Mia felt her stomach sink and tears filled her eyes.

Disgusted with herself, she went back to the couch, pulling the sheet back over her to protect against the cold air in the apartment. She remembered the times when Evan had told his friends she was a witch and then the expressions on their faces when he'd told them he wasn't joking. She'd wondered then if she was too different to find someone who could accept her for who she was. Now she knew. She was going to be alone forever.

Her thoughts were interrupted by the sound of the elevator doors opening in the hallway and two male voices talking quietly back and forth. She sat up quickly, fearing someone had found a way into the building. It sounded as if they were moving something heavy in the hallway. The squeaking of the wheels of the furniture dolly they kept in the basement was a familiar sound to Mia after all the construction and moving into her apartment. A loud thump shook the floor. She waited to see if they knocked on her door. They didn't. The sound of the elevator going back down to the lobby was the only sound she heard.

Mia cracked the door only a tiny bit to see if she was alone. She was, except for a huge wooden crate that sat next to her apartment door. There was a letter, addressed to her, stapled to the top. The return address was Charlie's gallery. She pried it off and opened it.

> *Mia, I wanted your work to put my gallery on the map, but not like this. Here are the remaining pieces that the police didn't take. I'm closing until the press stops harassing me. When I reopen, I think it best that I not show any of your work.*
>
> *Good luck to you, Charlie*

She carefully folded the letter and placed it back into the envelope. With shaking hands she set it on top of the crate. How long she stood there, she couldn't say. How she got back into Holly's apartment, she wasn't sure. The only thing she did remember was thinking that she wanted to go to sleep and not wake up until it was all over.

Mia popped the lid to her sleeping pills, dumped some of them out into her palm, and put them in her mouth. Three or four, she wasn't sure, and she didn't care. She just wanted it all to stop until she felt strong enough to take it.

She lay back on the couch and waited to feel the drugs take effect. Little by little, the open beams on the ceiling began to get fuzzy and the darkness crowded around her, growing closer and closer until she closed her eyes. That's when she heard the whispers come to her. "Take them all and it will be over. We will be together, forever."

For a moment, before she gave into sleep, she thought Nick had come back, but it wasn't his voice she had heard. Fighting to think through the haze of the pills, Mia knew she'd made a terrible mistake. It was Man and he was waiting for her to end her mortal life so he could take possession of her soul. Her heart thumped in her chest when she realized she was in danger. Was he the one making her feel so hopeless or was it her? She was so confused and she tried to figure it out, but she was too far gone. She couldn't hang on to consciousness any longer. Sleep pulled her down, down to where she didn't feel anything anymore.

CHAPTER TWENTY-FIVE

Nick left Mia's and called Kathy. "Kathy, I need your help. Can you meet me at Bloomingdales in thirty minutes?"

"Sure, but what for?

"I need to get some things for Mia, but I have no idea what to buy."

Nick drove as fast as he could without being reckless. He didn't want to leave Mia alone for too long.

As they went from department to department, Nick told Kathy about Mia.

"I'm worried about her. She is really depressed. I don't think she's been eating and she is still in the clothes she was wearing on Friday. Partly because she says everything in her apartment is ruined. I don't know why, but I'm sure she has her reasons. She has prescriptions for Prozac and Ambien with her."

"Well, that's something. It sounds like she knows she needs help. Getting to that point is the hardest part." Kathy picked out bath towels and put them into a shopping bag.

On the way to the clothing department, they passed bedding and Nick grabbed two down comforters and two heavy blankets. "The apartment she is in has no heat and it's freezing in there. All she has are a couple of sheets to keep her warm."

Nick had never been in the lingerie department before and he felt out of place when he saw an elderly lady looking at bras.

"What size is Mia?" Kathy asked as she looked at underwear.

"How the hell should I know?"

Kathy looked at him with raised eyebrows and took about five pairs of underwear off the rack. "What about bra size? I don't suppose you know what she wears, do you?"

Nick shook his head.

"You're disappointing me, Nick," Kathy said with a smirk on her face.

"It's not what you think."

"You've been practically living with her for a month."

"I know, but we haven't- I mean, it's not like- look, Mia is a virgin."

Kathy stopped dead in her tracks and stared at him. Nick felt his face get red. Strange how he was more embarrassed because they hadn't had sex than if they had.

"I can't explain it all right now and it doesn't matter because she says she never wants to get married now anyway, to me or anyone else."

"So, she's waiting for marriage. That's sweet. Really old-fashioned, but sweet."

"It was me who wanted to wait."

Kathy started to laugh, but stopped when she realized he was serious.

"Look, Mia is different from any other woman I've ever dated. I knew it from the moment I met her and I didn't want it to turn into another broken relationship, even though now, I may have ruined it anyway. I wanted it to be different because Mia is special."

"You really do love her, don't you?"

Nick didn't respond, he just moved onto sweaters, picking out a black one that seemed close to Mia's size. "I'm not sure that's going to matter in the long run. I just know I can't leave her hurting like this. I have to make it right."

It took another hour to finish buying all the little things he thought Mia needed and then they stopped at the market to buy her some food. Nick made a point of getting her some ice cream. As he held it in his hand, he wondered how everything got so complicated so fast. Then, the guilt settled in the pit of his stomach because he knew it was his fault. He tossed the ice cream into the cart and moved on.

"Nick, do you think I should go back to the apartment with you and check on her?" Kathy asked.

Nick wasn't sure what Mia would have to say about it, but after a minute he said, "I would appreciate that."

***

When they stepped out of the elevator, Nick saw the crate sitting by Mia's apartment door and the envelope sitting on top. He set the bags down and picked it up. He knew he had no business reading it, but he did anyway.

He scanned the letter and cussed under his breath. As if she didn't have enough facing her right now.

"What is it?" Kathy asked.

Nick handed her the letter.

Kathy read it. "With friends like him, who needs enemies?"

Picking up the bags, Nick headed for the apartment. Not bothering to knock, he opened it and went inside.

"Mia, I'm back. I brought you some food and some new clothes." Nick glanced at the figure lying prone. Mia was on her stomach with her face to the back of the couch, covered by the sheets.

"You weren't kidding. It's freezing in here." Kathy set a few of the bags of groceries on the kitchen island.

Nick dropped his bags and wiggled Mia's leg trying to wake her. She didn't move at all. "Mia? Mia!"

Alarm bells went off in his gut. He got on his knees and turned her over onto her back. "Kathy!" he called to her urgently.

Kathy was taking her pulse and checking her breathing before he could finish his sentence.

"Is she okay?" Nick was afraid to ask.

"Where are her sleeping pills?"

Nick looked around, but didn't see them. He lifted Mia so he could see if she was on top of them and the bottle fell out of her hand. Setting Mia down gently, he snatched it up and dumped the remaining pills into his palm. "It looks like she took three more, all at once."

Kathy breathed a sigh of relief. "She'll be fine once she wakes up, but that probably won't be for a while."

Nick watched her sleep. He was seeing her in a different way. Her skin had always been pale with purple shadows under her eyes, but now her skin was sallow and unhealthy looking and the shadows under her eyes were darker then he had ever seen them. It was the only color in her face. Even her lips were pale and waxy.

"Nick," Kathy said quietly, "should we put the groceries away?"

He could feel Kathy watching him, the way he was watching Mia.

"Sure. Although it's so cold in here, I don't think it will do them any harm to sit there for a while."

Nick took one step toward the kitchen, then turned around and opened one of the bags from Bloomingdale's. He took the new down comforter out of its plastic bag and shook it, trying to fluff it up. After three or four good shakes, he covered Mia from her feet to her chin and tucked it in around her. Then, he snagged one of the heavy blankets and put that over her too. "At least she won't freeze to death now."

Kathy put away most of the groceries and Nick put new bath towels and a wash cloth on the rod in the bathroom. The shampoo and conditioner Mia used were in green bottles and he hoped he got the right ones. He set them in the shower stall with a new bar of soap. This apartment wasn't as well appointed as Mia's was, but it was far from a shack. The shower floor was made of pebble stone and the walls were some kind of expensive looking tile. There were enough jets in the shower to make a person want to live in there. It put his little apartment to shame with its utilitarian fiberglass tub-shower combination.

He set the new comb and hairbrush on the vanity. For the life of him, he couldn't remember ever seeing her brush her hair, so he hoped these would be okay. He put the hair dryer in the drawer and left it open a crack, so she would be sure to see it. Kathy had picked out a few make-up things, 'just the basics', she'd said, that were right for Mia's coloring.

Talk about feeling out of your element. He had never bought this stuff before and he really hadn't paid attention to the brands Mia used. There was so much crap out there for women to buy, it made him glad he was a man.

When he came out of the bathroom, Kathy was sitting in the only chair with the extra down comforter over her.

"You don't have to stay," Nick told her. "You've done enough already."

"I don't have to leave for another hour, so I thought I would keep you company until then. Of course, that leaves you with no place to sit." Kathy laughed. She was always teasing.

"I'll sit here." Nick lifted the blanket and comforter at the end of the couch and slid underneath, pulling Mia's feet onto his lap. With the chair right next to him, they could talk quietly.

His touch must have made Mia uncomfortable because even in her sleep she moved away, curling up into a ball. Nick tried to hide the fact that it hurt his feelings by tucking the comforter around her feet. They had almost made love on more than one occasion. She wanted to be his wife and now she couldn't bear his touch. He had no one to blame, but himself.

"She'll come around, Nick. Overall, you're a good guy. Mia knows that."

"I don't know." He studied Mia's face. Even now, with her sleeping, he could see the sadness on her face. The damage was done. If he told Kathy that, she would think he was crazy, but he could see it. There was no peace in her expression.

Nick changed the subject and they chatted for almost an hour. All of the sudden Kathy's face paled of all its color and she began to tremble.

"Kathy, what's wrong?" Nick asked, wondering if it had something to do with her pregnancy. That's when he followed her gaze to Mia. At the other end of the couch, a lock of Mia's hair stood out from her head and some unseen being was running, what looked to be, fingers through it.

Nick jumped up so fast he almost fell over Kathy, who jumped up at the same time. His sudden movement didn't stop whatever was touching Mia. Her hair was still being played with.

"Wha- wha- what is doing that?" Kathy stammered.

"I don't know," Nick whispered back. He didn't feel like Mia was in danger. There was no hostility in the way her hair was being manipulated. In fact he felt like she was being caressed by a lover and that really pissed him off.

"Kathy, get the door. I'm getting her the hell out of here."

Nick scooped Mia up as Kathy opened the heavy steel door all the way.

Nick had only taken one step before the door was wrenched out of Kathy's grip and slammed with such force that dust floated down from the beams over their heads. The whole apartment shook so hard that he wondered if they could feel it in the lobby. Kathy tried to pull the door open again, but it wouldn't budge.

"It won't open. I think it's jammed." Kathy turned the lock both ways but it didn't help.

Nick set Mia down and went to see if he could get it open. He grasped the door handle and pulled. It was like the door had been welded shut. There was no give at all.

"Whatever is here, doesn't want us to leave," Nick whispered to Kathy.

"Whatever is here?" Kathy repeated in a strangled voice.

"It might be the demon Mia calls Man. She told me that he has been in her life, off and on, for many years."

"A demon?" Kathy said in the same tone. "I think I'm gonna faint."

Nick took Kathy by her arm, walked her over to the chair and made her sit down.

"This is really scary, Nick," Kathy whispered. "Really scary. Things like this don't happen to normal people."

"I know. I'm sorry you had to be here for this." Nick crouched down next to Kathy to see if she was going to be okay. "Do you still feel faint?"

Kathy shook her head and kept staring at Mia. "Will the demon hurt her?"

"I don't know. Mia never said anything about being hurt in the past."

They both stared at Mia, waiting to see what would happen next.

They had waited in silence for about ten minutes when the door made a clicking sound, as if someone had turned the dead bolt. Nick walked over and it opened on the first try. Kathy jumped up. He ran to where Mia lay, unaware, on the couch. As soon as he touched her, the door slammed closed once again, just as violently as it had the first time.

"I can't believe this is happening," Kathy said. "I don't think he wants you taking Mia out of here."

Nick put her down, and waited. Sure enough, after a few minutes, the door clicked again. When he tried to open it, it did so with ease.

"Kathy, get out of here!" Nick ordered.

"But what about you and Mia?"

"I don't know what will happen, but I want you out of here, so you don't get hurt."

"Nick…" her words trailed off.

"I'll be okay. If he wanted to hurt us, he could have a long time ago. I think he just wants Mia here, so I'm going to stay with her." Nick led Kathy to the door. "I'll be fine."

Kathy took his face in her hands and kissed his cheek. "I'll pray for you, Nick."

Nick nodded and closed the door behind her. He was relieved

that Kathy was no longer in harm's way, but he wasn't sure about Mia. Why was Man keeping her here? Was she in danger? And most importantly, how could he protect her?

CHAPTER TWENTY-SIX

Nick sat in the chair and watched Mia sleep until it grew dark outside. Wayne called him every hour, on the hour, to make sure he was still alive. Nick could only imagine what Kathy had told him about the incident. Of course, even if she only told him the basic facts, it would be enough to scare the daylights out of most people.

Nothing else strange had happened so far, but Nick couldn't shake the feeling that he was being watched. He dozed off around ten and woke up when he heard Mia tossing and turning on the couch. By his watch, it was after one in the morning.

"Mia? Are you awake?"

"What are you doing here, Nick?" Mia's tone was less than hospitable.

Nick got up out of the chair, searched the wall for the light switch, and flipped it on. Even though the only light that went on was in the kitchen, it was too much for Mia. She flinched and covered her eyes.

"I'm glad you're awake."

"I'm not." Mia covered her head with the comforter.

"Mia, we need to talk."

She sat up. "No we don't need to talk. *You* need to leave. Why can't you understand that I want to be alone? I am better off alone."

"You are not alone. When Kathy was here, something—""

"What do you mean, when Kathy was here? You had Kathy here while I was sleeping? Boy, you've got nerve."

"Kathy went shopping with me. I needed help to get the right stuff."

"What stuff?"

Nick reached down and took a handful of the down comforter in his hand and showed it to her. "I got some blankets and some towels. And we bought groceries. Kathy helped me get you some clothes, new underwear, shampoo, and make-up. I know they're probably not the brands you usually use, but we wanted you to be..." Nick stopped talking when he saw the tears in Mia's eyes.

He couldn't tell if the tears were because she was touched they had gone to all that trouble or if she was about to freak out at him, so he waited.

After what felt like forever, Mia sat up on the edge of the couch, her hands in her lap, staring straight ahead. "I don't understand you," she said finally. "Why would you do all this?"

"I'm worried about you."

"You don't need to be. I've been here before and it will pass."

"What do you mean, you've been here before?"

"This isn't the first time I've lost everything and had to start over."

"You haven't lost everything, Mia. You still have your art—"

"Haven't you read the papers? Thanks to your friends creating that scene at the gallery, in front of the press, I couldn't get a job designing greeting cards. And I lost both of my teaching jobs. I really loved them. Now, I can't even teach for free and my art will never be taken seriously again."

Nick had a sick feeling she was right. "You still have your dad's business."

"Not for long. Due to this mess, my uncle and my cousin are trying to get me kicked off the board of directors. It's a shameless grab for control, but with all the bad publicity, they may succeed this time. If they do, I give them ten years tops, before they have destroyed everything my dad and my grandfather worked to build, everything that I was supposed to guard and protect. "

"Your apartment?"

"An apartment that I designed myself, that I put my heart and soul into, but that I can't live in anymore." Tears pooled in Mia's eyes. "I loved that place. I was content there."

"With all your money, you can find a new apartment."

Mia smiled a sad, broken smile. "It always comes back to the money, you know? And, that is the most isolating thing ever. You don't know what it's like having the people around you being so friendly and caring, and all the time knowing that all they want is your money. Maybe that's why I give away so much of it to people who don't hunger for it. It's so rare."

"Mia, I have never cared about your money."

"I know."

A tear ran down her cheek and Nick reached out to wipe it away. Mia turned away, awkwardly.

"Don't touch me, Nick. I couldn't bear it right now. I'm not strong enough to feel your emotions while I'm trying to fight my own."

Nick put his hand down. "Okay." He felt like his insides had turned to ice. Everything inside of him was screaming to touch her, to take her in his arms and tell her how sorry he was for hurting her, but he understood that the wound was still too fresh. It was going to take time, a lot more time.

"Where are the shampoo and clothes you brought?" she asked with a listless tone.

"In the bathroom, waiting for you."

Mia gazed at him in silence. For the life of him, he couldn't read her expression at all. It was like looking at the face of a stranger, a familiar stranger.

"I'm going to shower." Mia got up and walked into the bathroom.

When Nick heard the water turn on, he rummaged through the fridge, trying to decide what to make for her to eat. An omelet would be perfect. She liked omelets. And he and Kathy had bought enough stuff to make a decent one. Today's little trip had set him back a pretty penny, but he didn't care as long as Mia had what she needed.

Nick shivered in the ice cold air. Now that he wasn't under the blankets, he remembered how cold the apartment was. He set the onions, cheese, mushrooms, and some ham on the island.

"And to keep from freezing to death," he muttered to himself as he grabbed his coat off of the back of the chair and slipped it on. He was going to be a sight cooking in a winter coat, but it was better than getting frostbite.

Nick wanted to wait until the water went off to start cooking. That way it would be nice and hot for her when she came out of the bathroom. He got everything cut up and ready. Thankfully, there were a couple of pots and pans left behind in the cabinets because he hadn't thought to buy any. To cut up the food he was using a plastic knife, but it seemed to be working just fine.

Nick leaned against the island for twenty minutes and finally went back to his chair and covered himself with the blankets. After another twenty minutes, the water was off and the hair dryer went on.

The omelet turned into more of a scrambled egg mess, because there was no spatula to turn it with. When he took a bite, however, he thought it tasted pretty good. He was just putting it on a paper plate when Mia came out.

"You're still here?"

"I made you an omelet."

Mia glanced at the plate. Her dark brown eyes seemed sunken into her face, though her cheeks had some color in them, probably from the hot water.

"I'm not hungry." Mia was swimming in the sweats Kathy had bought for her to sleep in.

"You need to eat something. You look too skinny."

Nick saw the flash of anger in her eyes and her teeth clamped shut.

"Go ahead and say it," he told her, "because I know exactly what you're thinking right now.

"Good. Then I don't need to use such an ugly and vulgar phrase, do I?"

"Please eat something, Mia. I think you'll feel better." Nick handed her a plate with his egg concoction and a little plastic fork on it.

She took it reluctantly and sat on the couch, as far away from his chair as she could get. He set a plastic cup of orange juice on the floor for her, without saying a word. Then, he sat in his assigned seat and ate his eggs, sneaking glances at her plate every now and then to see if she was really eating.

"Did you get a good enough look?" she asked as she showed him her empty plate. She set it on the floor and picked up her juice.

"Was I that obvious?"

"Yes."

"I wanted to make sure you ate." Nick told her as he set his empty plate on the floor too.

"I don't need a babysitter."

"Yes, you do. You're not safe here. I want you to come back to my place with me."

Mia laughed sarcastically. "Not a chance."

Nick could feel his temper rising along with his blood pressure. He didn't want to make things worse, so he took his plate, picked up Mia's too, and went into the kitchen. After spending a few minutes putting the food away and wiping down the counter, he went into the bathroom.

He stood over the sink and looked at his reflection in the mirror. There was a time, in his youth, when he would have punched his own reflection, but he had out grown his teenage fits of anger. That didn't mean he wasn't pissed off at himself.

"She was the best thing to happen to you in years and you screwed it up. You're an idiot." He splashed some water on his face and dried it with one of the new towels. Before he turned off the light, he checked the time on his watch, two-thirty in the morning.

Somehow, he had to convince her to come home with him. That was not going to be easy. He was going to have to present his case in a logical, non-intimidating way, and hope she could see reason through her anger.

Mia was once again lying on the couch with the blankets up to her chin. Her eyes were closed. Nick sat on the very end by her feet, careful not to touch her.

"Mia, I need you to listen to me."

She opened her eyes, but didn't say anything.

"There is something in this apartment with you. When Kathy was here, your hair was…it was standing out from your head and it looked as if someone was running their fingers through it. I picked you up and was going to get you out of here, but the door slammed shut on its own and wouldn't open."

Mia remained silent.

"Did you hear what I said?"

"Yes."

"I'm worried about your safety. Come and stay at my place. If you don't want me there, I'll go stay at a hotel."

"I'm not in danger, Nick." Mia closed her eyes and snuggled down into the covers.

"Mia!" Nick couldn't believe she was going back to sleep. Suddenly it dawned on him that it had to be drug induced. He searched for the pill bottles and found them just under the edge of the couch. He dumped the sleeping pills into his palm and counted, she had taken three more.

"Damn it, Mia! Why did you do this?" She didn't respond, but he could tell she could still hear him by the way her eyelids flickered.

"It doesn't hurt this way," she mumbled as she turned her back to him and fell asleep.

Nick plopped down in his chair and pulled the comforter over him. As he started dozing off, he felt the blanket sliding down his arm, the cold air chilling him instantly. He snatched at it, pulling it back up. He knew it had been no accident.

"I'm not leaving her, so you can take a hike." The air around him grew even colder than it had been and began to move. It felt like he was in a whirlwind. Nick jumped to his feet, fists clenched, ready to fight. Even though he knew it was insane, he yelled, "Get out and leave her alone!"

In the kitchen, the pan he'd cooked the eggs in went sailing across the room and landed with a thud on the wooden floor. The silence grew around him and he waited to see what else would happen. The freezing air that was surrounding him began to feel less frigid. The hairs on Nick's body, which he hadn't realized had been standing on end, started to relax.

He walked around the apartment to make sure everything was okay. Whatever that meant, when you were dealing with some creature you couldn't see to beat the crap out of. Back in his chair, he tried to get comfortable, but he kept one eye and ear open to make sure Mia was okay.

Finally, the sky started to grow lighter and Nick knew he had to go. He couldn't miss work two days in a row. He covered Mia with his blankets and tucked them in around her. More than anything he wished he could go back and do things differently.

Mia had asked him not to touch her, but he leaned down and kissed her softly on the forehead. "I'm coming back tonight. I know that will probably make you mad, but I need to make sure you are okay."

CHAPTER TWENTY-SEVEN

Nick made it to work with only minutes to spare. Wayne, as usual, was already at his desk.

"I'm glad to see you. I was afraid to think of what might have happened at Mia's last night." Wayne wasn't being funny

"How's Kathy?"

"She's freaked out and she's scared for Mia. Kathy says that thing wants Mia's soul."

Two months ago, Nick would have laughed at that, but not anymore.

"The Captain's looking for you," Wayne said ominously.

"What for?" Nick wanted to know what to expect before heading in.

"I didn't ask him, but he didn't seem pissed off at you."

Nick nodded and headed to the Captain's office. After tapping on the door a couple of times, he poked his head in. "You wanted to see me?"

"Come in, Nick." The Captain pointed to the chair.

Nick felt the relief all the way to his toes. If he was going to get chewed out for something, the Captain would have made him stand and wouldn't have called him by his first name.

"I wanted to ask you about Miss Carrigan. How is she doing?" Captain Webster leaned back in his chair.

"She's not doing very well, to be honest. Her career is in the toilet, she has lost both her jobs, she's got reporters trying to find her, and there are death threats on her answering machine. Her life has been turned upside down and she's in a deep state of depression over it all." Nick left out the part about their relationship probably being history.

The Captain appeared to think over all that Nick had said before he spoke. "The position the department is taking is that she was only brought in for questioning and has been cleared of any wrong doing."

"With all due respect, Captain, that's bull and you know it."

"Yes, I do. Her attorney has some very powerful friends and he has been raising hell and talking lawsuit. I have been put in the unenviable position of being told to ask you to ask her to not sue the City of New York."

"Mia isn't going to sue. She's not a vindictive person."

"Then she hasn't talked to you about it?"

"She's hardly talking to me at all," Nick told him. "Right now, she's living on Ambien and Prozac. She's not concerned with getting money from the city. She just wants to be left alone."

"I am sorry to hear that. As soon as I saw her and heard her in the interview room, I knew Shilling had screwed this up. He'd misrepresented the evidence to me or I never would have approved him bringing her in for questioning. He's getting transferred to another precinct, by the way."

"What?" Nick felt his jaw drop.

"This was just the final straw. He has some serious attitude problems he needs to overcome if he wants to continue his career."

Nick didn't say anything.

"I am well aware of his dislike of anyone that isn't a white, middle-class male. And I believe that his animosity toward you may have been his motivation in focusing so intently on Miss Carrigan. Anyway, please extend to her my personal apologies and those of the department."

"Thank you, Captain."

"If there is anything I can do to help, let me know."

Nick was almost out the door when the Captain said, "By the way, several of her leads have panned out and there will be a couple of arrests shortly."

Nick nodded and closed the door behind him.

"What did he want?" Wayne asked as soon as Nick got back to his desk.

"He wanted to know about Mia." Nick was about to tell him about Shilling when Shilling walked through the door, stopped and stared at him, then turned and went to his own desk.

"What was that all about?" Wayne wanted to know.

"I'll tell you later."

"Kathy said Mia's not doing very well."

"I'll tell you about *that* later too. Let's get to work. What have we got for today?"

"We got the itinerary from James Stanton's flight to Hong Kong. It says he and Mrs. Stanton were scheduled for the eleven pm flight the night Kelly Langford was killed, but when I called the airline to confirm, they told me that Mr. and Mrs. Stanton missed the red-eye and had to take the next flight at six-thirty in the morning."

"Isn't it funny that he forgot to mention that? That would give him plenty of time to kill Kelly and make it home to get the missus."

"I think we should go and talk to James Stanton again."

"I think we should go and talk to *Mrs.* Stanton. Hell hath no fury like a woman scorned," Nick told him.

"You think she knows her husband was having an affair?"

"Most women do. Besides, James Stanton is just arrogant enough not to care if his wife knows."

As they drove to the Stanton residence, Nick felt like he had been away from work a lot longer than a day. His mind kept finding its way back to Mia.

He used the time to fill Wayne in on all the latest, including the incident early that morning with the comforter and the frying pan.

"That is some freaky stuff. Are you going back there?" Wayne wanted to know.

"I have to. Mia's there."

"I really need to talk to her about this house situation. Kathy wants to move in."

Nick glanced at Wayne out of the corner of his eye. The expression on his partner's face told him that Mia giving them the house was causing major friction between them.

"So move in," Nick told him.

Wayne fidgeted with a paper clip. Nick could tell he was trying to work up the courage to say something. "Spit it out."

"I know you care about Mia, but what the heck is wrong with her? You don't go around buying houses for people without their knowledge. Kathy and I may not have millions of dollars in the bank, but we can buy a house for our baby." Wayne's face grew redder as he spoke.

"Do you feel better now that you got that off your chest?"

He took a deep breath. "Yes, I do."

"If it makes you feel any better, Mia told me just last night that she has been surrounded by people that pretend to like her, but are really only after her money. It's because of that, she likes to give it to those who "aren't hungry for her money." Those are her words. She must have known that you and Kathy liked her for her and because of that she wanted to do something nice for you."

Wayne stared at him for a minute. "Oh... I do like Mia. She's a little weird, but nice."

Nick chuckled.

"You're not pissed at me are you?"

"I know Mia's weird, so why would I be mad?"

The Stanton residence came into view and Wayne whistled under his breath.

"You and I are in the wrong profession," he said.

"You're not kidding."

Wayne got out and pushed the intercom button.

A woman answered. "Hello, Stanton residence."

"I'm Detective Coleman from the NYPD. We need to speak to Mrs. Stanton.

Within minutes they were sitting in a formal living room, waiting for Mrs. Stanton to make an appearance.

"Look at the size of this place." Wayne glanced around the room. "Do you think Mia grew up like this?"

"Probably." Nick was less concerned with their surroundings and more concerned with what James Stanton's wife was going to tell them about her husband.

Mrs. Stanton strolled into the room as if they had taken her away from something more important than them.

"What can I do for you, gentlemen?" she asked as she perched on an overstuffed chair across from the couch.

"We're investigating the murder of one of your husband's business associates," Nick explained as he prepared to take notes.

"Kelly Langford. Yes, I know. Such a tragedy."

"What can you tell us about Kelly, or more specifically, Kelly and your husband?"

"They worked together. James mentored Kelly for quite a while. She wouldn't have gotten where she is without him. I guess I should say where she *was*."

Nick couldn't help but feel as if he was being fed the words straight out of James Stanton's mouth. "It didn't bother you that your husband and Kelly worked so many long hours together? I mean, she was a beautiful, young woman."

The fake smile on Mrs. Stanton's face began to quiver. "No, Not at all."

"Mrs. Stanton, it has come to our attention that you missed your flight to Hong Kong the night Kelly was murdered and that you and your husband took the early morning flight instead. Can you tell us why you missed your flight?"

"James had some last minute details to take care of at work."

"I see," Nick said as he wrote every detail down. "What time did Mr. Stanton come home that night?"

"You can't honestly think that James had anything to do with her murder. Why, if it wasn't for him she would be waitressing in some rat-trap diner. James made her what she was. She was a product of the foster care system, you know. Stanton and Bingham Financial has a program for kids in the foster care system to help get them out of the ghettos and to give them a chance." Mrs. Stanton suddenly became defensive. "I am willing to bet that Kelly Langford was murdered by someone from her past. James told me she had a shady boyfriend, long hair and tattoos. He owns a motorcycle shop or something like that. Heaven only knows what someone like that is capable of. Have you investigated him?"

"We are checking all the possibilities, ma'am. That is our job." Nick subtly tried to calm her nerves.

"Oh, of course, it is. I'm sorry. It just seemed like you were thinking James had something to do with this."

Nick smiled as he stood. "Thank you for your time Mrs. Stanton. Oh, one more thing." Nick took the picture of Kelly Langford's ring out of the file and put it in Mrs. Stanton's face. "Does this look familiar to you?"

"That's my ring. I thought I lost..." Mrs. Stanton grew quiet.

Nick watched as different emotions crossed her face. First shock, then hurt, and then the anger.

"I have nothing further to say to you and I would like you to leave, right now."

Wayne led the way to the front door with Nick on his heels. As they stepped out onto the front step, Mrs. Stanton slammed the door behind them.

Nick took out one of his cards and rang the doorbell once more. It took a few minutes before the maid answered it.

"Give this to Mrs. Stanton and tell her if she changes her mind about talking with us, she can call."

The maid nodded and shut the door quickly.

"She's never going to call," Wayne told him.

"You never know." Nick shrugged. "When she starts to stew about her husband giving his mistress her ring, she might want to talk about it."

They spent the rest of the day following up on leads from two other cases and doing paperwork. Nick was about to leave for Mia's, when they got a call about another murder.

"You'd think, for just a few days, people could keep from killing each other."

"I'd better call Kathy and tell her I'm gonna be late."

It was three hours before Nick pulled up in front of Mia's apartment, a bunch of red roses in hand. He thought she might enjoy looking at something pretty when she woke up. The reporters and paparazzi had finally found other things to do, thankfully. As he walked through the lobby, the doorman said nothing, but he had a strange look on his face.

When the elevator door opened onto the fourth floor, Nick sensed something was different. The crate with all her paintings was gone from the hallway and the wood floor had been swept. Nick went into Mia's new apartment and flipped on the light. It was empty.

"Mia?" The comforters and blankets he bought were gone and so was Mia. Nick went to the bathroom and found all the things he put in there for her just the day before gone.

He opened the fridge, it was totally empty. A sick feeling settled in the pit of his stomach as he wondered what it all meant. The thought entered his head that maybe she got tired of freezing in this apartment and went back to her own. Nick hurried to Mia's old apartment and opened the door. He felt for the light and what it revealed shocked him. Everything was gone, the couch, the TV, even the bed. As Nick stepped inside, his footsteps echoed eerily. All of her secret cabinets were empty. The closet had nothing in it. All the shoes he'd matched and stacked back into the boxes were gone. It was the same in the bathroom, even *his* stuff was gone.

Nick's thoughts were all over the place as to what she was doing or thinking. If she had gone to a hotel, she wouldn't have taken *everything*. Could she have moved? A cold sweat broke out across his skin. Mia had the money to do anything she wanted to do. For all he knew, she already had another apartment waiting for her. Hell, she could have a hundred apartments.

The dining table was gone with all the chairs. The walls were bare of Mia's art. The kitchen cupboards were empty, as was the fridge. Nick noticed the phone on the counter. The message light was blinking the number twenty- three. He hit the play button and listened as the messages played, one after the other. There were reporters, hang-ups and three more psycho's threatening her life. Is that why she left?

If that was it, she would have left after the first day. The only thing different was him. He had found her. He stood in the silence, trying to take it all in. Eventually, he became aware of the sounds of the city outside. It only added to the loneliness he felt.

Nick wasn't sure what he should do next, except leave. That was when he saw an envelope taped to the inside of the door. It had his name on it and it was in Mia's handwriting. He snatched it and opened it as fast as he could, sure that Mia had left a note telling him where she was. He was wrong.

Inside the envelope were the two receipts from his shopping trip yesterday and a check for the full amount of both. That was it. Nick didn't know what to think anymore.

"I never wanted your money, Mia," he said out loud. And, then he yelled it like maybe she would hear him wherever she was. "I never wanted your money!"

The four floor elevator ride was the longest of his life. When the doorman saw the expression on his face, he got up out of his chair and took a step back.

"Where is she?"

"I don't know where she went. We spent the day clearing her place and then she left."

"Where did she take her stuff? Did she move to a new apartment?"

"No. She gave it all to charity. Her furniture, bags of clothes, and all her paints and stuff, all of it went to charity."

"What about her paintings? There was a crate of paintings sitting in the hallway. She wouldn't have donated those to charity. Where are they?"

"She told Carl to take them to the dump."

"What?" Warning bells went off in Nick's head.

"He took them down to the basement and covered the crate with a tarp. He didn't think he should be throwing away her art when she is in such a bad way."

Nick nodded. "Tell Carl I said, thank you."

"Detective?"

"What?" He wasn't in the mood to be nice.

"Miss Carrigan asked me to give this to you." He held out a couple of shopping bags.

Nick took them and left without looking inside. When he got to his car he tossed them on the seat, started the engine, and turned on the light. The clothes Mia bought him were inside, neatly folded. The other bag had all of his toiletries in it.

When he got home, he went through the bags, hoping he had missed something, but he hadn't. Nick sat on the couch and went over everything in his mind. He felt sick inside. He wondered if Mia had decided to end her life. It sure looked as if she was wrapping up the details like some people do before committing suicide. How was he going to live with it, if that was what she was planning?

He dug for the cell phone in his pocket and called Mia. He knew she wouldn't answer, but he had to try. At the sound of the tone he left a message. "Mia, I went to your apartment and everything is gone, including you. I'm so worried about you. Please, please don't do anything stupid. I'm sorry about everything. I know it's my fault." Nick's voice cracked and he had to clear his throat to continue. "Please call me and let me know you are okay. Just once, please. I need to know you are okay." Reluctantly, he hung up. His next call was to Wayne. He told him everything.

"I'm afraid for her. She's so sad and alone." Nick wiped a tear off of his cheek with the back of his hand.

"Nick, listen to me. We will find her. I'll help you search every hotel, motel, and under every rock until we do. Now, try to get some sleep. I'll see you in the morning."

CHAPTER TWENTY-EIGHT

Nick was at his desk when Wayne came in at eight-forty-five.

"What are you doing?" Wayne wanted to know.

"I'm waiting until nine when I can call Richard Sharpe. If anyone knows where she is, it's him."

"Isn't he her lawyer?" Wayne asked. "You think he'll tell you?"

"He will after I beat the crap out of him." Nick checked his watch once more. Eight-fifty one, close enough. He picked up the card Richard Sharpe had given him the night they'd met and punched the numbers on the phone.

A woman answered.

"Richard Sharpe, please. It's urgent."

"May I ask who's calling and what it's concerning?"

"This is Detective White and it's in regards to Mia Carrigan."

"One moment please."

He was placed on hold. As he waited, easy listening music played in his ear.

"I'm sorry, Mr. Sharpe is out of the country for the next three days.

"There has to be a way to reach him. This is urgent."

"If you would like to leave a contact number, I'll be sure he gets it when he calls in," the woman offered.

Nick gave her the pertinent information and slammed the phone down on the receiver.

"No luck?" Wayne asked as he took a sip of his first morning coffee.

"He's out of the country for three days."

Nick racked his brain for any place she may have gone. It would have to be someplace she felt safe. "What was the name of that hospital that Mia went to when she was a teenager? Do you remember?"

Wayne tried to remember. "It was a tree name, Oakdale, Oakhurst, no it was Elmhurst."

"That's it! It was in Connecticut." Nick started searching the computer for any information he could find.

"White, Coleman." The Captain's voice was not pleased, "my office."

They walked in and sat down, waiting to see what he wanted.

"What's going on with you two?" he asked.

"Sir?" Nick replied.

"White, you've walked in that door right on time or a few minutes late every day since you started here. Today, you're here before me and you have a panicked look on your face, so I want to know what's going on."

Nick looked at Wayne and then back to the Captain. He hadn't realized he was that transparent.

"Mia has disappeared. I went to her place last night and the whole thing was empty. I have no idea where she is and I'm worried about her."

The Captain nodded. "Fill out a missing persons report and check to see if there has been any activity on her credit cards."

"I want to check that hospital, Elmhurst, where she spent time several years ago."

"Do it. I don't want this on my head if anything should happen to her," the Captain said.

Within the hour, Nick and Wayne were driving to Connecticut.

Nick stared out the window, saying nothing.

"You get any sleep last night?" Wayne wanted to know.

"Not a wink."

They drove the rest of the way in silence. Nick was exhausted, but he had a million different thoughts going through his head. He wondered what Mia's reaction would be when she saw him? Would she be drugged out when he found her? What if she didn't want to see him at all? What if she wasn't at the hospital? Then, he was going to have to find somewhere else to look. He hoped wherever she was, she was okay.

"Please, be okay," he mumbled to himself.

After another hour, they found the turn off for the hospital. Wayne followed the long and winding driveway to the small parking lot. The hospital was small, much smaller than the image Nick had in his head. The center portion was two stories with large arched windows and it was flanked by a one story wing on either side of it."

As soon as Nick got out of the car, his stomach sank. "She's not here."

"What?" Wayne looked at him like he had lost his mind. "We haven't even gone inside."

Nick walked into the lobby and glanced around at the fancy carpet and expensive furniture. Straight ahead was a large staircase with an ornate iron railing. A huge desk sat to the right of the door with an older woman sitting behind it. The place felt more like a five star hotel than a mental hospital.

Nick took out his badge and showed it to the lady. "I'm Detective White, NYPD. I'm looking for Mia Carrigan. I believe she may be a patient here."

"I'm sorry, we don't have a Mia Carrigan staying here."

"Who's in charge around here? Is there someone I can talk to?"

"One moment." The lady picked up the phone. "Dr. Whitaker, there are two police detectives here who would like to speak to you about a Mia Carrigan." The woman glanced up at them in surprise. "Yes, sir." When she hung up, she pointed to the stairs. "You can go right up. It's the first door on the right."

Nick was headed up even before she'd finished speaking, with Wayne right behind him.

The sign on the door said, Dr. David Whitaker. Nick knocked and then opened the door.

The doctor was getting up from behind his desk. He met them half way across the large office and offered his hand.

"I'm David Whitaker. Come in. I've been expecting you."

The doctor was younger than Nick expected, only a few years older than him, if he'd guessed right. He was also tall, lean, and good looking enough to be on magazine covers.

Nick's hopes rose. "I'm Detective White and this is Detective Coleman. We are looking for Mia Carrigan. It's urgent that we find her. Is she here?"

"Are you going to arrest Mia? I assume you are here because of the incident that has been on the news lately."

"No, I'm not here to arrest her." Nick explained hastily, before the Doctor got the wrong idea. "Mia is my fiancée and she has disappeared. I'm worried about her. She wasn't in the best state of mind when she left."

Dr. Whitaker leaned back in his chair and nodded. "That explains a lot."

"I know you have been in contact with her because you ordered her prescriptions for Prozac and Ambien. I saw your name on the bottles."

"Mia called me, sounding despondent about what was happening to her. I asked her to come here so we could talk about it, but she told me she couldn't leave her apartment because the press had surrounded the building. So, I renewed her medications."

"So she is here?" Nick asked anxiously.

"No, I haven't talked to her since the day she called about the medications and you."

"Me?" Nick was totally confused.

"Yes," the doctor said. "She told me a homicide detective named White would be coming to see me and she told me to give you copies of everything. After what's been on the news, I was hesitant, but she insisted. So, I've made copies of everything I have."

The doctor got up and went and picked up a box that said, 'copy paper' on the outside and set it on the edge of the desk.

"It's all there, the files, the pictures, the tapes, all of it."

Nick nodded as if he expected to get it all. He'd figure out what it meant later.

"How well do you know Mia?" Nick asked.

"I treated her when she came here at seventeen and we have been in contact off and on over the years. When Mia needs to talk things over with someone, she will call. She has my private cell phone number."

Something about the way the doctor was implying a close relationship with Mia made Nick's blood pressure rise. "I never told Mia I was coming here."

"Well, if you are Mia's fiancée, you know she has certain…gifts. She is one of the most fascinating patients I have ever worked with."

Nick decided to ignore the doctor's comments and cut to the chase. "Tell me something, Dr. Whitaker, do you think Mia is capable of hurting herself?"

"As a homicide detective, I'm sure you know that anyone is capable of doing anything, given the right circumstances. And Mia did sound desperately unhappy when she called me, so I don't know. I wish I could say no, but I can't. I would hope before she got to that point, she would reach out to me. I helped her before and I can help her again."

Nick placed one of his cards on the desk top for the doctor. "If she calls you or shows up here, will you please call me? There is a missing persons report out on her and the sooner we find her the better."

The doctor reached into a desk drawer and took out a card and handed it to Nick. "If there is anything else I can do, feel free to call me. I hope you find her soon, Detective." The man stood and walked them to the door.

Nick hurried out to the parking lot, afraid the doctor would change his mind and ask for the records back. He sat down in the passenger seat and opened the box.

Wayne got in and started the car. "Why do you think Mia told him to give you copies of all of her records?"

"I don't know. How did she even know I would wind up here talking to her doctor?"

"That *is* weird."

Nick took a large manila envelope out of the box and opened it. Inside were pictures of Mia. The first one was a profile of her face. Her long hair had been pulled back and a purple bruise ran from her jaw bone up to her ear.

"Look at this." Nick held it out so Wayne could see.

Nick went to the next one. Mia had no shirt on, but her arm covered her breasts as the photographer focused on more deep purple bruises on her shoulder, chest, and ribs. The next six pictures were similar to the first, Mia with bruises and scratches on her thighs, back, neck and her upper arm. The last one, showed Mia's face straight on. Someone had grabbed her face hard enough to leave behind marks that could be made out as fingers on the left side of her chin and a thumb on the right.

Nick stared at it. He couldn't put it down, not because of the violence it implied, but because of Mia's eyes. She looked so hopeless, alone, and confused. Those same emotions had been in her eyes at the police station. Knowing he was the reason they'd been there, made a deep sense of shame settle in the pit of his stomach. It was true, he hadn't meant to hurt her, but the real truth was, he hadn't thought about *her* at all. He'd only thought of himself and what might have happened to his career if she had been involved with the murders somehow.

He knew he wouldn't be able to fix this. He'd thought if he went to her apartment and explained why he'd reacted the way he did, maybe she would understand. She'd understood all right. She'd understood that he is a self-centered, egotistical jerk, who doesn't deserve to be around her. That had to be why she took off. How many times had she said she'd wanted to be alone and he'd ignored her? He'd been trying to help, but it was too little too late.

"Those look like rape photos to me," Wayne said. "Her cousin must be a real prince."

Nick slid the pictures back into the envelope and put it back in the box.

"Aren't you going to see what else is in there?" Wayne asked as he turned onto the highway headed back toward New York.

"Maybe I'm making a mistake looking for her. She's an adult. If she doesn't want to be around people, maybe I should respect that."

"What are you talking about? I thought you were worried about her?"

"I am, but maybe I'm not the one that needs to be looking for her. Maybe it's me she's running from."

Wayne was silent for a few minutes. "That may be, but if you don't look for her, who will? The only other person I can think of is her attorney and he's gone. What if something happens to her because you didn't keep looking? Could you live with that?"

Nick knew he would never forgive himself if something happened to Mia on his watch, and this was his watch, there was no one else. "No, I couldn't." He had to find her, make sure she was going to be okay, and then he would let her go on with her life.

They rode back to the station in silence. Wayne dropped Nick off next to his car.

"Go home and try to get some sleep. I'll go take care of the paperwork."

"Thanks." Nick put the box in his car.

"Nick," Wayne called to him. "It's going to be okay."

He wished he had Wayne's faith. Nick nodded and got in his car.

CHAPTER TWENTY-NINE

Drive home in rush hour traffic was the last thing Nick wanted to do, but that was life in the Big Apple. When he arrived at his apartment, he set the box from Dr. Whitaker on the coffee table so he could go through it all. His stomach growled and even though he didn't have much of an appetite, he decided to call for Chinese. In the kitchen, he searched for the paper menu he always kept on hand. When he picked up the phone, he saw that his answering machine had recorded sixteen messages. Thinking that maybe Mia had called, he hit the play button.

"Nick, call me." He recognized his grandfather's voice instantly. The next fourteen were also from him. The last one was from the dry cleaners, telling him to pick up his clothes. Nick was afraid something had happened to his grandmother or one of his cousins. His grandfather never called unless it was bad news.

"Grandfather, it's me."

"Nick, something is wrong, what is it?"

He should have known his grandfather would sense something was wrong. He toyed with the idea of saying nothing, but he knew that wouldn't satisfy the older man. So, Nick spent the next half hour telling him everything that had happened, Mia being taken in for questioning, the bad press destroying her career, her reluctance to go into her old apartment, her disappearance, and everything in between. He even told his grandfather that he was afraid she might be suicidal.

"You must find her, Nick. This is not how it is supposed to be."

"Even if I do find her, she may not want me anymore." It was hard for Nick to admit it out loud.

"She needs to go home. Can you find white sage in that city of yours?" There was hesitation in his words. "Will you do a cleansing of her apartment?"

Nick thought about what his grandfather was asking him to do. It was more than a simple cleansing ceremony and Nick knew it. He remembered times as a child when his grandfather would do cleansings for others to drive away evil spirits or to cure an illness. His grandfather had taken him along and taught him all that he knew.

Nick was ashamed he hadn't thought of it himself. Mia was sensitive to the energies around her, maybe it would help.

"Yes, I could do that."

Nick hung up, determined to find the things he needed as fast as possible. If she came back to the apartment, he wanted it to be comfortable for her again. He got out his laptop and searched for local shops that would have what he needed. It was easier than he thought to order the supplies. On the way to work, he would stop and pick them up.

With that done, he took the lid off of the box from Dr. Whitaker. He set aside the envelope with the pictures of Mia, not wanting to have to look at those again. There were several thick files of paperwork dealing with the medical side of her stay and then there were pages and pages of what looked like transcribed conversations with her doctor. At the bottom of the box was another larger, bulky envelope. Nick opened it and dumped out about fifteen cassette tapes. Each one had Mia's name on it and a date.

Nick went to his bedroom closet and searched for an old cassette player he had. He'd meant to donate it to charity when he'd moved, but had never gotten around to it. He plugged it in, popped in one of the tapes, and pressed play.

Dr. Whitaker's voice was the first one he heard. Then Mia's voice came on sounding so young and scared.

"Mia, I'd like to talk about your family."

"I don't have any family left. They're all gone."

"Why do you say that?"

"Because a family is supposed to care about you and none of those people care about me."

"Why do you think they don't care about you?"

"I'm not a part of their family and they let me know it as often as they can. Living there is like being at a party where no one likes you."

"Can you give me an example?"

"I came home from school for Christmas break and they had all gone to Disney World without me. They left me home alone for Christmas with the household staff."

"How did that make you feel?"

"Alone and sad."

Nick could hear Mia crying quietly on the tape. He couldn't

believe how cruel her own family had been to her. She'd been just a kid. No wonder she hadn't wanted to see them.

"What about your Aunt Silviana and your Aunt Mirella? They fought for custody of you when your grandma died. Would you rather live with them?" The tape continued.

"The judge wouldn't let me live with them because they are gypsies and they didn't have the money to keep fighting it in court, so that was the end of that. Besides, they don't really want me either. One of the first things my aunt asked me after my grandma died was if I had access to my trust fund. Don't you see? It's all about the money, not me."

The tape droned on with Dr. Whitaker asking stupid questions and Mia doing her best to be brave. The whole thing made Nick sick to his stomach. All those years he was away from his family, first in the Marines and then settling in New York, he still had family who cared. It was true his parents were gone, but his grandparents loved him and so did his aunts and uncles and his sixteen cousins. His family would have welcomed him home with open arms. And Mia, with all her money, was alone in the world.

Nick put in another tape and listened as Mia talked about her parent's death.

"They were on the plane, coming home because I was sick. My mom was worried about me. There was a loud explosion…There was smoke and flames. I saw my father take my mother's hand and the last thing she did was cry out my name."

Mia's voice gave him the chills as she described it all.

"Mia, I think maybe you dreamed that."

"No, I was on board when it happened."

"But then, you would be dead too, wouldn't you?"

"Only my soul was there, my body was back at my grandmother's house."

"Mia, that's impossible."

"Not for me."

Dr. Whitaker was silent for a long time. "Tell me what else you think you are capable of doing."

"No."

"Why not."

"Because you won't believe me, anyway." There was a hint of anger in Mia's tone.

"Give me a chance."

"Okay. Go and get something that belongs to someone else, a piece of jewelry or something like that."

The tape clicked as it was shut off years ago, then another click as it was restarted.

"Here." Dr. Whitaker could be heard moving around.

Nick figured he must have handed Mia something.

"This postcard was in a book." Mia was quiet and then she said, "It is valued greatly by the owner, who is a man. Niagara Falls has special meaning to this person. He was there once, when this post card was purchased. It has both happy and sad memories attached to it. It was given to him by a woman who is no longer living. Your mother died shortly after this trip."

The doctor's gasp could be heard clearly on the tape.

"You were sad for a long time. Nothing was ever the same after that."

Mia's words were followed by a long time of silence. Then Dr. Whitaker's cracking voice came on.

"How could you know that?"

"Your mother is still with you."

"What are you talking about?"

"She is here, right behind you."

"What?"

"She was young when she died and she didn't want to leave you. She fought hard against the illness that took her life, but she couldn't fight any longer."

"Stop it! Stop it right now! I don't know how you have all that information but stop!"

Nick could hear the panic and anger in the doctor's tone.

"She wants me to tell you to stop hiding in your work and find someone to love."

"This session is over!"

The click of the tape player, as Dr. Whitaker shut it off, echoed through Nick's apartment. He leaned back and as he tried to picture the doctor's face he smiled.

"You showed him, Mia."

Nick turned the tape over and started it.

Dr. Whitaker's voice was first. "I would like you to talk to Dr. Steinberg. I want you to show him what you can do."

"No."

"Why not?"

"Because I don't want to be treated like a freak." Mia was adamant.

"Someone with abilities like yours is so rare, it's a shame not to study you further, to find out why you can do these things when others can't."

Nick got angry at that. He wished he could go back in time and tell the doctors where to go, but he continued listening.

Mia was quiet for so long that Nick thought the tape had stopped. He picked it up and saw that it was still on.

"You want to study me. You only see me like a puzzle to be solved. You don't see me as the girl that I am."

"Okay, tell me who you are?"

"Mia Ileana Carrigan, the daughter of Paul and Nadja Carrigan. My parents are dead and I have no home, no family, no one." Mia sighed deeply. "I should have been on that plane with my parents and then none of this would have happened and I would be happy."

"Mia, are you saying that you want to die?" The tape went on.

Nick could hear the concern in Dr. Whitaker's tone.

"It's not like it sounds. I know what it's like on the other side when these fragile bodies of ours no longer can sustain us in this life. The spirits I see have told me and shown me, death is just another part of the journey we are all on. I'm not afraid of death. I'm more afraid of life here, alone. I wouldn't be alone on the other side. Can you understand the difference?"

"It sounds like you're thinking of ending your life and it has me very concerned."

"Life is the greatest gift we have, but we are not meant to walk in this world alone. We're supposed to find the joy in life. That is the journey. That is why we are here. I don't know if I can do that alone."

Nick sat up when he heard those words, his heart sinking in his chest. If she thought she would have been better off dead then, what must she be feeling now? He had to find her and fast. He stacked all the files so he could read through them. There had to be a clue as to where she might have gone somewhere in the midst of all the stuff the doctor had given him.

"Then we need to talk about ways for you to find the joy and continue on the journey. Your parents would want you to find your way in this world before joining them in theirs. Don't you think?"

Once again Mia was quiet. "I don't know if I can."

"We'll start there in our next session."

The now familiar click of the tape recorder being shut off was recorded on the tape.

Nick went through all the tapes and lined them up in chronological order. He was going to listen to each and every one of them until he found her, but first he had to shower. He was really feeling the strain of no sleep.

After he showered, he put in the first tape and started it. His eyes were burning. He closed them and he must have dozed off.

Nick saw Mia from a distance, he kept calling to her, but she kept walking away. He started to run after her, still it made no difference. That was when he looked down and saw the blood on the snow. Little drops at first and then more.

"Mia!" He ran faster, gaining on her. When he was within ten feet of her she turned to him and held out her hands. They were covered in blood.

Sirens blared, getting closer, and then he woke up, covered in sweat, as if he had been running. The sirens continued from the street outside of his apartment.

Nick staggered into the bedroom and fell face down onto the bed.

"Mia, you're making me crazy," he mumbled as sleep overcame him.

CHAPTER THIRTY

Nick watched the clock all day. Finally, it was time to go.

He was slipping into his coat when Wayne asked, "Where are you off to in such a hurry?"

"I have something I have to do. I'll see you tomorrow."

"Nick, it's been four days. You have got to get some sleep."

Nick didn't want to admit that he couldn't sleep because of the nightmares he'd been having. Every night, as soon as he fell asleep, he would dream of Mia and every time there were the same three components in the dreams, Mia, snow, and blood. It didn't matter what else changed in the dream, those things stayed the same. "I'll try."

He fought the rush hour traffic for an hour and a half before arriving at Mia's apartment. He grabbed the brown paper bag from the back seat and went inside.

Carl, the doorman, sat at his desk. "Detective. I haven't seen you around much."

Nick nodded. "Have you heard from Miss Carrigan?"

"Not personally, but her lawyer called and told us that the contractors are going to start working on the second floor apartments. I guess the boss wants to finish them and rent them out."

Nick found this information very interesting. He had been trying to get in touch with Richard Sharpe since Mia disappeared. On the elevator ride up to the fourth floor, Nick wondered if Sharpe was back in town and just ignoring the fifty messages he'd left him, or maybe the bastard had never left town at all. That really ticked him off.

Mia's apartment was cold, dark, and lifeless when he went inside. Nick wandered around and tried to change his mood. He had to be in the right frame of mind to do the cleansing.

"I hope I remember how to do this," he muttered to himself as he pulled the small bundle of white sage out of the bag. He removed the white tissue paper it had come in. Next, came the clay bowl and the feather. All similar to the ones his grandfather used.

Nick sat in the middle of the floor and cleared his mind. He tried to open himself to the energy around him. Closing his eyes in the dark silence, he let his mind go wherever it wanted to. He found himself back on the reservation with his family. He could feel the cold bite of winter on his skin and smell the manure from his grandfather's horses.

His childhood home was in front of him, light shining from every window. Memories of the times he'd spent there with his relatives came to him. His Aunt Ruby, with her contagious laugh and his Uncle Joseph, who'd taught him how to ride a bike. He saw all of his cousins and heard the chaos that shook the small clapboard house whenever they were all together. For the first time in a long time, he noticed the happiness that was there. It was comforting and familiar and Nick was discovering how much he missed it all.

He also felt regret, knowing it was him who had walked away. It was him who had shut them all out of his life, all because he hadn't wanted to be controlled by his heritage and all it entailed. Yet, here he was. He'd come back to where he had begun.

Nick opened his eyes and struck the long wooden match. He let it burn until he was sure it wasn't going to go out and then he lit the bundle of dried leaves. He turned the sage one way and then the other to make sure the glowing embers were well established and then tapped it on the bowl to put out the flame. The smoke rose from the leaves. The pungent smell brought back different memories, ones of faith and tradition.

He remembered his grandfather using the feather to guide the smoke to his body, so Nick did the same. His grandfather explained how the smoke was purifying. It would cleanse and bring peace.

Nick walked all around the apartment and used the feather to move the smoke into every corner, he even opened all the doors, cupboards, and drawers, and waved the smoke into them. He mumbled the prayers he had heard his grandfather say, hoping he was remembering them correctly.

As he walked into the bedroom, a loud bang shook the floor and some of the kitchen cabinets slammed shut. Goose bumps pimpled his flesh when he knew he wasn't alone.

Nick smiled. He was pissing off someone or something. He continued on as if he hadn't heard the commotion. Another bang shook the floor, only this one came from farther away. This vibration wasn't as strong as the first. Nick moved to Mia's hidden cabinets and waved smoke into each one. Next, was the closet and the bathroom and then, for good measure, he circled the entire apartment once more. The heavy smoke from the sage burned his throat.

When he finished, he tapped the leaves into the bowl and extinguished the embers. Then, he opened all the windows, letting the smoke out and fresh air in. He almost felt light-headed from inhaling so much of it, but he was at peace in a way he hadn't been in years. The underlying anger he had carried with him for so long was gone.

Now, he only noticed the loneliness. He wanted to see his family and that included Mia. She was now as much a part of him as the blood in his veins. He wouldn't rest until he found her.

Nick went home and fell into bed, sleeping soundly for the first time in almost a week.

When he got to work the next morning, Wayne was smiling like the Cheshire Cat.

"You won't believe who called me not two minutes ago!"

"Who?" Nick hung his coat on the rack.

"James Stanton's wife. She gave me the name of the jeweler who custom made the ring that James bought for her, that somehow found its way onto Kelly Langford's finger."

"Really? Maybe she figured, instead of dividing up the china and the good linens, she would get it all if the hubby was in prison."

Wayne nodded in agreement. "That's not all, she has given us permission to come and search the house and the cars. She also told me that James was late getting home and that he had been driving the Cadillac, his favorite car, but hasn't driven it since."

"Now, we're getting somewhere. Where should we start?"

"The jeweler. We have to wait for extra man power for the house and car."

Nick knew the forensics team had to be there so nothing got missed. A strand of hair, a broken fingernail, or a drop of blood could make or break a case. He put his coat right back on.

***

When they arrived at the jewelers, they rang the buzzer and flashed their badges. The man hit the security lock to open the door. Nick was surprised once inside. It wasn't what he was expecting. The place was small and cluttered with the usual glass cases, but it didn't look like a fancy store.

He had time to check out some of the merchandise while the owner was finishing a phone call. It was some of the most unique jewelry he had ever seen, not that he was a big fan of the stuff, but he had bought the occasional necklace, bracelet, or anklet for whatever girlfriend he had around the holidays.

In the last case, a necklace with a heart caught his eye. It was a simple heart, but it was heavily engraved with vines and flowers. It reminded him of something Mia would sketch. Her birthday was coming up and he wondered if this was something she would like?

"What are you looking at so intently?" Wayne asked as he glanced at the items in the case.

"I was wondering if Mia would like that heart," Nick responded.

"I think that's going to cost you a month's pay."

Nick sighed. "Probably."

The jeweler finally got off the phone. "What can I do for you, officers?"

"I am Detective Coleman and this is Detective White. Are you Malcolm Tate?"

"Yes, why? Am I in some kind of trouble?"

"We would like to know if you can tell us about this ring?" Wayne took out a close up picture of the ring and handed it to him.

"I can tell you anything you want to know. I designed it." The man shook his long brown hair, pulled it back, and put it into a pony tail, revealing his tattoo covered arms.

"Who did you sell it to?" Nick asked.

"James Stanton. Why?" The jeweler looked from Wayne to Nick and then back to Wayne.

"Are you sure about that?" Wayne pressed.

"Of course, I'm sure. It was a custom design. He was in deep with his wife for crawling into the wrong bed one night and he was trying to get back into her good graces."

"He told you that?" Wayne asked, a disbelieving tone in his voice.

"You would be surprised what people tell you in here. It's almost like a shrink's office, but he wasn't confessing, he was bragging. The guys a real piece of work, but he pays up front."

"Do you have any paperwork on the ring, a bill of sale or something like that?" Nick asked, feeling like he'd hit the lottery.

"I keep records of everything. Hang on a minute." The man went into the back room and while they waited, Nick drifted back over to the case that held the necklace and gave it the once over one more time.

When Tate came back, he was holding a file folder, which he opened and let them flip through. The file held the written instructions of what the ring should look like and then a sketch that didn't look anything like the ring. The next one did, however, and it had James Stanton's name written on the bottom of the page.

"I always do a drawing or two to show the client before the work begins and then if they approve the design, I have them sign it. Mr. Stanton went through two test runs before he approved this one. And here's a copy of his credit card receipt."

"We are going to need to take these, Mr. Tate. I will make sure you get them back."

Tate nodded. "Okay." Then he turned to Nick. "I saw you looking at something in that case. Is there something you're interested in?"

"I wanted to know about this heart, the engraved one."

"That's a nice piece. It's made of white gold and the design on the heart is my own. The thorny vines and roses represent the pain and glory of love."

"The pain and glory of love?" Wayne asked.

"Yeah, if you can take the pain of a woman's thorns, then you deserve the glory of her love." Tate had a smile on his face. "If you're married, you know what I'm talking about."

Wayne started laughing. "I've been married for four years. I know exactly what you're talking about."

Nick bought the necklace. The smile on the jewelers face, quickly faded when Nick made the man cut it in half, from just to the right of the little loop for the chain to the left of the point at the bottom. An angled cut ran through the precious metal.

Nick put the box in his pocket as they left.

"I thought he was going to throw you out on your butt," Wayne chuckled as they got in the car. "Why'd you ruin an expensive piece of jewelry like that?"

"I have my reasons." Nick wanted the questions to end there.

They headed straight to the Stanton's residence, where they met up with the rest of the crew, to begin a methodical search of the place. Which was no small task. They had James Stanton's Cadillac impounded and taken away. Mrs. Stanton had them start in her husband's study and then the small room in the garage that he kept locked.

When Nick first crowbarred the door open, he didn't expect much. Shelves full of motor oil and other fluids for his collection of six cars, tennis rackets with eight cans of unopened tennis balls, bags of brand new rags for wiping the dust off of his cars, and a gym bag were all sitting there. A set of expensive looking golf clubs were leaning in front of the shelves.

Nick picked up the golf bag and dumped out all the clubs, searching every pocket and pouch. He found nothing. Then, he took the gym bag off of the shelf and unzipped it. The only thing inside that seemed unusual was a pack of condoms.

Nick showed them to Wayne. "Check this out."

"I always take condoms to the gym, don't you?" the sarcasm in Wayne's tone was obvious.

They had searched everywhere except the trash can in the corner. Nick dumped it out onto the floor.

"Just the usual kind of garage trash," Wayne observed.

"Yeah, if you're filthy rich." Nick pointed to the twenty, or so, barely used rags on the floor, mixed in with an empty motor oil container, a Starbuck's coffee cup, and a brown paper lunch bag. "James Stanton doesn't strike me as the brown bag type." Nick opened it and dumped out a woman's black pump.

Nick held it up by the heel with a pencil for Wayne to see. "Does this look familiar to you?"

Wayne smiled, "I think we just hit pay dirt. That looks like a match to the one found on Kelly Langford."

Wayne began picking up the rags on the floor with what looked like dried blood on it and showed Nick. "I bet you a million dollars that's her blood."

"I'm not taking that bet." Nick had the forensics team take all the appropriate pictures and document everything.

They were just about finished when James Stanton pulled into the driveway.

"What the hell is going on here?!" he yelled as he hurried up the driveway.

"We're searching your house Mr. Stanton." Nick informed him.

"You can't do that without a search warrant."

"Yes, we can, if we have the home owner's permission. And your wife was kind enough to give it."

"We'll see about that."

James Stanton headed toward the house with a look on his face that left Nick with no doubt he was capable of murder. Luckily, two uniformed officers stopped him and took him into custody.

"What am I under arrest for?" Stanton asked incredulously.

"The murder of Kelly Langford," Wayne told him as he held up the shoe, now encased in a plastic bag.

"You think you can get away with this? I'll have both your badges before this is over. Kelly was a nobody, a slut who thought she could sleep her way to the top. She got what she deserved!" Suddenly, James Stanton went white, as if he just realized what he had said.

Nick smiled with satisfaction. "Make sure those cuffs are nice and tight, boys," he told the uniformed officers taking him away.

On their way back to the city, Nick couldn't help but think about Kelly Langford and all the other girls like her whose deaths he had investigated over the last four and a half years. He looked over at Wayne, "Does it ever get to you? The violence that we see every day?"

"The meaninglessness of it, you mean?"

"Yeah." Nick stared out the window. "So many of these cases end up like this, with us arresting someone the victim had trusted. Someone they should have been safe with. They'd no idea they were as vulnerable as they were."

"Are you thinking about Mia?"

Nick was silent for a minute. "I need to know she's okay, that she's safe."

"What do you want to do?"

"I need to go to the Wentworth building. Do you know it?"

"I have a bad feeling about this." Wayne shook his head.

There was only one stone left that he hadn't over turned in his search for Mia and he was going to take care of that, right now.

Wayne pulled to the curb and stopped the engine. "So, tell me."

Nick was already half way out of the car when he said, "This is Richard Sharpe's office building."

Nick heard Wayne mumble, "I don't think this is a good idea."

He ignored him and went inside, with his partner on his heels.

The building directory placed Sharpe's office on the 29th floor. Nick found the right elevator and wasted no time going up. When the doors opened, Nick realized Sharpe had the whole floor.

A young woman sat at the desk with a phone to her ear. "Yes, sir, Mr. Sharpe is expecting your call. I'll put you right through."

"I see Mr. Sharpe has returned from his trip."

The girl looked confused, just like Nick thought she might.

"His trip?" she asked confused.

"Yes, wasn't he out of the country for the last three or four days?"

She caught herself before she answered. "Can I help you, gentlemen?"

"Tell Sharpe that Detective White is here to see him." Nick could feel his fury starting.

The girl pointed to the leather couches across the room, "Have a seat and I'll let him know you're here." She picked up the phone.

"I think I'll stand," Nick replied.

"He's on the phone right now and can't be interrupted," the girl told him as if it was final.

"I'll wait."

Wayne put his hand on Nick's arm. "Maybe we should come back tomorrow when you've had a chance to cool down."

"I don't think so."

Nick didn't move for over twenty minutes. He'd stand there all night if he had to.

The receptionist picked up the phone, whispering into it. When she put the phone down she looked scared. "I'm sorry, Mr. Sharpe can't see you today."

"We'll see about that." Nick went down the hallway opening every door and looking inside. He figured sooner or later he'd find the right one. He was right. The fourth door led to Sharpe, who stood up behind his desk when he saw Nick.

"You have a lot of nerve showing up here after what you've done! Get out!"

"Where is she? And don't tell me you don't know!" Nick demanded at the top of his lungs.

Both men were yelling at the same time.

"You've got a snowball's chance in hell of me telling you

anything!" Richard pointed at the door. "Now, get out!"

Sharpe's face quickly turned bright red with anger.

"I have been looking for her for days! I've left message after message for you! I have to talk to her!"

"Do you have any idea what you've done? It has taken her years to make a life for herself after what her family did to her! Years! I can't believe I fell for your, 'I don't care about her money' routine. I wish you *had* been after her money. Then, I would have made sure you didn't get within a thousand feet of her! I stepped aside for you once and look how that ended. It won't happen twice. How you got past her radar is beyond me!"

"I want to help her!"

"Like you helped her at the police station? She doesn't need that kind of help. She has her uncle and cousin to do that! Now get out!"

Nick took a step closer, only to have Wayne get in front of him and hold him back.

"That's not your decision to make. It's Mia's!"

Sharpe looked past Nick. "Melissa, call security and have Detective White thrown out of here! Now!"

"If you think you can keep me from finding her, you're wrong!" Nick swore.

"I will do whatever it takes to keep you from hurting her again and I do mean whatever it takes! Do you understand that?"

"Are you threatening me?"

"I'm telling you like it is. Take it how you will! Melissa, where the hell is security?"

Wayne forced Nick out the door and to the elevator. Two burly security guards were there to make sure he left the building.

"Are you out of your mind?" Wayne screamed at him as soon as they were back in the car.

"He knows where she is. I know he knows."

"Of course, he does, but he's not going to tell you, especially now." Wayne shook his head in frustration. "He'll probably have bodyguards on her within the hour."

"Good, then at least I'll know she's safe."

"What are you talking about?"

Nick told him all about his nightmares. "I think Mia's in danger. I have to find her and make sure she's okay."

"I think you've spent too much time together, you're starting to sound like her."

Nick didn't respond. Until that moment he hadn't realized how afraid for her he was. "Maybe I am going crazy, but I have to find her."

CHAPTER THIRTY-ONE

Nick opened his eyes, the sunlight momentarily blinding him. He must have forgotten to close the curtains when he finally fell asleep. These late nights were killing him.

"What the…" Nick sat up and turned to the clock on his nightstand, ten-twenty. His heart started to pound as he jumped into the shower. He had never been this late before. Getting dressed as fast as he could, he grabbed his coat and ran out the door. He hit number three on his cell phone as he pulled out of the parking garage. He had to let Wayne know he was on his way.

"Hello."

"I'm on my way. I overslept."

Wayne just laughed. Nick figured he would be ticked off, so his reaction caught him by surprise. "What's so funny?"

"It's Sunday. We have the day off."

Nick stopped at the red light, feeling like a moron.

"Nick? Are you okay?" Wayne's tone changed to one of concern.

"Yeah," Nick drove on when the light turned green, but now he had no destination.

"Listen, since you're up and out, why don't you come over and have breakfast with us? Kathy is making her Spanish omelets."

"I might as well." Nick made a left and headed to Queens. He pulled up in front of the small house that Wayne and Kathy had been renting for as long as he had known them.

When he knocked on the door, Kathy answered wearing a chef's apron and her red hair in a ponytail. "Nick! I'm so glad you came." She gave him a quick hug as he walked in. "This is a big day for us."

"It is?" Nick wondered what was going on.

"Come on in," Wayne called to him. "It looks like you finally got some sleep."

Nick sat at the tiny kitchen table. "Why is this a big day?"

"Wayne has finally given in and is going to let us live in the house Mia gave us."

Nick saw Wayne grimace. "Good. That will make Mia happy."

Kathy put her hand on his shoulder. "I'm sorry, Nick."

Wayne must have told her all about the confrontation with Richard Sharpe.

"You haven't heard anything from her at all?" Kathy asked.

"No."

"I keep trying to call her, but no answer." The doorbell rang and Kathy hurried to answer it. "Levi, hi. Come in."

Whoever Levi was, Nick could tell by the sour expression on his face, that Wayne wasn't happy to see him.

"Nick," Kathy said, "this is Levi Greene. He's Mia's real estate agent."

Levi was a small man with slicked back hair and an expensive suit.

He offered Nick his hand and Nick shook.

"Nick is Mia's fiancée," Kathy told him.

"Really? I didn't know Mia was engaged. You're a lucky man."

Nick cringed inside. He didn't know if he was even her friend, let alone her fiancée. "Thanks."

"Okay, I have these last few papers for you to sign." Levi reached into a large manila envelope and pulled out a thick stack of papers. He then took out a pen and pointed to where Kathy had to sign. Each spot was marked with a sticky note with an arrow on it. Kathy must have signed twenty times and then it was Wayne's turn.

He hesitated. "What happens to the house if we don't accept it?"

"Wayne, what are you talking about?" Kathy asked with a worried tone.

"Well, I suppose if you didn't want it, you could sell it and keep the money or give the money to charity, but legally, the house is already yours."

"Honey, just sign the papers," Kathy pleaded with him.

Wayne signed, but he wasn't happy about it.

When he was through, Kathy wrapped her arms around his neck and kissed him. "Our baby has a home now."

"Congratulations." Levi dug in his pocket and handed them the keys. "Enjoy your new house." He turned to Nick. "I don't know if you've met Dr. Whitaker, but he's very good. He'll have Mia back to her old self before you know it."

Nick had to think fast. "Yes, I met Dr. Whitaker."

"Mia's at Elmhurst?" Wayne asked the younger man.

"She was when I talked to her yesterday." The young man glanced at each of them in turn and then his gaze settled on Nick. "Was that supposed to be a secret? I hope I didn't speak out of turn."

"It's okay." Nick tried to play it cool. "I talked to Dr. Whitaker about Mia just last week."

"That's a relief." He turned back to Kathy. "I'll tell Mia it's a done deal when I take her house hunting on Wednesday."

"Mia's going to buy a new house?" Kathy asked.

"I believe that's her plan, but with her you never know what she's got up her sleeve. She's full of surprises, but I don't have to tell you that?" Levi smiled at Nick. "Well, I better go. I hope you like the house."

"I know we will," Kathy assured him.

As soon as the door closed behind him, Nick looked at Wayne.

"Go." Wayne told him as he pointed at the door.

Nick's mind raced as he made the long drive to Connecticut, pushing eighty-five almost the whole way. There was such relief in knowing that Mia was safe, but he had so many questions. Where had she been, because he was pretty sure that Dr. Whitaker hadn't seen her when he was at Elmhurst? Would she be glad to see him or would she be mad that he had tracked her down? It was obvious she didn't want him to know where she was. The relief he felt in knowing she was safe was replaced by anxiety in not knowing exactly what he was going to find. Still, he drove on. One way or the other, he had to know.

He walked into the hospital and passed the front desk like he knew where he was going. Nick passed a couple with open doors and saw large TV's and down comforters on the beds. A woman, who looked like a patient, walked toward him in the hallway.

He stopped and asked, "Do you know which room belongs to Mia Carrigan?"

"I don't know who that is."

"She's small. Dark hair and dark brown eyes."

"Oh, her. She's in room 12, but she's not there now."

"Where is she?" Nick was going to lose it if she was gone again.

"She's outside. If you go out the door at the end of the hallway, it takes you to a path that circles the grounds. She walks out there a lot."

"Thank you, ma'am."

Nick felt like he had entered a different world when he went outside. The gravel path was surrounded by trees. The deciduous ones had no leaves, but the pine trees towered overhead, blocking the sun's rays. The edge of the path was lined with a couple of inches of snow. The footsteps of many passersby had worn away the snow on the path. The gravel was wet and icy and it crunched as Nick walked on it. First, the path turned to the right and then it veered back to the left. After about fifteen minutes, he crossed a wooden bridge with a small creek running under it.

At any other time, he would have stopped to enjoy the beauty and the quietness, but now, all he could think about was finding Mia. As he rounded one more bend in the path, he saw her sitting in the sunshine on a small wooden bench at the edge of a snow covered meadow. She was dressed in black from head to toe and she just stared ahead, at what, he couldn't guess. He made his way to her and sat on the bench. Still, she didn't turn to look at him.

"Where have you been, Mia? I've been searching for you."

"Why?"

"Why? Because I was worried sick about you. You weren't in very good shape when I saw you last and then you just disappeared without a word. Your apartment was empty. It scared me. *You* scared me."

Mia turned to look at him as if she was confused.

"Did you leave to get away from me?" He had to know.

"I left to get away from the darkness…and you."

"Where did you go? I came here and Dr. Whitaker said he hadn't seen you. Did he lie to me?"

"No. I went to my father's cabin for a few days, but I realized I couldn't get better on my own, so I came here."

Nick was relieved. He usually had good instincts for when he was being lied to and he hadn't sensed that with the doctor.

They sat in silence for a few minutes. The sun was warm, but every now and then, the breeze would blow and when it did the air chilled him.

"What happened to you?" Mia asked out of the blue.

"What do you mean?"

"You're different."

Nick looked into her soft brown eyes and thought about telling her he was different because of her, but he didn't think she would believe him, at least not now. "What makes you think I'm different?"

"I can feel it. Your energy is different. You're more at peace than you have ever been."

Nick thought about the night he did the cleansing at her apartment. He *had* felt different ever since. It was as if his personality had been altered. That deeply imbedded anger he'd had since his teenage years was gone.

"Come to the city with me. There's something I want to show you. Can you leave here?"

"I'm not a prisoner. I can come and go as I please."

"Then come with me," Nick pleaded. "I have something I want to show you. I'll bring you back whenever you want me to. I promise."

Mia bit down on her bottom lip for a second while she thought it over. "I have to change my clothes. While I do that, will you go and tell Dr. Whitaker I'm leaving with you, but I'll be back. He's in his office. Do you know where that is?"

"Yes." Nick almost took her hand to help her up, but he stopped short. She may not welcome his touch and he didn't want to give her any reason to change her mind.

"I wouldn't want him to worry," Mia continued.

Nick bit his tongue at that. She didn't want *the doctor* to worry.

He found Dr. Whitaker in his office, just as Mia said he would be.

"Detective, I heard you were here."

"I'm taking Mia to the city for a while. She wanted me to let you know."

His disapproval was obvious. "I don't think that's a good idea. She needs intensive therapy."

"For how long?"

"At least a month."

Nick knew it was the skeptic in him, but he wondered if Mia was poor if the doctor would think she needed such intense therapy.

"What exactly is wrong with her?" Nick asked.

"Normally, I don't discuss a patient's diagnosis with anyone but immediate family. However, Mia told me to give you any information that you wanted and since she feels she has no one else…," the doctor shrugged. "Mia is having a major depressive episode, characterized by insomnia, hopelessness, lack of appetite, and thoughts of suicide, among other things."

Nick felt like the breath had been sucked out of him. "Suicide?"

"Yes. She feels worthless and sometimes thinks she would be better off dead."

"How can I help her?" Nick saw the doubt on the doctor's face. "I *need* to help her."

The doctor tapped a pencil on his desk. "Do the one thing that no one has done for her since the death of her grandmother. Be there for her, emotionally. If you can't do that, then don't take her from here."

"I don't know what Mia has told you about me, but I love her and I want to marry her. If it takes a month for her to get better, or six months, or a year, I'll be here."

Dr. Whitaker watched Nick closely for a minute. "I hope you mean that."

"I do."

***

Nick drove as Mia stared out the window, saying nothing. Her body pressed against the door, about as far away from him as she could get. So many things went through his mind. He wanted to say he was sorry. He wanted to beg her not to do anything stupid and most of all he wanted to say how much he realized he loved her and wanted her in his life, but he couldn't bring himself to say any of them.

When he pulled up near her apartment, Mia turned to him. "Why are we here?"

"There's something I want you to see." Nick went around to her side of the car and opened the door.

When they went inside, the doorman jumped to his feet. "Miss Carrigan, I didn't know you were coming home." He looked like he got caught sleeping on the job.

"I'm not staying, Carl. Has the contractor been working on the second floor?"

"Yes, ma'am. The crew wasn't here today, but they worked a full day yesterday."

"Thanks. You're doing a good job and I appreciate it."

Nick couldn't believe how normal Mia seemed. If he hadn't ridden in almost complete silence with her for the entire trip he would have sworn she was her old self.

They rode the elevator with nothing said between them. Nick unlocked the door to Mia's apartment.

"I don't want to go in there."

"Please, just for a minute. If it's uncomfortable for you, we'll leave."

She stepped into the apartment hesitantly, one step and then two. Glancing over her shoulder at him she asked, "What did you do?"

"I did a cleansing, like my grandfather used to do when I was a kid."

Mia walked into the kitchen and then to the dining area, glancing out the window as she did. Then, she headed into the bedroom where she stared at her hidden cupboards for a moment and then moved to the bathroom. She pushed the door open and peered inside.

"What do you think? How does it feel to you? Being in here, I mean?"

"It's better." Mia glanced around the apartment one more time and then walked back to the dining room window. "I always loved this view. I was happier here than anywhere else."

"Does that mean you could move back in here?"

"Is that what you were trying to do?"

"Of course. I'm trying to fix this, so you can come home."

"I can't come back here, Nick. It's too painful. I had so many hopes and dreams and they're all gone now. This place would just be a reminder that I failed. I have to start over and make a new life for myself, if I can." Mia's chin began to quiver.

His heart sank to his knees. He got the feeling her new life didn't include him. It dawned on him that it might really be over. Nick took a deep breath to give him strength. If this was it, he wanted to spend as much time with her as he could before he had to take her back to Elmhurst.

"Come on. I'll buy you dinner."

"I'm not very hungry."

Nick took her to the same Italian restaurant where they'd had their first date. They talked about nothing of consequence. He wanted so badly to break through the wall she had built around herself, but he didn't know how. Neither of them had much of an appetite, so Nick paid the bill and they left.

"I guess I should take you back now. It's already late." Nick slid behind the wheel and started the car.

"You can't drive me all the way to Elmhurst tonight and then all the way back to the city."

"But, I told you I would."

"Don't you have to work tomorrow?"

"Yes."

"You'll be exhausted if you do that."

"I'm getting used to it. I haven't had more than three hours of sleep at a time since you left." Nick regretted the words the minute they were out of his mouth.

"I'll stay at a hotel and take a cab back in the morning. That way you can get some sleep."

Nick smiled. "I don't think I'll sleep either way. Besides, I'm not going to abandon you in the city. You can stay at my place and I'll go to a hotel."

Mia thought it over for a minute. "I've never been to your apartment."

"Don't get your hopes up. It's nothing like yours."

It took forty-five minutes to get to his place. Nick unlocked his door and pushed it open so Mia could go inside. She inspected the small living room with the attached kitchen and then he pointed down the short hallway. "The bedroom's at the end and the bathroom's to the right. You can check them out if you want to, but be forewarned, I didn't make the bed."

Mia wandered through the rest of his apartment, "It's just like I thought it would be."

"How's that?"

"Comfortable, functional, masculine…" Mia stopped speaking.

When Nick followed her gaze he found her staring at the painting she had given him, their hands were linked together, his tanned skin against her white skin. He had spent hours just looking at it, wondering where she was.

He took her by the arm and turned her toward him. Moisture shined in her eyes.

"I was so sure about us. How could I have been so wrong?" Tears rolled down her cheeks. "I'm so confused."

"I don't blame you for hating me, Mia." With his thumb he wiped the tear from her cheek.

"Hate you? If I didn't love you so much, it wouldn't hurt this bad." Mia sat down hard on the couch, as if her legs wouldn't hold her any longer, and covered her face with her hands.

"I'm so sorry, Mia. If I could do it all again, it would be different. I swear." Nick sat down next to her and put his hand on her leg. He had to offer some kind of comfort. "I feel like a different man than I was then. I know that isn't worth two cents now, but it's the truth."

Mia put her hands down and looked him right in the eye. "You were ashamed to know me, I felt it. You broke my heart and tossed me aside like I was nothing to you, just like everyone else I've ever known." Mia was shaking with emotion. "And now, when you touch me, I feel tenderness and concern. How can that be? I don't understand."

"I only thought about myself. I never even considered how scared you must have been. I was worried about my career. I've had to work so hard to get where I am today. I was my usual self-centered self. Other than that, I have no excuse and I can only say I'm sorry."

Nick took her into his arms as she sobbed. He kissed the top of her head, his own tears wetting his cheeks and her hair. "I'm sorry, Mia. I'm so very sorry." He told her, but he knew it would never be enough. Richard Sharpe's words haunted him, "You have no idea the damage you've done." The man was right, he'd had no idea. It was going to take a lifetime to make up for it. Luckily, he had a lifetime to offer. If she would only give him the chance.

CHAPTER THIRTY-TWO

Mia woke up in Nick's bed with his arms wrapped around her and the warmth of his breath on her back. She didn't move because she didn't want him to let go of her. For the first time in over two weeks, she'd slept through the night without sleeping pills.

The clock said six thirty-seven and it was still dark outside. Snuggling closer to his body, she waited another half hour until she had to get up and go to the bathroom. She was almost out from under Nick's arm when he reached for her.

"You're not leaving yet, are you?" His voice was raspy from sleep.

"I'll be right back."

Mia went to the bathroom and brushed her teeth. Luckily, she'd thought to grab her toothbrush just in case she stayed the night in the city. She studied her reflection in the mirror, her eyes still swollen from crying last night. Her face grew hot with embarrassment when she thought about crying like a child in his arms. Part of her regretted coming to his apartment, another part of her was comforted just by being near him. She looked ridiculous in one of Nick's old T-shirts. It hung to her knees and made her look like a homeless person. Mia wondered what Nick saw when he looked at her. Someone to be pitied probably. All the money in the world and she couldn't pull herself together.

The sinking feeling in the pit of her stomach started once more.

"Please, not now." Mia splashed water on her face, and then wiped it off with a hand towel hanging from a small hook next to the sink. Sitting down on the edge of the tub and resting her elbows on her knees, she tried to push all the negative thoughts out of her mind, but couldn't.

There was a quiet knock on the door and it cracked open. "Hey," Nick said, "Are you all right?"

"Fine."

Mia could feel his doubt.

Nick came into the small bathroom and crouched down in front of her. "Tell me the truth."

"I'm sorry about last night." Mia stared at the floor, humiliated.

"I'm not." Nick's large, warm hands moved up and down her thighs. "You don't know how relieved I am that I found you and that you're safe. Promise me that you won't do anything stupid."

"What are you talking about?" Mia asked, even though she thought she knew.

"Dr. Whitaker told me you've talked about hurting yourself. Please, please promise me you won't do anything like that."

Mia's humiliation was so strong it was painful and she couldn't stop the tears that filled her eyes, which only added to her misery. "He shouldn't have told you that because he doesn't understand." She tried to stand up, but Nick's hands went to her hips and he held her there.

"I want to talk about this."

"Why?"

"Because I love you."

"Don't confuse love with guilt... or pity."

Nick pressed his lips together and Mia couldn't tell if it was in anger or disgust because her own emotions were so volatile. She went back to staring at the cheap linoleum on the floor.

"I should go. You have to get ready for work." Mia tried to stand, but Nick just tightened his grip on her hips.

"Mia, I want to help."

"You can't help me. I have to do this on my own. I have to start over."

Nick thought about that for a minute. "Why do you have to start over? Why can't you just pick up where you left off?"

"Because everything has changed. All my plans, all my dreams and all the things I worked for since I was seventeen. I don't even have a home..." The lump in Mia's throat made it impossible for her to finish.

"But, I thought your apartment felt better to you now that I did the cleansing?"

Mia could see the disappointment on his face. "It does. It's just that...that apartment was the chrysalis for my new life. It was the perfect place for me to work on my art. I had all the privacy I wanted. And then, you came along and my life was perfect. Now?" Mia shook her head in confusion. "I just don't know."

Nick tipped her chin up and wiped the tear off her cheek with his thumb. His eyes were black in the early morning light just beginning to come through the small bathroom window. "Come with me, there's something I want to give you."

He helped her to her feet and took her back into the bedroom.

"Sit here." He guided her to the edge of the bed, then went into the front room. He came back with his overcoat across one arm and was searching the pockets.

Mia watched as he pulled out a black jewelry case and sat on the edge of the bed right next to her. "I wanted to give this to you for your birthday, but I didn't know where you were."

He opened the case and Mia saw a necklace with a heart dangling from the chain, at least one piece of it was. "The heart's been cut in half."

"I had the jeweler do that." Nick hesitated. "I know I hurt you, Mia. I know I broke your heart, just like this heart is in two pieces. I want the chance to make it right, to make it whole."

Mia touched the heavily engraved pieces with her fingertip, not sure what she should say. Nick seemed to sense her indecision.

"You don't have to wear it. I just want you to keep it and give me a chance. I want to prove to you that you can trust me."

"Why? You would be better off without me. I'm not a normal person. My life isn't normal and your life would be a lot less complicated without me in it."

"Who's normal anyway?" Nick shrugged.

"Don't trivialize this. When I met you, you didn't believe in anything outside of yourself. How can you accept who I am now, when you couldn't only two weeks ago?"

"One of the first things you said to me at Elmhurst was that I was different. I'm a different man than I was when I was standing in that interrogation room, Mia. You have to believe me. I've learned so much since then. Give me the chance to prove it to you. Please."

Mia continued to trace the vine that swirled, this way and that, over one of the pieces of the heart. "It's beautiful."

"Does that mean you'll keep it?" Nick's arm went around her shoulders and she snuggled closer.

"I'll keep it."

Nick kissed the side of her head and whispered. "I love you, Mia."

She whispered back, "It's so nice to hear something good for a change."

"What do you mean?"

"There's this darkness around me. Sometimes, there are voices. They're the ones who want me to hurt myself, not me. That's one of the reasons I had to leave Holly's apartment. I could hear them in my dreams and feel myself being pulled into the darkness by hands as cold as ice." Mia began to shiver from the cold morning air and the fear that was around her.

Nick reached behind her and tugged down the blankets that he must have tossed together when he'd gotten out of bed. He slid under the covers and took her in his arms until she grew warm again. Mia turned to him and kissed his chin, which was prickly with morning stubble. Nick's dark eyes studied her face, looking for something, and then his lips touched hers, so gently it was almost like a first kiss.

Mia slid her arms around his neck and brought his lips to hers once more. What started as a tender kiss, suddenly burst into flames and she was sure her skin was on fire as their tongues explored each other.

For the first time in two weeks Mia felt human again. Human, and alive. Her heart pounded in her chest so hard she could hear it.

The heat of Nick's hand on her breast only made her want more. She pressed her body against his, feeling the urgency within him. He was all tension and need.

"Make love to me, Nick," Mia begged.

His only answer was a groan from deep in his chest. Mia wound her fingers in his hair and put his face to her breast. Even through the t-shirt, she felt the heat from his mouth. She was sure she was going to make love for the first time when Nick rolled over, onto his back. "I can't do this now."

Mia gulped in a breath. "What? Why not? What do you mean you can't?"

Nick laughed. "Oh, I can. And I want to, but it's late and it's your first time and I'm not going to rush through something that should be this special. Besides, I want to make love to you when you're feeling better, not when you are depressed and wondering if you can trust me with your heart."

Mia told herself he was right, but it didn't change the fact that her body was on fire in a way it hadn't been before.

He leaned up on one elbow and looked down at her. "Mia?"

"It's okay."

"Are you sure?"

"Yes. Now, go get ready for work or you're going to be late."

"I will be late unless I get in the shower right now."

Mia smiled. "Then go. I'll call for a cab to take me back to Elmhurst."

Nick thought about that. "Maybe I should take the day off and take you back myself."

"I can take a cab all by myself. I've been doing it since I was thirteen. Besides, I don't want to make this a big deal. You do what you have to do and I'll do what I have to do. Now, go. Wayne doesn't like it when you're late, remember."

"I remember." He smiled and got out of bed, heading to the bathroom, then suddenly he turned around and came back, kneeled on the bed with an arm on either side of her, and said, "That was the best night's sleep I've had since you left. That means something." He kissed her quickly and hurried to shower.

Mia lay in bed and knew he was right, but it was going to take all her courage to find out what *that* was exactly."

***

Nick kissed her cheek before she slid into the cab. He shut the door and leaned in the open window.

"Will you call me tonight? I mean, I don't want you to break any of Elmhurst's rules, but I'd like to talk to you tonight."

"I can do whatever I want. I'm there voluntarily."

"Then, will you call me?"

Mia could feel his anxiety. He was afraid she would say no. "Yes. I'll call."

Nick tapped twice on the roof of the cab and the driver pulled into the flow of traffic.

All the way to Elmhurst, Mia thought over the events of the last twenty-four hours. She couldn't logically understand why she would let Nick back in to her life after he hurt her so badly. It just felt right. He had changed. She'd sensed it right away. The underlying anger he had buried deep inside of him was gone.

Mia took the necklace case out of her purse and opened it. She didn't take the necklace out. She didn't even touch it, so strong were the emotions emanating from it. He was desperate and unhappy when he held it last. Nick's energy was all over it.

The last twenty-four hours gave her hope that, maybe, he could love her for who she was. Perhaps she had been right after all when she'd felt that Nick was her soul mate. That thought was enough to push some of the darkness away and make her feel lighter.

"Slow down, Mia. Take it one day at a time," she mumbled to herself.

"Did you say something?" The driver, who had been blessedly quiet the whole way, asked.

"Just thinking out loud." Mia snapped the case closed and put it back into her purse. She stared out the window at the dark gray clouds.

The cab finally pulled into the parking lot at Elmhurst. Mia paid the driver and went inside, just as the snow began to fall.

She walked into her room to find Richard Sharpe sitting at the small table tucked in the corner.

"Where have you been?" His tone was calm, but Mia could feel his worry and irritation.

Mia sat her purse on the bed and began taking off her coat. "I spent the night in the city."

"With him?"

Mia could have pretended she didn't know who Richard was talking about, but there was no point. "Yes."

"After what he did to you? Why?" Now, his irritation had turned to outright anger.

How could she explain it to him when she wasn't quite sure herself? "I'm not a child, Richard, and you're not my father."

Richard stood there with his mouth hanging open. Mia had never talked to him that way before.

"Mia, come and sit down."

Mia did as he asked.

"I know I'm not your father, but I'm the closest thing you have. I care about you and I want nothing more than for you to be happy. I have known you all your life and yet, you keep me at arms-length, like I'm nothing but a business associate.

I never told you this, but I even thought about trying to get custody of you when Maggie died. The only reason I didn't was that I knew I wouldn't have stood a chance with all of your blood relatives lining up to take you in."

Mia was stunned. "I didn't know."

"It's to be expected that you would be on guard, what with your family and all the others who have tried to take advantage of you over the years. And that intuition of yours has helped immensely, so I don't understand how you let that cop get so close to you so fast and why on earth you would let him back into your life after what he did to you. Is it just the physical side of things?" Richard studied her for her reaction. "I just want to understand."

Mia felt her face get red. She'd never dreamed that Richard would ask such a personal question. She started to tell him it was none of his business, but there was a wave of deep concern radiating off of him that stopped her.

"Richard, I appreciate that you're worried about me, but you have to let me work this out by myself."

"I don't want to see you get hurt, again."

"You said yourself that you didn't think Nick was after my money."

"That doesn't mean he's good for you. Can you honestly tell me that he's good for you?"

Mia thought about it for a full minute before she answered. "Yes, I think he is."

Richard leaned back on the sofa in resignation. "I hope you're right. I really do, because we have other problems to worry about."

Mia's momentary joy didn't last long. "What are Uncle David and Evan up to now?"

"They're moving forward with their plan to get you kicked off the board."

"They have been trying to do that since I turned twenty-one." Mia wasn't being flippant, something had changed or Richard wouldn't be worried.

"This time, I think they may have a majority vote of no-confidence from the board. The murder investigation was devastating and your stay here at Elmhurst has them concerned that you can't fulfill your responsibilities."

"If they kick me off the board, Evan will ruin everything within two years. I can't let them destroy everything Dad worked to build." The weight on her shoulders increased tenfold. "What do you suggest?"

Richard leaned forward and put his hand on hers. "You have to get out of here and be a strong presence at the next board meeting if you're to stand half a chance."

Richard wasn't telling her everything. His deception wasn't malicious, however. He was trying to protect her. "I'm not ready to leave here yet. I do feel better, but I'm not where I need to be to leave."

"I was afraid of that. Your health has to be your number one priority, Mia, but you have to know there are other things at risk."

Mia nodded. "Thanks, I'll be in touch."

Richard leaned over and kissed the top of her head as he got up to leave. "Take care of yourself."

As the door closed behind him, Mia flopped down on her bed. She didn't have the emotional energy to fight all of this at once. Just thinking about it made her tired. Her eyes closed and she drifted off to sleep. When she woke up it was dark outside.

Mia noticed her purse on the bed next to her was open. She sat up and looked inside. The necklace case was gone. She started to panic and turned her purse upside down, letting its contents spill everywhere. The necklace was gone.

CHAPTER THIRTY-THREE

When Mia's cell phone rang at eight-thirty, she knew it was Nick. She felt awful about the missing necklace and was determined to keep that information to herself until she found it.

"Hi," Nick began. "How was the drive back to Elmhurst?"

"Fine. Richard was here when I got back. He wanted to know where I was and who I was with." Even through the phone Mia could sense his apprehension.

"Did you tell him you were with me?"

"Yes," Mia admitted.

"I bet that didn't go over real well."

"I told him that he needed to let me handle my own life, such as it is."

"I'm pretty sure he's never going to think that I'm good enough for you," Nick said.

"What makes you say that?"

"Just a guess."

Mia was silent for a minute. Nick was trying to work up the courage to tell her something. She could sense it even through the phone. His indecision almost made her laugh. He was usually so sure of himself.

"What is it that you are trying to decide whether or not to tell to me?" Mia asked.

"I went to Sharpe's office when I was trying to find you. It didn't go very well."

"What do you mean, it didn't go very well?"

"I demanded to know where you were. He told me to go to hell. I told him, I wouldn't stop trying to find you. He called security... it went like that." Nick sounded embarrassed.

"Richard will get over it sooner or later. Now, tell me what you really want to tell me."

"I'm never going to be able to get away with anything with you, am I?"

"No, so you better think long and hard about that." Mia meant it.

"I already have. I had two of the longest weeks of my life to think about it. I'd rather live with you than without you. That's why I bought two round trip tickets to Oklahoma for this weekend. I want you to meet my family."

It was a good thing she was already lying on her bed, because she might have fallen over with shock.

"Mia? What are you thinking?"

"I'm not sure. Can I think about it?"

"Yeah, but let me know as soon as you decide."

They talked for another two hours until both of them were getting tired. "You better get some sleep, you have to work tomorrow," Mia said.

"It won't be the same without you here. Last night was the best night's sleep I've had in a long time."

Mia smiled. His words touched her heart. She had to admit, it felt right when they were together. Her hope for their future was growing. There was a small voice inside of her, however, that warned her not to get too close. It reminded her, "you trusted him once before."

Her heart ached when she remembered how it hurt when he wouldn't look at her at the police station. Could she find the courage to trust him again? To really trust him?

"Mia? What's wrong?"

"Nothing." She tried to keep her voice steady.

"Yes, there is."

"I have some things I need to work through." She was going to have to talk to Dr. Whitaker about all this during tomorrow's session.

Nick seemed to sense that what she needed to work through involved him.

"If I could turn back time, I would do things so differently."

She believed him, whether it was because he was telling the truth or because she wanted to, she wasn't sure, but she believed him. "I'll go with you."

"To meet my family?" Nick sounded so hopeful. "Are you sure?"

"Yeah, I'm sure." Mia smiled at how happy he was.

"That's a relief. The tickets are non-refundable."

"I can pay my way or I can pay for both of us if you want me to. It's not like I can't afford it."

"I may not be rich, but I can afford a couple of airplane tickets.

Besides, I invited you on this trip. It's my treat."

"Okay." She could hear Nick yawning. "You need to get some sleep."

"I know. I'm beat."

"I'll talk to you tomorrow."

"Mia," Nick hesitated. "You won't be sorry."

"About what? Going to meet your family?"

"No, for giving me another chance."

The lump in her throat was back and she couldn't speak. Her emotions were so out of control.

"You don't have to say anything. I'll call you tomorrow night."

Mia nodded, even though she knew he couldn't see her. She kept the phone to her ear long after he was gone. She was lonely for him already.

The next day she searched her room for the missing necklace, but there was no sign of it. Mia knew there wouldn't be. The necklace was gone or she'd have been able to feel the energy coming off of it.

At three she met with Dr. Whitaker. Mia talked about her trust issues and Dr. Whitaker helped her to see that she was going to have to trust someone sooner or later, or spend her life alone. "In my head I know you're right, but in my heart it's still scary."

"Putting yourself in a position to be hurt is always scary, but those are the times when we, as human beings, grow the most."

Mia thought about that. "Nick has asked me to go to Oklahoma to meet his family this weekend and I told him I would."

Dr. Whitaker was silent, but Mia felt his instant disapproval. That unsettled her and made her question her decision. Her new found confidence was evaporating.

"Why did you make that choice?"

"Because..." Mia thought it through. "He wants to mend our relationship and I want to see if we can make it work."

"When you got here, you thought your relationship with him was a mistake."

"Not the whole thing. I knew that he cared about me, for me." She was sure of that.

"What are your plans when you get back?" he asked.

Mia sensed a shift in his emotions and it raised her defenses instantly. "What do mean?"

"We agreed that you should stay for a six week course of treatment. It has only been a week since you arrived. I don't think you've given yourself enough time. Decisions like these can be life-altering. Don't you think you should wait a few more weeks?"

There was truth to what he was said, but Mia could tell there was something else behind his words. The realization hit her like a slap in the face. It was the money. He was concerned about the money. A six week stay at Elmhurst would cost over fifty-thousand dollars. Her stomach sank to her toes.

"I have a necklace missing from my room. It's white gold and it's in a black case. The necklace is a heart that has been cut into two pieces with vines and flowers engraved on it. If it turns up will you let me know?"

Dr. Whitaker seemed confused by her sudden change of subject. "Of course. We've never had anyone's personal property go missing here before." He studied her carefully. "Are you okay, Mia? You look a little pale."

"You've given me a lot to think about today."

"That's good. We'll talk more tomorrow."

Mia got up, went back to her room, and began to pack her things. Why did it always come back to the money? As soon as she had recognized what had been bothering him, she could feel his hunger for it instantly. Mia could count on one hand the people she had gotten to know who didn't think about it whenever she was around. Richard was one, but he didn't need her money. He had plenty of his own. Holly never gave it much thought, even though she came from a middle class family. Nick didn't care about it. Neither did Kathy or Wayne. Everyone else seemed to see her as a workable asset, someone to be manipulated into sharing the wealth.

Her own family was the worst of the lot. Silviana and Mirella always had their hands out, even though her mother set up trust funds for them when they came to the United States. No matter how much money Nadja had given them, it had never been enough. They always spent more.

Her uncle's family wanted all her money and control of Carrigan Industries. Their greed was dark and deep. Evan's was the strongest of them all. When he was near, she could feel his hunger for everything she had. Mia had no doubt that if he could find a way to leave her penniless, he would embrace it. Getting her kicked off the board of directors would only be the beginning.

Mia turned on the TV and waited. She was leaving as soon as Dr. Whitaker left for the night. If she had the courage, she would walk right out the door, but she wanted to avoid a confrontation. By the time she saw his car pull out of the parking lot it was almost nine. She wouldn't get to the city until midnight.

She left an envelope for Dr. Whitaker with Margie, the lady who sat at the front desk all night, and hurried to her car.

Grabbing her phone, she dialed Levi's number. It was ironic that they had met at Elmhurst when she was seventeen and he was nineteen. They had run into each other a few times over the years and when he went into the family real estate business a few years later, she called him to help her with a few real estate purchases.

"Hello."

"It's Mia. I need to know about those three houses I had you research."

"I think the first one is going to be a problem. The owner's are still living there and they seem to be having second thoughts. The other two are both empty and the sellers are ready to unload them. I think we could make them an offer they couldn't refuse." Levi did his best Godfather impression and Mia couldn't help but laugh.

"Can you show them to me in the morning?"

"In the morning?"

Levi went quiet and Mia knew what he was thinking. She had told him she would be at Elmhurst for at least six weeks. "I checked myself out."

"Mia, are you sure you should have done that? I mean, I know you weren't there for substance abuse, but still. What about your meds?"

"I have a few left and if I have to, I'll find a new doctor and get a new prescription."

"You and the doc have a falling out? I thought you two were thick?"

"I don't think we were working toward the same thing." Mia left it at that. "So, are you available tomorrow or not? I need to find a place to live, fast."

"I'll make myself available."

"Thanks. I'll meet you at the Harvest Street property at ten am."

"I'll see you then."

Mia's next call was to Nick, but he didn't answer. She didn't leave a message because she didn't know how he would react when she told him she had left the hospital. That was news she wanted to deliver personally.

She kept her phone on her lap the whole way, but Nick never called. Mia found herself pulling up in front of her old apartment. It was just after mid-night. Only the lights in the lobby were still on. The construction workers, who were finishing the apartments on the second floor, were long gone for the day. Mia grabbed her suitcase and went inside.

Carl was sitting at the front desk watching TV. When he saw her come through the door, he turned off the TV and jumped up from his seat.

"Miss Carrigan, what are you doing here this time of night?" He came and took her suitcase from her hand.

"I just got in from out of town," Mia said. It was sort of true. She had been out of town. "How's the work going on the second floor apartments?"

"It's good, you want to see?" Carl didn't wait for a response before heading to the elevator, her suitcase in hand.

When the doors opened onto the second floor, Mia was surprised and pleased with what she saw. Instead of an open space there were walls and doorways. It would have the same footprint as the forth floor when it was done.

"Come this way and I'll show you the two apartments."

She followed Carl into the first one where he fumbled to turn on a couple of the lights the workers had set up. The drywall was newly hung, but hadn't been mudded or sanded. As she walked around, she could see where everything was going to be placed. In the bathrooms and kitchens, all the pipes protruded from the floor and wires stuck out from holes in the walls where the lights would be. "It looks good. When we get these rented it won't be so quiet around here."

"After that mess a few weeks ago, I don't mind the quiet."

Mia changed the subject. "Let's go look at the other unit." It looked the same as the first. "The apartments on the third floor will be next." She walked around the apartment once more, decided to call it a night, and headed back to the elevator.

"Are you going up to your old apartment?" Carl asked with a

strange look on his face.

"Yes, why?"

"If it's okay with you, Miss Carrigan, I just as soon take the stairs back down to the lobby."

"That's fine with me, but why?"

"The fourth floor creeps me out. I always feel like I'm being watched when I go up there. And sometimes, we hear strange noises coming from there, like moaning and heavy footsteps." Carl visibly shivered. "I don't like the fourth floor."

Mia smiled to reassure him. "I understand." She rolled her suitcase into the elevator and hit the number four. When the doors opened, the dimly lit hallway was spooky enough to be in a horror movie. Three of the four sconces that lit the hallway were burned out.

Mia opened the door to her old apartment and stepped inside. She had given away all the lamps, so she had to turn on the light over the stove. It wasn't much, but it was something. The apartment seemed so much bigger with no furniture in it. The open space was what had appealed to her to begin with.

When the memories of the police confronting her at the gallery, the implosion of her career, and the way Nick had reacted that day came back to her, she knew she couldn't live here anymore. She needed a fresh start. *They* needed a fresh start. Pulling out her cell phone, she checked once more to see if he had called. The icon on the screen showed no missed calls. It was almost twelve-thirty in the morning. She couldn't call him now.

Walking around the apartment, she had to admit that the cleansing Nick did had changed the energy in the apartment. This space had felt so good to her when she'd first moved in, now it was neutral, which was better than the hostility she'd felt after the police had turned the place upside down, but it was no longer home.

The stress of the day had taken its toll. She was tired. The couch was still in Holly's old apartment, so Mia decided to stay there since she hadn't been able to get a hold of Nick.

After changing into her pajamas and spreading out the blanket and down comforter, she set up camp on the couch and fell right to sleep.

"Mia. Mia." She opened her eyes to a pitch black room. At first she thought Nick was there.

"Nick?"

"Come to me."

The voice sounded like Nick's. She walked carefully toward the door, trying to make her way in the dark. Once she was in the hallway, Mia glanced one way and then the other, blackness was all she saw. The voice called to her again.

"I need you. Come to me." It was farther away this time. Mia ventured down the hallway. Reaching out, her fingers touched the rough, cold brick. It was like a life-line, guiding her in the dark. She walked and walked. Long after she should have come to the end of the hallway she was still walking.

"Nick, where are you?"

"I'm here. Hurry, Mia."

She began to walk faster even though she couldn't see anything. The hairs on the back of her neck were warning her that something was wrong.

"Mia, help me."

Somewhere, just ahead, there was a lighter shade of blackness. A figure moved. It looked like Nick. His height, his broad shoulders, but she couldn't see his face. He wore a hooded jacket that kept him hidden in the shadows.

"I have something for you."

A hand appeared out of the darkness, Nick's hand, with something shiny resting in his palm. Half of a heart on a chain.

"My necklace!"

His hands went behind her neck as he put it on her.

"Say you'll be mine forever."

Mia held out her hand and waited. The other half of the heart was placed gently into her hand. Her fingers closed around it and she held on tight. His hands rested on her shoulders, warm and soft.

"You know we belong together. Tell me you'll be mine forever."

Mia opened her mouth to say the words, but what came out was, "I will never be yours."

Instantly the hands on her shoulders turned to ice and doubled in size, the clawed tips digging into her back as he shook her violently.

Her arm flew forward and knocked the hood off of his head. Mia stared into the face of the most hideous creature she could have ever dreamed of. His skin looked as if it had been scorched and melted. Fangs hung from his mouth and his eyes were blood red.

With his hand still on her, his emotions flowed into her,

unheeded. The mindless rage he had inside of him filled her with terror. He would possess her or no one would. The images in his mind come to her like a fast moving movie reel. One after the other, she saw her body, bloody and torn to pieces, being fed to the canines of demons.

Her heart pounded in her chest as she waited to die. His laughter filled the air as her body was pulled backward, faster and faster. She couldn't breathe. Death felt only seconds away when she was slammed into the ground.

Her eyes flew open and Mia stared at the beams overhead. She tried to take air into her lungs, but the wind had been knocked out of her. Pain ran through her from head to toe. Little by little, she took in quick, shallow gulps of oxygen. Every one of them hurt. If she'd had the strength she would have cried. Her head told her to move, to get up and escape. Her body, however, was weak and shaky. Finally, she managed to roll off the couch and onto her knees. After a few more breaths, she used the couch to push herself to her feet.

Mia stumbled to the bathroom and turned on the faucet. She cupped her hands in the ice cold water and brought it to her face. As she did, she heard the sound of something metallic falling into the sink. The predawn light wasn't enough to see by. She reached for the light switch. There in the sink, next to the drain, was half of a heart. The water flowing past it to the drain made it flutter like an autumn leaf in the wind. The water spilled from her hands and she could see the deep purple creases on her fingers and palm caused by her holding onto it so tightly. The seconds turned into minutes and still she stared, trying to make her mind accept the fact that it hadn't been a dream.

Slowly, she forced herself to a standing position and looked into the mirror. Hanging from her neck was the other half of the necklace. The light faded from her eyes as she sank to the floor, trying desperately not to let the darkness take her.

CHAPTER THIRTY-FOUR

When Mia could get to her feet, she grabbed her things and went back to her own apartment. She felt safer there. Her hands still trembled as she ran the hot water for her shower. As soon as she stepped into the water, she cried out in pain. Her back was burning. She stepped out of the shower and looked over her shoulder, into the mirror. Across her shoulder blades were six bloody gouges in her skin, three on the left and three on the right.

Mia's head began to swim again. Her hands gripped the edge of the sink. It hadn't been a dream at all. In the two years she had lived in her loft, she had never been hurt. The spirits that came and went were sometimes ornery, maybe even obnoxious, but never violent. This was something more. This was Man and he was furious. He had declared war. If he couldn't possess her, he was going to try to destroy her.

"Think, Mia, think," she whispered to herself. Silviana would know what to do.

If she hurried, she would have just enough time to go see her and still meet Levi at ten.

Traffic was especially bad and it took her longer than she'd expected to get to Silviana's. Mia would probably be late to her appointment with Levi, and she hated being late. Her hands still trembled as she rode up the elevator.

It took a few minutes for Silviana to come to the door. Her long, gray hair hung loose over her nightgown. Rubbing the sleep from her eyes, she looked at Mia and seemed to come to life. "Mia, what are you doing here so early?"

"I need your help." As quickly as she could, Mia told her aunt the whole story, the missing necklace, the dream that wasn't a dream, and the scratches on her back. "I don't know what to do. I'm afraid he is going to try to kill me or maybe Nick."

Silviana leaned back in her chair and for the second time in less than twenty-four hours Mia felt the energy around her change. Even as she was begging for her aunt's help, Silviana was trying to figure out a way to manipulate her for more money. Unlike Dr. Whitaker, who didn't seem to want it for himself, Silviana's hunger was plain, old greed.

Mia wanted to laugh and cry. Why she'd thought this time would be different she wasn't sure, maybe because she felt as if her life was in danger and that it might matter to her aunt.

"I can see if Olga can help, but her charms are expensive."

Mia sighed. "How expensive?"

"They are very powerful. They will protect you."

"How expensive, Silviana? Five thousand, ten thousand?" Mia had to know how far her aunt would take this.

"It could be around ten thousand dollars."

Mia let that sink in for a moment. "How much of a cut do you get from that ten thousand? Fifty percent? Seventy-five? Or, are you going to give me some ten dollar trinket and keep the rest for yourself?"

Silviana feigned offence. "What do you accuse me of, Mia?"

"Never mind, Silviana. It was a mistake coming here." Mia headed for the door which not only surprised her aunt, but made her mad.

"You come here, ask for my help, and then insult me. Help is not free. It costs money to make these things happen. *I* need money to make these things happen."

"If you need more money to live on than what you get from the trust fund, maybe you should get a job." Mia slammed the door behind her and left.

***

Mia made it to the Harvest Street house in record time. Levi pulled up right behind her. As she got out of her car and saw the massive house in person, she knew it wasn't the right one. Out of respect for Levi she let him lead her through it, pointing out all the upgrades and remodeling the last owners had done.

When they made it back to the front door he asked, "You hate this house, don't you?"

"I don't hate it."

"But, you're not going to buy it?"

"No, it doesn't feel right."

"Let's go check on the other one. It's only two blocks from here."

Mia let Levi drive her in his car. The second house was worse than the first. She'd had such high hopes that she would find a new home quickly and now those hopes were gone. It was strange that she'd been so off. When she had seen the Harvest Street name under the picture of the first house, she was surprised by the sudden rush of warmth that had surrounded her.

Her cell phone rang in her purse.

"Go ahead and answer it. I don't mind," Levi said,

Mia was afraid it was Silviana, but when she glanced at the number, she saw it was Dr. Whitaker. She let it go to voice mail. The last thing she wanted was to be analyzed over the phone.

As Levi drove her back to her car, they passed a house where a brand new real estate sign was being put up in front of a heavily wooded yard.

"Are we back on Harvest Street?" Mia asked.

"Yeah. Hey, that's Karen Dempsey. She used to work for my dad before she started her own company."

"Turn around," Mia told him.

Levi and Karen exchanged greetings and he introduced Mia. The two women shook hands.

They were joined by an older man who came walking down the driveway from the direction of the house. "All locked up," he said as he noticed her and Levi.

"This is John Reed," Karen Dempsey explained. "His mother used to live here and I just listed the place."

"May I see inside?" Mia asked before anyone else could say another word.

Levi shrugged his shoulders. "She didn't like the other two houses I showed her," he said to Karen.

Karen's smile grew when she realized that Mia was a serious buyer. The middle-aged woman began to give her sales pitch as they walked up the winding driveway. "It's a Tudor style home with seven bedrooms and five and a half baths. It has over eight thousand square feet of living space on an acre lot."

Mia could hardly see the house with all the trees in the front yard, but as they got closer, her spirits grew brighter. The house had a good feel about it. Karen Dempsey talked faster when they walked inside. Mia knew why when she saw the dated interior of the house. It would drive most people running in the opposite direction.

The entry opened to a formal living room on the left and a dining room on the right. A staircase leading to the second floor was set back about ten feet. It needed restoration badly, as did all the wood floors. Beyond the dining room was the kitchen, which was closed off from the large family room that led to the back yard. A second, less formal staircase, led upstairs from the family room. The bottom floor had a real library with floor to ceiling shelves built in, and a half bath right across the hall, a good sized laundry room, and maid quarters with an attached bathroom.

"How long has the house been empty?" Mia asked the agent.

"Mrs. Reed lived here until nine months ago when she passed away."

The upstairs master bedroom was small and the master bathroom had hideous coral colored tile. To the right of the master bedroom was a small bedroom that had been used as a nursery. Mia knew she could use it to enlarge the bedroom and bathroom. The other five bedrooms upstairs were large. Two had their own bathrooms and the other two had a Jack and Jill bathroom to share. The last one, the smallest, would be perfect as a nursery.

Despite the awful condition of the house, Mia saw the way the house could be rather than how it was. The deep set windows at the front of the house still had the diamond shaped panes of glass, though the wood was rotting.

"Is there a basement?"

"Yes, but it's not finished," Karen said, trying to distract Mia from wanting to see it.

"I assume that is where the mechanics of the house are?"

Karen and Mr. Reed glanced at each other, which would have set off warning bells for anyone seeing the house, but Mia sensed both of their apprehension right away.

"Yes." Karen smiled.

"Then, I need to see it."

Mia was grateful that her parents had dabbled in real estate and had taught her a thing or two about what to look for.

When they came back upstairs, Levi, Karen, and Mr. Reed were anxiously awaiting Mia's decision.

"If you don't mind waiting a few more minutes, I have to make a phone call."

Mia walked into the kitchen by herself and called Nick's cell. He answered right away.

"Nick, is it possible for you to get away for a few minutes?"

"Why, where are you?"

"I'm in Queens looking at a house and I want you to see it."

"You're in the city? Mia, what's going on?"

"I'll explain everything later. Can you come?"

"Give me the address," Nick said.

"1271 Harvest Street."

"I got it," Nick told her. "Wayne and I are only fifteen minutes from there."

True to his word Nick and Wayne pulled up the driveway fifteen minutes later. As he got out of the car and walked toward her, her heart started beating harder. She had no idea how he was going to react to everything and she was nervous. She took him by the hand and led him inside the house.

As she started pointing out the different things she liked, he interrupted. "Mia, what's going on? You were at Elmhurst last I heard and now you're here looking at houses. What happened?"

"I left."

"I can see that, but why? And when?" Nick's dark gaze bore into her.

"I left late last night." Mia headed toward the kitchen. "Can we talk about all that later? I want to show you the rest of the house." As she started to walk away, Nick put his hand on her back and she cried out in pain.

Nick took her by the arm so she couldn't go any further and lifted her coat and blouse. When he saw the marks on her back, he turned livid. "What the hell happened to you? Who did that? Is that why you left Elmhurst? Did Whitaker do that to you?"

"No." Her excitement over the house sank when she realized he wasn't going to take 'later' for an answer. "Dr. Whitaker and I, well, things weren't working and I checked myself out and came to the city. I tried to call you, but you didn't answer. I had no where to go so I spent the night in Holly's apartment—"

Once more Nick lifted her blouse and took a better look at the damage on her back. Mia felt his fury and thought it was directed at her.

"Mia, why would you go there?"

"Don't get mad at me, Nick. I don't think I could take it right now." Tears welled in her eyes and her chin quivered. "I've cut ties with Dr. Whitaker and had a huge falling out with Silviana. I can't go back to my apartment..." Mia took a shaky breath. "I'm trying to move forward. Can't you see? This house could be a new start for me, for us. With all the drama the past few weeks, we haven't spelled it all out, but when you said I wouldn't be sorry if I gave you another chance, I thought that meant..." The look on his face made the words stick in her throat.

Nick didn't respond. He was staring at her like he didn't know who she was.

"I need to know where I stand. I can do this on my own, I think, but I don't want to. I need to know if I am on my own or if we are going to do this together."

He pulled her into his arms, holding her as tight as he could without hurting her. "Mia, I love you and I'm here for you, but you're scaring me." Nick took her by the chin and looked down at her. "Are you healthy enough to be checking yourself out of Elmhurst, because right now I'm having my doubts?"

"I was in a lot better shape when I left there than I am now. The last twenty-four hours have been bad, really bad, but I'm trying to make a new start like Dr. Whitaker told me."

Nick kissed her forehead and held her once more. "If you think this house is the way to start over, then let's have a look."

Mia wrapped her arms around him. "Thank you...thank you."

"Tonight, I want to know exactly what happened, from the minute you got back to Elmhurst to right now, so don't think you're getting out of anything."

Mia walked him through the rest of the house, talking about all the things she wanted to do to fix it up. When they got back downstairs Mia asked him, "How does it feel to you?"

"I don't think anything has been done to this place since 1960 and it's really big."

"I know, but that's not what I need to know. How does it *feel*?"

"Mia, I'm not like you. I don't get impressions about things like that."

Mia took both of his hands in hers. "Close your eyes and tell me what you saw in your mind when we went upstairs?"

"I could picture us waking up on a Sunday morning with the sun coming in the windows."

"Did the room look like it does now?"

"No," Nick thought for a minute. "It was lighter, brighter. The ugly curtains that are on the windows were gone."

"See, it has a good feeling."

"What are we going to do with all those bedrooms?" Nick smiled a naughty smile.

"Well, we either have to have some babies to fill them up, or rent them out."

"This place is going to cost a fortune to fix."

"It's a good thing I have money. We can give it the attention it deserves. That will make her happy."

"The house is a she?" Nick chuckled.

"Not the house, Nora, the last owner. She's embarrassed because the house is in such disrepair."

Nick stopped dead in his tracks. "You mean this place is haunted?"

"Not really. She's just curious as to what we're going to do to it. Nora wants it to be pretty again." Mia could tell that Nick was having doubts. "It's always been this way for me," she tried to reassure him.

"I know, but I'm not used to it yet."

Mia waited, holding her breath, for him to commit, one way or the other.

"Let's go buy a house," he said with a smile.

Levi, Karen, Mr. Reed, and Wayne were waiting in the driveway when they came out.

"What are you asking for the house?" Mia asked.

"One point one million," Karen informed them.

Mia tried not to laugh. "With the extensive repairs it's going to need, you won't be able to get more than eight hundred thousand, and you know it." Turning to Mr. Reed, Mia said, "I will give you eight hundred and fifty thousand, on one condition."

"Which is?" Mr. Reed wanted to know.

"I'll call my attorney and have him transfer the funds to your account today and we can sign papers whenever it is convenient for you. I will also forgo a home inspection, but I want the keys right now. I need to move in as soon as possible and I need to meet with my contractor and architect this afternoon."

"You're paying cash?" Mr. Reed turned to Levi, as if to confirm that it wasn't a joke.

"She always pays cash," Levi confirmed.

Karen started to negotiate, but Mr. Reed interrupted her. "It's a deal." And he handed over the keys.

As Levi, Karen, and Mr. Reed walked away to hammer out the details, Nick leaned closer to Mia and whispered, "I've never seen you as a business woman before. That was impressive."

Wayne laughed. "I can't believe you bought a house just like that. It seems like that's becoming a bad habit with you."

Mia shrugged, choosing to ignore the pointed remark. "I needed a new place to live."

"You're not thinking of staying here tonight, are you?" Nick questioned her.

When she didn't answer right away, he grew irritated. "You are not going back to the loft. If you're not at my place when I get home, I'm going to come looking for you." Nick took out his keys and handed her the key to his apartment. "Remember, we have things to talk about later on." He kissed her on the cheek and left.

Mia made a slew of phone calls starting with Richard, who couldn't decide if he was angry or relieved that she had left Elmhurst. He was irritated she had bought a house in one day without a home inspection, but he was happy that she got it for less than market value. And he definitely wasn't pleased that she was back with Nick.

By seven that night, she was on her way up to Nick's apartment. Her hands were full and straining with the weight of all the stuff she had picked up on the way there.

Mia didn't have a hand to knock with, let alone try the key, so she kicked the door several times. Nick answered and took some of the bags from her.

"I was just calling you. I picked up some Italian."

"Good, I'm starving. I haven't eaten all day." As she said it, Mia realized she really hadn't eaten all day. She was too excited about the house to even think about food.

"What is all that stuff?"

"I bought a new lap top, a printer, a case of paper, extra ink cartridges, and a few other bags of miscellaneous supplies. If there was one thing the loft renovations taught me, it's that Internet access is imperative. We have a million decisions to make before we leave for Oklahoma on Friday night."

"We do?" Nick sounded less than thrilled.

"Yes, we do." Mia set the rest of the bags down and worked the knots out of her fingers. "But first, let's eat."

When they were done, Nick took her hand and led her into the bathroom.

"Now, take off your blouse."

"Excuse me?" That certainly wasn't what she'd expected to hear.

"I want a closer look at those scratches on your back."

Mia unbuttoned her blouse, slipped it off of her shoulders, and then used it to cover her breasts. She was blushing, even though she still had on her bra. Nick turned her toward the light.

"Let's get something on these before they get infected."

Nick pulled out some gauze pads, medical tape, and a bottle of medicine she didn't recognize. He put some on a cotton ball, unhooked her bra with one hand, and started dabbing it on her back.

"Ouch! That hurts," she cried as she watched him in the mirror.

"Cuts usually do."

"What are you putting on them? Kerosene?"

Nick chuckled. "Stop being such a baby."

"This is the twenty-first century, you know. There are medicines that don't sting."

He carefully covered the gouges with the gauze and taped them down. "That should do it."

"Don't think I didn't notice the one-handed bra removal trick."

"I perfected that in high school." He had the gall to wink at her.

Mia groaned and walked away while Nick laughed out loud. Slipping her blouse back on she went into the living room, sat on the couch, and started to set up her computer.

"I have to go back down to my car and get the printer and case of paper."

"First, I want to know why you left Elmhurst." The tone of his voice told Mia that he expected answers.

Her hands froze and she sat still for a minute. "Because… when I told him I was going to Oklahoma with you, he was irritated, and when he thought I wasn't coming back to Elmhurst, his first thought was about the money." She couldn't bring herself to look at him for fear he would see the tears in her eyes.

Nick crouched down next to her. "Just because he thought about money doesn't mean that's all he cares about. When I met him, he seemed genuinely concerned about you."

Mia blinked and the tears slipped down her cheeks. "And when I came to the city I tried to call you, but you didn't answer."

When Nick saw that she was getting upset, he sat down next to her and pulled her into his lap. "I know. I'm sorry. We got called out on a case right at quitting time. I didn't get home until two-thirty this morning. That's when I saw the missed calls, but I figured you were asleep by then. I'm sorry, babe. Everything in this apartment is yours from now on, okay?"

She nodded.

"Now, tell me what happened in Holly's apartment?"

"Oh, Nick, it was awful. The worst it's ever been. I had this dream, only it wasn't a dream. I heard you calling me from far away. It was so dark and I kept walking down the hallway at the apartment, but it never ended. And then, I saw you, only I couldn't see your face. You put the necklace on me and told me to say that I belonged to you. Then, you put the other piece of the necklace in my hand and put your hands on my shoulders. That's when I wanted to say I belonged to you, but some how my subconscious mind knew it wasn't you and what came out was, 'I will never be yours'.

"He transformed right before my eyes into this inhuman creature and he was consumed by rage. He dug his claws into my back and I ran. When I woke up I still had the necklace on and the other piece in my hand. I was so scared. I thought Silviana would know what to do, but all she cared about was manipulating me for more money. Even after I told her what had happened. She didn't care, just like the rest of my family. I wish I had been born poor." The tears ran down her cheeks

Nick tucked her head under his chin. "Don't say that. Your money is a blessing."

"How can you say that? It has brought me nothing, but trouble."

"It's a blessing because of what you do with it."

Mia leaned back enough to see his face. "What do you mean?"

"You bought Wayne and Kathy a house. Now, they have no mortgage. Wayne told me today that Kathy has cut back her hours at the hospital and when their baby's born, she is going to get to be a stay at home mom. You helped that family whose son died of cancer. And what about all the ex-cons you have on the payroll. Those are only the situations I know about. I have a feeling you have been doing good deeds for people all along. So, your money is a blessing."

Mia let his words sink in.

"Don't forget, you also bought a house today, which is a blessing, isn't it?"

"It's not just *a* house, Nick." Mia couldn't stop the smile from returning to her lips. "It's *the* house. It has everything, at least it will when I'm through with it. It's going to be the place where we live our lives."

"Including a studio for your art?" He waited for her to respond. "Mia?"

Mia thought about it. "I know what you're saying, but the way I'm looking at it right now, the house is my blank canvas." She looked at Nick and smiled. "Speaking of the house, do you want to see some of the drawings I worked on with Robert?"

"Who's Robert?"

"My architect. He came to the house today, after you left. So did Jerry, my contractor. They helped me convert the loft, from the empty shell that it was, to what it is today. When I call, they come, because they know I mean business. I have so many plans for the house..." Mia stopped for a moment, "I mean, if you like the plans that we sketched."

"As far as I'm concerned, you can do whatever you want and I'll love it.

"I'm so glad you love me." Mia held onto him tightly, her heart healing a little bit more.

CHAPTER THIRTY-FIVE

Nick woke up alone in bed. The clock read two-fifteen. He wandered into the living room where Mia was asleep on the couch with pile of papers resting on her chest. Her head was turned to the side and her dark brown hair lay across her face. She looked so young when she slept, and innocent. Not at all like someone who has a demon after her.

He deserved an Academy Award for pretending to stay calm while she'd told him all about it, when inside he'd wanted to rush over to Holly's apartment and call the demon out. If he could make that thing mad enough, maybe it would come after him instead of Mia.

Nick slipped the papers out of her hands and looked through them. Picture after picture of kitchen cabinets, tile and furniture, it looked like she was organizing the entire house remodeling project in one night.

It made him happy to see her enthusiastic about something, but he had no illusions about her depression being a thing of the past. He had watched his mother suffer with it for years before her death. Of course, he didn't know what it was at the time. He'd only grown to understand it as a man.

"Mia," he whispered, trying not to startle her. "Mia, you need to come to bed."

She opened her eyes and looked around, confused for a moment as to where she was. "What time is it?"

"It's after two in the morning."

"You should be sleeping," she murmured.

"I was, but I sleep better with you next to me. So, come on."

Mia smiled a sleepy little smile that made his heart do something funny in his chest. He held out his hand to help her to her feet and she staggered into the bedroom, plopping down like she was exhausted. He covered her up and made his way to his side of the bed. Nick turned out the light and held her close.

When he heard the quiet rhythm of her breathing and knew she had gone back to sleep, he whispered into her hair, "I'll watch over you, babe. I won't let him hurt you."

When Nick woke up, Mia was already in the shower. It was only a minute or two before the water shut off. She must have gotten up early. When she came out of the bathroom, she was already dressed, but she still had wet hair.

"You can get in now. I'll dry my hair out here."

"Why are you up so early?" he asked, trying to stifle a yawn.

"I have to be at the house when the workers get there. I don't want them knocking down the wrong walls."

"You're knocking down walls?"

Mia laughed. "That's just the beginning. The entire heating and air conditioning system needs replacing and so does the plumbing. I don't want to have to tear the house apart again later, so it's easier to do it all at once. The kitchen has to be gutted and reconfigured and all the bathrooms are over fifty years old."

"I can't even imagine how much this is going to cost."

"I'll find out today. Jerry should have some of the estimates done by now. Robert started working on the plans last night. He emailed me some of the rough drafts. Do you want to see?"

"You'll have to show me tonight. You know how Wayne is if I'm late."

Nick was half way to the bathroom when she asked, "Do you have a crock pot?"

"A what?"

"A crock pot. It's a kitchen appliance that you put food in in the morning, turn it on, and at night it's done."

"I think so. It would be in the kitchen on the bottom shelf of the pantry," Nick told her.

When he was ready to leave, Mia was sitting on the couch with the computer on her lap. She had set up her office right on the coffee table, which was now missing in action. It had to be under there somewhere, but he couldn't even see the legs with all the stuff she had piled everywhere.

Mia saw him staring at it all. "Is it okay if I have all this stuff here?"

Nick leaned down and kissed her softly on the lips. "Mi casa es su casa. Did you find the crock pot?"

"You don't have one." Mia laughed. "What you have is a bread maker."

Nick shrugged. "Someone gave it to me as a gift. I've never used it."

"I know. That's okay. I've got to go shopping today anyway, so I'll pick one up."

Nick was on his way out the door when he turned back to her. "By the way, where's your engagement ring?"

Mia's smiled faded quickly. "It's in the basement at the loft. There were a few bins of personal things I left there. Why?"

"I'm glad you didn't give that to charity."

"I'd never part with that." Mia grinned. "Have a good day."

"I'll call you later," Nick told her as he left.

***

Nick and Wayne spent the day running all over the city, trying to tie up loose ends on several different cases. Next week, when he got back from Oklahoma, he and Wayne were going to be spending most of the week in court, so they had a list of things to get done before then.

They were on their way back to the station when Wayne's phone rang. He dug it out of his pocket and glanced at the caller ID.

"It's Kathy," he told Nick as he answered. "Hello."

Nick could hear the hum of Kathy's voice through the phone. She was talking non-stop.

When Wayne didn't say a word for several minutes, Nick looked at him questioningly.

Finally, Wayne said, "I'm glad you had so much fun. Don't get any more ideas."

Kathy was once again speed talking, causing Wayne to roll his eyes. Nick tried not to laugh too loud.

"Okay, I'll see you when I get home." Wayne hung up and chuckled.

"What was that all about?" Nick asked.

"Apparently, Kathy went over to your new house today to see it. Mia invited her to go shopping. Now, Kathy is having a meltdown because Mia spent like a hundred thousand dollars in one day."

"What?"

"They started with kitchen cabinets, worked their way through all the appliances, and ended the day with furniture. And somewhere in there, she said something about a fireplace. Kathy is so excited. I think she may have a stroke before I get home." Wayne paused for a minute. "I think Mia is a bad influence."

"Why?" Nick was laughing out loud now.

"How am I supposed to keep up with Mia's money? Now that I gave in on the house, Kathy wants all new furniture. She says she's not taking any of our old stuff into the new house, including my favorite sofa."

"That green thing?"

"Yeah." Wayne's tone was defensive.

"I don't blame her. That is one ugly couch." Nick laughed.

"Whose side are you on?"

"Yours, except when it comes to that couch." Nick needled him some more.

"Laugh if you want to. You'll come to appreciate a comfortable couch when you've been married for a few years."

Nick decided not to comment on that remark, but he couldn't stop laughing.

When they got back to the station, Wayne got out of the car. "All kidding aside, I'm glad you and Mia worked it out. You're not such a hard ass anymore."

Nick was surprised that Wayne could see the difference in him. He hadn't realized it was so obvious to others. "I'll see you tomorrow." Nick pulled away and headed to Mia's apartment. He wanted to find Mia's engagement ring and ask her to marry him again. Only this time, he was going to do it right. The first time in the park, he hadn't thought it through. The words had just seemed to come out before he could stop them. Looking back now, he was only sorry he hadn't planned it out and made it more romantic. He'd make it special this time.

He pulled up in front of the building and wondered if the doorman would object to him going through Mia's things.

Luckily, Carl was sitting at the desk. "Don't you ever go home?" Nick asked.

Carl laughed. "I'm the go to man when someone is sick, or just doesn't want to work. I take home a nice fat paycheck thanks to Miss Carrigan." Carl glanced past Nick, looking for his boss.

"She's not here. I need to get something for her. She said it's with some stuff she stored in the basement. Can you show me how to get down there?"

Carl nodded and took Nick to a door that he opened. It was like taking a trip back in time. The outside lobby was clean, modern, and updated, but when Nick stepped through the door, it was all old wood and brick. The lighting was dim and there was a feeling of dampness all around.

"To the left you'll find a staircase that will take you to the bottom. The light switch will be on the right when you get down there."

"You're not coming with me?" Nick questioned the man.

"I don't go in the basement and I don't go to the fourth floor unless I have to. They both give me the creeps."

"Thanks," Nick mumbled as he started down the tight staircase.

When he got to the bottom, he could barely see his hand in front of his face, let alone a light switch. He reached out and skimmed the cold, rough brick until he finally found it.

The light didn't make the place much more welcoming. There were metal drums here and there with the remnants of some of the construction still evident. One was filled with bricks. Another was filled with stuff that must have been left in the building when Mia first bought it, rusted pieces of machinery and a length of iron chain that was as thick as Nick's wrist. There were several sets of tall cabinets with peeling paint. Each cabinet had a number on it. The workers must have used them like lockers. Everything in the basement was old, and not in a cool, antique kind of way.

The basement smelled musty, as if it hadn't had a breath of fresh air in decades. In the corner Nick spotted some plastic bins. They had to be Mia's. He opened the first bin and found the baby clothes Mia'd had hidden away in her apartment. He stuck his hand inside the bin and searched for anything that felt like it might hold jewelry. Nothing but fabric touched his skin.

He moved onto the next bin and opened it. Mia's camera equipment was inside, along with stacks of pictures she had taken. There were a few letters and some old diaries from when she was a little girl. One had a pink bunny on it.

A loud bang from the top of the staircase made Nick jump.

"Hello? Is someone there? Carl?"

As Nick took a few steps toward the stairs, an ice cold pocket of air surrounded him and he had the feeling he wasn't alone. His heart started beating harder and the hair on the back of his neck stood up.

Not again, he thought.

He needed to find the ring and get the hell out of there. The next bin had some canvases in it and that was it. From behind him he heard the creaking of someone on the steps. Someone or something was watching him. He was sure of it. Nick didn't turn around. He didn't want to see whatever was there.

With shaking hands, he crouched down and opened the next bin. Inside were all kinds of little things, boxes with perfume inside, and some of Mia's ice skating awards. Nick pushed the things around, feeling for the ring case. At the very bottom, in the corner, his fingertips touched something velvety and square.

As he grasped it, a voice whispered right next to his ear, "Mine."

Nick jumped up and was ready to fight. He turned one way and then the other. Beads of perspiration ran down his temples, his fists clenched. All of his senses strained to see or hear anything that meant him harm. He had never wanted to get out of a place more than he wanted to leave that basement, but he had to make sure this case had the ring first.

He opened the velvet box. Mia's mother's ring caught the light and winked at him.

Nick snapped the case closed and shoved it in his pants pocket, put the lid back on the bin, and was headed toward the stairs. The light bulb popped and he was in pitch blackness. It was no accident and Nick knew it. He could feel something moving around him, faster and faster, the ice cold air swirling. He gasped for breath, as the dust and dirt of past decades choked him. All the air was being sucked out of his lungs.

He tried to move to the stairs only to find the cold brick wall where the stairs should have been. He staggered to the left and to the right. No wooden railing met his grasp. Nick wondered if he was still in the basement at all or if he was in some other place. It felt like he was on a ship in rough seas, swaying one way and then the other.

Nick knew he was in trouble. He couldn't fight back with his fists. He had to fight back with something much deeper. He slammed into the wall on the right. Leaning on it for strength, he steadied himself and tried to mentally fight against the wind. In his mind, he pictured himself pushing against it, corralling it, controlling it, and finally calming it.

When he opened his eyes, he could see the light from the top of the stairs. After dragging several deep gulps of air into his chest, he stumbled to the steps. He was half way up when he stopped and peered back into the dark and dreary, crypt-like room. In the back corner was a shapeless figure, hovering in the air with two red, glowing eyes staring at him. Nick blinked several times to make sure he wasn't imagining it. He knew it was Man when the waves of fury radiating off of the demon washed over him. Man's one word, whispered so quietly into his ear, rang in Nick's mind.

"She will never be yours," Nick snarled. With that, he took the steps two at a time and slammed the door behind him.

An unholy and inhuman screeching sound, long and loud, resonated through the lobby.

Carl came running from the front desk. "What the hell was that?" When Carl saw Nick, he stepped back in shock. "What happened to you? Are you okay?"

Nick was still so shaken he wasn't sure how he should answer Carl's question. So, he just said, "I'd stay out of the basement if I were you."

Carl nodded. His face lost all color.

When Nick saw his face in his car's rear view mirror, he knew why Carl had looked so scared. He was covered in dust. Running his fingers through his hair, a smoky cloud fell and settled on his suit jacket. It was a good thing it was one of his old ones and not one of the expensive suits that Mia had bought for him.

His hands were still a bit shaky when he got home. Thankfully, Mia hadn't gotten there yet and he had time to shower and change into clean clothes. He'd also had time to make a few phone calls and put his plan into action. After going through hell to get the ring, he wasn't going to wait to get it back on her finger.

He heard several thuds on the front door. When he opened it, Mia staggered in with her hands full of packages, just like the night before.

"You're home." She smiled as he took the bags from her hands. "How was your day?" When her hands were empty she threw her arms around his neck and hugged him tightly.

Nick slipped his hands around her waist and he held her close. It was comforting, after the day he'd had. Her hug made all the drama and fear worth it.

"I was hoping to get home before you, so I could make us some dinner." Mia pulled away enough that he could see the smile on her face.

"Forget cooking, I have something planned. Go change or whatever you need to do, just be ready to leave in twenty minutes." Nick couldn't stop the smile from growing on his face.

"Twenty minutes! You don't give a girl a lot of time. I still have some bags in the car I need to bring up."

"We'll bring them up later, hurry." Nick pushed her toward the bedroom.

***

"Where are we going and why are you being so secretive?" Mia asked with a grin on her face.

"It's a surprise. You're sure in a good mood tonight."

"I always feel happy when I get a lot accomplished and today was one of those days." Mia grinned, obviously pleased with herself.

"So I heard. Kathy called Wayne on a shopping high."

Mia laughed out loud. "I think I'll take her shopping with me all the time. It's way more fun spending money with a friend."

"I'm glad you two get along so well. I think we'll be seeing them more often once we move into the house. It's only about fifteen minutes from theirs."

As Nick found a parking space, as close to the Central Park Ice Skating Rink as he could, Mia turned to him, "Are we going ice skating?"

"We can if you want to."

He helped her out of the car and found a bench as close to the original spot he'd proposed as he could. Taking Mia's hand in his he sat down next to her. It was funny how he was feeling nervous now, even though they had already talked about living in the house and making a life together. There was just something about having the ring in hand that made a man's anxiety level go up.

"I wanted to bring you here for two reasons," Nick said. The first is to thank you for giving me a chance to redeem myself after being such a jerk." Mia's eyes closed for a moment and Nick knew she still felt pain from memories of that night. When she opened her eyes once more, Nick took the ring case out of his pocket and opened it, so she could see what was in it. He got down on one knee in the middle of the park, with people walking by every few minutes. "The second is, will you marry me and be my wife forever?"

"How did you get the ring?" Mia's smile faded.

"I went to the apartment, into the basement, and searched through your things until I found it." Nick could see by the expression on her face that she knew exactly what that had entailed. "It's okay. I got out alive, though he didn't like it much."

"That doesn't make you question your judgment in asking me to marry you?"

Nick hesitated for a minute. "In my head, I know it should make a difference, but in my heart I know you're the best thing that has ever happened to me. That's such a cliché, I know, but I've come to accept all of that stuff as being a part of loving you. And, I don't ever want to be away from you again. It was a lifetime in hell condensed into two weeks. Never again. I figure the best way to keep you by my side, is to make you my wife. So, will you marry me?"

"I would be honored." Mia blinked back tears and after Nick put the ring on her finger, without waiting for him to stand up, she wrapped her arms around his neck for the second time that night. "I love you."

"I love you, too." He held her tight. "I have another surprise for you. I planned a special dinner."

When they got to the restaurant, they were led to a back booth. On the table, Nick was relieved to see that the bouquet of red roses he'd ordered had arrived and was in place.

"The flowers are beautiful," Mia commented as she smelled them and smiled.

The prime rib dinner went beautifully and Mia chatted about all the things she had bought that day for the house.

"So, what do you think?" she asked excitedly.

"It's up to you. It's your house." The minute the words were out of his mouth he had this strange ache in his chest.

Mia took a sip of her water and started to get up from the table.

"Where are you going?"

"To the ladies room."

Nick sat at the table alone, trying to figure out what was going on. He had never felt this way before. There was this weird sinking sensation in his gut.

"Will there be anything else, sir?" The waiter asked as he set the bill on the table.

"No, we're good." Nick slid his credit card into the black check holder and nodded to the waiter. When the waiter returned with his credit card and Mia still wasn't back, he started to get worried. After scribbling his name on the receipt, he got up and headed for the ladies room.

He knocked on the door, but got no response. He pushed the door open a few inches and called her name. "Mia, are you okay?"

"You're not supposed to come into the ladies room."

He opened the door wider and saw her standing at the sink.

"Technically, I'm not *in* the ladies room. I'm still outside the door."

When she turned around, Nick could tell she'd been crying. His cocky attitude changed instantly into one of concern. "Babe, what's wrong?"

"I need to go home."

"Let's go. I already paid the bill. I'll grab your flowers and meet you in front."

Nick handed Mia her roses as they walked to the car. "Why are you crying? What's wrong?"

Mia just shook her head.

Nick took her by the arm and made her face him. "Please talk to me."

"You wouldn't understand. It's stupid and childish and I don't want to talk about it."

"I don't care if it's stupid and childish. If you're upset, I need to know why."

In the glow of the street lights, he could see tears pooling in her brown eyes and her chin quivering. She blinked and the tears that were waiting there rolled down her cheeks. He had the feeling she was trying to work up the courage, so he gave her all the time she needed.

"When you said that the house was mine…it hurt me. Even though I know you didn't mean it the way it sounded. My stomach just sank. I can't help the way I feel sometimes. I'm trying. I really am. It's just that my emotions are so hard to control."

Nick listened to every word, silently cursing himself for being such an idiot. "I didn't mean it like that, Mia. I swear."

"I know. But I've been alone for so long the thought of living in the house by myself…" Mia shook her head. "It scared me, a lot. I bought the house for us. It's supposed to be *our* home. Without you, it's just a roof and some walls," Mia scoffed. "This all makes me sound like someone who's very needy and pathetic doesn't it?"

"It makes you sound like a human being. I'm sorry I hurt your feelings. I wish I could say it won't happen again, but it will and I won't mean it then, either."

Mia studied him and a grin broke out on her pretty little face. She must have known he meant it.

"Let's go home," she said quietly.

"Mia, when you said your emotions are hard to control, it made me wonder if you're taking your medicine?" Nick asked her once they were in the car.

Mia kept looking out the car window.

"Mia?"

"Dr. Whitaker and I didn't part on the best of terms, asking him to refill my prescriptions, as I was leaving, didn't seem appropriate."

"I'm not an expert, but even I know you're not supposed to stop taking anti-depressants cold turkey. We have to do something about this tomorrow. I don't want you to suffer like this needlessly."

They rode the elevator in silence until they got to Nick's floor. When it stopped, his stomach grew tense and once again that awful sinking feeling overcame him. *What the hell,* he thought. *That's twice in one night.*

Mia's gaze was suddenly drawn to the closed doors. "Oh, no."

"What? What's wrong?"

"I don't want to do this now."

"Do what?" he asked as the doors opened.

In the hallway, outside of his apartment door, was Dr. Whitaker.

Mia made no attempt to move until Nick put his hand to the small of her back and gently forced her down the hall.

"I apologize for showing up on your doorstep unannounced, Detective, but I have been trying to get a hold of Mia since she left Elmhurst, with no response."

"That's okay. Would you like to come in?" Mia shot him a look that told him she was not pleased.

"Yes. I won't stay long."

"We were just talking about you."

"Well, then maybe it was meant to be," Dr. Whitaker said as he walked inside. "I'll make this quick, since it's late. I have this for you, Mia." He reached into his coat pocket and pulled out an envelope. "Inside you will find a refund check for the overpayment on your account. I'm not sure why you left so abruptly, but I suspect it has something to do with money and I just wanted to tell you in person that whatever upset you, was not intentional. I have been worried about you and your health. Have you been taking your meds?"

"No," Mia replied.

"I was afraid of that." Dr. Whitaker reached into his pocket and took out two pill bottles. "There are three refills available on both. If you need more later, please call me."

Mia took the medicines from him, but said nothing.

"I'll be leaving now," Dr. Whitaker said to Nick. "Sorry to interrupt your evening."

Dr. Whitaker was half way out the door when Mia called him back. "Dr. Whitaker?"

The man stopped and looked at her. "Yes?"

"Thank you. It was kind of you to come all this way just for this."

"You're welcome. You know you can call me, if you need me."

Mia looked relieved. "I know."

When the doctor was gone, Nick put his arms around her. "You're feeling happy right now, aren't you? Happy and a little shaky."

"Yes."

"And, at the restaurant, when I said the house is yours, you had this sick sinking feeling in your stomach, didn't you?"

"How did you know that?" Mia had a concerned, yet knowing expression on her face.

"It's the strangest thing. All night I've been having the oddest feelings and I think they are coming from you."

Mia didn't say anything, but her Mona Lisa smile made an appearance.

"You're not surprised, are you?" Nick needed an explanation.

"It was the same way between my mother and my father. He knew instantly if she was upset, or scared, or angry. She said it was because they knew each other's souls."

"So, now I'll feel all of your emotions?"

Mia laughed. "You're gonna love it when I have PMS."

"Oh, man. I didn't sign up for this. That's something I only want to observe from far away." Nick shook his head, but he couldn't help joining Mia in her laughter.

"Don't worry, you won't have PMS, you'll just sense how I am feeling at the moment. Think of it like checking the weather. If it's sunny and warm, it's all good, but if it's stormy with thunder and lightning, duck and cover."

Nick couldn't tell if she was kidding or not and at that moment he didn't want to know. "Let's go to bed. I'm going to need some time to think this over."

Mia just giggled.

CHAPTER THIRTY-SIX

The week was gone before Mia knew it. She spent all day, every day, at the house making sure things got done the way she wanted them, and Nick worked overtime every night. They got home exhausted and ate whatever Mia had put into the crock pot that morning.

They were packed and ready when Friday afternoon came. As they sat on the airplane, waiting for take off, Mia stared out the window. She was so nervous.

The engines whined as they taxied down the runway. The louder and faster they went, the more fearful Mia became. Bad memories came into her mind of loud explosions, fire, and screaming.

Nick took her hand, leaned over, and said into her ear, "It's going to be okay."

"Every time I do this, I remember my parents." She tried to smile, but couldn't.

"I know." Nick pressed her fingers to his lips and kissed them.

Once they landed, they got their rental car and were headed to Nick's grandparent's house.

As they drove onto the reservation, Mia stared out the window, barely noticing that while some of the houses were well tended, many weren't. There were rusted out old cars and washing machines sitting in front yards and dogs chained to trees. It was nothing like the world she had grown up in, but that wasn't what was foremost on her mind. "Do you think your family will like me, or were they hoping you would marry an Indian girl?"

Nick chuckled to himself. "They'll like you because you're you."

Mia didn't say anything, but she wasn't reassured. She had so much on her mind, including the house and the board of directors meeting. She was waiting for word from Richard about what he'd been able to find out. It all weighed on her mind and now she had the added stress of meeting Nick's family.

When they turned down his grandparent's street, Nick pointed to all the cars in the driveway and spilling out into the street. "It looks like the whole family is here to meet you."

Mia sighed. As much as she wanted to meet Nick's family, she was wondering if she had made a huge mistake in the timing. Her palms were sweating and her heart was pounding.

Nick helped her out of the car. "Don't be so nervous. It'll be okay."

As they walked through the door, a cry went up from all of his relatives. Mia watched as one after another hugged him, punched him, or chastised him for staying away so long. She didn't count, but with all the kids running around, there must have been thirty people crowded into the small house, not that anyone seemed to mind.

He introduced her to everyone, except his grandfather and grandmother, who were nowhere to be found. Mia knew it would take much longer than the weekend to remember all their names, let alone get to know them.

"Where is Grandfather?" Nick questioned his cousin, who she thought was called Joe.

"He's taking care of Grandmother. She's been sick." As Joe finished speaking, an older man came out of the bedroom.

He didn't look at all like she'd expected. His short hair was white with age, and his face was deeply lined, but his eyes were those of a much younger man who saw everything. The house went silent as everyone waited to hear what he would say to her. Without a word, the older man came to Mia and took her hand. She wanted to be witty and charming, but she said nothing as he laid his other hand on top of the one he already held. For a full minute, it was as if they took inventory of each other's souls.

The emotions flew between them like leaves in a whirlwind, love, loneliness, pride, devotion, helplessness, joy, ambition, despair, vulnerability, gratitude, acceptance and hope, along with many others and some so complex there were no words for them. Mia had never experienced anything like it in her life. It made her feel exposed and naked and yet, she knew she was safe.

Mia placed her hand over his. His knowledge and power were pure, strong, and uncorrupted. She couldn't help the sadness that came to her when she realized this was how it should have been with Silviana and Mirella, but it never would be. Her money would always be their first desire.

He gently let go of her hands, took her by the shoulders, and kissed her cheek. "Welcome home, granddaughter."

His words touched her deeply. Tears filled her eyes and she was afraid she was going to embarrass herself by crying like a baby. Mia felt love and acceptance surround her in a way she hadn't since her parents had died, so long ago. And oh, how she'd hungered for it.

Nick came and put his arm around her and tucked her close to him.

The older man put his hand on Nick's shoulder. "She's too good for you."

That broke the ice. All of Nick's family hooted, hollered, and laughed.

"I know that already, Grandfather. You don't have to tell me." Nick squeezed her shoulder once more.

"It's good to have you home, Nick."

"It's good to be here." The two men embraced.

"You should go see your grandmother and introduce her to Mia."

Mia was more relaxed, now that his grandfather had been so kind. Nick led her to a bedroom in the back of the house that was the size of their closet in the new house.

In the bed, an old woman dozed. When they walked in, she woke up and squinted to see who was there. "Osiyo, Nick? Oh, Nick. You've come home." She appeared much older than her husband.

"That means, hello," he whispered to Mia as he went to his grandmother's bedside and hugged her.

Mia knew his grandmother didn't have much time left in this world. "

"I'm so happy to see you. I've missed you so much. You've been away too long." There was no attempt to make Nick feel guilty in her words. They were her honest feelings.

"I know, Grandmother. I'm sorry. I should've come home to visit sooner." Nick glanced at Mia and held out his hand to her.

"I want you to meet Mia. She's going to be my wife. Mia, this is my grandmother, Josie."

"Come closer so I can see you. My eyes are bad from the diabetes." She shifted in her bed.

Mia moved closer. Nick grabbed a chair from the corner of the room and brought it to her, so she could be more comfortable.

"Your name is Mia? I like that." She shooed at Nick with her hand. "You go be with the others while Mia and I get to know each other."

Nick glanced at Mia with raised eyebrows, as if to ask if it was okay. Mia nodded.

When the door shut behind him, his grandmother wasted no time. "You're going to marry Nick?"

"Yes."

"Tell me what it is about my Nick that you love."

So many thoughts went through her head at once she didn't know what to say. The old woman was looking for something specific, Mia could feel it. She just wasn't sure what it was.

"There are so many things to love about Nick. When I first met him, I knew he was different from most men. He was sure of himself, almost cocky, but still kind. He loves his work. He's a loyal friend."

The old woman waved her hand. "You are talking about a dog. Tell me about Nick."

"Okay," Mia made a mental list of all of his qualities, good and bad. "Nick works twice as hard as anyone else to prove to them that he is as good at his job as they are. On the outside, he can seem jaded and uncaring, but he's not. He can be hard-headed, stubborn and rash. He's not quick tempered, but once he's mad, he has to work to keep his temper under control. He also likes to be doted on. If he feels like the center of my world, it makes him feel important and needed."

Josie pursed her lips and then laughed out loud. "You know him pretty well. Franklin told me you did. It's important to see the flaws before you are married and then to ignore them afterward."

Mia made a mental note to remember that piece of advice.

"You have opened his heart. It has been closed to us for a long time. Thank you for bringing him home, even if it is only for a few days."

Mia thought about telling her that coming home was Nick's idea, but she didn't think it would matter to her. "You're welcome."

"Go now and be with my Nick. I need to rest." An old wrinkled hand reached out and patted hers.

As Mia got up to leave, the hand tightened. "You'll take care of him for me, Mia?" Tears shone in her eyes. She knew she was dying.

"I will, for the rest of my life." Mia touched her hand. "Though he hasn't been home for a long time, Nick has carried all of you in his heart. He was a part of you, even when he didn't want to be."

"You *do* see him for who he is."

"Yes," Mia knew she had given her peace of mind. The calmness the old woman felt flowed into her.

The rest of the evening was spent getting to know Nick's family. His Aunt Ruby was a character, her laugh infectious. All of his male cousins were friendly, but didn't pay her much attention beyond the occasional glance. His female cousins, however, asked her a million questions. They started out wanting to know how she and Nick met, how Nick could afford her engagement ring on a cop's salary, when they were getting married, and then moved on to how many children she wanted.

His cousin, Tawna, let Mia hold her new baby boy, Franklin. The baby had a mop of black hair with black eyes to match. He lay in Mia's arms and stared at her with a wrinkled brow, as if he were trying to figure out who she was, and then he smiled. She was smitten in seconds.

Nick came to her and took the baby's tiny hand in his big fingers. "Hey, little man. I haven't met you yet."

"He's beautiful, isn't he?" Mia asked him.

"Yes, he is." Nick smiled as if he knew what was in her heart.

Mia touched the baby's silky cheek. "I want one."

"I think we should get married first, don't you?" Nick chuckled quietly.

"One might not be enough."

His eyebrows shot up. "Just how many are you thinking?"

He was amused. Mia could see laughter in his black eyes. "One for each day of the week."

"I think we should have one or two and see how we feel." He leaned down and whispered in her ear, "That doesn't mean we can't practice making them."

Mia tried to hide her grin as her face turned pink and hot. She held onto the baby until he got fussy and needed his mama. Everything about him intrigued her, from his baby smell to his drooly smile. It was hard to hand him back.

Later that night, when they were in their hotel room, Mia had just finished brushing her teeth. Through the crack in the bathroom door she observed Nick as he leaned against the headboard and stared at the TV, remote in hand, and channel surfed. His black hair was due for a haircut and his skin seemed even darker against the white sheets.

After watching him with his nieces and nephews all day, Mia was sure he was going to make a great father. She could picture his smile as he held their first baby in his arms. It made her heart beat faster just thinking about it. She wondered what it would be like making that baby.

When she climbed into bed, she slid over and pressed the full length of her body against his, her head resting on his chest. His arm went around her. He didn't take his gaze from the glare of the screen until he felt her hand skimming across his bare belly, slowly moving lower and lower.

"I know what you're up to and it's not going to work." He told her as he tossed the remote and slid down until they were face to face.

Mia feigned innocence. "What are you talking about?"

"You held the baby today and now your baby hungry, big time."

Mia pushed against his chest and cried, "I am not."

Nick chuckled, but didn't say anything more.

Mia could feel the warmth of his breath on her neck and it made her wonder. "Haven't you even been tempted to make love to me? We've been sleeping in the same bed for over a week."

Nick was quiet for a moment. "Yes, but all my life I've been a leap first and ask questions later kind of guy and it has come back to haunt me. I don't want to make that mistake with you. I want to do it the right way. You told me once that I would know when the time was right. It's getting close, but it's not tonight." Nick gave her bottom a light pinch. "Don't think it hasn't taken Herculean strength to keep my hands off of you though. I even dream about it."

"You do?" Mia was intrigued.

"Yeah, and it's always the same dream. I'm in this room with huge windows—"

"Stop! Don't tell me anymore." Mia clamped her hand over his mouth.

"Why not?" he mumbled through her fingers.

"I have my reasons. Please," Mia pleaded.

"Okay." Nick wore a confused expression on his face.

"Besides, it's not easy for me either, you know."

Nick nibbled on her neck and then kissed the same spot. "At

least I'm not suffering alone."

She rolled into her usual sleeping position, her back against his chest. "Go to sleep, Nick or all your good intentions are going to be in trouble."

He held her so tight, that when he laughed she could feel the vibrations of it go all the way through her. Mia fell asleep with a smile on her face.

They spent all day Saturday with his family at his grandparent's house. Sunday morning they drove out to say goodbye before heading to the airport. Most of his cousins stopped by for a quick farewell and then made Nick promise to come home for a visit again soon.

Nick and his grandfather went outside to walk his cousin Joe and his family to their car. Long after Mia had heard the car drive off, neither of them had returned to the house. Out of curiosity, Mia peeked through the lace curtains. Nick and his grandfather were nowhere to be seen.

She knew he hadn't gone far because she could feel his presence. It was more than an hour before they came back into the house.

"Mia, we have to get going." Nick's face looked ashen.

"What's wrong?"

"We're running late. Let's go," he answered too quickly.

They said goodbye to his grandmother, who hadn't left her bed since they'd arrived and Mia watched Nick embrace his grandfather. "I'll call more often. I promise."

As they drove down the road, Nick remained silent. Mia sensed the turmoil, but didn't ask again what was wrong. When, and if, he wanted to tell her, he would. She had to give him the space he needed.

Dark clouds rolled across the sky all around them. In the distance, Mia could see the clouds had unleashed the rain and it was pouring. If they hit thunderstorms, it may make them late for their flight.

Without saying a word, Nick jerked the wheel to the right, pulled off to the side of the road, and stopped. His hands gripped the wheel so hard his knuckles were white.

Mia looked at the open highway ahead of them, not another car insight. Behind them it was the same. They were the only travelers on the road, at least for now.

"My grandfather wanted me to thank you for bringing me back home to them."

"I didn't do that, you did."

Nick turned to her for the first time since he'd stopped the car. "No, Mia, it's all you. If I hadn't met you, I would never have come back here. My grandmother would have died without ever having seen me again." Nick's voice was choked with emotion.

Mia could feel his regret and guilt. She didn't know what to say, so she put her hand on his arm and tried to comfort him.

"I didn't want to be an old man who hadn't lived a life worth anything. There was so much I wanted to see and do and none of it included following in my grandfather's footsteps. I saw him as a man who lived in the past at best, and was a little crazy at worst. I thought he had wasted his life staying here, but I was wrong. I see that now, thanks to you. I ignored all the things my grandfather tried to teach me about his spirituality, but I can't ignore them anymore. You've shown me that there are things beyond ourselves, beyond what we can see and touch.

"I thought of my family as a burden. Then I saw how horrible it was for you to not even have people worth calling family…" Nick choked out his next few words and tears ran down his face. "I abandoned my own family. And I almost ruined everything I had with you because of my being a… a…"

"A human being," Mia offered. "One who makes mistakes?"

Nick turned away from her and stared out his window. "I'm so ashamed of what I've done and how I've treated the people around me who just wanted me to love them back."

Mia took off her seat belt, spun in her seat, and with her knees on the rental car's center consul, took his face in her hands. He wouldn't look at her at first. Then, he let her turn his face to hers.

"Your family loves you. Surely, you can see that. You can make it up to them for the past. It's not too late. Nothing is unforgivable with them, or me."

Nick took a minute to think over what she'd said, "Mia?" he pressed his forehead against hers. "Would you marry me?"

"Yes."

"Would you still marry me if I changed my name back to Whitecloud?"

"Mia Ileana Carrigan Whitecloud. It has a ring to it, I think."

Nick laughed with relief. "Promise me, if I ever do something stupid, or come close to ruining what we have, that you'll tell me."

"You won't. I won't let you." Mia kissed him softly on the lips.

The taste of him always made her heart beat faster. He kissed her back. With his teeth he tugged on her lower lip, his tongue caressing hers until she was breathless. They had never kissed so passionately or with such hunger before. She wanted more of him, but she knew this wasn't the time or the place.

"Shouldn't we get to the airport?" Mia managed to gasp out the words.

Nick's dazed expression snapped back to reality when her words broke through the fog. "Oh, crap. Our flight! We're going to miss our flight."

Mia sat back in her seat.

"Put your seat belt on! This is going to be one crazy ride!" The dirt and rocks flew as he pulled out.

They made their flight only because it had been delayed thirty minutes.

Mia held Nick's hand so tight her fingers went numb. She didn't let go until they were on the ground in New York. Another hour went by before they got their luggage and were out of the airport.

"I want to stop by the house," Mia said, knowing it wouldn't be high on Nick's list of things to do.

"Are you serious? It'll be another two hours before we get home and I have to work tomorrow."

"Please? It's important. There's something I want to show you."

He studied her closely and then relented. "Okay, if it's *that* important."

When they stopped in the driveway, Mia hoped and prayed that Jerry had been able to do all that he had promised. She unlocked the door and Nick walked in and immediately headed toward what used to be the dining room.

"Didn't there used to be two doorways here?"

"Yes, we're going to have one larger one."

Nick looked around the room. "You do know there is a huge hole in the back of the house, right?"

Mia giggled. "Of course. I'm making the family room bigger. The easiest way was to blow out the back wall and just go out in the yard. We're going to need the space."

"My apartment's not even a thousand square feet, how much space do two people need?"

"It won't always be just the two of us, which brings me to what I wanted to show you. Follow me." Mia led the way up the stairs. Right in front of the master bedroom door, she stopped and with a huge smile she asked, "Are you ready?"

"As ready as I'll ever be."

She swung the door open and picked up a remote that sat on the nightstand. Slowly, the lights grew brighter, just enough to be able to see. Then a fireplace went on and the room was filled with a warm golden glow. The bed was made with all the bedding she and Kathy had picked out in rich browns, ice blue, and silver. The dark walnut headboard and matching nightstands gleamed in the muted light.

Above the bed, a crystal chandelier sparkled, even with the bulbs so dimly lit. It was perfect, but what Mia was most proud of was the fireplace. The wall had had a long bank of windows that had run horizontally. She had them taken out and replaced with two, almost floor to ceiling arched windows with the fireplace in between. The stone veneer that covered the fireplace had flecks of quartz that caught the light and the fireplace itself was made up of crushed glass that was the same ice blue as the bedding. It was romantic, sparkling, and beautiful, at least to her. However, the fact that Nick hadn't said a word started to worry her. She had been so sure he would love it.

Nick looked around, taking everything in, but said nothing. Mia waited until she couldn't stand it anymore.

"Please tell me you don't hate it."

"Hate it?" He moved to her and took her hand. "Mia, this is the room from my dream, the windows, the fireplace, the light fixture, everything right down to the rug. How did you do this? How did you know?"

"This is how I saw the room the first day I walked in. I saw the whole house not as it was, but how it should be."

"This is where we made love for the first time in my dream. I thought I was going to have to search thousands of hotels in the city to find this and here it is."

"So, you do like it?"

"I love it. I see your creativity everywhere I look. It's nothing like your loft, but it has the same feel to it. Does that make sense?"

"It makes perfect sense."

"How did you pull this off in a week?"

"You'd be surprised what money can do, just don't go into the bathroom it's not finished. Time is one limitation that can't be bought."

"Now, I have to see it." Nick opened the door and turned on the light.

The bathroom was still in the raw stage. It had no tile, no vanity, no shower, but Mia was happy to see that her bathtub had been delivered.

"Is that the bathtub from your loft?" Nick asked with a smile on his face.

"It's the same as my loft tub. I can't live without a hot soak once in a while. Besides, it's big enough for two."

"I like the way you're thinking." Nick flipped off the light and strolled over to the fireplace. "We should set a date. How long will it take to put together your dream wedding?"

"My dream wedding?" Mia was confused. "What are you talking about?"

"I saw all those wedding magazines in your loft a while back. I figured you must have been dreaming of a huge wedding."

The cloud she had been walking on burst right under her feet and she came crashing down. Mia sat on the end of the bed and twisted her engagement ring.

Nick came over and got down on the balls of his feet and looked at her face.

"I felt that. I felt your happiness get sucked right out of you. Now, tell me why."

"Who would I invite? Holly and Joe, Richard and his wife, maybe Dr. Whitaker? Charlie won't even talk to me after all the bad publicity and I don't like his wife anyway. Wayne and Kathy, but they are more your friends than mine."

"They're our friends." Nick put his hands on her knees.

Mia could feel the tears starting. "I have all this money, which the world thinks can buy you happiness, but I can't even fill a small church with real friends and family who care about me. It's pathetic. *I'm* pathetic."

Nick put his hand on her cheek. "They're the pathetic ones. Let's just go to the courthouse then."

"No courthouse. Marriage is a commitment you should make before God in a church. It means something."

"Okay, we can have a small church wedding. How long will it take for you to put it together?"

"I could put it together in a few days."

"Really?"

"Yes."

"Then let's get married next Saturday."

"Really?" Mia's good mood was returning quickly. "I would love an evening wedding with candles burning. I have to call Holly and see if she will be my matron of honor."

"Sounds great. We'll just invite the friends we really care about. Maybe have dinner and dancing afterward."

Mia smiled. "Leave it to me."

Nick kissed her. "And leave the honeymoon to me."

CHAPTER THIRTY-SEVEN

Nick sat at his desk after spending the morning in court, testifying against a man who killed his wife. He hated those cases more than anything.

Shoving aside the paperwork he couldn't concentrate on, he said to Wayne, "We should have gone to lunch first."

"Man, you're in a mood today. Did you and Mia have a fight?"

"No, everything's great." Nick didn't want to go into the nightmares he continued to have about Mia or the warning his grandfather had given him. It was always the same, snow falling, Mia bleeding, her face ghostly white as drops of her blood mix with the snow on the sidewalk. He could never see where they were or any other details, but it was freaking him out.

Nick scrubbed his face with his hands, wishing he could forget the words his grandfather said the day they'd left Oklahoma, but they were burned into his memory.

"There is a dark presence around her, powerful and dangerous. If it can't possess her, it will try to destroy her. Be careful." His grandfather's somber expression told Nick he was worried about the situation.

His nightmares and his grandfather's warning were linked somehow, he was sure of it, but Nick had no idea what to do about it. There was still a part of him that wanted to believe it was all imagination and superstition, but in his gut, he knew it was more and that's what was making him crazy.

Wayne leaned over and whispered, "I think you have a visitor."

Nick glanced up to see Richard Sharpe coming through the doorway. Mia's attorney had a sour look on his face. Apparently, he didn't want to be there any more than Nick wanted him there.

"I wonder what he wants." Wayne walked away as the attorney came to Nick's desk.

I am not in the mood for this, Nick thought to himself.

"Detective, I need to speak with you in private, if that's possible."

Nick led the way to room six, motioned for Sharpe to go inside, and closed the door behind him. "What can I do for you?"

Richard stood on the other side of the table and set his brief case on it. "Mia called me this morning and told me about your wedding plans and asked me to give her away. Under the circumstances, I thought it would be best if I came down here and talked to you about a few things."

Nick grimaced, but remained silent.

The attorney hesitated for a minute, as if he were deciding just what to say. "Mia's father, Paul, was my best friend. I won't go into how much I owe him. I just want you to know that when he and Nadja died, I stood over their graves and promised I would look after Mia to the best of my ability. I've done what I can to make sure she has been protected from those who would harm her, financially, physically, or emotionally. I'm not ashamed to say that I went so far as to pay off one of her college boyfriends to get lost. He was only too happy to take the money and run."

"If you're here to try and pay me off again, I will throw your ass out on the street and I don't care who you are." Nick could feel his blood pressure rising. "I'm not after Mia's money."

Richard's eyes narrowed. "If I thought for one second you were after her money, I wouldn't be here and you would be working third shift as a security guard. Don't underestimate the strings I can pull, or the favors I can call in."

Nick started to tell the man to go to hell, but Richard held up his hand. "Let me finish. I know Mia loves you and she says that you love her."

"I do love her."

"Mia's intuition usually protects her from those who aren't being truthful, so I have to believe that. I want to believe that. But, just so there is no misunderstanding, if you ever hurt her like you did before, or you cheat on her, or mistreat her, there are no roads I won't go down to make you suffer."

"I usually appreciate candor, but don't threaten me. I'm not a man who won't push back." Richard looked surprised. "What happens between Mia and me, is none of your damn business. You take care of business and I'll take care of Mia. It's as simple as that."

"When it comes to the Carrigan Empire, you'll find that nothing is as simple as that. There are those who would love nothing more than to see Mia fail, but she is smart, smarter than most give her

credit for. Keep that in mind. I have some papers for you to sign."
Richard sat down and opened his briefcase. Taking out an inch thick
folder, he began sorting through everything. "Mia won't listen to my
advice in getting a pre-nuptial agreement, but there are still several
things that you need to sign. Mia wants to allow you access to the
bank accounts."

"Bank accounts? There's more than one?"

"Mia has five different bank accounts that she uses personally
and I believe, when I last checked, they totaled about nine million
dollars." Richard informed him. Of course, the bulk of her wealth is
in the business and in various investments."

"Nine million dollars? Are you serious?"

"One she uses for day to day expenses. One's for real estate
purchases, such as the loft and the house she's renovating for the two
of you." Sharpe stopped talking and studied him carefully. "You
have no idea how much Mia is worth, do you?"

Nick sat down hard in the only other chair. "I knew she was rich,
but nine million in her personal bank accounts? I had no idea." All
kinds of thoughts went through Nick's mind at one time. None of
them good. "Just how much is Mia worth?"

"When you are talking about an estate of this size, a slight drop
in the stock market can cost you hundreds of thousands of dollars, so
it's hard to say exactly."

"Give me a ballpark figure." He was getting frustrated.

"If I were to liquidate all of Carrigan Industries' holdings world-
wide and hand Mia a check, it would be close to a billion dollars. Not
in Bill Gates league, but still a lot of money."

Nick didn't know what to say. He felt like he had been lied to,
only Mia hadn't lied, she just hadn't told him the whole truth. In all
fairness, he hadn't asked either, because he hadn't wanted to know.

"I think I'm beginning to see why you are such a hard ass. This
changes everything," Nick mumbled.

"How so?"

"I've seen junkies kill each other over a nickel bag of weed and
Mia walks around New York City all alone. If the wrong people
found out who she is and what she's worth, she could be in real
danger. Her loft didn't even have a security system."

"Now you're beginning to see what I've been up against.

There's a fine line between trying to live a normal life, as Mia wants to do, and being careless."

Nick realized he was going to have to swallow his pride and try to make it right between Sharpe and himself.

"Look Sharpe, I know you and I got off on the wrong foot and it's gone down hill since then. I know Mia won't ask me to sign a pre-nup, so I am going to make you the same offer I did the first time we met. If, at some time in the future, she doesn't want to be married to me, I will walk away with what I have right now. Which is about seven grand in savings and eight or nine hundred in my checking account."

"But you want something in return."

"I want a truce. I'd like to know that I can call you if I'm worried about Mia for one reason or another and not feel like I'm consorting with the enemy. And I think it would make her happy if we could at least be civil to each other."

"I'm willing to give it a try, for her sake," Richard stated unenthusiastically. "Mia wants you on all the checking accounts, savings accounts, and as the beneficiary of her life insurance policy, and all the rest."

"I only want one joint checking account, which my paycheck will be deposited into, and that's it. Make it the one with the least amount of money."

"That's not what Mia wants. And the balance of the accounts changes all the time."

"I'll talk to her and get back to you. I'm not in any rush."

"I think you will find when Mia sets her mind on something, she usually gets it." Richard closed his briefcase with a click. "So, good luck with that. I'll see you Saturday, if not sooner, depending on what you two decide."

Nick took his lunch break and went to the house. Wayne tagged along for good measure. Mia was sitting on the stairs with her laptop when he walked in.

"Hey, I was just going to call you. I reserved tuxes for the two of you for Saturday, but you need to go and get fitted. Both of you."

"Okay, we'll deal with that later. I need to talk to you."

"What's wrong?"

"I'm going to check out the house while you two hash this out," Wayne said, making himself scarce.

"Let's go into the library," Mia said with a worried look on her face. "It's the only room downstairs that isn't torn apart."

The previous owner's massive desk and leather chair were still in the library.

Mia sat down on the edge of the desk and waited for him to speak. "I had a visit from Richard. He wanted me to sign a bunch of stuff."

"Oh, good. I'm glad that's all taken care of." Mia smiled.

"I didn't sign any of it." Nick felt her mood shift immediately.

"Why not?"

"I don't want to be a part of all that. And, why didn't you tell me how much money you're worth? I mean, I knew you had money, but for crying out loud, you could have warned me." His irritation was obvious in his tone.

"Oh."

Nick waited for her to say something more, but she didn't. He felt a sick feeling in his gut.

"Mia?"

"I imagined that our marriage would be like my parent's was and we would share all of it, like they did." Mia blinked rapidly. "I guess it wasn't fair for me to expect that, at least not without talking to you first."

"Mia?" Nick couldn't decide if the tightness around his heart was his or hers.

"I'm sorry. I…" Mia stopped in mid sentence. "I'm sorry."

"It's okay. Do you want to go to lunch with us?" Nick asked.

"I really can't leave right now. I have a meeting with Jerry, the contractor." Mia's voice was unusually quiet.

"Okay. Where's the tux shop?"

"I'll have to look up the address. I'll text it to you later." Still, she didn't look at him. Nick got the feeling she was angry.

"Okay, I've got to go. We'll barely have enough time to grab something and eat it on the way back." Nick kissed her cheek and headed out the door.

"I can't believe how the house has changed in a week. It's hard to believe it's the same place." Wayne commented as they got into the car. "So, how did it go?"

Nick had told Wayne the whole story on the way over. There was very little they didn't share with each other. "I told her I didn't want any part of it."

"And she was okay with that?" He sounded doubtful.

"Yeah, she understood." As the words left his mouth, he grew uncomfortable.

"Man, it must be nice to be able to pick and choose which parts of her life you are going to be a part of. If I had my way, I would choose a few of Kathy's relatives and cut them out of the picture. Unfortunately for me, it's a package deal."

Nick stopped the car at the end of the driveway. "A package deal?"

Wayne raised his eyebrows. "Yeah. You know the good with the bad, one for all. The relatives you like along with the ones you don't. That's marriage."

Wayne's words hit him like a ton of bricks. "I wish you would have shared that bit of wisdom before I made an idiot out of myself." Nick jammed the car into reverse and gunned it back up the driveway.

Once he was back inside the house, he glanced around for Mia and didn't see her. He opened the library door and there she was standing at the window looking out at the overgrown backyard. He swung the door closed behind him.

"Did you forget something?" she asked.

He didn't have to feel her emotions to know she was irritated. "Yeah, I forgot that this is supposed to be a fifty/fifty proposition. And I don't have the right to pick and choose what parts of your life I want to share. If you want me to be a part of all the financial stuff, I will."

"I know how intimidating it can be, believe me. There are times I don't want to deal with it, but it would mean a lot to me if I didn't have to do it all by myself anymore.

"I'm sorry. It seems like I keep having to say that. I'll try to do better next time."

"I'm glad you came to your senses." Mia smiled.

"Oh, and before I forget, we need to talk about a security system for the house. Top of the line, the best your money can buy."

"Our money," Mia reminded him.

"Our money." Nick kissed her neck.

"I already have the security company coming to install their best system next week. Despite what Richard thinks, I do try to take precautions."

"I really have to go." Nick was almost to the door once again. "I'll see you at the apartment tonight."

"Okay." Mia smiled.

Two hours later, Nick was still trying to finish his paperwork.

"What's the matter with you today? Are you getting cold feet about the wedding?" Wayne wanted to know.

Nick tapped his pen on the desk in exasperation. "No." When he'd left Mia she was okay, but now he couldn't shake the feeling that something was wrong.

"Then, what is up with you today?" Wayne stared like he didn't recognize him.

"Mia's really upset about something." Nick hit her number on his speed dial and after three rings she picked up. "What's wrong?"

"I can't believe it. Holly won't come to our wedding," Mia cried. "She said she couldn't get away from work, but that wasn't why. She admitted, finally, that Joe doesn't want her near me because of the things that happen around me. She said he thinks I'm too weird and that her old apartment was haunted."

"Holly's old apartment *is* haunted," Nick tried to reason with her.

Wayne, who could hear the whole conversation, nodded emphatically.

"Do you think Kathy would be my matron of honor?"

Nick looked to Wayne who once again nodded his head.

"I'll call her right now and ask her." Wayne already had his cell phone in hand.

"I can't believe she won't come to my wedding, after all these years." Mia had stopped crying and was angry again.

"Kathy said she'd be honored to do it," Wayne told him.

"Mia, Kathy said she'd be honored."

Mia's emotions shifted instantly. "She will? Have Wayne tell her I'm coming to get her, so we can get her a dress. Is that okay with her?"

Nick looked at Wayne. Wayne relayed the message to Kathy.

"She'll be waiting," Wayne told Nick and Nick told Mia.

When Nick hung up, Wayne was staring at him funny.

"What?"

"How did you know Mia was upset, when she's thirty minutes

away?"

Nick leaned closer so he wouldn't be overheard. "I know it sounds crazy, but there are times when I can feel what she's feeling."

Wayne sat back in his chair and thought it over. "Nick, I like Mia. She's sweet, pretty, and generous, but are you sure you want to marry her? When it comes to being strange, she's over the top."

"I've never been so sure of anything in my life."

"Good enough."

Tuesday night Nick and Wayne went right after work to get their tuxes fitted. Wednesday, Richard showed up again and Nick signed all the paperwork the attorney had for him. Richard gave him six different credit cards and the not so subtle reminder that it's customary for the groom to buy his new wife a gift and make it something nice. Nick knew that was code for expensive. Thursday, he went shopping and bought Mia a wedding band that matched her mom's ring, and two different wedding gifts. He wasn't sure she would like the first one, so he had a back up, just in case. Friday night he slept on Wayne's ugly green couch because Mia didn't want him to see her before the ceremony.

***

Saturday turned out to be a perfect day. The sky was blue with big puffy white clouds. Mia and Kathy had early morning appointments at the spa for massages, manicures, pedicures, facials, and make-up. They finished with time to spare. With their dresses in the back of the limo, they headed toward the church. Mia needed to make one stop along the way.

"Are you sure we have time to stop?" Kathy asked her.

"Yes. Besides, they can't start without us."

Kathy laughed. "Well, they can't start without you."

The limo driver stopped at the cemetery and Mia got out and walked among the headstones, clutching a dozen red roses. She knew right where she was going, even though she hadn't been there in a while.

A large granite headstone marked her parents' resting place and a small bench had been placed at the foot of their graves. Mia always sat there whenever she went to visit.

"It's my wedding day, mama. Do you remember when I was four and I would look through your wedding album over and over again as I sat on your bed and you would do my hair?" Mia's tears slipped down her cheeks as the familiar ache started in her chest. "You were so pretty, and dad was the handsomest man. I still have the album and I look at it when I'm lonely and missing you both.

"I picked out a dress that reminded me of the one you wore that day. It's very Audrey Hepburn, scoop neck, tea length, long sleeves, with buttons down the back." Mia had to swallow back a sob. "I wish you were here to help me dress for my wedding. I'm using your ring. I thought you would like that. It's my way of having you near me on my big day." She touched the ring on her finger.

"Remember how you told me that hardly anyone came to your wedding, but you said you didn't need anyone, but dad? My wedding is going to be the same way. All I need is Nick. You'd both like him. He's a detective and he loves me for me, not the money. And I love him. I love him *so* much.

"Daddy, I wish you were here to walk me down the aisle. When I was little, I always imagined you would be here for this day." Mia had to take another breath. "Richard is going to do it. I know that will make you happy. He's been a part of my life since the beginning. I didn't realize how much I depend on him until lately. Still, it's not the same as if you both were here." Mia couldn't hold it back any longer and she cried. "It's been so hard to be alone for so long. I miss you."

Mia heard the crunch of footsteps behind her and then Kathy sat down next to her on the bench. Without saying anything, Kathy put her arm around Mia's shoulders and hugged her.

"They should be here for my wedding day." Mia barely managed to get the words out.

"They will be. They'll be watching over you." Kathy had tears in her eyes.

Mia could feel that her intentions were pure. Kathy cared about her, just like Nick. She took a deep, but shaky breath. "Thanks, Kathy, for everything."

"You don't need to thank me. That's what friends are for." She smiled. "They are also to make sure you get to your own wedding on time." Kathy stood up and offered Mia her arm, like a man would. "Shall we go?"

Mia laid the roses on her parents' grave, linked arms with Kathy and walked back to the limo. On the way to the church, Kathy fixed her make-up, which had almost been ruined by her crying.

At the church they both dressed as quickly as possible. When Mia saw herself in the full length mirror, she had to admit, she looked pretty.

"Is that the necklace Nick gave you, the one he had cut in half?" Kathy asked.

Mia's fingers touched the heart. "It's a surprise for him. I had it repaired. I picked it up yesterday with his wedding ring."

"You look amazing. I can't wait to see the look on Nick's face when he sees you."

"So do you, and in the black satin, you can't see your tummy at all."

"I'm glad you chose black. It's slimming and it goes with my hair. I won't be able to hide this growing belly of mine much longer though." Kathy smiled and rubbed her hand over her rounding tummy.

"When he gets here, it will all be worth it." Mia patted Kathy's tummy also.

"He? It's a boy? How do you know? I haven't even had my ultra-sound yet."

Mia shrugged. "It's a boy."

"Wayne wants a boy so bad. I can't wait to tell him."

The wedding coordinator poked her head in the door. "It's time ladies. Kathy you're first. Mia, you follow along, but stay out of site in the hallway."

"Are the photographer and videographer in place?" Mia wanted to know. Nick's family couldn't be here, but she wanted to be able to send them DVDs of the ceremony, especially his grandmother.

"They're all ready."

Mia handed Kathy her bouquet and she grabbed hers. It was a beautiful arrangement of cascading red roses.

In the hallway, Richard waited for her. His mouth dropped open when he saw her. "You look just like your mother."

It was the nicest thing Richard could have said.

"I truly hope that you and Nick will be as happy as your parents were, Mia. I always envied the relationship they had. They made marriage look so easy."

It made Mia smile that she wasn't the only one who had noticed that what her parents had was special. "I hope so too."

She heard the bridal march start and took Richard's arm, then a deep breath to calm her nerves before they walked down the aisle. The small stone church was over one hundred and fifty years old and it looked amazing with red roses and candles glowing everywhere.

The minister, in his black robes, waited for her, but it was Nick who had her attention. Through her veil, she could see him watching her every move. He looked more than handsome in his tux. He could have been on the cover of a magazine, he looked so good.

Mia saw his lips move as he said something to Wayne. Nick's emotions overwhelmed her. He was nervous, happy, and at peace, all at the same time.

Mia's heart beat faster when she realized this was really happening. She slowed down a little bit, wanting to make the moment last. When she took her place next to Nick, she saw the tears in his eyes. And she noticed when he caught site of the necklace that hung around her neck.

"My heart isn't broken anymore," she whispered.

The grin on his face filled her with warmth.

"Who gives this woman to be wed?" The minister asked.

Richard answered, "On behalf of her mother and father, I do."

Nick took her hand and the minister continued. Mia must have said the right things at the right times because the next thing she remembered was hearing the words 'you may kiss your bride.'

Nick lifted her veil and kissed her softly on the lips.

"Ladies and gentleman, may I present Mr. and Mrs. Nickolas Whitecloud."

The chapel erupted into applause. That was the first time Mia saw that there were about fifty people sitting in the congregation. Most of them were police officers who knew Nick from work, but she found out later that some of them were friends from his time in the Marines.

Mia and Nick accepted congratulations from everyone. Then they got into the limo and headed to the reception.

Nick smiled at her, then leaned over and kissed her much more passionately than the kiss he had given her in the church. "Do you think anyone would notice if we skipped the reception and headed into the honeymoon part of this event."

His naughty grin made Mia laugh. "I think if the bride and groom didn't show, they might notice, yes."

"Damn!" Nick grinned.

"What did you say to Wayne when I was walking down the aisle?" Mia wanted to know.

"I said, 'Wow, I can't believe she's marrying me.'"

Mia smiled. "I love you." Framing his face with her hands, she kissed him, once, twice, three times. "We do have to show up, but we don't have to stay all night."

CHAPTER THIRTY-EIGHT

Nick picked Mia up into his arms, pushed the bedroom door open with his toe and carried her across the threshold.

When she saw inside their bedroom, she couldn't believe it. The fireplace was on and there were hundreds of red roses everywhere. On the bed, rose petals were strewn about and a bottle of sparkling cider was in a silver bucket on a stand. It was the most romantic thing anyone had ever done for her.

"When did you do this?" she asked.

"This afternoon, right before we left for the church. Wayne helped me."

"Wayne helped you?" Mia's cheeks grew warm with embarrassment and Nick laughed at her.

"He won't be here for our wedding night." He let her down until her feet found the floor.

"Thank goodness." This was one night she wanted to be alone with only Nick.

"Are you nervous?" Nick asked as he ran a thumb over her bottom lip, his voice soft and reassuring.

Mia shrugged and then nodded. "I've never done this before and you have all this experience, and..." Mia's words faded.

"And what?"

"I've never considered myself very sexual. In fact, until I met you I'd never thought about it much. I was always focused on other things, like school, work, and my art."

Nick grinned. "Until you met me?"

Mia ignored his comment. "What if I'm not very good at this?"

Nick pulled her close. "Relax, we'll take it one step at a time." Nick's lips touched hers softly at first. When he would have pulled away, Mia brought her mouth to his again. She wanted to do this right.

"Help me with my dress," she whispered, turning around to let him unbutton her.

The back of her dress was all buttons, from her neck down to her bottom. One at a time, Nick shoved each button through the tiny loop of fabric. "Is this some kind of endurance test for new husbands on their wedding night? How about I just tear it open?"

"Don't you dare! A little patience builds character." Mia giggled.

Her dress parted little by little. Mia could feel the air on her naked skin. When Nick undid the last button, he ran his finger down her spine from her neck, over the clasp of her strapless bra, to the top of her white lace panties and the garter belt that held up the sexy, shimmering stockings Kathy had insisted she buy. Mia took a slow breath and slid the dress off of her shoulders and let it fall to the floor.

"Oh, babe, you look good." Nick's gaze was riveted on her, her face, her breasts, and her legs.

Mia just smiled as she stepped out of her dress. She picked it up and walked across the bedroom, laying her dress gently on a chair, so it wouldn't get wrinkled. Nick watched her every curve as she came back to him.

He sat down on the edge of the bed, toed off his shoes, and reached out to put his hands on her waist. They were cool against her skin, which was already heated.

He leaned forward and kissed her belly as he slid his hands to her breasts, cupping them and running his finger tips over the lace. Mia's heartbeat went into overdrive. Her chest began to move up and down, faster than before. Through his touch she could feel his desire for her. The intensity of it surprised and pleased her.

She pushed his coat off of his shoulders and helped as he shook his arms out of the sleeves and tossed it to the floor. His tie was next. With one tug it came loose. Mia pulled it from around his neck. It landed on his coat.

The scent of his cologne and of Nick himself filled her and she knew she would never get tired of it. Mia worked the buttons of his shirt as his fingers ran down her back. Surprised, she gasped as her bra fell to the floor. Her arm went across her breasts out of instinct.

Their eyes met. He grinned a naughty, sexy grin that turned the butterflies in her stomach into skyrockets.

He took her by the wrist and kissed the palm of her hand, exposing her breasts to his gaze. Her nipples were already hard and achy and he hadn't even touched her. He remedied that. Cupping her breasts, he ran his thumbs over them making them draw up even tighter. The sensation went straight to her belly, deep and low. Mia tipped her head back, and moaned deep in her throat. He pulled her into his lap and held her, stroking her back to relax her, one hand still toying with her. His kisses found a pathway from her neck to her lips, where he tasted her with his tongue.

Mia couldn't get close enough. She slipped her hand under his shirt and felt him. The movement of his muscles under his hot skin was new to her. Even after all the times they had slept in the same bed, she had never touched him like this before. Every touch, every taste, confirmed that they belonged to each other and always would.

Nick's fingers ran up and down her thigh, unclipping the garters and sliding the stockings down her feet. He hooked her shoes with his thumb and off they came. Only her white lace garter belt and panties covered her now.

With his eyes he devoured her. "You are so sexy. I can't believe you had these on under your dress. If I had known, we never would have made it out of the limo."

"Kathy helped me pick them out." Mia almost didn't recognize her own voice as she spoke. "She said men love them."

"She's right." Their lips met again. They kissed, tongues mingling and tasting.

Nick's fingers ran up Mia's thigh until she could feel the pressure on the outside of her panties. Her body was on fire. He pressed his finger against her, until she wanted to cry out with pleasure. She opened her legs wider for him. He took the cue and slid his finger inside her panties. Between her legs moisture had gathered and he spread it over her most delicate skin. Mia's heart pounded in her chest and she couldn't seem to get enough air into her lungs.

Nick swung her in his arms and laid her down on the bed where the sheets had already been turned back. He kissed her, brushed the hair out of her face, then stood and began taking off the rest of his clothes.

His body was beautiful, so strong and masculine. It all pleased her, from his brown skin to his broad shoulders, the narrowing of his hips, even his large hands. It called to her as a woman, like nothing ever had before.

Nick slid her garter belt and panties down her legs, until the only thing she had on was her necklace. He then joined her on the bed, holding her close. She enjoyed the warmth of their bodies and the sensation of skin on skin. He nibbled her ear lobe, following an invisible trail down her neck to her breasts.

"You smell so good," he whispered to her as his lips found a taut nipple.

Mia's back arched as he licked it. Her fingers ran through his hair, taking hold, and keeping him in place. His tongue manipulated her nipple in his mouth, his lips sucking forcefully. His hand went to her belly and with one finger circled her navel. She couldn't keep her hips on the bed, they kept coming off the sheets seeking for what he wanted to give her. Slowly and seductively he worked his way down her body until he slipped his finger between her nether lips.

She couldn't stop the cry that escaped her when he brushed over her throbbing nub, Mia cried out, "Oh, oh, please." Her skin was on fire. Nick kissed her belly, licking and tasting all the way down.

"Open your legs, babe."

When she looked down at him, it was through dazed eyes. She moved her legs and Nick slipped between them. His kiss, so intimate and tender made her breath catch in her throat.

When his mouth covered her most private parts, Mia moaned out loud. "Oh, Nick! Oh, please."

She was quaking with excitement when Nick forced his finger all the way inside of her. Mia stopped moving for a second and then wiggled her hips to test the feeling of it so deep inside of her. He didn't give her any time to think before his next sensual assault on her body.

Mia gasped. Moving his finger in and out in time with her hips she felt the stretching, but didn't notice any pain through the pleasure he was giving her. The intensity of it was growing, spiraling out of control. "Don't stop, don't stop," she pleaded. He didn't.

As the passion became unbearable, she left reality and went to a new place where only her desire existed. Her body had taken control of her, moving to its own rhythm until she shattered into millions of pieces. Without thought she cried out as wave after wave of ecstasy washed over her. His touch grew slower and softer as she floated on another plane of existence. It was someplace new and wonderful and she wanted to stay there forever. As the minutes passed, she came back to a new reality. It left her weak, but so fulfilled.

Nick climbed up her body kissing every inch along the way. By the time he got to her mouth she was smiling. Mia took his face in her hands. "Come inside of me now." With that she pressed her body against his. She wanted to give him the same kind of pleasure he had given her. She didn't have to ask twice. With his arms braced on either side of her and his body poised at her entrance, he started to press into her.

"Am I hurting you?" he asked.

"No,"

He pulled out and pressed in again, going just a little bit further this time.

She reached up and wrapped her arms around his neck and brought his body down to hers. Mia ran her hands down his back and kissed his neck.

Now that her own desire had been quenched, she could once again feel Nick's. There was power, passion, and desperation to his need. As their bodies joined so did their souls. She could feel his every emotion and desire. He moved slowly at first, letting her body become accustomed to his.

The pace of their love making increased. Mia felt the heat from his breath as his need became uncontrollable.

"I can't hold back any longer," he managed to say between gritted teeth as he drove deep inside of her. He tried to be gentle, but he was beyond control. His seed filled her as his body quaked with his release.

Mia's arms were around him and she held him tightly. She kissed his neck and stroked his hair. His breathlessness pleased her. It made her feel womanly to know she had brought him to this uncontrollable and exhausted state.

"Am I hurting you?" he asked, between gulps of air and when he could once again form words.

"No. I want to stay like this forever."

Mia felt him chuckle against her neck. "I'm going to get pretty heavy in a few minutes.

"I don't care." She just wanted the moment to last. A healing had taken place within her. They truly were one. The tenderness of it brought tears to her eyes.

When Nick saw them he quickly rolled to the side and pulled her into his arms.

"Are you okay?"

"I'm more than okay." Mia touched his face. "That was

beautiful."

As they lay in bed looking at each other, Nick picked up the heart that dangled on its chain around her neck and looked at it.

"Whoever repaired this did a good job. I almost can't tell where it was cut."

"I had the jeweler that made it repair it."

"How did you know where I got it?" Nick looked at her suspiciously.

Mia laughed. "The name of the store was printed on the inside of the box."

"Oh." Nick laughed too. "I didn't even notice that."

"The jeweler sure was mad at you for making him cut his artwork in half."

Nick laughed even harder.

"I bought your wedding ring from him to make up for it." Mia took his hand and looked at the ring she had put there hours earlier. "It's perfect."

"It has a lot of diamonds," Nick commented.

"Twelve," Mia told him. "I knew it had to be this one the moment I saw it."

"Really?" His dark eyes looked at her as if to see if she was teasing him.

"Do you love it?"

Nick laughed at her. "I'll get used to it." He touched the tip of her nose with his finger. "You looked so beautiful today. I can't believe we're married."

"Forever," Mia whispered.

"Forever," Nick repeated.

It wasn't long before Mia started dozing off.

"Mia, don't go to sleep yet."

"Why not?" she looked at him sleepily.

"You need to go pee."

"No, I don't."

Nick laughed at her. "If you don't go after sex, you could get a bladder infection. They don't call it the honeymoon disease for nothing."

Mia searched his face for a clue. "How do you know that?"

"It doesn't matter, just go." He pushed against her hip until she got out of bed.

When she came back, she climbed into bed and asked, "Just how many girlfriends have you been with in the past?"

"It doesn't matter, because I didn't love any of them." Nick pulled her close. "I was fond of a few of them, but I didn't love them. I do love you, though."

"You're just trying to change the subject." Mia snuggled closer to him.

"What subject was that?" Nick pretended he didn't know what she was talking about.

"That's what I thought." She knew he wasn't going to tell her.

"Go to sleep, Mia," he said as he kissed her on her head.

CHAPTER THIRTY-NINE

Mia woke up Sunday morning with the sun streaming in through the windows. Nick was sitting up against the headboard watching her.

"What are you doing?" she mumbled, still groggy with sleep.

"Watching you sleep." He smiled. "It's nine-thirty already."

"I guess I should tell you now, I'm not a morning person. I used to work at night."

"I know. That reminds me, I have a present for you. Actually, I have two presents for you." Nick got out of bed, still naked, and went through the bathroom into the new walk-in closet Mia had designed. He came back with sweats on carrying a big box and a tiny box. "Open the little one first."

Mia sat up, excited to see what he had gotten her. She tore the wrapping off a small black velvet jewelry box. Inside, were diamond earrings. "They're beautiful. You have good taste."

"I know. I married you." He gave her a quick kiss on her cheek.

Mia's heart swelled in her chest. "You're setting the bar really high. All these sweet things your saying, I'm going to want to hear them forever and when the newness wears off and you don't say them anymore, I'll be disappointed."

Nick grinned. "I'll have to keep telling you how lucky I am then, won't I?" He tapped the big box with his finger. "This is what I really wanted to get you. The earrings were a back-up in case you didn't like this one."

Mia wondered what it could be that he thought she wouldn't like it. She could sense his excitement and anxiousness.

"Go ahead and open it."

She unwrapped the box, opened the lid, and took out the tissue paper, revealing all kinds of art supplies.

"I tried to get the same brands that you had, only I couldn't remember them all."

Mia took out a pack of colored pencils, charcoal sticks, art paper, water colors, and oil paints. She had always dabbled in the different mediums, depending on her mood and the subject.

"I know you got rid of your stuff, but babe, you're too talented to quit and I like looking at your work." Nick shrugged.

As she studied all the different things Nick had picked out, it brought back such a strong desire to create that she was stunned. "I didn't realize how much I missed it. The drawing, painting, and sketching have always been a huge part of me."

"I know you're busy working on the house right now, but when you're done here, maybe you could take it up again?"

"Maybe." Mia ran her fingers over the charcoal. She looked at Nick's dark eyes. "I'm sorry, but between working on the house and the wedding plans, I didn't get you a gift."

"Sure you did. You gave it to me last night."

When Mia saw his wicked grin, she blushed and Nick laughed.

"Go get ready and I'll take you out for breakfast."

***

Mia scooped a piece of her vegetarian omelet onto her fork. "Should we go back to your apartment until the house is done?"

"How much longer do you think it will take?"

"I think the kitchen will be done by the end of next week. The family room about a month and the basement at least another two months. And then, we can move in while they finish the rest. The kitchen is the biggest concern. It's hard to live without one."

"What do we need a kitchen for? We're newlyweds. We only need a bed." He smiled and winked at her.

Mia almost choked on her food. "Nick, be serious."

"I am serious. Besides, you've been making dinner in that pot thing almost every night. Why can't we do that at the new house?"

"We don't have a fridge, or a dishwasher, or even a kitchen sink."

"I see your point, and as long as were together, it doesn't matter. I really like the idea of starting off our new life in the new house though. It feels like a fresh start that way, but if it's easier for you, we can stay at my place."

Mia liked that he thought that way. "Let me think about it."

"Okay." Nick shoved another lump of pancake into his mouth. "You're finishing the basement? When did that happen?"

"Why have all that space if you can't use it? I am putting two small bedrooms down there with a bath in between. The rest of the space will be open, but finished. I'm thinking about a home gym."

"I could cancel my gym membership and save some money. Oh, wait, I don't need to save money anymore, do I?"

"Nope, you can pay off all your debts and spend freely."

"I have to admit, when I went shopping for your wedding gifts, it was pretty cool when I bought the earrings and didn't have to ask how much they were and then figure out in my head how long it was going to take me to pay them off, like I did with your necklace."

"You went into debt to buy me my necklace?" Mia touched the heart hanging around her neck.

"I could have used my savings, but I don't like to use that unless it's an emergency."

Mia leaned across the table and kissed him. "I love you."

"Prove it," he challenged her.

"Get the check," Mia told him saucily.

"To hell with the check." He dropped two twenties on the table and helped Mia up.

***

Mia had her refrigerator and freezer delivered. She had them out in the living room. She also set up a card table with four chairs and picked up paper plates, napkins, and plastic utensils. It was like camping in the living room.

When Nick got home from work, he took one look at the commercial refrigerator and separate freezer and said, "Are we stocking up for The Apocalypse or something? Why do we need such a huge fridge and freezer for just the two of us?"

"What if we want to entertain? And I'm hoping it won't be just the two of us for very long." Mia smiled.

Nick studied her for a minute, then went a little pale. "We didn't use any birth control. I can't believe I didn't think of that. That isn't like me at all. Are you trying to get pregnant?"

Mia wanted to laugh at him. "Trying is such a strong word," she teased.

Nick didn't smile. He looked perplexed.

"Would it be so horrible? I told you I wanted a family." Mia slipped her arms around his waist and held him tight.

"I guess it wouldn't be horrible." He held her and ran his hands up and down her back. "After all, it would be a good nine months from now. How many babies are you planning?"

Mia shrugged. "I thought we'd keep having them until the money runs out."

"Babe, that's not funny." The serious expression on his face made Mia laugh out loud.

"Do we have to make that decision tonight?"

"I guess not. What's for dinner?"

"Crock pot lasagna."

"I love Italian. By the way, on Friday I want to take you out for a belated birthday dinner."

"That sounds great. Why don't you invite Wayne and Kathy to come along?"

"I already did. Let's eat."

Mia's cell rang and she looked to see who it was. "It's Richard. I have to take this."

Mia was on the phone for only five minutes, but Richard told her exactly what she wanted to hear.

"What was that all about?" Nick asked as he put a plate full of lasagna on the table in front of her.

"I'm trying to make some changes to the manufacturing division of Carrigan Industries which, in the long run, will begin to limit how much power my Uncle David and Evan have. It will take a while, but Richard thinks I have the backing of the board."

"That will piss them off."

"Probably, but I'm tired of all the drama they create. It's hard enough doing all this, but when I have to deal with them manipulating things behind my back, I really hate it."

"You hate being in charge of Carrigan Industries?" Nick asked shocked.

"I do it because I know it's what my father and Richard expect of me. If I'd had a choice, I would have majored in art and done nothing but create every minute of everyday."

Nick's mouth hung open. "I'm shocked to hear you say that. I thought you loved it."

"If I could find someone I trust to do what my father would have wanted with the business, I would turn the whole operation over to him or her and Richard and just collect a check every month."

"Really? I never would have guessed that's how you felt."

Mia smiled. "I'm glad you don't know everything about me. It adds a little mystery."

***

Friday morning, Mia's cell phone rang right in the middle of an argument with one of the construction workers about which wall the TV was going on.

"Hello," Mia said, straining to hear with all the banging going on around her.

"Mia? It's Kathy. Can you hear me?"

"Barely. Hang on." Mia made her way into the library and slammed the door in frustration. "Sorry, it's crazy here today."

"Oh, is it too crazy for you to go shopping with me today? I had my ultrasound this morning and you were right, I am having a boy. I want to start getting some ideas for the baby's room and I wanted you to come. You have such a good eye for what goes together and what doesn't." Kathy finally took a breath. "And then, I thought we could meet Wayne and Nick at the restaurant when we're done."

"That sounds perfect. I need a break from this place. Give me an hour to talk to the contractor and take a quick shower and I will come pick you up."

"I'll see you then." Kathy hung up and Mia smiled. She had felt her excitement over the phone.

Mia touched her belly and wondered if she was carrying a baby yet. They hadn't even been married a week, but they had been working as hard as they could on it. Mia smiled again. She was truly happy with every aspect of her life and it had been a long, long time since she could say that. Picking up her cell phone, she texted Nick, "I love you."

After talking to Jerry and going over the plans for the family room one more time, she was headed up the stairs when Nick texted her back, "I love you more." Mia was pretty sure she could float up the stairs if she wanted to.

On the way to pick up Kathy, Nick called Mia. "I wanted to remind you that we are having dinner with Wayne and Kathy at The Steakhouse. We have reservations at six and it's supposed to snow, so drive carefully."

"Kathy and I are going shopping today, so we'll meet you there."

"Okay. See you then."

***

Mia and Kathy's third stop was La Belle, the posh baby store, where they spent hours going through everything.

"I can't believe this place. It's like heaven for pregnant women," Kathy said gleefully.

"It makes me want to have a baby, no, ten babies all at once, because I don't think I could pick only one bedding set. They're all too cute." Mia concurred.

"It would be such fun if you got pregnant right away. Our babies would only be four months apart."

Mia smiled at her, but said nothing.

Kathy gasped. "You're trying to get pregnant, aren't you? Does Nick know?"

"Of course." Mia tilted her head. "At least, he does now."

Kathy laughed and laughed. "I wish I could have been there when that was going down. I would have loved to have seen the look on his face."

"I thought he was going to vomit, or pass out. It was hard to tell."

Kathy laughed so loud the clerk shot her a dirty look. She responded by looking at the clerk. "You better be nice. She's really rich," she said while pointing at Mia.

Kathy then went on to make derogatory comments about the baby stuff she didn't like. "My mom raised seven kids without ninety percent of this crap and we all turned out fine, except for my brother Kevin. He's weird." She picked up a pacifier. "Twenty-four dollars for this? Can you believe it? I'll just pop a boob in the kid's mouth. It's free."

"And you can't lose them." Mia couldn't stop laughing. She always had fun when she was with Kathy. "I just had a great idea. I want to give you a baby shower."

"Are you serious? No way. You've done enough already. Because of you, I can quit work and stay home with the baby. You don't know what that means to me."

"Yes, I do. That's why I bought you the house in the first place. I wanted you to have the chance to be the kind of mom you want to be."

Kathy didn't laugh then. Tears filled her eyes. "I never had a chance to tell you thank you. Thank you, Mia. It was and is the nicest thing anyone has ever done for us." She wiped her eyes. "Damn hormones. Laughing one minute and bawling the next."

"So, which one do you like better? The sail boat theme or the zoo animals?" Mia asked changing the subject.

Kathy took a deep breath. "Wayne is going to hate them both. He's going to want the baseball bedding. He used to be a baseball player, you know?"

"I didn't know that."

"He was being scouted by a couple of teams when he ruined his shoulder. He was so hot in those baseball pants."

Mia glanced at her watch. "It's getting late. We better go. With traffic and the snow outside we'll be lucky to get there on time."

"You're right. Wayne hates it when I keep him waiting, especially when he's hungry."

Mia was sure they were going to make it on time, but a mile from the restaurant, they hit a traffic jam. It looked like a car had slid into the intersection on the icy roads and smashed into another one. She put her car in park as they waited for the cops to sort it out. Every few minutes, she had to clear her windshield with the wipers.

Kathy's cell phone rang. "It's Wayne," she said with dread in her voice.

As Kathy talked, Mia had a creepy feeling she was being watched. She looked in her rear view mirror and then the side mirrors, but she couldn't see anyone who seemed to be paying her any special attention.

Kathy hung up. "He gets so grouchy when he's hungry. I think he must have low blood sugar or something. Oh, look, they're starting to send cars around the accident."

"It's about time." Mia made her way around the smashed up cars, thankful they were out of that mess. The closer they got to the restaurant, the heavier traffic became. By the time Mia pulled into the parking structure across from the restaurant, it was dark.

Mia found a spot and pulled in. As soon as she got out of her car, she felt it. The rage washed over her like acid, turning her stomach and making her heart pound in her chest. She froze in fear and searched the darkness for any sign of life.

With all the traffic on the street, it struck her as odd that the parking structure was void of anyone but them. His eyes were on her, she could feel it, and he was moving closer, silently stalking her. She was being hunted.

She turned to her left and then to her right. Her hands trembled.

"Are we going or what?" Kathy asked, watching Mia with an odd expression on her face.

Mia took a few steps toward Kathy and whispered, "We're in trouble."

Kathy must have heard the panic in Mia's tone because she whispered back. "What are you talking about?"

Mia stopped and turned around to look into the blackness. He was getting closer. She couldn't see him, but she could feel him. He was watching them both. It was Mia he wanted, but he would kill Kathy too. She couldn't let that happen.

"Get out of here! Get out now!" Mia said as forcefully, but as quietly, as she could.

Kathy was confused. "I can't leave you."

"If you want to see your baby born, get out of here now. Go!" She pushed against her back to get her going.

Kathy turned and ran like the devil was after her soul.

Mia stood in the dark, waiting for what she knew she couldn't escape.

***

Nick sat at the table looking at his watch. He was agitated and angry and he didn't know why. Suddenly, a horrible, sick feeling settled in his gut.

He looked at Wayne. "Mia!"

"What about her?"

Nick jumped up from the table where he'd been sitting, almost knocking over the waiter as he ran past.

"Nick! What the hell are you doing?" Wayne asked as he followed on his heels.

He slammed the door open so hard the glass almost broke. Out on the sidewalk, he searched for her.

"What is going on?" Wayne yelled at him.

Kathy came running around the corner just then and Nick was sure he would never forget the look on her face.

Before Kathy could say a word, two loud pops rang out in the night. Their echoes, bouncing off the buildings, made it hard to tell where they'd come from.

Nick and Wayne knew instantly what they were.

"Those are gun shots," Wayne said.

"Mia's in the parking garage across the street. She's in trouble," Kathy screamed on the edge of hysteria.

Nick pulled out his gun as he broke into a full on run.

Wayne followed, but yelled to Kathy as he did. "Call 911! Tell them 'shots fired!'"

Nick shielded his body at the edge of a block wall that supported the parking structure. He took a quick look inside and saw nothing. Not one person was around. He crouched down and ran inside, darting behind cars as he went. He knew Wayne was behind him somewhere, but he didn't look to him. He had to find Mia.

He saw her car, but there was no sign of her. He tried to listen to see if he could hear anything, but his heart was pounding so hard he couldn't hear a thing.

"Mia?" he called quietly. "Mia?" a little louder. "Mia?" he screamed.

From far away he heard a metal door slamming shut, followed by the screech of tires.

Nick ran from cover to where he thought it had come from, exposing himself to whoever might be there.

"Don't be stupid, Nick!" Wayne hollered, yet his partner followed him anyway.

"It's so damn dark, I can't see anything." Nick yelled to him. "Mia!"

He saw light from the street lamp outside coming in through a crack in a door. He ran his free hand over the wall, looking for the door knob. When he found it, Nick swung open the door and stepped outside, into another world.

Everything moved in slow motion as the snow blew around him. On the sidewalk at his feet were drops of blood. A few at first, but the further his gaze went on the sidewalk, the more blood there was. It was his dream in real life, even before he looked up he knew he would see Mia, just down the sidewalk about fifteen feet away.

"Mia!" he screamed. It sounded hollow, like it didn't come from him.

She turned slowly like a movie in slow motion. He tried to go to her, but it was as if he was trying to run under water.

She didn't move. Her face was ghostly white as she held out her blood covered hands and sank to the ground. Nick turned her over and opened her coat. Blood was everywhere. He only knew she'd been shot because he'd heard it.

"I'll call for an ambulance," Wayne yelled as he started back to the restaurant.

"No! Get the car! She won't make it if we wait!"

She stared at him, sheer panic in her eyes. The way she gasped for breath told him the bullet had punctured her lung. Mia mumbled something he couldn't understand.

"Stay quiet. You're going to be okay." He wished he believed his own words, but she was losing too much blood.

Wayne and Kathy came careening around the corner, the car sliding on the slush as they stopped.

Mia moaned in pain as Nick scooped her up and climbed into the back seat. Kathy climbed into the back with him and put pressure on the wounds.

Kathy's eyes met Nick's and they both knew it was bad. There was no need for words. Mia tried once more to speak.

"You're going to be okay. We're taking you to the hospital." He tried to sound reassuring, but was failing miserably.

He felt her slipping away as he held her in his arms. With one hand she reached out and touched his cheek. Her eyes closed and she went limp in his arms.

"Wayne, she's dying, hurry!"

CHAPTER FORTY

Wayne picked up the radio once more and started yelling at the dispatcher. "Tell the hospital to have a trauma team standing by. The gunshot victim is the wife of a cop!"

"Mia? Mia!" Nick called to her, trying to get her to open her eyes.

"Wayne! We don't have anymore time," Kathy cried.

Wayne cut across three lanes of oncoming traffic and went in the exit to pull up to the emergency entrance reserved for ambulances. A medical team was waiting.

They took her out of Nick's arms, put her on the stretcher, and ran. Nick jumped out and followed to the doors of the trauma unit.

"Stay here. You can't come in." He was stopped by a nurse.

"I need to be with her," he pleaded.

"Let us do our job." The nurse's hand was against Nick's chest, keeping him from pushing past her. "I know you're worried. I'll come for you when we have word of her condition."

Nick stood there like he had turned to stone as the door shut in his face. He couldn't move. All he could do was think about the lifeless body he'd held in his arms. Through his haze, he noticed someone talking to him and pulling on his arms. Wayne and Kathy were speaking words he couldn't hear over the ringing in his ears.

Somehow, they managed to get him into a chair in the waiting room. People moved about all around him. He could feel the chaos, only he couldn't think of anything but Mia. Images of her, memories he hadn't even known he had made, flashed in his mind. Her smile, her fingertips covered in charcoal dust, her eyes filling with tears, her laugh, it was all there like some weird mental recording.

When his mind examined the possibility that she could die, it was like being split into two different people. One was logically trying to look at the situation and the other, rejected it entirely.

He turned to Wayne. "Is this really happening?"

Wayne put his hand on the back of Nick's head and brought it to his until they touched at the forehead. "No matter what, we're here for you."

After an hour, a nurse came out. "Your wife is in surgery. The doctor will come and talk to you when it's over."

Nick could only nod.

Wayne put his hand on Nick's arm "That's good news."

Kathy whispered something to Wayne.

"Come on, Nick." Wayne helped him up. He followed wordlessly. They went into the bathroom and Wayne turned on the faucet. "You need to get washed up."

Nick looked at his hands and arms. They were covered in blood. When he glanced in the mirror, he saw Mia's hand print on his cheek, in her own blood.

Placing his hands under the running stream of warm water, the sink turned pink and then red. Pumping the soap dispenser and scrubbing, he tried to get it all off. Maybe then, the smell would go away. He cupped his hands and splashed his face, rubbing and washing until it was all gone. There was nothing he could do about his clothes, however, so the scent of her blood stayed with him.

Nick turned off the hot water and when the water was ice cold, he splashed his face once more. "I need you to find out what is going on at the scene. We have to find out who did this."

"It's already being taken care of. A witness saw a car speeding away from the scene right after the shots were fired. Every cop up and down the state is looking for it, but don't worry about that now. You need to focus on Mia."

They went back to the waiting room and sat. Nick couldn't take the silence any more. He turned to Kathy. "What happened?"

Kathy swallowed hard and her eyes got glassy. "She knew the minute we got out of the car that something bad was going to happen. She told me if I wanted to live to see my baby born, to run."

Wayne put his arms around her as she collapsed against his chest and sobbed.

"You didn't see anything? Someone lurking about?"

"It was too dark." Kathy didn't look up as she spoke.

Just then, Captain Webster came into the waiting room. "Nick, I heard what happened. How is your wife?"

Nick got to his feet. The shock was starting to wear off. The anger taking its place. "She's in surgery. Tell me what you know!" Nick demanded.

The Captain thought about it for a second. "Okay. Let's sit

down." He pulled a chair closer, so he could speak quietly. "A witness at the scene saw a Jaguar pull away after the shooting."

"A Jaguar?" He knew in an instant who had shot Mia. "Evan! That bastard! I'll kill him!"

"You missed your chance. He's dead."

"How?" Nick asked through clenched teeth.

"His car was spotted by a patrol car. They tried to do a traffic stop, but there was a high speed chase. He exited the highway and couldn't make the turn. He plowed into a block wall at seventy miles an hour. The rescue workers are still trying to get his body out of the wreckage."

"He got off lucky," Nick said.

Captain Webster stayed with them until the doctor came out several hours later.

The doctor, Myra Hicks, took them into a small conference room, just off the waiting room. "She's alive and doing better than we expected, considering everything. The first bullet entered the bottom part of her right lung. We've repaired that as best we could. The second bullet hit her spleen. We had to remove it."

"So, she's going to be okay?" Nick inquired.

"We don't know yet. Due to the amount of blood she lost, well, she may have gone a long time without oxygen to her brain." The doctor spoke quietly. "There may be significant brain damage. We won't know until she wakes up."

"When will that be?" Wayne asked for him.

"She could start coming around in a few hours or not until morning."

The words 'brain damage' hit Nick hard. "Can I see her?"

"Yes. Only you, for now," the doctor said.

"I'm going to take Kathy home to get some sleep," Wayne told him. "I'll be back."

"There's no point in you coming back right now. Go home and stay with Kathy. You can see Mia in the morning when she wakes up."

Wayne glanced at Kathy, who was exhausted. "Are you sure?"

Nick nodded, "I'd like to be alone for a little while."

"Okay. We'll be back in the morning," Wayne said. "If you need me before then, call me."

"Would you like me to stay?" Captain Webster offered.

"There's nothing anyone can do for her right now," Nick told the Captain. "I'll let you know her progress."

Nick was escorted to the surgical ICU a while later. Mia lay in bed, so pale and fragile looking. He stood over her, watching the machine breathe for her. There must have been twenty different kinds of medical equipment around her, making all kinds of noise.

After a while, he didn't even notice the sounds anymore. He sat right next to the bed, in the most uncomfortable chair ever manufactured, and held her hand. One a.m. came and went, then four and six. He dozed off here and there, never for more than twenty minutes at a time. Outside the window, the sun came up on a city covered with a white blanket of fresh snow, but the sky was blue and cloudless. Nick felt like it was a good omen.

Nurses came in checking on Mia and changing her IV bags. Hospital administrators had him filling out forms he didn't give a damn about.

At nine, a nurse came in. "There is a man here named Richard Sharpe. He says he's family."

"Yes. Let him in."

A few minutes later, Richard walked into Mia's room. "I was out of town or I would have been here sooner." He sounded almost apologetic.

"It didn't even occur to me to call you. How did you know?"

"Your partner, Wayne Coleman, called and left a message. I also heard what happened from David, Evan's dad." Richard stood next to the bed, looking at Mia. "I can't believe this happened. I knew Evan was unpredictable, but I never would have suspected he would go off the deep end like this. It doesn't make any sense."

"How he ever thought he could get away with it, while leaving the scene in his Jag, that's really stupid."

"It's out of character. Evan was smart, greedy, and manipulative, not careless. If he had hired someone to try to kill her I could see it, but not this."

Richard stayed with him until afternoon. Still, Mia didn't wake up. Wayne and Kathy showed up with clean clothes for him.

"I stopped by your house and brought you these." Wayne handed him a small duffle bag with his toothbrush, shampoo, and some other stuff. "I know you won't leave her, even to go home and shower, so here you go. Jerry, Mia's contractor, heard about what happened and he wants to know if he should keep working or not. I told him you would call him."

Nick heard the information Wayne was giving him, only he didn't care about any of it. He could tell the nurses were getting worried that Mia hadn't woken up yet and they were trying not to upset him.

At four in the afternoon, a neurologist, named Dr. Stanhope came in and checked Mia over, ordering all kinds of tests as he talked to Dr. Hicks.

When Dr. Stanhope left, Dr. Hicks sat him down. "This isn't a good sign. I suspect the lack of oxygen has caused severe damage. We will know more about the extent of it after the test results come back and then we'll talk again about how we want to proceed."

Kathy cried quietly and Richard and Wayne both had tears in their eyes.

Nick sat back down in the chair he'd placed right next to her bed and continued holding her hand, like he had been doing all night.

If Wayne, Richard, and Kathy talked amongst themselves, Nick didn't hear. He held Mia's hand and prayed in his heart, begging God to spare her, crying out at the unfairness of it all. They had just gotten married and had their whole lives ahead of them. What about the children that Mia wanted so badly and the house that she had put her heart and soul into? What about him? Strange how he couldn't picture his life without her, when three months ago he hadn't known she existed. The sick feeling in his gut settled in for a long stay.

At nine that night, Richard left, promising he would be back after his morning deposition.

Wayne and Kathy went down to the cafeteria and brought him back some food. "You have to eat something, Nick. There is no sense in you getting sick too. When Mia wakes up, she's going to need your help," Kathy coached him.

"We'll be back tomorrow night," Wayne told him. Wayne had to go to work. He had already taken the day off to sit with him. It was inevitable that others would go on with their lives. Sitting in Mia's hospital room day after day wasn't going to help and Mia wouldn't want them there, he knew that. Still, it left him feeling as if they were accepting the fact that all hope was gone.

First thing in the morning, different people started coming in and doing different tests. Some of the tests he couldn't be there for, so he used that time to take a quick shower down the hallway in a special bathroom for family of patients. He forced himself to eat some food and resumed his place in the chair next to the bed.

Hours slipped by. Nick kept track of everything that was going on around him by the hands of the clock. He found it odd, he'd never been very aware of time, until now. He couldn't help but feel that every hour took Mia further away from him.

Wayne showed up after work. Nick glanced at the clock, six p.m.

"How is she doing?" he asked as he stood at the end of the bed.

"She's still sleeping," Nick replied, knowing that wasn't what was really going on. There was something else wrong. He could feel it in his gut, but what?

Nick said nothing more and Wayne sat in a chair and waited with him. The hands on the clock continued their journey while they waited.

Dr. Hicks came in and looked at Mia, checking her pupils and all of the machines that never ceased buzzing, beeping, and humming.

Nick knew right away something had changed. She was trying to figure it out and couldn't. "What is going on?" he asked in a tone that said he expected answers.

"We are going to run all the tests again. I think we have some—inconclusive data."

"What do you mean *inconclusive data?*"

"The tests we ran show very unusual brain activity for someone in a coma. Her brain waves are those of someone under extreme stress or panic. Dr. Stanhope is doing all the tests over and if we get the same results, he's calling several of his colleagues in for a consultation as to what's going on."

Nick glanced over at Wayne, who leaned forward in his chair, listening closely.

Dr. Hicks left.

"You haven't told her about Mia being psychic have you?" Wayne asked.

"No. And I'm not going to. It's enough that they don't think she's brain dead."

Wayne stayed for a couple more hours and then headed home.

At ten that night, all the nurses were busy and the doctors had long since gone home. He took the rare moment of privacy to talk to

Mia, hoping to get some kind of response.

He stood over her and brushed the hair out of her face. "Mia, open your eyes. You need to wake up now. Please, babe." He waited to see if he got any kind of reaction, a flicker of an eye lid, a twitch of her mouth, but he got nothing.

Nick felt someone's presence in the doorway and glanced in that direction. He was shocked to see Mia's aunt standing there like an apparition who'd appeared out of nowhere.

"Silviana? I'm surprised to see you here," Nick told her as she came into the room and stood next to Mia on the other side of the bed.

The old woman took Mia's hand. "She is my niece. I'm concerned about her."

"About her or the money?"

"She has so much." Silviana shrugged, as if that justified her greed.

Silviana held Mia's hand and gently rubbed her fingers up and down her arms. She said nothing for the longest time, but the expression on her face changed from one of familial concern to fear. Nick heard her gasp under her breath.

"What? What is it?"

Silviana just shook her head.

"Don't tell me no. I know you have the same gifts as Mia. You sensed something, didn't you? Tell me what you saw." Nick's voice grew louder. "Tell me why she isn't waking up."

The old woman's dark eyes looked at him with defiance, but Nick didn't care. He wasn't going to let her leave until she told him whatever it was she was seeing or feeling or whatever.

"She's not waking up, because she is not here. She's gone into the darkness," Silviana whispered, "and she's not alone."

Nick's stomach turned into knots. He was pretty sure he knew who was with her. "Man?"

"Yes. He is keeping her from returning to her body."

"What can we do?"

Silviana shook her head. "There is nothing we can do. Mia has to fight him herself. She is the one who let him in in the first place."

Her attitude ticked Nick off. "Are you blaming Mia for this?"

"There is no blame. It just is. A demon cannot attach itself to a person, in most cases, unless they allow it through their deeds. Mia was different though, her gifts allowed him to enter her world. She was a very lonely child. He has used that loneliness to manipulate her into thinking he was a friend, like one of the harmless spirits she sees. She let Man into her life and she has to be the one to shut him out of it. If she doesn't, or can't…"

"What?" Nick demanded.

Silviana shrugged. "She may never wake up."

Nick felt a cold sweat break out all over his body. "How can you be so callous about this?"

"Death is not the end. You do not know this, but I do. Mia does. Our souls are never ending. The death of our bodies is just the next part of the journey. Perhaps, this is what was meant to be." Silviana looked at him as if what she'd said would make it all okay.

"*This* is not meant to be. She's supposed to be with me." As Nick said the words out loud he knew they were true. After everything that had happened between them, he was sure they were supposed to be together. "We are going to have a life together."

Silviana said nothing more. The old woman held Mia's hand for a long time.

A nurse came in, changed Mia's IV bag, and left without a word.

Silviana laid Mia's hand down gently on the bed. "I will pray for her." With that she turned and left.

The clock moved on to almost midnight. Nick was exhausted and sore from sitting in the crappy chair. There was a recliner type chair, for family members to sleep in, across the room, but he needed to be closer to her than that allowed him.

He got up and walked around, stretching his muscles and trying to shake off his feelings of dread. Out the window, a storm had moved in and it was snowing again. The city lights made the snowflakes glow in the night. Already, a layer of snow covered the cars in the parking lot below.

His mind recalled Mia's blood in the snow, then the blood on her hands and the shocked look on her face as she'd held them out to Nick. Tears filled his eyes. This isn't how it's supposed to be. It's not. She's mine and I want her back. When he blinked, the tears rolled down his cheeks.

He hadn't been this close to breaking down since his mother died. What he needed was a good night's sleep in his own bed with Mia in his arms. Was that ever going to happen again? One thing he was sure of, he couldn't sleep in their new house without her, not with the memories of making love in their bed to haunt him. It would be a new form of torture.

Nick stood over Mia and kissed her forehead. "You have to come back, you have to. Find your way, Mia." He took his place on the chair, ignoring the pain in his back and held her hand. His eyes grew heavy and he let his head fall on top of their hands. The softness of Mia's skin against his cheek was the last thing he remembered before he drifted off.

Somewhere in the darkness he heard Mia's voice, calling out to him.

"Nick? Nick? Where are you? Help me."

Nick opened his eyes and tried to figure out where he was. It was dark all around him, but not due to the absence of light. This darkness was different from anything he had ever experienced before. Wherever he was, there was an absence of hope, of happiness, of any positive emotions. He was being oppressed with negative emotions, darkness, despair, and anger. Was this Hell? *Hell is supposed to be fire and brimstone and all that,* he thought.

It was cold here. The darkness and the cold pressed against him like a physical force. All around him he could feel others trying to find a way out. He couldn't see them, but he could feel them. He shouldn't be here.

In the distance, he could hear someone crying softly. Was it Mia? It didn't sound like her. Something stirred the dank, wet air around him. He turned quickly, only to see nothing.

A voice whispered in his ear. "Find her." It had been a long time since he'd heard words spoken in Cherokee. "Find her."

"Where?" There was only the distant moaning of those he couldn't see. He took a step forward and called out, "Mia," as quietly as he could.

An ice cold hand brushed over his arm, another on the back of his neck. He swung his arms to push whoever it was away from him and took another step. "Mia," he said, louder this time.

Somewhere, far away, he heard his name. It was Mia. Panic filled his chest when he realized she was farther away than she was the first time. She was being taken away from him

"Mia!" he yelled. "Where are you? Mia!" he screamed with every ounce of will he had.

In the darkness he heard something moving toward him, running at him. More than one, it sounded like a pack of animals. Deep threatening growls grew louder as they got closer. Nick tried to see something, anything. He had to know what he was going to fight.

His mind told him this couldn't be happening, but the pounding in his chest told him it was. The sound of snapping of jaws was to his left and then his right. He could see nothing, but he felt pain when long sharp teeth sank into his thigh, his arm, his hand. Nick thrashed about, trying to move. His flesh was being torn away. They were going to kill him. "Mia!" he screamed into the darkness once more.

Nick tried to fight back, but they were all around him. He heard himself cry out, "Help me!" in Cherokee. A language he hadn't spoken in years.

Instantly, they were gone. Nick stood shakily on his feet. He could feel the blood from his wounds running down his limbs. Pain and fear made him tremble. He could see the silhouette of a man in the distance. A man with darkness gathered all around him, his red, glowing eyes stood out.

Nick knew the demon's thoughts without any words being spoken. He was warning Nick to leave or he would die. "She is mine." He heard the words in his head.

"No! She's mine," Nick said out loud causing the creatures, thirsting for his blood, to howl.

The atmosphere around him changed and filled with rage. Man didn't like being challenged.

"Mia! Where are you? Come to me."

"Nick." He heard her, closer this time. Still, he couldn't see her.

"Mia, I'm waiting for you. Come back to me."

"Where are you?" She was scared. Her words were quaking with fear. "I can't find my way."

"Mine!" Man cried out.

Nick heard a hint of doubt in the demon's one and only word. It gave him the insight he needed. "Mia, come to me. Come to the sound of my voice. I love you. We are supposed to be together. You don't belong here."

With a wave of his hand, Man unleashed the dogs as he shrieked in uncontrolled fury. Nick was sure it was over as his body was being torn to shreds. Pain filled every inch of him as he tried to fight off beasts he couldn't see.

"Nick, where are you?" Mia was close now.

"Mia, I'm here. Mia!" he cried out, thinking those may be his last words. The pain stopped and Mia was in his arms. He held her and cried. "I thought I'd never see you again." He looked down into scared brown eyes.

The air around them began to move, to swirl about. The cold sank into his already weakened body. Nick tightened his grip on Mia and Man continued to screech and gnash his teeth in anger. The whirlwind they were in spun faster making him unsteady on his feet. "Hang onto me, Mia."

"I'm trying."

Nick's head began to pound and there was ringing in his ears. Still he held on as tight as he could to Mia. Something began crawling on his body. It felt like insects stinging and biting. His arms, his face, his back, his legs, nothing was safe from the assault. Mia's body was being pulled away from him.

"Hang onto me," he yelled to her, but he barely heard his own words in the rush of wind around him.

Mia cried out, "Nick!" as she was ripped from his grasp.

"Mia!"

Nick slammed hard against something, knocking the wind out of him. When he opened his eyes, he was on the floor, looking at the hospital room ceiling. He tried to take deep breaths, but it hurt. He was soaked in sweat or was it blood? Glancing at his arms he saw it was only sweat. Still, the pain seared his skin like fire. His body was intact, but it felt like he had been torn apart.

On the other side of the bed Mia's monitor started going crazy. Her heart was racing. The beeps were one on top of the other.

Nick was barely on his feet when the nurses came running into the room, calling out all kinds of stuff. Mia's body jerked all over the place. A doctor, Nick didn't recognize, came running in.

"She's seizing," were the only words Nick heard. A nurse pushed him out of the room as they began pumping her IV with drugs.

Nick stumbled to the bathroom and ran the water. It was cold, but not as cold as Hell or wherever he'd been. His body shook and he could hardly hold the water he was using to splash his face. He went over it again in his mind. Only he had no answers, just questions. Would she wake up now or had he blown his chance when she was torn from his arms?

Leaning against the wall for support, the strain overtook him and he slid to the floor. He didn't know how long he'd sat there. It wasn't until he heard a knock on the door and it opened a crack that he knew it must have been a while. The nurses had been looking for him.

"It's okay, Detective, we have her stabilized. You can go back in." The nurse helped him up. "This is never easy," she sympathized. "Are you sick? You're soaked with sweat."

"I'm fine." He made his way back to Mia's room.

Nick stood over Mia, hoping beyond hope she was back, but he felt nothing. He should be able to feel her if she was inside her body. He'd failed. He'd had a chance to bring her back and he'd failed.

CHAPTER FORTY-ONE

Nick didn't watch the clock anymore. He didn't need to. It had been three and a half days since he'd tried to bring Mia back from Hell or wherever. He had tried to get back to where she was, but couldn't. It had now been eighty-four hours of misery.

Dr. Hicks came in, making her morning rounds. "I think we should start thinking about moving your wife to a place where she can get the kind of care she needs."

Nick was confused. "What do you mean, the kind of care she needs?" His beyond tired brain was having a hard time functioning.

"I'm talking about a long-term care facility. Her wounds are healing and now her brain waves are what we would expect from a person in a coma. There is really nothing more we can do for her here."

It took Nick a minute to be able to speak. "I'll take care of it." After Dr. Hicks left the room, he kissed Mia on the cheek and went home for the first time in almost a week. He needed a shower, clean clothes and some sleep. And he was going to have to go back to work sooner or later.

He'd call Richard and have him find the best place available for Mia. When he walked outside, he realized he didn't have his car. Where was his car? He couldn't remember. Did he leave it at the station or was it at the house? His brain was fried. Processing a coherent thought was beyond him, except for one, this isn't supposed to be happening.

He hailed a cab and went home to his old apartment. When he opened the door, the air inside was stale and it felt strange being there. He wished Mia was sitting on the couch, waiting for him. Nick cracked a window, showered, and fell face first onto the bed, where he slept for four hours without moving. It was nearly two in the afternoon when he woke up.

Nick wandered around the apartment and came to the conclusion he didn't belong here anymore. Most of his stuff had been moved to the house, at least the stuff he cared about. This apartment was just a few walls and a fridge with rotten food in it. He wasn't ready to go back to the hospital, but he didn't want to stay here. He wanted to be someplace where he could feel close to Mia. He couldn't feel her at the hospital and he couldn't feel her here.

He hailed a cab and gave the driver the address to the house. On the way, he took out his cell phone. The desire to call Mia was so strong. In his mind she would answer, tell him where she was and that she loved him, like she always did. Her cell phone was in the cupboard at the hospital, with her purse and all the clothes she'd had on the night she'd been shot.

It was dead for sure. He hadn't charged it. There was no point. Before he could think about how crazy it was, he started texting her. "Mia, I'm sorry. I'm trying to find u, but I can't. How am I going to go on without u? You're my heart and soul. Can't feel u anymore. There's nothing, but darkness."

Nick's fingers hesitated for a second as he tried to decide what else he needed to say.

"Come back to me. Please, come back to me." He hit send and put his cell phone away.

The cab pulled into the driveway. There must have been ten trucks and cars parked there belonging to all the workers remodeling the house to Mia's specifications. A house she may never see again.

Nick walked into the entry and the workers, who were installing the old stair railing that Mia had stripped and re-stained back to its original state, went silent for a moment and then awkwardly went back to work.

Jerry, the contractor, saw him and came over. "Detective, how are you?"

"I've been better." Nick took the hand offered.

"Sorry, that was a dumb question. We have the kitchen and family room almost done. The hardwood floors and cabinets are in and the backsplash is being grouted right now. The appliances are all here, they just need to be installed. There's still the painting to do and the carpet that needs to be laid in the family room. The curtains your wife ordered haven't come in yet, but when they do, we'll get them hung. I want it to look nice when she comes home."

Nick walked into the kitchen and looked around. The transformation was amazing. Mia had tried to tell him all the things she wanted to do for this part of the house, but he could never picture it. He just hadn't had the vision she'd had.

"It looks great, doesn't it?" Jerry went on.

The kitchen was double the size it had been. Mia had eliminated the formal dining room in the front of the house, took down the walls that separated it from the kitchen, and made it all one huge room. On the east wall, the small window had been replaced by a long bank of windows just above the sink.

"What goes there?" Nick asked pointing to the two holes on either side of the sink.

"The two dishwashers," Jerry said like he should know.

"Two dishwashers?" Nick asked.

"She said you were planning a big family. That's why she designed the eating area this way." Jerry pointed to the long bank of topless cabinets sticking out from the island like a big T, only they were shorter. "She's planning on granite counter tops here with an overhang for chairs. No need for a dining table and you can seat up to fourteen."

The eating area was huge. Mia must have been planning a lot of parties. Nick had always imagined Wayne and Kathy coming over for the Super Bowl and birthday parties. Now, it may never happen.

Nick walked around the kitchen and studied the backsplash. Mia had searched high and low for the right one. It was some kind of stone with different shades of brown, tan, gray, and rust. Mia said it would pick up the richness of the walnut floors. The hardwood floors were covered with paper to protect them, so Nick used his toe to peel back the paper and see the deep brown on each plank.

"She was right. The stone backsplash picks up the color of the floor."

"She has quite the eye, your wife. I have talked to her a couple of times about coming to work for me as a project manager. She had all the decisions made and most of the stuff ordered within three days of starting this project and this is one big project."

Nick remembered Mia sitting on his couch with her laptop, clicking away until the early hours of the morning.

"So," Jerry seemed hesitant to speak. "When is she coming home? I'm anxious for her to see all that we've accomplished."

It suddenly occurred to Nick that with Mia in the hospital, Jerry hadn't been paid. His life had stopped a week ago, but, for everyone else, life went on. "I'm not sure when she'll be back. She's pretty sick. I'll get you a check before I leave."

"I'm sorry." Jerry couldn't look him in the eye. "I know it's rude to think of money at a time like this, but these guys have families to feed."

"I understand. Mia would want you to be paid. You've done a great job. It's turning out just how Mia would have wanted." Nick felt sick inside when he realized what he'd said and how he'd said it. He talked about Mia in the past tense.

He couldn't talk any more. He left Jerry standing there and hurried up the stairs. Closing and locking the bedroom door behind him, he lost it. Everywhere he looked he saw Mia. In the new windows, the fireplace, the paint, the curtains, even the linens on the bed.

The bed. Nick lay down on his side of the bed and put his hand on Mia's pillow. It was cold. He brought it closer, her scent was on it. Tears flowed as he covered his face with her pillow. It wasn't supposed to be like this.

Memories of making love to her were like an assault on his soul, painful and permanently scarring. In this room, he felt her. He didn't think he could be here without her, but this is where he belonged. It's where they belonged. The pain would fade, he hoped, and he would make it through today. Tomorrow, he would worry about tomorrow.

Nick took a deep breath and tried to close off his mind to all of it. He needed some downtime.

When he opened his eyes, he realized he had fallen asleep. The sun was setting.

In the bathroom, he splashed some water on his face and brushed his teeth. He had promised Jerry a check. He hoped the contractor hadn't left for the day.

Downstairs, most of the workers were gone. Nick went into the library where Mia kept the contract and all the paperwork for the house project. After searching for a few minutes he found the payment schedule and saw that there were two payments that hadn't been made. Nick wrote out a check for the delinquent amount and wrote a bonus check to Jerry, for all the hard work he was doing. Mia would like that.

When he handed Jerry the checks, the man was taken off guard. "What is this one for?"

"It's a bonus for you. I know she would've appreciated the job you're doing."

He had done it again. He had talked about Mia in the past tense.

"That's not necessary," Jerry said.

"I know, but she would want you to have it."

"Thanks."

Nick nodded and headed for the door.

"Detective?" Jerry called to him.

Nick turned back to the man.

"I'm praying for your wife."

"Thank you. I'll tell her."

Once he was outside, he remembered he didn't have his car. He called Wayne. "Do you know where my car is?"

"It's in the garage at your new house. The keys are on the hook on the wall."

Nick had no idea what he was talking about because he had never been in the garage. "Okay, thanks."

"How's Mia today?" Wayne asked hesitantly.

"They want me to move her to a long-term care facility."

Wayne was silent. "I'm sorry. Kathy and I are coming by the hospital after I get off work."

"Okay." He found his car and the keys. As he pulled out of the driveway, he glanced at the house in his rear view mirror. He couldn't get past the feeling that this was all wrong.

***

Nick had been away from the hospital for too long, but his stomach was growling. He stopped in the cafeteria and grabbed a sandwich. He ate half of it on his way up to see Mia.

She was so still and pale. If it wasn't for the heart monitor beeping along with her, he might think she was gone. Nick sat back down in the chair that was going to give him a permanent kink in his back.

"Jerry wanted me to tell you he's praying for you." Nick picked up Mia's hand and laced his fingers with hers. "You should see the house. It's amazing. I know you would be so happy to see that the floor, the cabinets, and the backsplash are all in. Everything is perfect, just like you imagined it would be."

The heart monitor started beeping faster. Nick jumped to his feet and studied her face for any sign of movement or recognition of his voice. Had she heard him? None of the nurses seemed to be paying them any attention and he didn't want to get his hopes up.

"Mia? Mia, can you hear me?"

The heart monitor went back to its normal rhythm. "Don't do this to yourself." Nick whispered under his breath as his hopes came crashing back down.

There was a loud knock on the open door.

Nick looked over to see Richard standing in the doorway. His expression said he didn't want to be there. "I brought you some info on two long-term care facilities." He handed Nick two different brochures. "This one is the best as far as care. This one is good, but much closer. You're going to have to choose."

Nick glanced at the covers and thought he was going to puke. It had come to this. He had to find a place to keep Mia until her body withered away and she died. "I'll look them over later."

The two men stood there, looking at each other, not knowing what to say.

Richard broke the silence. "I keep wondering what I could have done differently so this wouldn't have happened, but I'm not coming up with anything."

"This wasn't your fault. Mia's blood is on Evan's hands. I hope he rots in Hell."

"I hope you understand that I always had Mia's best interests at heart. I wanted her to find someone who would love her and not just for the Carrigan name, or her money. I didn't think you were the one. I was wrong. I can see how much you love her. I had to let you know that."

Nick nodded, afraid to try and speak. He offered Richard his hand and the attorney took it with no reservations.

"Call me if anything changes or if you need help making any of the financial decisions. It's a lot to get used to so quickly."

"What financial decisions?" Nick asked him, feeling like he'd missed something.

"All those papers you signed before you and Mia were married, they give everything to you in the event of her death or her being incapable of making decisions on her own."

Nick's mouth hung open for a full minute while he tried to wrap his mind around that thought. He shook his head. "Who could have thought all that money would feel like such a burden. I understood that when I signed them, but I never thought…it isn't supposed to be like this."

Richard put his hand on Nick's shoulder. "I know."

Nick told Richard about the checks he wrote to the contractor.

"Mia had me shift a few deposits into that account last Friday morning. There is more than enough to finish the renovations on the house. When it gets down to a few hundred thousand I'll let you know."

Richard left and Nick opened the first brochure. Mia didn't belong in a place like this. She belonged at home, with him. Nick tossed them on the bedside table and vowed he'd think about all that later.

Wayne and Kathy walked in a few minutes later. Kathy came in and hugged him without saying anything. Nick knew Wayne had told her about the long-term care business and hope was fading.

When Kathy let go, she was crying. "I can't believe this is happening."

"Me either," Nick agreed.

"I've only known Mia for such a short time, but it feels like I'm losing my best friend. We had so much fun shopping together."

"You should tell her that," Nick encouraged her.

Kathy moved to the side of the bed and started talking. "Mia, I had fun shopping with you. I want to go again, so wake up. It's your turn to buy lunch."

Mia's heart monitor sped up. Kathy looked at Nick as if she wanted him to explain what was happening.

"That's the second time that's happened tonight."

"Is it good or bad?" Wayne asked Nick.

"Damned if I know. Keep talking, Kathy."

"Mia, can you hear me? Open your eyes if you can hear me."

Nick watched Mia closely, but there was no movement. Nothing to indicate she had heard. After a few minutes, Mia's heart rate went back to its normal rhythm.

The dark cloud of disappointment that settled in the room was heavy. Kathy and Wayne stayed a few hours, keeping him company, and then went home.

Nick knew that tomorrow he would have to choose a place for Mia. He wished Richard had made that decision. It was too final, too painful to think of. He held her hand and watched her sleep. Eventually, his eyelids got heavy. He thought about going home and spending the night in a bed for the first time since Mia had been shot. He wasn't doing her any good being here and his back was killing him, but when he looked at her face he knew he couldn't do it, not yet.

He laid his head on the edge of her bed, closed his eyes and started to drift off. His mind took him back to Mia's loft, to the times when they would watch TV at night while lying on her couch. He would lay his head in her lap and she would absentmindedly run her fingers through his hair. Mia would work her way down his neck and then start all over. He'd loved the feeling of being petted like a big cat. The memory was so strong he could feel her hand on his head, starting at the top and working its way down to his neck.

Nick's eyes flew open, but he didn't move when he realized he was really feeling it. Several times a hand ran down the back of his head to his neck. He sat up and was shocked to be looking into Mia's brown eyes.

"Mia? Can you hear me?" he grabbed her hand and held on tight, afraid to let go for fear she would slip away again.

"Throat...is...sore," she struggled to say.

"Up until two days ago you had a tube down your throat," he told her laughing and crying at the same time."

Nick glanced at the nurse's station out in the hallway, but didn't see anyone. "She's awake!" he yelled to anyone who may be near by. Still no one came.

He hit Mia's call button and finally a nurse answered. "Can I help you?"

"She's awake. She's talking. Get a doctor in here." Nick leaned closer to her.

"I can't believe you're awake. Tears rolled down his cheeks. Mia put her hand on his cheek. Then with her thumb she wiped them away.

"What?"

Nick guessed she was asking what had happened to her. "You were shot. You had surgery and you've been in a coma for a week."

Mia look confused.

"Don't worry about that now. How do you feel?"

"Tired." Mia closed her eyes and started to drift away again.

"Mia, don't go to sleep again! Please!"

Her eyes stayed closed, but she squeezed his hand. By the time the on call doctor got there, she was back to sleep. Nick was worried sick that she wouldn't wake up again.

He was relieved when the doctor pinched her really hard and she opened her eyes. "Stop it," she told him.

Nick laughed out loud. "Those are the best two words I've ever heard."

"She's out of the coma, but she's not going to get better overnight. This will take a while. She may drift back and forth for a few days. Her body has been through a lot."

"I don't care how long it takes, as long as she comes back." He grabbed his cell phone and called Wayne. Nick had to force the words out. "She's awake and she's talking."

"We'll be right there."

Thirty minutes later they walked in, but Mia was sleeping. "Mia, Wayne and Kathy are here," he told her. She didn't move. Nick pinched her skin like the doctor had done and Mia pulled her hand away from him.

"Mia!" Kathy said loudly. "Mia, open your eyes. We've been waiting for you to wake up."

Mia's eyes opened and she looked at each of them in turn. Kathy took her hand and started bawling. There wasn't a dry eye in the room.

When Mia saw them crying, she asked, "What's wrong?"

Nick brushed the hair off of her forehead. "Nothing's wrong. We're happy you're back with us."

"I had to come back… because of the baby." Mia's eyes closed once again.

Nick looked at Kathy and Wayne and then back to Mia. "What baby? Mia, what are you talking about?"

"We were talking about you two having a baby when we went shopping. She must be thinking about that," Kathy said.

"Oh, okay."

Mia shook her head. "No…my…baby girl."

When Mia fell back to sleep, Nick didn't wake her up.

"She was right about me having a boy. Maybe she knows something we don't," Kathy said with a shrug.

"What about the trauma her body's been through and all the drugs she's been given." Nick was trying not to panic.

"Let's not go off half-cocked," Wayne was trying to be the voice of reason.

"She could be dreaming, or even wishful thinking. You said she wanted a baby. It's probably something that's just in her head."

Kathy looked at Nick and he knew they were thinking the same thing. Mia was usually right about these kinds of things.

"Time will tell, I guess," Kathy said. She and Wayne stayed for over an hour, but Mia didn't wake up again.

After they left, Nick moved the recliner closer to her bed and went to sleep. When he woke up in the morning, Mia was awake.

"How are you?" he asked.

"I hurt." She spoke slowly as if she were still coming out of the coma.

"You got shot," he told her. Nick wondered if he should tell her the rest. "It was Evan."

Mia shook her head no and Nick thought she didn't want to believe it.

"It was Evan, Mia. I'm sorry."

"Red eyes. Not Evan." Mia closed her eyes and drifted back to sleep.

Nick tried to comprehend what those few words meant. If Man had somehow possessed Evan, it would explain his uncharacteristic behavior. It also explained how desperate Man had become. The memory of the red eyes staring at him in the basement of Mia's loft and when he had followed Mia into the darkness, made him shiver and goose bumps rose on his skin. His mind raced as he tried to figure out what it all meant.

Mia woke up again in only an hour. Each time she woke up, she was a little more alert, but she tired quickly, so he tried to make the time count.

He decided not to bring up Evan again. Someday, they would talk about him, maybe, but not now. "Tell me what you remember," Nick asked her, "from when you were sleeping."

She smiled. "You came for me. I was alone in the darkness and you came."

Nick felt the blood drain from his face. He had tried to tell himself it was all a dream, but if Mia remembered it, it couldn't have been. "I couldn't bring you back with me. I failed and I almost lost you.

Mia shook her head. "No, you gave me the strength I needed to get away."

"Silviana was here. She said you were in the darkness and Man was with you. She said you let him into your life and it was up to you to cast him out."

"She's right. I know that now. He only wanted to use me. He couldn't have me in life, because of you, so he tried to possess me in death. He hates you because you love me. His hate and our love aren't compatible. He had to cast me out of the darkness."

"But you didn't die," Nick pointed out.

"Yes, I did."

Nick held his breath while he waited for her to explain.

"I was given a choice. I chose you and our children."

"Mia, are you pregnant right now?"

"Barely. She won't be here for a long time."

"She?" It felt like his heart swelled in his chest. "We're going to have a little girl?"

"Yes. I chose to come back for you, and for her, and the other babies. I saw them all."

He held her hand. "I was so afraid you weren't going to wake up. I wasn't sure how to go on without you. I've planned my whole life with you in it. It just felt wrong."

Mia slowly and carefully scooted over on the bed and then patted the empty spot. Nick lay down next to her and held her in his arms. "*This* feels right."

***

Five days later, Nick was helping Mia out of their car and into their house. She was moving slow, but she had a smile on her face. He watched her eyes light up when she walked into the entryway and saw the stair railing back in place and looking brand new.

Mia walked up and ran her hand over the wood. "This turned out beautifully."

"Why do you sound surprised? You did it all."

"I know. But the vision doesn't always translate into reality."

"You're telling me. I like this version of reality." Nick gently pulled her close and kissed her on top of her head. "Let's check out the kitchen and the family room."

Mia didn't smile like he thought she would. Her gaze moved from one place to the next, slowly and methodically. He was afraid she didn't like it.

"I need to sit down."

Nick quickly grabbed one of the fourteen chairs that now surrounded the huge granite table and guided her to it. "Are you okay?"

"I'm a little overwhelmed. This is how I envisioned this room the first time I saw it. I can't believe how perfect it's turning out."

"Jerry told me the couches are going to be delivered and the curtains hung tomorrow. After that, they'll start working in the other rooms again."

Mia nodded. "I wanted this area done as soon as possible, so we could start our lives here."

"I think an army could live here. We have the commercial refrigerator, freezer, and the sixty inch stove with a double oven and two wall ovens in case that isn't enough. To top it all off, we have two dishwashers and seating for fourteen. And that's just in the kitchen. What more could two people need?"

Mia laughed. "You think I'm crazy now, but you just wait."

Nick crouched down on the balls of his feet until their faces were right next to each other. "I don't think you're crazy. I think you're beautiful."

"I love you," she whispered as she took his face in her hands and kissed him.

"Let's go upstairs, so you can relax. We have the rest of our lives to admire our house."

Mia had to rest part way up the stairs, but she made it. When she pushed the door open, she cried out with joy. Red roses were everywhere. "Oh, Nick, they're beautiful. It reminds me of our wedding night."

Her cheeks turned pink. He had to laugh. "Unlike our wedding night, you are getting into bed to sleep and to recover, right after your bath." He led her into the bathroom where the tub was full and hot. Red rose petals floated in the water.

"Are you up to it?" he asked, afraid she may be too tired.

"I would love to get the smell of hospital off me."

He helped her get undressed and when the last of her clothes were off, he noticed she kept her hand over her new scars. It had never occurred to him she might worry that he would find them ugly. He could feel her apprehension, however.

He sat down on the edge of the tub and took her hand and pulled it away from her body. The surgical scars were red and rough looking. He leaned forward and kissed one and then the other.

Tears filled her eyes and one slid down her cheek.

"I love you, Mia."

She smiled and laughed through her tears. He held her hand as she got into the water and sank up to her neck. "Get in with me."

"I don't think it would be a good idea."

"The tub is big enough for two and I need you to wash my hair."

Nick dropped his clothes where he stood and entered the water. Mia leaned against him. They soaked for a while and then he made a bunch of lather with the soap. He ran his hands all over her making sure he didn't miss any important places. Then he put shampoo in her hair, washed it really well and rinsed it with an old-fashioned hand-held shower wand.

"You really thought of everything, didn't you?"

Mia smiled one of her Mona Lisa smiles and moaned quietly.

"I think you're clean enough," he said as he climbed out and dried off quickly, wrapping the towel around his waist.

Mia pulled the plug and he helped her up, so she wouldn't fall. When she stepped out, he cocooned her in a towel and dried her hair and skin.

"Do I still smell like the hospital?" she asked.

He leaned toward her and inhaled the scent of her shampoo. "No more hospital smell."

He held her panties as she put her foot in, one and then the other. Her pajamas were next. He brushed her hair out and dried it as she sat at the new vanity. He wondered what he would have done if she hadn't come back from wherever she'd been.

They climbed into bed and Nick took Mia in his arms. "This is how it's supposed to be," he said and he meant it. This felt right. Every night, for the rest of his life, he would remind himself how close he'd come to losing her. He would hold her tighter, from now on, so she would never face the darkness alone again.

CHAPTER FORTY-TWO

Nine months later

Mia waited on the front porch steps for Kathy to get there. She usually took a minute to appreciate the fall foliage, but not today. She had been having contractions that had come and gone for days. These ones meant business, however.

Kathy pulled into the driveway and helped her into the car. "Are you okay?"

"No. I need drugs and lots of them," Mia told her, trying to catch her breath.

"Really? It's that bad?" Kathy asked with a worried look on her face. "Did you get a hold of Nick?"

"He's meeting us at the hospital." Mia glanced into the back seat, wanting to say 'hi' to baby William, but his car seat was empty. "Where's William?"

"My sister, Regina, was visiting today. She has him."

"Is she still--" Mia's words were cut off due to another contraction. She gasped and panted in pain. "I think I've changed my mind about this whole pregnancy thing."

"That's what they all say." Kathy laughed until she saw Mia's face. "We'd better get you to the hospital." She slowly backed down the driveway.

"I never realized how bumpy these streets are," Mia said, gripping the armrest.

"Hang in there. We'll be at the hospital soon and they can give you something for the pain." Kathy swerved to avoid a pot hole.

When they finally pulled up to the main entrance, Nick was waiting with a worried look on his face. Mia could feel his anxiety.

She put her hand in his as he helped her out of the car. She tried to seem calm so he wouldn't be so nervous, but her anxiety became much worse when she took one step and a wave of warm water ran down her legs.

"My water just broke!" The words were barely out of her mouth when another pain started low in her belly and grew more and more intense. Mia moaned out loud.

Nick tried to move her toward the sliding doors.

"Don't touch me!" Mia cried out, grabbing her belly. When the contraction started to ease, she took his hand again.

She was about to apologize when Nick said, "You don't need to. I know you're in pain."

Kathy, who was still waiting by the curb, yelled to her. "Thanks for holding that in until you got out of my car."

Nick started to laugh and so did Mia. They couldn't help it. Leave it to Kathy to find the humor in a situation like this.

"I'm going to go park, I'll be right up."

"Can you walk now?" Nick asked before he tried to move her this time.

Mia took a breath and had made it four steps when another contraction started. "This baby is coming fast." Mia gasped as the pain made her double over.

Someone inside finally noticed them and came out with a wheelchair. "Do you need some help?"

"Yes!" They both said at once.

"And I need drugs! Strong ones." And she wasn't kidding. Mia sat down and they hurried to the elevator. "Is Dr. Schulman here yet?"

"Honey, that isn't my department. You'll have to ask when we get you up there." The woman's pink blouse indentified her as a volunteer. "Is this your first baby?" she asked Mia as she rolled her into the elevator.

"Yes."

"First baby's usually take a long time. How long have you been in labor?"

"For days," Mia said.

"Two hours," Nick said at the same time.

The next contraction started and Mia squeezed Nick's hand with everything she had. "I don't think I can do this." She was starting to panic. After reading everything she could find on childbirth, Mia thought she was prepared, but the pain was so much worse than she'd thought it would be. If she could just hang on long enough to get something for the pain, she might make it.

The elevator doors opened and the volunteer pushed her to the desk.

"What's your name?" the nurse behind the desk asked, without even looking up.

"Is Dr. Schulman here?" Mia asked instead.

"First things first. What's your name?" she repeated.

"Mia Whitecloud," Nick answered for her.

Mia tried not to move as the deep, twisting pain started all over again.

"Hang on, babe. We'll get you some pain medicine soon." Nick turned his worry on the nurses. "Let's get her into a room, get her comfortable, and then we can take care of the rest of this."

Mia loved it when he went into cop mode and made people do it his way.

The nurse rolled her into her room and laid out a gown. "Help her get undressed and I'll call the doctor."

As she struggled to get undressed, two more contractions came and went, each one progressively stronger. "I don't think I can do this," she said, her voice cracking.

"Let me help you into bed." Nick held her arm as she climbed in. "Now, take my hand. When the next one comes, don't let go, but relax and look into my eyes."

The words were barely out of his mouth when Mia felt the now familiar pulling starting in her belly once more. The contraction kept increasing in strength, until she couldn't believe she was able to stand the pain without screaming. "Nick, go find out where Dr. Schulman is and where my drugs are," Mia told him in a tone that sounded much calmer than she felt.

The minute he left the room the mother of all contractions started and decided to stay a while. Mia was sure the gut wrenching pain was never going to stop. She could hardly catch her breath. At the end of it, something changed. The pressure moved from inside her belly to a place much lower.

The baby was coming and she was all alone. Mia found the call button and hit it. "I need help! I'm having this baby, right now! Where is the doctor and where is my husband?" Mia was getting close to hysterical.

Nick walked in with Dr. Schulman, who obviously was not ready to deliver a baby. She still had her street clothes on.

"Mia, let's check you and see how dilated you are." She pulled on a glove, lifted back the sheet. "Oh! You are ready to have this baby." Then, to Nick she said, "Hit the call button."

The nurse answered from the station down the hall. "Can I help you?"

"This is Dr. Schulman. I need help in here, right now."

Within seconds, three nurses came running in. After pushing twice, a tiny baby girl slipped from Mia's body, wet and blue. Dr. Schulman laid the baby on her belly. As one of the nurses wiped their daughter dry, the other cleared her throat.

Mia and Nick watched as the tiny bundle turned pink and opened her eyes for the first time. A quiet cry filled the room and at the same time filled Mia's heart.

"Look at her," Nick said softly. "She's perfect."

Mia held her and watched as she took her first few breaths and then started to wail. It only took a second for Mia to memorize every curve, every crease, the very essence of her daughter. The emotions hit her fast and hard. This was what she was here for. This was what life was all about.

"She's a tiny one. No wonder you didn't have to push much," Dr. Schulman commented. "Dad, do you want to cut the umbilical cord?"

Nick took the scissors and cut the cord. And then, his attention was drawn back to the squirming little creature in her arms. "She's the most beautiful thing I've ever seen. She looks like you. And look at all that dark hair."

Mia couldn't talk. Her throat was closed with emotion. Her heart felt like it was going to burst, it was so full. She'd never missed her mom more than at that moment.

"Mia? Are you okay?" Nick asked.

She nodded. "I was wondering if my mom felt like this the first time she held me." A sob broke through and tears ran down her cheeks.

Nick kissed her cheek, her forehead, and then her lips. "I'm sorry your mom isn't here."

He didn't say anything else. He didn't need to. Mia could feel how much he loved her and that was enough. She still missed her mom and dad, but she wasn't alone anymore.

Nick put his giant finger into the baby's hand. She wrapped her fingers around it.

"She's already got you in the palm of her hand," Mia told him.

Nick laughed softly. "Is her name still going to be Tessa Rain

Whitecloud?"

"Yes." Mia smiled as she said it.

"Okay, but you don't get rain from white clouds."

They'd had this discussion before. "I still like the name."

Kathy walked in just then. "I can't believe you had her in three hours."

"And I never got my drugs," Mia told her.

Kathy came and looked at the baby. "Oh, she is a cutie. I can't wait until William sees her for the first time. I've got to call Wayne." Kathy whipped out her cell phone and told Wayne the whole story, with her usual embellishments and colorful exclamations.

Mia gazed at her baby and then at her husband. His dark eyes were watching Tessa's every tiny breath. "I love you, so much," she whispered to him.

Nick smiled. "And I love you, so it works out."

He kissed her once, but that wasn't enough. Mia took a hold of his shirt collar and pulled him back for another kiss.

"You know, that's what got you here in the first place," Dr. Schulman teased, still on a stool at the end of the bed.

Nick chuckled and Mia felt her cheeks start to burn.

"They're still newlyweds," Kathy told the doctor. "It's disgusting. They've only been married for nine months. It took me four years to get pregnant and she gets knocked up on her wedding night."

Nick winked at Mia and said quietly in her ear, "And what a night it was."

Mia adored her husband and new baby girl and thought about how this almost didn't happen. Her memories were choppy and scattered, but she would always remember that cold blackness that had not only surrounded her, but had felt like it had entered her soul with every breath and through every pore like black ink spreading within her being, consuming any positive emotion.

Everywhere she'd turned, Man had been there, stopping her from moving on, until Nick came for her. He'd brought with him the positive energy of his love. The simplicity of it still amazed her that positive and negative energies can't exist together for long. Some would call it the battle of good and evil. One or the other has to have dominion. Man couldn't endure being in the presence of love. Mia understood that that was why he had become so hostile when Nick had entered her life.

Looking back now, she could see it was the times when she was lonely or felt unloved that he came to her. After her parents and her Grandma Behan died, when she was living with her Uncle David and his family, was when he'd become a big part of her life. Man had used those negative emotions to try and possess her, so he could use her abilities to do his will. Chills ran up her arms as she thought about it.

How she could have been so stupid and so blind to it all, when it was all so simple, she wasn't sure. Mia kissed her baby's head and said a prayer of gratitude for the new little spirit in her arms. "You will never feel unloved, Tessa. I promise."

***

Three weeks later, they were lying in their bed at home. Mia was nursing Tessa and Nick was watching as she greedily gulped down her mother's milk.

"I don't think she only weighs six pounds anymore. Look at the little rolls she's getting on her hands and neck."

"She eats every two hours, so I hope she's gained weight."

Nick continued to stare until Mia couldn't take it anymore. "What?"

"You amaze me sometimes." Nick smiled at her.

"I do? Why?"

"You're such a good mother. Tessa demands so much of you, but you never complain, even though I know you're tired."

"I'm trying to commit every minute, every smile, and every smell to memory, because I know she won't be this small for long."

"Every smell? That can't be good," Nick teased.

"You know what I mean, that sweet baby smell." Mia kissed Tessa's head while she inhaled. "She's perfect and I love her more than anything."

"More than me?" he pretended to be hurt.

"I love you in a totally different way," Mia said, trying to sound sexy.

"You better watch it. It's been a long few weeks, if you know what I mean."

"So, if I leaned over and kissed you like this…" Mia pressed her lips against his and let her tongue slip inside his mouth for just a second. "It would be a problem for you?"

Nick didn't say a word. He just moaned.

"We may not be able to make love, but I'm sure we could use our imaginations and come up with something."

"I like your way of thinking," Nick whispered as he nibbled her neck.

When the baby was done nursing, Mia took her to the newly redecorated nursery and put her in her crib. She checked the baby monitor to make sure it was still on and went back to Nick. He was waiting with a cheesy grin on his face.

Mia hesitated in the doorway for a second.

"What's wrong?" Nick asked.

"Nothing, I just wanted to remember this moment too."

Nick patted the bed. "Come over here and we'll make some memories worth remembering."

He was true to his word and Mia couldn't have been happier.

Two hours later, as sure as clock work, Tessa woke up. This time Mia stayed in the nursery and fed her, so she didn't wake up Nick, who had to go back to work in the morning.

As she climbed back into bed, Mia glanced at the clock, it said one thirty-five a.m. That meant she had until three thirty to sleep before Tessa woke up again.

She drifted off right away. Only to wake up an hour later with a strange feeling that something was wrong. The baby monitor was still on and she didn't hear any crying from the baby's room, so what was it?

Mia climbed out of bed into the freezing cold air. Her heart sank to her toes when she realized what was wrong. "Nick, wake up."

"What? What's wrong?" Nick sat up as the baby monitor flickered to life, but it wasn't Tessa they heard. It was the sound of demonic growls coming from her room. The baby started screaming. Without waiting for Nick, Mia flew down the hallway and rushed in to get her daughter. She scooped Tessa up into her arms and held her.

Nick was right behind her. He turned on the light, his face as pale as hers must have been. "I thought this was over with? He knows he can't have you." Nick was furious.

Mia started sobbing hysterically. Exhaustion and fear for her daughter made it hard to get her emotions under control. Nick held them both in his arms, rubbing her back to make her feel safe.

"Babe, don't cry. You cast him off once, you can do it again."

"Oh, Nick, it's not me he wants this time. He wants Tessa. He's going to bide his time until she's old enough and then he's going to try to take control of her just like he did me. This was just a warning, he wanted me to know that he won't quit."

Nick was silent while he mulled over what she had said. "Then we are going to have to find a way to fight him off again and protect her. He's not going to insert himself into our lives again. Do you hear me, you bastard?" Nick shouted to the ceiling. "It'll be okay, Mia. I promise."

Mia stayed in his arms, with her baby in between them, and wondered if it would be as easy as that? She doubted it. Somehow, Man had found his way out of the darkness to torment her once more.

Nick took her face in his hands and made her look at him. "We're going to fill this house with so much love that Man won't be able to get near us."

Mia nodded and leaned against his hard, warm chest. Nick was right they had the power to keep Man at bay and they would. Together.

Excerpt from Out of the Darkness

Book Two in the Darkness Series

Mia slipped out of bed trying not to wake Nick. The house was silent and dark. She knew all four kids were sleeping, but she needed to see them for herself. In the nursery Madison was sound asleep in her crib. The pain medicine Mia had given her for her teething seemed to have done the trick. Next she checked on the boys.

Blake and Ryker were resting peacefully in their cribs. Both of their blankets had been kicked off as usual. They weren't quite two and couldn't hold still for more than a few seconds when they were awake and it was the same when they were sleeping. No blankets ever stayed on them. Tessa was in her big girl bed. Her dark hair draped across the pillow. None of the kids stirred as she moved between them. Everything was as it should be. Mia took a deep breath and tried to fight off the uneasy feeling sitting in the pit of her stomach.

Mia closed the door silently, turned and walked right into a huge mass standing in the hallway.

"Nick! You scared the life out of me," Mia whispered. "What are you doing up?"

"I was about to ask you the same question."

She couldn't see his face in the darkness, but she knew the expression he wore just the same. It was one that was studying her to see if she was going to tell him the whole truth.

"I was checking on the kids." Mia moved passed him and started down the stairs to the kitchen. He followed behind her. She turned on the light and got a glass out of the cupboard for some water.

"This is the third night in a row you've been up. What's going on? And don't tell me it's nothing." His dark eyes were watching her every move.

Mia sipped her water.

"Babe, I can't help if you don't tell me."

"I can't tell you what I don't know." She looked at him. "Something's not right. I can feel it. The vibrations around me are making me anxious and scared. I can't sleep."

Nick was quiet for a moment. "Is it one of the kids?"

"I don't know." Mia shook her head in frustration. "I haven't felt like this since right before Detective Shilling and Detective Wentz took me in for questioning about the murders."

Nick made a face at the mention of the time in their past when their relationship almost didn't survive and neither did she. Mia felt the guilt settle in his gut. She set her water on the counter, went to him and slid her arms around his waist. "I'm only bringing that up because it's the same kind of fear."

Nick's hand running up and down her back helped to calm her. Whatever was coming their way, she knew he would stand beside her this time.

"Let's go back to bed. There's nothing we can do tonight."

About the Author

Amberly Evans was born and raised in California but moved to Utah five years ago with her real life hero. She is the mother of ten children who keep her very busy.

She has written all her life and loves a happy ending. To keep up with her works in progress check out her Amberly Evans author page on Facebook or her website at www.amberlyevans.com.

Made in the USA
Las Vegas, NV
08 December 2021